The

DEVIOUS
DR. JEKYLL

ALSO BY VIOLA CARR

THE ELECTRIC EMPIRE
The Diabolical Miss Hyde

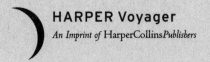

HARPER Voyager

An Imprint of HarperCollins*Publishers*

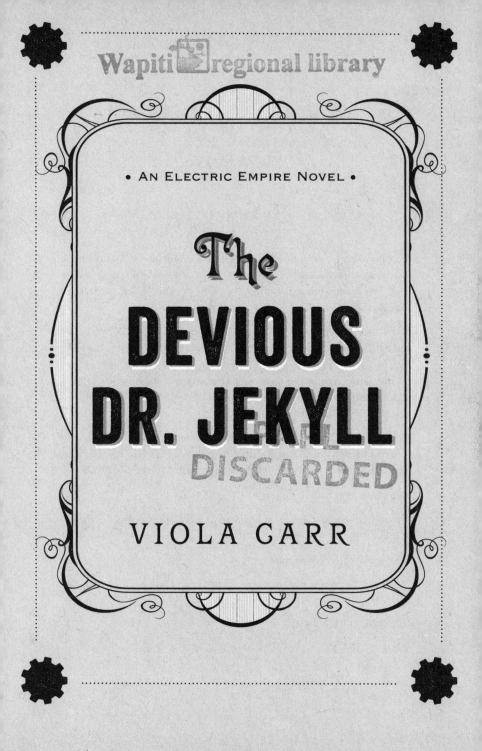

• AN ELECTRIC EMPIRE NOVEL •

The
DEVIOUS
DR. JEKYLL

VIOLA CARR

THE DEVIOUS DR. JEKYLL. Copyright © 2015 by Viola Carr. All rights reserved. Printed in the United States of America. No part of this book may be used or reproduced in any manner whatsoever without written permission except in the case of brief quotations embodied in critical articles and reviews. For information address HarperCollins Publishers, 195 Broadway, New York, NY 10007.

HarperCollins books may be purchased for educational, business, or sales promotional use. For information please e-mail the Special Markets Department at SPsales@harpercollins.com.

FIRST EDITION

Harper Voyager and design is a trademark of HarperCollins Publishers L.L.C.

Designed by Janet M. Evans

Library of Congress Cataloging-in-Publication Data has been applied for.

ISBN 978-0-06-236310-7

15 16 17 18 19 OV/RRD 10 9 8 7 6 5 4 3 2 1

Dr. Watson
Orange and white
A sleek, satisfied fellow of no small size
Who liked to sit on the keyboard
and help
2000–2015

THE ELECTRIC EMPIRE PRESENTS

The Devious Dr. Jekyll

an Artful Tale of Diabolical Drama!

....

STARRING

DR. ELIZA JEKYLL

intrepid practitioner of legal medicine,
also appearing as the bold adventuress

MISS LIZZIE HYDE

AND FEATURING

CAPTAIN REMY LAFAYETTE

Investigator for the Royal Society and reluctant lycanthrope

MARCELLUS FINCH

of the fabled Worshipful Company of Alchemists

The French spy and cut-throat called HARLEQUIN
and PROFESSOR MORIARTY QUICK

purveyor of dubious beauty products and snake oil

ALSO ONSTAGE, in various haunts and dreadful guises:

ADA, COUNTESS OF LOVELACE

a fanatical Scientist with a mechanical heart

The inimitable Philosopher, SIR ISAAC NEWTON
rumors of his death exaggerated

MR. MALACHI TODD, a Homicidal Lunatic,
alongside his eldritch cohort MR. SHADOW; *and*
MR. EDWARD HYDE, the malignant and maniacal
KING OF RATS

As Always, the Splendid Scenery, Machinery, and Effects
produced by MISS VIOLA CARR

....

The

DEVIOUS
DR. JEKYLL

A STAIN OF BREATH

• • •

WHERE'S THE BODY?" ELIZA JEKYLL SKIDDED eagerly into the frame-maker's shop, clutching her doctor's bag—and rocked back in dismay.

Not a corpse in sight.

The shop had been ransacked. Blue-coated police constables milled about, clambered over scattered oil paintings and frame parts. Arc-lit chandeliers crackled, shedding the stormy scent of aether, and through the windows glared a sullen, fogbound yellow sun.

Inspector Harley Griffin of the Metropolitan Police— immaculate suit, sharply combed dark hair—waved her over. "What do you make of this, Doctor?"

Eliza pushed up her spectacles, frustrated. "It's a pile of paintings, Harley, not a cadaver. Surely you need no crime scene physician to avail you of that."

"Ah," said Griffin imperturbably, "but it's the art you *don't* see that we're interested in."

"State-of-the-art police work, I'm sure." Eliza sidestepped a constable, who promptly tripped over a rug in the crush and blundered into the scattered artworks, likely obliterating any trace evidence. "A dozen murders a night, the city bursting with bloodthirsty French spies, and our good Chief Inspector has the finest detective in London investigating a petty theft."

Hippocrates, her clockwork assistant, jigged on hinged brass legs at her skirt hem. "Human remains absent," he proclaimed in his tinny little voice. "Does not compute."

Griffin tugged neat mustaches. "To be fair, the scenario does exercise the mind. The villain filched twenty-one artworks on Saturday night—"

She snorted. "And now it's Monday. The evidence venerable as well as trampled. An even more irritating waste of my time."

"—from under the noses of four security guards," continued Griffin with a knowing smile. "Law-abiding citizens all, naturally. No one saw or heard a thing. No alarm raised, locks intact, every key accounted for."

"A locked-room art heist," she muttered, intrigued despite herself. "Impressive. What does Reeve want me to do about it? Test for incompetence?"

"Don't get smart with me, missy." Chief Inspector Reeve—newly appointed to that lofty rank—waddled up in an ugly brown suit, puffing self-importantly on a cigar. "You're late. Getting your hair done?"

"My apologies, sir. Looking so pretty takes *such* a long time."

Her sarcasm struck Reeve's glaring aura of *chauvinistic pig* and bounced off. "Quite right, too. Put some color in your cheeks. All that unladylike science makes you peaky."

Behind Reeve, Griffin rolled his eyes. Eliza barely noticed, possessed of a creeping, all-too-familiar itch to claw Reeve's skin off . . . but it wasn't *her* craving. It belonged to Lizzie Hyde, the shadowy second self inside her, thrashing to break free.

I'll make YOU peaky, you sniggering prat. Lizzie's disembodied urgings seared Eliza's flesh. Suddenly her plain gray dress itched like fire ants. Her hair rippled, alive, trying to spring free of its coil, and Lizzie wriggled and swelled beneath her skin, threatening to burst out . . .

"Eh?" Eliza blinked, heart thudding. Suddenly, all was still. Her vision bounced back into focus. The cramped shop, the fat frame-maker hovering in one corner, the scattered paintings. "What did you say?"

Reeve puffed cigar smoke, rocking on smug heels. "I said, police work isn't all murders and mayhem. You're always complaining no one but young Griffin here takes you seriously. Well, here's a case. Do you want it or not?"

Eliza swallowed Lizzie's compulsion to slam Reeve's nose into his brain. She *needed* this job. When she and Harley caught the gruesome killer known as the Chopper, she'd imagined her career as a physician would at last take off. But Harley was still her only friend on the force. Police work—especially the newfangled crime scene medicine—was still a man's world, and even more so when said crime scene was owned by a thoughtless donkey like Reeve.

Her employment at Bethlem Asylum had dried up, too. She wasn't exactly popular there. Understandably, given that the surgeon in charge who'd employed her had been killed, and the Chopper had turned out to be an asylum orderly—and one of her closest friends. Not to mention the trifling matter of Razor Jack, a lunatic killer who'd taken advantage of the mayhem to escape.

In short, she needed all the work she could get. Even petty larcenies, instead of cases that *mattered*. "I merely remark that my expertise is hardly—"

"Burglary beneath your attention, is it? Couldn't care about some louse-ridden criminal type wiping his greasy fingers all over Her Majesty's new portrait?"

"Oh." Her curiosity piqued. No one had seen the Mad Queen in public for years. People whispered that she'd died of cholera, been starved by her wicked advisers, or had been bewitched by sorcerous spies for the terrifying new French Republic. "New, did you say?"

Griffin consulted his notebook. "Apparently. Painted by a court artist, name of Wyn Patten."

"Never heard of him." But it explained Reeve's attendance: ingratiating himself with the Palace and the Police Commissioner.

"Not the kind of thing a villain can sell, is it?" Reeve stuck a belligerent thumb into his braces. "Ergo, not a simple theft. Her Majesty could have a crazed admirer. It could be Froggie agents, stirring up trouble! But you've better things to do, have you?"

Aye, whispered Lizzie. *Come closer and I'll show you.*

"Not at all." Eliza smiled through clenched teeth. "Pleased to assist."

Reeve grinned. "Not so smart as you think you are. Lads, make way for the good *lady doctor.*"

Thwack him. Lizzie slithered up into Eliza's throat like a serpent, making her splutter for air. *Tell the woman-hating little bastard to go screw himself. Better still:* I'll *tell him to go screw himself. Just let me at him . . .*

Hippocrates snuffled disconsolately at the floor. "Remains. Samples. Does not compute."

"Hipp, take a recording, please." Eliza yanked on a pair of white cotton gloves. "Wooden frame on trestle legs, about seven feet by three. The Queen's canvas was tensioned here with these pegs—"

Reeve sniggered. "Never would've figured that for myself."

Eliza shot him an oily glare. "So you've solved the case already, then? No? Whatever will the Commissioner say? Do you want my help, or shall I return to my embroidery?"

"Embroidery," chirped Hipp, muffled beneath her skirts. "Irrelevant. Logic failure."

Shall I return to my embroidery? Lizzie mocked. *Shall I break your pox-ridden nose with my forehead? Shall I grab your tiny balls and squeeze until your face turns black?*

"Carry on, if you must," muttered Reeve. "I've witnesses to examine." And he strutted away.

Eliza's fingers flexed of their own accord, and she shuddered in cold sweat. Her skin felt stretched too thin, like overstressed rubber. The urge—no, the *need*—to carry out Lizzie's creative revenge burned all too fresh and real.

Panic blinded her momentarily. The metamorphosis wasn't meant to happen on its own, without her elixir to control it. If she *changed* . . .

Wouldn't be the nicest pair of trousers we've ever shoved our hand down, agreed Lizzie silkily, *not that you're any help in that department.*

"Shut up," hissed Eliza frantically, fiddling with the empty pegs. "I'm trying to work."

Fine. You work away. I'll just sit over here and think of fun ways to rip his nuts off.

"If it makes you happy. Just do it quietly. You're embarrassing me!"

"Doctor, are you quite well?" Griffin eyed her strangely.

Eliza flushed. Talking to herself again. "It's nothing. Shall we get on?"

She uncased her brass-framed optical and strapped it to her forehead. She'd built the gadget herself, modified from her late father's designs. The array of lenses and spectrics detected all manner of substances, from bloodstains to stupefying drugs and poisons. Not strictly classical optics. Such unorthodox contraptions could get you dragged from your bed in the dead of night to answer uncivil questions in electrified dungeons at the Tower.

But none of Henry Jekyll's dabblings had been suitable subjects for tea party conversation. As a girl, she'd been fascinated by her father's dusty laboratory, the bold young men in shirtsleeves with their illicit experiments on light, air, the substance of life itself. Not to mention outlawed elixirs and the search for eternity.

She slotted a magnifier over her spectacles and examined the wooden frame. "Nothing's damaged, no oil flakes. This art was not snatched. Our thief took his time, confident he'd remain undisturbed. And . . . hold on, I see a handprint on the adjoining wallpaper."

Griffin coughed. "Pity this isn't the Paris *Sûreté*," he murmured. "I hear they're collecting copies of convicted felons' handprints for comparison."

"Along with their severed heads? Away with your treason-
ous Republican sympathies, Inspector." She peered closer.
"Coal dust, or iron. Smallish hands, perhaps a youngster.
Hmm." Surreptitiously, she flipped in an experimental lens
she'd borrowed from her pharmacist. Multi-dimensional res-
onance, Mr. Finch had claimed. Highly unorthodox, when
the Philosopher's doctrine allowed for four dimensions and
no more. The stuff of torture and witch burnings.

The smudged handprint glittered in her lens, greenish-
yellow. "I say, how extraordinary—"

"*You're* extraordinary." A whisper, sparkling in her ear.

Startled, she teetered. Big hands caught her waist, a familiar gunflash scent of steel and thunder.

Hippocrates danced a clumsy jig. Griffin winced. Inwardly,
Eliza groaned.

Oh, bother.

I lied, whispered Lizzie with a grin. *Ain't leavin' this alone.*

A FACE IN THE MIRROR

· • ·

ELIZA STEPPED AWAY, CASUALLY SLIPPING THAT incriminating optical from her forehead. "Good morning, Captain Lafayette. I note your manners haven't improved."

"My manners shall never improve, Dr. Jekyll. You may rest assured." Remy Lafayette made a flashy bow. Gold braid glittered on his scarlet cavalry officer's tailcoat, with arc-pistol, sword, and spurs all fighting to outdo each other for shine. A decorative fellow, no mistake. Lush chestnut curls, brilliant electric-blue eyes fit to melt an iceberg—or a lesser woman's heart. Until, of course, one noticed the iron badge on his lapel, engraved with the words NULLIUS IN VERBA.

"Why? Is there a new Royal Society moratorium on gentlemanly behavior? Or heaven forbid, is your incorrigible buffoonery unauthorized?"

"Admit it: it amuses you to scold me." Lafayette bent to pet Hippocrates. "If I failed to outrage, my entertainment value would swiftly degrade to negligible."

"And it has *such* a long way to go. Hipp, come away."

Harley Griffin nodded amiably. "Lafayette, how we've missed you. Still inflicting yourself where you're not wanted?"

A jaunty tilt of sword. "I'm a Royal investigator, Griffin old boy. Being unwanted is my job."

"And you perform it peerlessly."

Lafayette laughed, and the fat frame-maker shuffled and averted his gaze. Even Reeve's constables edged away. A dangerous thing, this Royal investigator's mirth. The all-powerful Royal, under the dubiously enlightened guidance of their immortal Philosopher, made the rules. Science or superstition, orthodoxy or a burning for heresy—who was to know from day to day? And lately, the Royal's efforts to weasel out scientific heretics had escalated from irritating and invasive to over-zealous and violent. No one was safe. Especially not Eliza Jekyll, alchemy addict, dabbler in dubious crime scene science—and afflicted with what her father's notebooks liked to call a *transcendental identity*.

Inwardly, she shuddered. Remy Lafayette, IRS, hid uncanny secrets of his own, cursed with a metamorphic monster more terrible than anything Henry Jekyll had envisaged. They'd reached an understanding while they'd worked to solve the Chopper case—hadn't they?

Nullius in verba: "take nobody's word for it." An exhortation to see for yourself, to question blind assumptions. A rule she ought to keep in mind. She barely knew the man, after all. Any moment, he could lose his nerve and betray her to save himself a burning.

Bollocks, whispered Lizzie gaily. *Ain't the real reason you've got ants in your knickers, is it?*

Lafayette clapped a constable on the shoulder. "Fantastic work, chaps. Keeping the streets safe, all that. I say, Griffin, do you mind if I borrow the good doctor a moment?"

"Oh, dear," she said smoothly, "I'm afraid I'm urgently occupied. Perhaps next week—"

"Be my guest, sir," interrupted Griffin, with a wicked grin. "I'll muddle on without her." And he wandered off, pretending not to see as she crossed exasperated eyes at him.

She swallowed on Lizzie's jubilation. "What can I do for you, Captain?"

Lafayette tucked his hands behind his back, a flip of scarlet coattail. "I'd hoped to ask you the same. I can't help but observe you've been avoiding me."

She sidled around him, skirts squashing against the cluttered shop's wall. "Nonsense. Terribly busy, you know. Must go, can't stand around all morning indulging in chit-chat."

He jumped into her path. "Up to your neck in it, are you?"

She sidestepped a pile of carved frame parts. "Didn't I tell you? I've a new job, at the parish workhouses."

"I'm all admiration—"

"How gratifying."

"—but enabling society's exploitation of the poor? Hardly up to your enlightened standards." He blocked her way again, brandishing that disarming smile.

In fact, she'd already been dismissed from the job, for accusing parish officials of embezzling church funds. It was true, but that greedy beadle had fired her anyway. Despicable man, stealing food from impoverished mouths. Just the thought of him tickled an indignant itch up her arms. "I take what criminal cases I can, thank you."

Lafayette glanced at the crime scene, faking a shudder. "Villainy in the foulest! The Empire's fate surely rests upon solving this enormity."

Again, she tried to slip by in the cramped space. "Scoff if you will, sir. Police work isn't all murders and mayhem. Now, if you'll excuse me—"

"What if I could get you a *real* case?"

She halted, pulse thudding.

A knowing smile. "Gruesome, suspicious, the threat of sinister enemies unknown. A perfect chance to test your skills. Did I win you over yet?"

"Whatever are you blathering about?"

"A society murder, of course. High-profile case, get the jump on your charming constabulary colleagues. Naturally, you'll be paid for your expertise. If you're interested." Lafayette let his gaze wander. "Perhaps you aren't. Perhaps you enjoy being insulted by idiots and working misdemeanors for pocket change."

"Burglary's a felony," she corrected automatically. But temptation warred with caution in her mind. Never mind the payment, which she could surely use. To solve a big case, yet again prove herself worthy of a proper job . . .

"Not a very glamorous one. So are you in, or shall I call the next on my list of stunningly attractive medical geniuses?"

She snorted. "Is that what passes for charm at the Royal these days? Since when is homicide your purview?"

A flippant shrug. "It isn't. But from time to time—I can't imagine why—people like to whisper to me of certain peculiarities. And this case is very peculiar."

"Your spies, you mean. To save their own skins. Such public spirit."

"Call them what you please. I thought you might enjoy it, that's all. Told you I could use a crime scene physician, didn't I?" He hesitated. "Perchance you recall that conversation?"

She fidgeted.

"In your consulting room, one evening six weeks ago? When I asked you to marry me? Whereupon the conversation abruptly ended?"

Light suddenly glared into every crevice, leaving her nowhere to hide. The constables grew deeply entranced by their tasks. Even Griffin examined a pile of coiled wire with unwarranted intensity.

Smiling blandly, she dragged Lafayette into a corner, beneath a pair of ugly spaniel portraits on the wall. "This is hardly the time nor place, sir," she hissed. "If you're hoping to embarrass me into an answer, it won't work."

Lafayette winced, and tugged his chestnut curls. A little too ragged for decency. A creature such as he needed frequent haircuts. "I didn't mean it like that. If you want the case, it's yours, regardless." An irrepressible glint of bright eyes. "But I note you haven't yet said no to either. Dare one hope?"

Reeve strutted up, brandishing his cigar stub. "Are you two love bunnies quite finished?"

Eliza sprang a foot backwards, certain her face outreddened Lafayette's coat. "Chief Inspector. We were just—"

"Spare me the sordid particulars, missy. I pay you to work, not pursue your little affair d'amours."

Piss off, you rude little rat, yelled Lizzie in her ear. Eliza fought to keep still, nerves jangling.

Lafayette bristled, stroking his sword hilt. "Were your French not such a tragedy, sir, I should take you to task for that insulting plural."

Honestly. Add "gallant" and "idiotic" to his list of maddening attributes. "Gentlemen, please. Such primitive hostility."

Reeve just grinned bullishly. "Watch it, Captain. This isn't 1815, and you're not the Duke of bloody Wellington. I could arrest you, Royal Society or not. Dueling's a capital crime."

"Only if I kill you." A chilly Lafayette smile. "Perhaps I'll just leave you to bleed."

"With a dozen armed constables at my back? I don't think so." Reeve chewed his cigar. "Now clear off. I don't remember inviting you to my crime scene."

Lafayette didn't budge. "What a pity I don't need your invitation."

Let Remy kill the little squeezer, hissed Lizzie. *Better still, let ME tear the rude bastard's face off. Stuff that stinking cigar up his nose. Squeeze his scrawny neck until his eyeballs bleed . . .*

Sweating, Eliza laid a hand on Lafayette's arm. "Captain, be so good as to refrain from gutting our Chief Inspector, at least not this morning."

"If it please you, madam." Lafayette's stare didn't defrost. A flat, disturbing, metallic shine. A *wolfish* shine. Oh, dear. Was it that time again?

Shakily, Eliza faced Reeve, with Lizzie roiling and thrashing beneath her skin. "As for the crime scene, sir? No forced entry, and your witnesses claim they saw no one. Either they're lying and someone let the thief in—in which case I've no doubt a man of your impressive stature will beat the truth out of them directly . . ."

Finally, Reeve scowled. "Or?"

She smiled brightly. "Or they're telling the truth, and the burglar has covered his tracks with an unorthodox trick."

Ha ha ha! Lizzie cackled. *Stick that in your cigar, weedbrain!*

"Makes sense," put in Griffin airily.

"Unorthodox, eh?" muttered Reeve, with a sharp glance at Lafayette. "Clever of you, I'm sure."

Eliza widened her eyes. "Are you ill, sir? Or was that a glimmer of grudging regard?"

Reeve flicked away his cigar stub. "Don't push me, missy. I can't scour the streets for an invisible thief."

"Can't you? And here I thought you were the expert."

"Sting me with your wit, will you?" He gave her a hurt look. "Last time I do you a favor."

Eliza stared, taken aback. Reeve was old-fashioned in more than his condescending attitude. He'd thrived on the old thief-taker's methods: informers, tip-offs, bribes exchanged in dark corners, confessions beaten from yowling unfortunates. But epic mulishness made him dogged, not incompetent, and impressing the Home Office with a swift result was his idea of a good day's work. Reeve truly thought this petty theft an important case.

What if he'd honestly intended to help her?

But Lizzie's rage made her shudder and sweat, and her mouth stung with sour need for the elixir. She wasn't inclined to show mercy. "Shall I do your job for you yet again? I suggest you put the hard word on your security guards and smoke out the burglar's accomplice. Otherwise, I believe only one invisible thief of note is at work in London, and that's Harry the Haunter."

Reeve gaped like a half-skinned eel. "Harry the who?"

"The mythical miscreant who stole the Balmoral Diamond and robbed the Royal Exchange? Perhaps you'd have read of him in your divisional reports, if you weren't too busy hobnobbing with the Commissioner to pay attention to real detective work."

She stuffed her optical into its leather case and shouldered her bag. "I shall forward my account in due course. Good day, Chief Inspector." And in a satisfied swirl of skirts, she stalked out.

———◦◦◦———

Outside, on Great Portland Street, acid bubbled in her throat, and her hair coiled like wound springs, yearning to *change*. She swallowed a scream. *It's not your turn, Lizzie. Stop it!*

Hippocrates scurried after her, brassy feet clattering over the curb. Uncaring traffic hustled by, the din roaring in her ears. She inhaled deeply, then again. It didn't help. The foul air only wrung her throat dry with unbearable thirst.

The crowd jostled her, a barrage of skirts and coattails and careless elbows. She fumbled for her little phial of remedy—a drug to relieve the symptoms of her darker dependency on Lizzie's elixir—and gulped a mouthful.

Her eyes watered. The horrid salty flavor made her gag. Gradually, her squirming skin subsided, but still, the craving for that warm, strangely bitter drink that set Lizzie free writhed, a ghost trapped in a bottle, swirling in ever-tightening knots, until . . .

"That went well." Effortlessly, Captain Lafayette matched her stride, dodging loping clockwork servants and costermongers yelling about strawberries or salted fish.

Curse him, but the man didn't give up easily. "Did someone speak? I'm afraid I heard only childish babbling."

A sheepish glance. "Fair enough. I apologize. I lost my temper with him. Your hair looks stunning, by the way. Is that a new hat?"

"Lost your temper? If I'm not mistaken, you grabbed for your sword to defend my honor. I rather think you've lost your mind."

"Well—"

"Or is it that you imagine yourself some swashbuckling Georgian highwayman, to duel at dawn for a lady's favor? Either way, I recommend a swift pistol shot as the better solution."

He opened his mouth, and shut it again.

"Wise," she remarked, wedging past a flower-seller, who waved a basket of red chrysanthemums. "I'm glad we're agreed you're a romantic fool, Remy Lafayette."

"I prefer 'foolish romantic,' but point conceded. I'm sorry."

"Apology noted."

"And accepted?"

"Your credit is limited, sir. Don't waste it all in one day." But uneasily, she recalled that glint of wolfish eye. An impending full moon did strange things to those who *changed*. "I trust you're in good health," she added belatedly. "It being, er . . . Friday quite soon."

"Never better," he announced, too readily. "Your concern touches my heart."

"How quaint. From your daft behavior, I imagined it had touched your wits."

"Ouch. Is it wrong that I've missed your tongue-lashings?"

"No, but it's timely." She smiled sweetly. "I've been polishing my store of insults on the off chance you should show your irritating face."

They reached Oxford Street, where electric omnibuses rattled amongst horses and clockwork carriages. Glowing purple coils crackled amidst the whir of cogs and the thundery smell of aether. Tall brass velocipedes weaved in and out on teetering wheels, their riders holding on to the handlebars for dear life.

At length, Lafayette chuckled. "Harry the Haunter, eh? Or did you invent that to annoy Reeve?"

She waved at a one-legged paper-seller, whose headlines today yelled EMPIRE PREPARES FOR WAR—LAST CHANCE FOR PARIS EMISSARIES and DEPORTATION SQUADS RAID ENEMY ENCLAVES IN WEST END and RADICALS PUSH FOR COMMONS REFORM. "Don't you read the broadsheets? Harry's responsible for every grand theft since the Crimean Gold, they say. In and out like a ghost, they say, seen and heard by no one."

"Except you."

Her optical with its unorthodox lenses suddenly weighed her down, incriminating. Secrecy and suspicion died hard. She laughed to cover her unease. "It's all nonsense. Likely the thief overpowered the guards with some stupefying concoction, and they were too embarrassed to confess. Reeve will have a fine time closing this one without me."

"Dr. Jekyll, did I ever tell you you're magnificent?"

She frowned. "Your idiotic remarks make such limited impression, I'm afraid I don't recall. You uttered some flattering nonsense about my hat?"

"If you'll take my murder case, I'll happily flatter you all over."

Temptation warmed her skin again. Money, prestige, a case that mattered . . . "I can barely wait. Good day, Captain." She swept around the corner, dismissing him.

But Lafayette jumped into her path, unsheathing an utterly unfair smile. "That's a yes, then?"

Her skirts were jammed between his thigh and the centipede-like brass legs of a waiting omnibus. She tugged. They wouldn't come free. "Do you deny your ulterior motive?"

"Not for an instant. Doesn't change the fact that you want me desperately. My case, I mean."

She sniffed. "I suppose a mild diversion could amuse."

"There you are, then. Admit it: you've missed me."

Eliza sighed. "Very well, if you insist. Show me what you've got." She eyed him sternly over her spectacles. "For the case, that is."

A dazzling twinkle of blue. "Naturally. Whatever else could you mean?"

THE OLD-FASHIONED WAY

• • •

HOW BURLESQUE," REMARKED ELIZA AN HOUR later, as grimy mid-morning fog crawled through the broken window of a grandiose drawing room in Grosvenor Square. Peevish yellow sunlight glared at a set of Queen Anne armchairs, a green-baized billiards table, expensive Indian carpets. The grit stung her throat, driving away even the meat-copper stench of clotting blood.

The dead man sprawled on his side in a pool of black gore. A hunk of bronze poked from a ragged wound in his neck—a crucifix, complete with emaciated Christ—and the victim's face was missing. Peeled away, leaving a sticky crimson mess in which his lidless eyeballs glistened. His starched shirt front was torn open, and a bloody hole gaped below his sternum. On the carpet, in a splash of blood, sat his heart.

"I promised you gruesome." Lafayette made an ironic bow. "Meet Sir Dalziel Fleet, baronet. Painter, culture critic, society's arbiter of artistic taste. Fashionable fools hanging on his every breath. A genuine waste of space, in fact. They ought to have elevated him to the peerage."

"I've heard the name. Poor silly fellow." She knelt by the corpse's skinned face, and a swift ache knifed her heart. In life, this man had been rich, privileged, powerful. What was he now? Dead, mutilated, his effects poked into by strangers.

No matter the victim, murder demanded justice. And she, Eliza Jekyll, would make certain he got it.

Behind the body, in one papered wall, yawned a secret door. The hinged panel had swung inwards, revealing a large private closet. Ransacked, papers and books littering a desk and a plush red chaise. A wall safe hung open, the picture that had covered it torn down and crushed.

"Love and money," she murmured. "The two most common motives for murder. Which is this, I wonder?"

"Add 'fear' to the list." Lafayette shielded his eyes from the bloodied crucifix. "Brr! Clandestine Roman Catholics, scourge of the Empire! We've suspected the good baronet for years."

His casual "we" made her squirm. The Royal preyed on anyone weak or vulnerable. She'd thought Lafayette to be different. But his offhanded charm made it all too easy to forget his defining characteristic: threat. "Persistent of you," she said tartly. "Last I heard, faith isn't a crime."

"But dangerous superstition is. It's difficult to reason with people who eat the flesh of their god." He grimaced. "Still, I wouldn't wish this horrid demise on anyone."

In a corner, a clockwork footman jigged on long hinged legs. It wore a tailcoat and tie over its narrow brass skeleton. Hipp galloped up and tried to climb it, flashing his blue *happy* light. The footman screeched, flapping hysterical arms. "Unacceptable! Unwelcome visitor! Recompute!"

"Do shut up," muttered Eliza. The machine whirred indignantly, but obeyed.

Beside it, the butler—a living one—was spotlessly turned out in black coat and white gloves. An unusually young and ornamental fellow, to be sure, for such a senior post, with dark-lashed eyes and startling coal-black curls. "The room's as I found it, my lord. Madam."

"Excellent." Lafayette winked down at him. "But flattery will profit you none. At least, not at this hour."

The butler blushed. "Effusive apologies, sir."

"No matter, Mr. Brigham. Easy mistake. You say no one else has seen this?"

Brigham licked a reddish bruise on his lip. "The household is from home, sir. I sent to you soonest when I discovered what 'ad 'appened." A trace of the East London accent he was trying to cover.

"Where might 'from home' be?"

"Hampstead, sir. Lady Fleet's country house. She goes every weekend, with 'er maid and the carriage and the first footman. We held a dinner party here last night. Twenty, or thereabouts. The guests didn't leave until nearly two. No visitors since."

"Outstanding work, Mr. Brigham. Don't go far." A tip exchanged hands, and Brigham bowed out.

Eliza eyed Lafayette archly as he closed the wood-paneled door. "How much did that cost?"

"Five pounds and a flirt? Least I can do for such a precocious lad. Twenty-one if he's a day, and already the senior manservant. Shouldn't surprise me if he gets fired after this. I rather feel for him, don't you?"

"Quite," she said, chastened. Doubtless, Lafayette had lived in a house full of servants from childhood, but it was just like him to *notice* people. For fair reason or foul. "So your solution is to make your pet butler the Royal's spy?"

"Don't look at me like that," protested Lafayette. "True, he'd get along better if he didn't blush quite so brightly at the sight of a gentleman in uniform, but that's hardly my fault."

"The poor deluded boy. His definition of 'gentleman' clearly leaves much to be desired."

Lafayette glanced at the ugly crystal-faced mantel clock. "Well, don't just stand there looking clever. Time is of the essence! The grieving widow will soon return, having called on our erudite friends at the Metropolitan Police. I'd say we've all of ten minutes until your fame-seeking Chief Inspector arrives."

"Excellent." She petted Hipp. "Have a sniff for organic traces, there's a good boy." Hipp ground eager cogs, *skrrk! skrrk!,* and snuffled off with his *happy* light blinking. He'd a catalog of organic samples stored in his tiny brain. If blood or other stains were present, he'd find them.

She poked her tweezers at the severed heart. "Torn out, not cut. That aorta has snapped at the weakest point, adjoining the heart." She slid her fingers beneath the corpse's armpit. "Quite cold, muscles stiff. Several hours dead. I'd say soon after the dinner party ended."

"Twenty suspects. How convenient." Lafayette examined a drinks tray that sat on the untidy desk, amidst tossed papers, and sniffed a dirty glass. "Scotch, single malt."

"Collar and cuffs removed," she mused. "Comes down *après* party, takes a drink . . ." She frowned. "Wait. Everyone was out of town. They held a party with no servants? Just Brigham and the clockworks?"

"Perhaps a secret, racy sort of party." Lafayette beckoned to the clockwork footman, which still jerked in the corner like a frantic marionette. "You. Tell me about last night."

Cogs rattled in its pointed head. "Dinner," it yammered, "ten o'clock. Twenty guests. First course, tuna fish wafers—"

"Delicious, I'm sure," interrupted Lafayette. "What time did the guests leave?"

"Last departure, ten minutes to two. Ten minutes to two. Ten minutes to two . . ."

Hippocrates popped out a glowing purple coil on a stick and jabbed the machine's legs. *Zzap!* "Fault! Inferior mechanism. Upgrade!"

"Ten minutes to two! Ten minutes to two . . ."

Eliza waved the footman off. "Enough, silly thing."

It dashed out, flailing frenzied arms. "Unacceptable! Ten minutes to two! Tuna fish!"

"Inferior," sniggered Hipp. "Upgrade futile. Recommend scrap heap."

Wryly, Eliza shook her head. "Practically manic. That's what you get for choosing a cheap substitute."

Lafayette shrugged. "It confirmed Brigham's story. Machines don't lie."

"You don't trust your blushing beau?"

A spectacular half-smile. "I'm a Royal investigator, Doctor. I don't trust anyone."

"I'm sorry, were you including me in that?" She peered at the corpse through her magnifying lens and swabbed crusted blood. "Look: markings cut into his chest. Quite precise. A

thin blade, like a penknife. A five-pointed star, encircled,
with . . ."

A half-circle, joined to a circle, joined to a cross. An alchemical symbol. Mercury.

Her nerves smarted. What did it mean? Was Lafayette
trying to trap her? "Looks like something from a bad gothic
novel," she amended lamely. "What is it?"

"Irrational," muttered Hipp, scratching the carpet. "Does
not compute."

Lafayette studied the cuts. "A pentacle. Used in, shall we
say, doubly unorthodox rituals? And the symbol for mercury,"
he added, "as if you didn't recognize it. Anyone would think
you were hiding something."

"Anyone would think *you* knew about this before we arrived. First a crucifix, now a pentacle. Tell me you don't believe in black magic."

"I did promise sinister enemies unknown."

Zzap! Hipp jabbed gleefully at the corpse with his glowing
coil, making it jerk. "Irrational. Logic flawed. Recompute."
Zzap!

"Stop it, Hipp," scolded Eliza. She eased one of the cuts
apart with her tweezers. "Look how pale this flesh is. The
cuts haven't bled. Post-mortem, same as the heart extraction.

You don't jam your hand into a living man's chest without making more of a mess."

"Unless he was insensible. He reeks of that single-malt Scotch, enough to fell a medium-sized horse. Also, that's Caribbean tobacco, laced with . . . Chinese opium, or some such. See, I come in handy sometimes."

"A veritable scent encyclopedia." She scraped ash into a test tube, and pointed at a long bloodstain at the desk's foot. "But look, the victim was standing when he was stabbed. Not so insensible after all."

"How's that?"

"That's arterial blood, sprayed under pressure. Imagine the victim standing here." She twirled to assume the position. "Crucifix in the throat, *whoosh!* Blood all over the assailant. Except . . ." She frowned. "The spatter is unobstructed. It doesn't make sense. If you're close enough to stab a man in the throat, there's no leaping out of the way. You'll get it all over you."

Lafayette eyed the carpet, dubious. "Perhaps the killer was very short."

"An opium-smoking dwarf brandishing a crucifix. How our theories deteriorate. No, the victim was attacked from behind. Which necessitates a killer of a certain height, to achieve that downwards angle of entry." Gingerly, she freed the bloodied crucifix. "Not exactly sharp, is it? A perverse choice of weapon."

"Spur of the moment? He grabs whatever was to hand."

"And lingers afterwards to carve up the corpse? No, this was the spur of no moment that I can perceive. The killer brings a knife, yet chooses this. Why?"

"A sense of theater?"

"Or something in particular to say." She eyed Lafayette expectantly. "So was Sir Dalziel dabbling in black magic as well as papistry? Is that the real reason the Royal are watching him? Is this a ritual gone wrong?"

The crystalline clock chimed the quarter hour.

"Three minutes to go, Doctor. You tell me." Lafayette began to rummage through the desk. "Drawer forced, letters and sketches ripped up. And that empty safe, key in the lock, contents missing." He indicated the mangled painting on the floor. "They knew where it was, or took an educated guess."

She eased the crucifix back into the wound. "Seems a lot of effort just to cover up a burglary. If I'd killed a man who'd caught me in the act, I don't believe I'd hang around to mutilate the body."

"You imagine the fellow who did that"—Lafayette pointed to the extracted heart—"is thinking things through?"

"I'm thinking he had a very particular purpose. Murder was his aim, theft an opportunity."

"Ah. So he breaks the window to enter. Stabs the old man, tears out his heart, rips his face off, *schllpp!* Job done. Filches the fellow's cash for good measure, and off he trots?"

"Plausible. Especially if the killer was hired, and looting the scene for a bonus." She tested the sliced edges around the dead man's chin with her scalpel. "A human face isn't strongly attached to the skull. Cut around the edge, it'll just peel off. But why?"

"For fun? No point trying to hide this victim's identity."

"Hmm. But to hide something else about him . . . ?"

"Like what?"

"I've no idea," she admitted. "Where is it? I wonder. The face, I mean."

"Perhaps the killer took it with him. Proof of a job well done. A powerful man like Sir Dalziel has enemies. Sending a message?"

She rose to examine the carpet, where Hippocrates snuffled and squeaked. "All this carving and stabbing. Surely he's left some traces . . . Aha!" She pointed triumphantly at a curved smudge of blood. "Difficult to make footprints when you're drowning in your own blood. Captain, meet our killer."

"Man or woman?"

Her brows arched.

"The wife's always the chief suspect, isn't she? I get the impression they didn't like each other."

"But peeling his face off? Hardly a society wife's specialty. Simpler to poison the fellow's port."

"Given it much thought, have you? Murdering one's husband, I mean."

"One should plan for every contingency."

"Indeed. I sleep with a loaded weapon for that very purpose. Just so you know."

"I'll bear that in mind." She squirted a sheet of paper with a clear solution and touched it to the footprint. The outline seeped gently through the paper, its shape copied. "In any case, this belongs to a man. A narrow shoe, a fashionable gentleman's type." She pointed to another smudge. "He's long-legged. So not our lovesick Mr. Brigham."

"A party guest?"

"Mmm. We must get a list of names." She walked to the window, frowning. "Smudges in the blood there, as if he strode back and forth. But no footprints back this way. So either he took a different exit, or . . ."

The front door slammed. Eliza groaned. "Ready or not."

The drawing room door burst open, and in stalked Chief Inspector Reeve, four constables on his heels. "Right, you two. Out."

Swiftly, Eliza backed towards the body before Lizzie could react. "I say, have the police not already attended? Captain Lafayette, you odious mischief-maker, you deceive me again. I'm terribly sorry . . . Oh!" She stumbled, swiping her skirt hem into the bloodstain. "Dear me. So clumsy."

Quickly, Lafayette thrust a sheaf of Sir Dalziel's papers into her bag behind her back. "No need for alarm. We were just leaving."

"Alarm unnecessary," chirped Hipp, kicking up his feet. "Exit imminent."

Furniture crashed in the hall. "Out of my way, you horrid monster-boy!" A flurry of black satin skirts swept in. Lady Fleet, presumably, surprisingly slim and pretty, trailing a dark veil over her elaborate blond chignon. She'd certainly laid hands on the appropriate mourning attire at a moment's notice.

Suddenly the idea of this fashionable young wife doing away her rich, elderly husband didn't seem so unlikely.

"You, sir!" Lady Fleet pointed dramatically at Lafayette. "Leave my house immediately. You and your preposterous accusations have hounded my poor husband to his grave. Dispatched in his own home by some vile scion of the criminal classes! Are you satisfied?"

Brava! cheered Lizzie ironically, and Eliza resisted the urge to applaud. If Lady Fleet had held a fan, or a pair of gloves, she'd probably have slapped him with it.

Lafayette bowed gravely. "My condolences, my lady. Who would do such a terrible thing? And in a secret closet, too. Is no one safe?"

Lady Fleet's eyes gleamed, calculating. Then—a moment too late—she burst into tears. "My poor Dalziel! How I shall miss him." She collapsed against Reeve in a paroxysm of weeping. Hippocrates squeaked, and scuttled for the hallway. Eliza could practically smell the onions the lady had rubbed into her eyes.

Reeve's ruddy face flushed even redder. Awkwardly, he patted Lady Fleet's hair and off-loaded her to a smirking constable. "We'll soon have it sorted, my lady. You have my word."

He fired a sharp glance around. "Window smashed, room ransacked. Burglary gone wrong, I'd say. Shouldn't take long to flush out the villain. My lady, why don't you have a nice lie-down, and mend your nerves? You there, fellow," he ordered, "fetch Lady Fleet some tea."

"You're very kind," Lady Fleet whispered, dabbing streaming eyes, and let the constable help her out.

"A command performance," remarked Eliza, once the door had closed. "You're not actually buying into that?"

Reeve didn't turn. "Still here, missy?"

Lafayette tugged her arm, but she resisted. Like any murdered soul, Sir Dalziel deserved justice, not Reeve's self-serving pig-headedness. "This man's heart is ripped out and his face cut off. Elaborate for a burglar, wouldn't you say? And how would a casual thief know about the hidden closet? Unless it's an inside job, in which case why—?"

"Yes, yes. Always complicating things, aren't you?" Reeve glared at her. "Never can solve a case the old-fashioned way. I swear, you're that upstart Griffin born again."

We'll solve you the old-fashioned way, you pumped-up turkey, whispered Lizzie darkly. *Come by the Holy Land late one night and I'll uncomplicate you with a knife in the guts.*

Eliza gritted her teeth. "How sad. Have I left you no one convenient from whom to thrash a confession?"

"Remains to be seen, doesn't it?" Reeve grinned. "Perhaps your friend Razor Jack did it. You know, the lunatic killer *you* allowed to escape?"

She flushed. "Razor Jack is *not* my friend, and I didn't *allow* anything—"

"Protesting too much, are we?" Reeve rounded on Lafayette. "As for you, Royal Society, I'll tell you once more, and then I'll get unpleasant: Homicide's a police matter. Stay out of it."

"As you wish, sir. I'm confident you have it fully in hand." Firmly, Lafayette ushered a squirming Eliza into the hall, with Hipp scampering ahead.

"And stay away from the servants," called Reeve, "or I'll nick you for obstructing my investigation." The door slammed.

"Shouldn't dream of it, old boy." Lafayette studied her as they treaded the long hall towards the front door. "Are you well, Doctor? Perhaps we should retire."

"Why must that man be so obtuse?" she fumed. "He's no fool, yet he refuses to countenance the simplest police work, let alone any attempt at science. You'd think he was put on this earth to infuriate me."

"Jealousy makes idiots of us all," murmured Lafayette.

"Reeve, jealous of me? That's absurd."

He laughed, easy. "Allow me to polish your spectacles, Doctor. You're young, clever, educated, and pretty, with the world at your feet. He's backward, middle-aged, and unattractive, with two unmarried daughters and a demanding wife who wants to be Lady Police Commissioner someday. I'm only surprised he hasn't wrung your neck already."

"What? Nonsense." But she sniffed, discomfited. She'd never met Mrs. Reeve. Hadn't wondered whether one existed. As usual, Lafayette was dangerously well informed. But it made her speculate. Could the murder motive be jealousy? A rival slighted, a woman scorned . . .

By the door, the manic clockwork servant jerked like a pecking chicken. A saturnine fellow in livery—Lady Fleet's footman, presumably—stoically ignored it, glaring in poorly veiled disgust at the butler, who was bailed up in the archway by an eagerly springing Hippocrates. Perhaps the clockwork servant's problem was catching.

"Mr. Brigham, are you and this fellow here the only human servants?" asked Eliza.

Brigham bowed. "Plus Lady Fleet's maid and the cook, madam. The rest are clockworks."

"Odd, isn't it, for a household to rely so heavily on machines?"

"Couldn't say, madam." Brigham ignored Hipp, who scrabbled at his trouser leg.

Eliza hid a grin. "This party last night. Who attended?"

A twitch of besieged knee. "The usual. Sir Dalziel's students and, um, other friends. We finished around two, and I went to bed."

"And his 'um other friends' would be . . . ?"

Brigham handed Lafayette a scrap of paper. "Thought you'd want a list, sir."

"Good man." Lafayette scanned it rapidly. "A bright bunch, I see . . . Why do they all invite *her* . . . ? Cartwright, M.P., eh? Of the new Reform Bill? Who'd have thought Sir Dalziel would rub shoulders with a radical?"

"You'd be surprised, sir."

"Would I?" Lafayette frowned at the list. "Zanotti. You don't mean Carmine Zanotti? His *Eve and the Serpent* is on show at the Academy."

"Indeed," murmured Eliza. "Who knew you were a fan of art?"

"I'm a fan of prodigious talent," said Lafayette with a quick smile. "It so often goes with malfeasance. Your own, for instance."

She ignored him. "You said no visitors after the party broke up?"

Brigham shrugged. "Didn't hear a bell."

"Bell!" Hipp head-butted Brigham's knee and bounced off, falling in a heap. "Bell-bell-bell . . ."

"Sir Dalziel might have expected someone," suggested Lafayette. "Then they wouldn't need to ring."

A baffled blink. "But weren't it just a ruckus? I mean, was the villain not some vile burglar?"

Eliza smiled. "The police certainly think so. Certain you heard nothing?"

"No, I . . ." Brigham toed Hipp away. "Come to think of it, I did, but I didn't come up. I thought . . ."

"Yes?"

"I heard breaking glass."

"The window? Why would you not come up?"

Stiffly, Brigham raised his bruised chin. "I thought it was Sir Dalziel throwing crystal. He was worse for drink. They'd been arguing politics. When he's in a temper, it's best not to be seen. He's not so patient." The lad licked his reddened lip. "With the crystal."

"Crystal," agreed Hipp, making another attempt to climb Brigham's leg.

Old tyrant had it coming, muttered Lizzie. *Bat his servants around as he pleased, did he? Arsehole.*

"I see. Can you estimate the time you heard the glass break?"

"Ten minutes to four, give or take."

Lafayette cocked one eyebrow. "So precise?"

"Checked my watch, sir. I sleep poorly, and I'd only just gone off when the noise woke me."

"Keeps proper time, does it?"

"The best, sir. It's my job to wind the clocks, and keep the monsters in good repair."

"Monsters?"

"The mechanical servants, madam."

"I see . . . Oh, pet him, Mr. Brigham, he won't relent until you do."

Cautiously, the butler offered his hand. Hipp bunted it, whirring happily. "A bit overstressed, aren't you, boy? Could use an overhaul."

"He certainly could," threatened Eliza, and Hipp whined, contrite. "Did you know about this secret closet?"

"Of course. Sir Dalziel kept personal things there. Letters and such."

"And did his friends know?"

"I expect so. It weren't secret so much as private."

Her nerves twanged. A person ought to be permitted to keep secrets. Now Sir Dalziel's were being exposed. "Any oddities in his behavior lately? Keeping strange company?"

"They're artists, madam. Behaving oddly's what they do."

"So you've no idea who might extract his heart and carve a magical symbol into his chest?"

Brigham shook his head, pale.

"One last thing," put in Lafayette. "How would you characterize Sir Dalziel's relationship with his lady wife?"

A blank look. "They were married."

"Yes, but affectionate or at war? Devoted lovebirds or playing around on the side?"

"Not my place to judge the upper classes, sir. Different rules for them."

"So I've heard. Supremely helpful as always, Charles. If ever you need a job, come and see me." Lafayette flipped Brigham another, larger tip.

"Flirt," whispered Eliza as they turned to leave.

"Is that an accusation, or an imperative?" Lafayette retrieved his hat from the scowling footman, whose elaborate livery involved breeches, lace-edged cuffs, and a braided coat, fresh from the previous century. The upper classes put their servants into such silly costumes. As if the class divide weren't clear enough. "What's your name, good man?"

"James, sir." Eyes front, chin up. Poor at concealing his hostility in hope of a tip. Lady Fleet must be paying him too well. Buying his silence, perhaps?

"Any point in my questioning you, James, or will you just glare bayonets at me and deny everything about any black magic in this house?"

Coldly, James yanked open the door. "I was in the country, sir. I don't know anything."

"Glad we've cleared that up." From the doorstep, Lafayette shot him an icy challenge. "One thing more. You'd better hope nothing nasty happens to Mr. Brigham this morning. Or ever, come to think of it."

"Sir?"

A bright, threatening Lafayette smile. "You've just made a new best friend. If I see any more bruises on his innocent little face? I'll come looking for you. Understand?"

THE NUMERICAL ENCHANTRESS

•••

OUTSIDE, SUNLIGHT STRUGGLED THROUGH THE gritty haze to bathe the grandiose houses of Grosvenor Square with their ornate plastering and grand brickwork. Their windows gleamed, dulled with greasy coal dust. Next door, a grim-faced maid in a drab apron scrubbed fruitlessly at her front steps. The coal-burning power station upriver had been blown up by home-grown republican outlaws a week ago—the demise at the Royal's hands of the relatively moderate Thistlewood Club had left the door open for a gang of dangerous radicals dubbed "the Incorruptibles," led by a cunning rabble-rouser by the unlikely name of Nemo. Since the explosion, which had been heard all the way down at Rotherhithe, London had smothered under a dirty pall of fog that crawled into every crack and crevice. Half the electric lights in town still languished unpowered, and everything was constantly filthy.

Eliza tucked a struggling Hippocrates into her bag, and she and Captain Lafayette walked east towards New Bond Street, beneath a row of trees. Clammy fog-fingers curled under her skirts. "So gallant, sir," she teased. "I'm practically a-faint. Brigham will fall over himself to earn another smile from you. Would you really employ him?"

"I might." Lafayette didn't offer his arm. Nothing so presumptuous. Just strolled at her side, hands tucked behind him. His scarlet-and-gold uniform glared like a bloodstain in the coarse light. "I feel sorry for the lad. I'm reminded unpleasantly of public school: always some witless oaf waiting to thrash your lights out."

"That explains a lot." She eyed his Royal Society badge. "A dish best served cold?"

"Never crossed my mind."

An electric carriage thundered by, purple coils crackling in the damp. A pair of harnessed horses sidestepped and rolled crazed eyes. Crossing sweepers darted beneath speeding wheels to scrape up dung. Housekeepers and kitchen maids loomed from the fog, balancing baskets of vegetables and meats from the market.

"I say, watch out!" Eliza dodged a sprinting clockwork servant with a bundle over its skinny shoulder. It whirred self-importantly and hared off, *clank! clank!,* scattering shoppers in its wake. She dusted her skirts angrily. "Stupid thing. They can build them so much better than that. But that's what happens when you debase science with commercial concerns. Cheap materials and shoddy workmanship."

"Stupid," echoed Hipp dolefully inside her bag. "Cheap."

A lady flounced by, a pet hedgehog on a chain tucked under her arm. Her decorative leather throat armor stretched from collarbone to chin, forcing her nose into the air at a comical angle.

Lizzie laughed, and Eliza snickered, too, earning a haughty glare. When Razor Jack had escaped from Bethlem, panic had ensued, spawning all manner of bizarre safeguards against that singular gentleman's favorite weapon. Naturally, the society set had turned the practical, if fanciful, armor into a fashion statement.

As if an expert like Razor Jack would be thwarted by a device so banal. If he wanted you dead, you perished. End of story.

Lafayette tipped his hat to the lady, who simpered, until she noticed his iron badge, whereupon she avoided eye contact.

Shivering, Eliza tugged her shawl tighter. "Burglary, indeed. Reeve will never solve this case. Your case, that is."

"Reeve doesn't solve cases. He plays angles. Swift results, no questions asked. Not the sharpest tool in the box, but he's accomplished at giving people what they want."

Her sense of justice bristled. "Who'd want the wrong man arrested for murder?"

"I say, did it rain crime scene physicians this morning? I must have missed the weather reports."

"Excuse me?"

"Black magic, secret debauchery, Lady Fleet's reputation at stake? Do you imagine anyone cares who actually did it?"

"I care," insisted Eliza. "Playing the angles, indeed. If this were my case—which it isn't, of course, what a shame I haven't time to assist further—I wouldn't let anyone's reputation pervert the path of justice."

"Did I mention that's why I'm besotted with you?"

"Really? I imagined you bamboozled by my exotic beauty."

"There's that. But mostly it's your fortune I'm after."

"Consider me forewarned." More from habit than interest, she fingered through the offerings on a book-seller's cart: *The Daily Telegraph*, Mrs. *Beeton's Book of Household Management*, a luridly illustrated edition of Burton's famous *Pilgrimage to Al-Madinah and Meccah*. A penny pamphlet entitled VARNEY THE VAMPYRE! sported a leering black-caped imp ravishing a swooning maiden on a canopied bed.

Newspaper headlines promised violence and mayhem:

ASSASSINATION FOILED
FRENCH ARSONIST ARRESTED IN COMMONS LOBBY

TOXIC FOG COULD DELAY GREEN PARK SKYSHIP LAUNCH

PALACE RISKS LAST-MINUTE DIPLOMATIC OVERTURES

"Massacre in Paris!" shouted the newsboy. "Blood in the Bois de Boulogne! Killer sorcerers run amok!"

Across the street, a pair of bulky brass-skeletoned automatons cataloged the crowd with glittering red eyes. Royal Society Enforcers, their white plaster faces impassive. Armed with twin pistols, electro-clockwork engines ticking indefatigably inside hollow chests.

Lizzie thrashed in Eliza's belly. *Dog-lickers! Turdbrains! Metal-dick freaks!*

Lafayette looked at her oddly. "I'm sorry?"

Had she muttered that aloud? Mortified, Eliza fanned flushed cheeks. "Friends of yours?"

"Practically family," he said cheerfully. "Morning, chaps. This horrid weather rusts the joints, eh?"

The machines ignored him, guarding a large cage that lumbered along, *clonk! clunk!,* on stodgy iron feet. An older lady twirled a sharp-tipped parasol in one iron prosthetic hand. Her steps jerked, out of kilter, twitching her silvery skirts. On her copper corsage gleamed a Royal Society badge.

Lafayette dipped a bow. "My lady."

The lady nodded mechanically. Her face would have been beautiful, but part of it was missing. One glinting steel cheek-bone lay exposed, scar-edged skin grafted with rivets. Her deep-set eyes glittered, one electric red, like an Enforcer's, the other a dead black.

Eliza shivered. "Congratulations," she whispered after they'd passed, "you've certainly charmed *her* sense of humor away."

"I flatter myself that there wasn't much to work with. Behold the Countess of Lovelace, my new observer. A formidable investigator with a jagged-toothed rat trap for a brain."

Eliza resisted the need to turn and stare. That metalwork was both fabulous and gruesome. "Why the prosthetics? Was she injured?"

"The Royal's instrument-makers rebuilt her after some terrible *accident.*" An ironic emphasis. "Blew her own face off with a ballistic pistol, they say, like Robespierre himself."

"A dangerous choice of comparison."

"An apt one, given the frightful things they did with that unlucky fellow's remains. She's using herself as the model for the new breed of half-flesh Enforcers she's developing. With limited success, I might add, which isn't improving her temper. François tells me she's quite the curiosity of the town."

Her mind whirred like Hipp's cogs in alarm. She'd heard tales of the Royal's artificial body experiments, mostly from her gleefully gossiping pharmacist, M

metal, grafted to living flesh and ne

make the Enforcers stronger, quicke

stimuli. But the flesh kept expiring fro

plant before it could recover from its wo

Eliza could have taught them a thin

changed, any scratches or wounds healed.   , were

remade afresh. An elixir like hers would solve Lady Lovelace's

problems for good.

Just another reason to keep Lafayette at a distance.

"I'm told your brother's quite the war hero," she covered hastily. "He'd do better not to repeat scurrilous tales."

"And how would you know, having avoided every opportunity to meet him?"

"Nonsense. I've been—"

"—very busy, yes. I don't doubt it." A tiny dog snarled at Lafayette, yapping. He arched an incredulous eyebrow, and it cringed away with a supplicating whine. "Scurrilous or otherwise: word is, Lady Lovelace went mad from unrequited love, and now she has a clockwork heart. Perhaps you've heard of the fellow. A certain Mr. Faraday, whom the Royal burned? They say it was she who betrayed him in the end. Isn't irony a killer?"

Henry Jekyll's colleague, in fact, executed for defying the Philosopher's notions of light and electricity. Eliza remembered him vaguely from her childhood, as a kind young man with an incorrigibly curious mind. Now she liked Lady Lovelace even less. "Does she . . ." Eliza lowered her voice, fearful. She trusted Lafayette enough to believe he'd never betray her on a whim. But to keep his own secret . . . "Does she know?"

d glance. "Relax. I've told her nothing about you."

flushed. "I meant about you. The wolf."

"Oh." A flash of bewildered smile, as if it surprised him she'd care. "Not that I'm aware. But I imagine the first I'll hear of it is when I wake up chained to a dungeon wall, with my blood dripping into a test tube and electrodes jammed into unfortunate crevices."

"Doesn't that bother you?"

"Please." Lafayette waved airily. "I proposed to you and walked out unscathed, didn't I? I can surely withstand Lady Lovelace's patented Glare of Epic Disapproval. Besides, her disdain for me is but a shabby façade. Secretly, she's all a-flutter."

"You think that about everyone."

"Deny it if you can." He waited, grinning. "Didn't think so."

"You're insufferable, do you know that?"

"And you're unreasonably enchanting, but I won't let it get between us."

Pedestrians sidled past the Enforcers, gazes downcast, hoping to escape notice. No such luck for one boy who flitted through the crowd, pointy-nosed, a strange green cast to his hair, as if he'd had a dyeing accident. People claimed such odd folk had fairy ancestors. Probably a thief, too, fingers too light for his own good in purses and pockets.

An Enforcer grabbed the fey boy by his suspiciously long ears. He yelled, struggling, but no one dared stand up for him. The metal machines nodded solemnly and tossed him into their cage.

He landed on his face—*blam!*—and the lid banged shut. Lady Lovelace jabbed him with her parasol through the bars.

Zzap! Electricity crackled, and the boy jerked and yowled. She nodded, satisfied, and cage and Enforcers stomped away.

Lafayette wriggled his shoulders. "Chilly around here, isn't it?"

Eliza's bones itched, deep inside where she couldn't scratch, and Lizzie's rage flushed her with ugly heat. "What exactly was that boy's crime? Looking too strange?"

"I'll ask him, if you like. No doubt she'll send me to pick his brains later." He sighed. "You glare at me as if I'm already peeling his fingernails off. I shan't, you know."

"Isn't that how the Royal extract confessions?"

Kill them god-rotted brass bastards and their iron-faced bitch queen, whispered Lizzie gleefully in her ear. *Tear their faces off! Ha!*

"If it pleased me to stoop to such atrocities, madam, I'd have stayed with my regiment in India. Or joined the Foreign Service. I hear they're having a fine bloodthirsty time in Paris these days. I say, are you well? Suddenly your face glows a peculiar shade of pink."

Eliza clenched sweating fists, willing Lizzie not to betray her now, not while Lady Lovelace watched. A pair of waiting brass horses creaked mildewed joints, their rudimentary clockwork driver motionless in its seat. She wanted to leap up and throttle it. "So . . . about this guest list. Since when did you care one whit for art?"

Lafayette grinned. "Did you imagine we soldiers to be all carnage and no culture? Carmine Zanotti's *Eve and the Serpent* is the surprise sensation of the Summer Exhibition. I'll get us an invitation, if you like. We could see what kind of people Sir Dalziel's hangers-on are. Care for an evening out?"

Hell, yes, whispered Lizzie, *don our fancy gown and go a-courting. 'Bout time he asked.*

Eliza squirmed, cornered. "I couldn't possibly impose—"

"Oh, and in case you wondered," added Lafayette, as if he'd said nothing of import, "Brigham telegraphed me just after seven. Got me out of bed, if you must know. Lady Fleet could have driven to town this morning after she learned of the murder."

"She could have killed Sir Dalziel at ten to four, and returned to Hampstead in time to pretend she knew nothing about it, too. Presuming we believe your pet butler's story."

"That clockwork idiot did confirm it. And Brigham seems artless enough."

"Mmm. Hardly likely to lie for an employer who mistreated him."

"Still, he could've killed Dalziel in anger. The old tyrant takes a hand to him once too often, he finally loses it, and *blam!* One dead baronet in a satisfying pool of gore. Always the quiet ones who pop."

"The butler did it," mused Eliza. "How cozy. But why the mutilations? And—unhappy infatuation aside—why call you, and not the police? Why stick around at all, in fact? Surely his best chance for a cover-up is police incompetence."

"Whereas my shining investigative skills would swiftly pin him for the cowardly felon he is?" Lafayette fanned himself. "Madam, you make me blush."

"And," she continued, ignoring him, "those footprints weren't Brigham's. Five feet three if he's an inch. Our man is taller."

Lafayette wrinkled his nose. "What odds on Lady Fleet's footman? Drives up from Wimbledon, bumps the old man off for her, *splat!* Makes a mess, knowing Brigham won't risk a beating by coming up. Legs it back to the country before seven, and *voilà!* Lady Fleet gets a dead husband, the 'stolen' loot returned in secret, and a butler she loathes upon whom to pin the blame."

They stopped at New Bond Street, where lamps in shop windows burned like beacons through the fog. Tree branches hung motionless in still gray air. A mare shied, clattering her ironclad hooves. Her eyes rolled in fright as Lafayette brushed past, and absently he edged away. Was his blossoming wolfish scent upsetting her?

A few yards up the street, Finch's Pharmacy beckoned. Eliza's head pounded, her skin rippling like a shedding snake's. This was unendurable. Lizzie was threatening chaos. What if she'd *changed* in public? In front of Lady Lovelace? Eliza needed her remedy. Now.

But like that mare, her mind danced, unsettled. "It doesn't seem right. Why would this murderous footman mutilate the body?"

"To throw us off the scent?"

"Surely. But why not just fit poor Brigham up for it properly? Without the ghoulish details, Reeve casts around for the closest thing with a motive and a heartbeat, and arrests our long-suffering butler. Case closed."

"Whereas now, Reeve must investigate?"

"Exactly. Why would Lady Fleet want that? Even Reeve occasionally stumbles across the truth."

"Perhaps her killer footman's an idiot," suggested Lafayette. "Did you notice him? Calves like a Greek god. I don't imagine she hired him for his intellect."

"But if Sir Dalziel was already suspected of black magic, why confirm it and risk Lady Fleet's reputation?"

"Because the killer didn't care?"

"Or he did it deliberately. Either way, something strange is going on."

Lafayette grinned, contented. "Don't look now, Dr. Jekyll, but you just took my case."

"Humph. One almost suspects you dispatched the poor fellow yourself, just to get my attention."

"It's possible. You should investigate." He offered his wrists to be cuffed. "Interrogate me thoroughly."

She eyed him sternly. "I said I'd look, nothing more."

"But you know you *want* more," he insisted. "You need the job. You're desperately intrigued. Reeve will be furious. What's stopping you?"

She smiled weakly. "I'm afraid I'm late for work," she lied. "How time's getting on—"

"Please, Doctor." Not threatening. Just sincere, a hint of disarming vulnerability that halted her in her tracks. "Lady Lovelace is watching me. I need your help."

She hesitated. He'd trusted her with his secret. Shouldn't she trust him? "Well . . ."

"You can't deny we work well together." A sly eye twinkle. "We might even have fun."

Of all the things he could have said, that was the worst.

"I'm sorry, I can't possibly fit it in." Briskly, Eliza shook his hand. "Lovely to see you again, Captain. I wish you luck with your case. Good day."

BEFORE THE DEVIL KNOWS
YOU'RE DEAD

•••

ELIZA MARCHED UP NEW BOND STREET TOWARDS Finch's Pharmacy, fighting for breath. Cloying fog swirled around her, stuffing her lungs like wet wool. Her corset was squashing the life from her, and this cursed acid air wasn't helping. She pinched her waist with both hands, trying to heave in a proper lungful.

Lafayette didn't follow, of course. Didn't try to persuade her. Nothing so crude.

"Freedom!" shouted Hipp, muffled by the bag. "Confinement unreasonable. Motion imperative!"

She fished him from beneath Lafayette's sheaf of letters. He sprang from her grip and screeched up the street, flashing his lights, *blue-red-blue-red!* "Finch! Freedom!"

At last, her cramping chest eased. She fanned her damp face, thoughts muddling like dark treacle. Lafayette knew how to engage her interest. His case, a blend of mystery and glaring inconsistency. His amusing conversation, unfettered by social pressures. His damnable flirtation, which thanks to Lizzie worked all too well.

Lizzie fought, a hooked fish. *Right. All my fault, is it? As if you ain't flirting right back.*

But what did he really want? The spectacle of those Enforcers—and steel-faced Lady Lovelace—had only underlined his dangerous hidden motives. Too cunning by half.

Pain stabbed between Eliza's eyes, an all-too-familiar symptom of her dependence on the elixir. Her wits clogged. Lafayette was tormenting her for his own murky reasons. Nothing else made sense.

"Aye," taunted Lizzie. Somehow, she'd clambered from the bag, too, and sauntered alongside, a shimmering red-skirted specter. "Almost as if . . . hell, I don't know. He likes you?"

Eliza hurried on, raking itchy forearms. Lizzie wasn't really there. How could she be? "It isn't that simple. Nothing's ever that simple."

Lizzie flicked transparent mahogany curls. "Only 'cause you're making it difficult."

"I am not! He's up to something. I know it."

"Bollocks. You're jumping at shadows. Delusions of persycootion, eh? That bonehead Philosopher lurking under every rock?" Lizzie danced a hop-step, skirts frothing. "Remy could've shopped us months ago, if he cared to, so what's he waiting for?"

"I haven't the faintest idea. I can't read his mind, can you? Now stay where you belong. Just because you're smitten doesn't mean I should let down my guard."

Lizzie cocked one hand on her hip. "Aye. 'Cause you ain't never acted the fool for a gentleman's bright eyes. Green, wasn't they?"

Eliza stomped up the pharmacy steps, where Hipp bounced impatiently. "Shut up. That's different. Did it escape your notice that said green-eyed gentleman was a razor murderer? That's enough to render anyone nervous in his company."

"Nervous? That what they call it these days? Have you lost your friggin' *mind*?"

In the street, an enormous mauve crinoline with a woman inside tilted to stare . . . but with a ghostly giggle, Lizzie vanished.

Had Eliza shouted those last few words aloud? Hallucinations, talking to herself. *Delusions of persy-cootion.* She grinned sickly. "Rehearsing for a comedy. Charity performance for addle-brained orphans. Won't you come?"

"Quite," muttered the crinoline, and flounced away.

Quite, mimicked Lizzie in posh tones, once again tucked safely away in Eliza's mind . . . for now. *I'll "quite" you, you uppity tart.*

The bell tinkled, and Hipp charged in, skidding across the polished floor and nearly bowling over a round-faced girl in blue velvet skirts who was examining the interior window display.

Out o' the way, brown-eyes! Comin' through! crowed Lizzie.

"My apologies, miss," cut in Eliza desperately. "Hipp, for heaven's sake, calm down."

"Finch! Finch!" trumpeted Hipp, oblivious. The girl muttered and hurried away.

Delightful warmth washed over Eliza, the familiar scents of possets and medicines and alcoholic solvents. Sheaves of strange-smelling herbs hung drying. Bottled liquids of every color lined the shelves. Smoke wafted from behind a leather curtain, bringing the throaty *bubble-pop!* of some viscous preparation boiling.

She leaned over the counter, where rows of Latin-labeled drawers were stacked to the ceiling. "Marcellus? Are you there?"

Mr. Finch popped up like a jack-in-the-box. Thin and angular, apron smudged with charcoal dust, blinking vaguely over a silver-rimmed pince-nez. "My dear girl, you look awful!" He rushed around to take her hands. "In twenty years I've never seen you so . . . floury."

"It's Lizzie." Her tongue stumbled in haste. "She's growing stronger. I can't hold her in."

"Remedy still inadequate?" Finch pressed his knuckles to her cheek. They felt dry, cold. Was she sweating?

"I dosed an hour and a half ago. It's not working." Finch brewed her elixir, but she'd grown cruelly dependent on it, and he'd also fashioned her a remedy to bring respite. "My dreams are worse. And during the day, I see her. She talks to me. It's as if she's a separate person."

Crash! A pile of boxes toppled. Hipp charged in a circle, doggedly chasing his own rear end.

"Hello, little fellow." Finch eyed him dubiously. "I say, is he overwound? Excess elastic energy, eh? A tonic, say what? I've just the thing!"

"Hipp's made of brass," she reminded. "A tonic won't do much good."

"Oh. Right. Never mind, then. May I?" Finch peeled back her eyelids with his thumbs. He smelled of spicy herbal tea, a happy scent that recalled her childhood. Little Eliza in a white pinafore, cross-legged by the fire, practicing her letters on a slate while Mr. Finch read aloud. Not fairy tales, but dusty tomes bound in cracked leather, inked with alchemical symbols. Treatises on forgotten pharmaceuticals, dissection notes, arcane Latin rhymes with compelling rhythms that spoke to her.

Finch had taken her in when she was orphaned. Until her uncouth guardian, Edward Hyde, took charge, leaving her alone in the gloomy Cavendish Square house, supervised by an endless string of strange tutors and absent-minded governesses.

Or so she'd thought. Until she'd learned Henry hadn't died after all. Hyde had consumed his better half, little by little, until Jekyll was eaten away. Hyde was but Henry in a darker, murderous guise. And who'd known all along? Marcellus Finch, who beneath his "vague old man" act harbored a secret sinister side. He'd fooled everyone, including her.

Finch squinted. "Your irises are cloudy. Eat more turnips, improve your digestion."

"Genius, Marcellus. I shall inform Mrs. Poole directly."

His face paled. "Must you encourage her? Last time I dropped by, your housekeeper—" He glanced left and right, beckoning her closer. "She *made conversation*," he whispered. *"Fiercely."*

Eliza hid a smile. "That only means she likes you."

"That's what terrifies me." He wriggled a finger into Eliza's ear and examined it, frowning. "That worthy woman has designs on my virtue. Elaborate, explicit ones."

She giggled. "Come, a dalliance might do you good. Have you never been in love?"

"Eek! Don't be absurd. Why should I want to fall in *love*? All that sighing and mooning about with your wits in a fuddle, stricken with the urge to vomit bad poetry. Not to mention the *kissing.*" He screwed up his nose. "Not scientific, dear girl. Dangerously irrational. I'd steer well clear if I were you. Now, don't blink." He brandished a glass dropper, filling it from a tiny bottle.

Drip! Drop! Her vision stung blue.

"I say, how curious." Finch leapt back around the counter like a white-haired locust. He wasn't as old or feeble—nor *quite* as insane—as he appeared. He rummaged in one drawer after another, pills and powders and herbs flying left and right. "We had these difficulties with your father's elixir. Henry, I'd say, Henry, you foolish old badger, you have to *tell* me when this happens. I can't be expected to read that decrepit dustpit you call your *mind,* and thank heavens for that, come to think of it, so you can't hold me responsible for titers and dilution regimes and molecular purity and so forth if you aren't being *honest* with me . . . Aha!" He unearthed a tiny tin and popped the lid. "Watch your teeth," he warned, and puffed green dust into her face.

Poof! Sweetness fizzed, blinding her temporarily. She sneezed, tears dripping. "Marcellus, really—"

"Egad! As I thought!" Finch tossed the tin aside and waved his arms, nearly knocking over a shelf of bottles. "But did the stubborn old parsnip listen to wise Marcellus? No! Of course he didn't. He'd just let Eddie gad about town willy-nilly, wouldn't he, swilling vats of gin and smoking frightful Oriental cigarettes and complaining of headaches and gout and itching eyeballs and forgetting to mention it if he should happen to *overdose.*"

Eliza froze, guilty.

Finch skewered her on his stare, no longer so vague. "Did *you* overdose, dear girl?"

She lifted her spectacles to wipe streaming eyes. "I might," she admitted, "have consumed more than sufficient. From time to time."

Finch clucked, scolding. "To be expected, with your dependency. But do be careful. The active ingredients will accumulate in your tissues. Once they reach toxic levels . . . well, you can ask Eddie about that."

"But I can't stop Lizzie drinking it," Eliza protested. "She thinks it'll let her stay longer."

A sharp glance. "Interesting. Does it work?"

"Sometimes," she admitted. "I'm losing my memory of her episodes." Not that she'd want to remember. Dark streets creeping with ghosts, horrid laughter, the stink of gin and sweat. "I don't suppose she's visited you?"

He blinked, innocent. "Why would she? Last time, she practically throttled the tripe out of me."

"I—I thought she might want medicines of her own. If she does . . ."

"Of course, dear girl. Goes without saying."

Inwardly, she despaired. Finch's curiosity and compulsion to experiment sometimes overwhelmed his good sense. Could she trust no one?

"Luckily for you," said Finch brightly, "I'm developing a new formula. Splash of alkahest, dash of hush-hush, all that. If you're game," he added gloomily. "It's erratic. I behaved quite bizarrely when I tested it. Perhaps you shouldn't . . ."

"I need to do *something*." Suddenly, unaccountable tears burned her eyelids. Science could cure any problem. Why was this remedy so elusive? "Lizzie practically popped out in public just now! She's putting us all in danger."

Finch gave a cunning grin. "Excellent! Intrepid voyagers into the unknown are we!" He plopped a bottle of luminous pink-purple liquid onto the counter. "This takes a different approach to your existing remedy. Instead of starving the, er, *need*, we feed it. It's a singular sensation, but . . . well, you'll see. Put one drop under your tongue, *hora decubitus.*" He wagged a warning finger. "A single drop only. Tastes vile, naturally. Can't abide strawberries. A dose now, if you would, and monitor tonight for any adverse reaction. Telegraph if your skin starts peeling off, eh?"

She took the bottle, fingertips sticking to the cold glass. The pink substance was frosty, calculating. Not like her elixir, seething with sinister heat.

She eased out the glass dropper. On the tip glistened a single berry drop. She licked it. Chilled fumes wafted, heady like gin with a sickly, sugared flavor. Her skin tingled, icy yet warm. Did her pulse slow, just a little?

"Good." Finch's expression darkened. "But from time to time, you *need* to drink the elixir. You must give Lizzie her space. Otherwise . . . well, you know what happened to Henry."

"You can rely on me." She slipped the bottle away. She'd no intention of giving Lizzie space. Not if it meant getting them both thrown in the Royal's dungeons. "I've crime scene samples for analysis, if you're able?"

He beamed. "Do my part for justice, all that. Saliva from suspected cannibals? Blood of a monster? You get all the good jobs, now you're so practiced at catching bloodthirsty killers. How *is* your young man, by the way?"

Her throat constricted. "Excuse me?"

"Smart regimental fellow, with the badge and the wolf problem. Haven't spied him for weeks."

"Oh." She hadn't told Marcellus about Lafayette's proposal. Hadn't told anyone except Harley, who'd expressed his approval by teasing her mercilessly at every opportunity, and Mrs. Poole, who'd been eavesdropping from the stairwell and knew all about it anyway. Not that Eliza didn't want anyone to know. Only that . . . well . . .

"He's disgustingly well, as ever," she conceded. "But that prophylactic you mixed him didn't work."

"Full moon too powerful, eh? A formidable furry foe! Never fear, we shall renew our attack!" Finch rubbed eager palms. "Did you say samples?"

She offered her test tube. "Cigar ash from a murder scene. Something odd in it."

He held the phial to the light, and his pince-nez polarized, glittering like prisms. "Odd, indeed. Let's see."

He disappeared behind the stiff leather curtain and Eliza followed. She pushed aside dangling copper cables. Acrid smoke and alcoholic solvent vapor stung her eyes. Gas flames darted, and in the corner, a coal fire glowed red. Upon it steamed a vat of a strange-smelling black substance that bubbled and roiled like a living creature.

Already, the heat made her perspire. No windows; secrecy was too vital. Just a ventilation shaft, the updraft billowing her skirts.

She stepped over a coil of carbon-wrapped wire. Like a magician's den, Finch's laboratory always seemed bigger on the inside. Potions in rainbow colors bubbled over hissing gas flames. Coiled electrodes poked into beakers, soldered to silvery anodes. Hinged tubes of mercury upended themselves like pendulums, and an aetheric generator hummed and glowed, its glass globes forked with blue lightning.

"The Royal could easily find all this. You ought to be more careful."

Ahead, Finch waved dismissively. "Pah! They investigated me already, years ago. Mr. Faraday's admirer, you know, stern young lady with big brains."

A chill stabbed her. "You mean Lady Lovelace?"

"That's the girl. Not a countess then, of course. Merely the daughter of some gloomy aristocratic poet. Endless rude questions about some magical ointment of mine. Witchcraft, love potions, a cure for piles, whatever it was. I don't rightly recall."

"Not the elixir?"

"Goodness, no. Far too clever for that! Something wrong with her, I should say, the way she muttered and kept on. But she never made anything stick. Ha-ha! Brave Marcellus, victorious! Down with the tyrants!"

Finch was already vanishing behind an array of brass scales and centrifuges, Hippocrates dashing at his heels. Charts and graphs were pinned crookedly to the walls, scribbled with formulae and alchemical symbols in Finch's copperplate handwriting, alongside an annotated periodic table and a diagram of Leonardo da Vinci's *Vitruvian Man*.

She recalled that crucified Christ, dripping with Sir

Dalziel's blood. "Do you know anything about devil worship, Marcellus?"

"Why? Planning to give it a whirl? A spell, say what, like Lady Lovelace, for the lover of your dreams?" Finch tinkered with a retort, adjusting a leaping yellow flame beneath an apparently empty flask.

"You have me, sir. All over London, witty scientific geniuses with obligingly hefty fortunes shall faint at my feet." She shoved past a pile of evil-smelling herbs. "You know I don't believe in hocus-pocus. This murder had ritual elements, that's all."

He turned a glass tap to trap some invisible gas in a phial, and jammed in the cork. "Behold! My new prophylactic against stupefying gas attacks. Steels the lungs, fortifies the intestines. Doubles as a hangover cure, *and* repels ants. A marvelous breakthrough!"

"Sounds fascinating . . . No, you're too kind, I oughtn't."

He thrust the warm phial into her hands. "I insist. Grimy-fingered republicans blowing things up on every corner, disseminating frightful toxic stenches, and who knows what. We're all doomed! Just don't inhale too hard. Rots the tonsils, eh? What were you saying? Ritual, bah! Bad excuse for debauchery. Still," he added happily, "one ought to try everything. No such thing as forbidden knowledge. True science knows no boundaries, all that."

"Bravo." She stuffed the phial into her bag. "It isn't as if we'll be flattened by lightning bolts from on high, after all."

"Let's hope not." Finch stirred a beaker of scintillating blue goo. "I do enjoy a lovely murder. Gruesome, was it?" he added hopefully.

"Particularly."

Finch popped the cigar ash onto a dish, poured in the blue substance, and brandished a sparking electrical wire. *"En garde!"*

Bang! The ash exploded, shattering the dish in a puff of blue mist.

Eliza cleared her throat. "Well. That was unexpected."

Finch sucked a scorched thumb. "Alchemy, as you say. Reactive to aether. An hallucinogenic intoxicant, by the spectral range. Did he smoke the whole cigar, perchance?"

"It looked like it. Something one might use in an unorthodox ritual?"

"Or a debaucherous one. Heightens the sensations, eh? Not that I'd know anything about that. Veritable stoic, that's me. Utterly sober at all times."

"I've the victim's blood sample, too. Might you test for toxins?" She scraped dried blood from her skirt onto a glass slide. Lafayette's olfactory analysis still dangled, a tantalizing loose end. *Chinese opium, or some such.* His wolfish nose was a precision instrument. If he couldn't identify it . . . or wouldn't?

Finch dabbed a forefinger into the blood, and licked it. "I say. Drunk as a skunk, was he? Scotch, single malt, well aged?"

She laughed. "You can taste that?"

"All eminently scientific, dear girl." Finch winked. "Fruits of hard-won experience. Your man was plastered. Sozzled. Up to his eyeballs, say what? And then he smoked enough hallucinogen to buy a week's holiday in la-la land . . ."

"Whereupon someone peeled his face off and cut out his heart." Eliza's skin tingled, anticipation and dread in equal measure. Did someone give Dalziel this drug to incapacitate him? Or had he taken it willingly? Black magic, indeed. What kind of insane shenanigans had Dalziel been up to?

———◆•◆———

Late afternoon had crept stealthily upon her before she finally returned to her town house in Russell Square. Her muscles ached and shivered, her throat sore. The singular flavor of Mr. Finch's pink remedy whispered across her face, lifted the hair on her arms, teased the back of her neck. She could still taste it, foreign yet sweet, like the breath of an absent lover.

No breeze disturbed her skirts. The park's iron railings glistened wet, rows of trees retreating into the gloom. The dirty London fog hadn't lifted, just turned sour and vengeful, biting at Eliza's eyes until they watered. On the corner, a pair of white-masked Enforcers surveyed the street with empty red eyes.

Shivering, she hurried by, recalling Lady Lovelace and the green boy. Was Captain Lafayette interrogating him right now? Had the Royal sniffed her and Lizzie out, just waiting for their moment to strike?

Inwardly, she fumed. Satisfying as it had been, this morning's debacle with Reeve left her in a pretty spot. She'd recently spent most of her savings on urgent repairs to her house—which she now owned, thanks to her former guardian—and was short of cash for expenses and servants' wages. Her infrequent police work paid poorly, her private practice was sadly non-existent, and as for Lafayette's murder case . . .

Of course, she'd access to funds in plenty, if she chose. Edward Hyde was generous with his ill-gotten gains. A doting father, by financial standards at least. She needed only to ask.

But the idea of accepting his charity stung her pride. She wanted to make her own living as a physician. And Mr. Hyde was an evil man. Unhinged. Murderous.

Aye, whispered spectral Lizzie, drifting alongside the fence, just a faint shadow in the fog. *Bloodied hands is a real turnoff for you. Never would dream of consorting with no killer.*

"I'm sorry, did you speak?" snapped Eliza, but tiny bubbles of hope prickled inside her. Was Lizzie *dimmed,* by that tiny drop of pink-purple remedy? Had Finch at last found a working formula?

Under her porch, the lamp shed a welcoming glow. She glanced up at her expensive, newly repaired roof, already coated in dirt from the filthy London air, and checked a sigh. The brass shingle on her doorpost—ELIZA JEKYLL M.D., it announced politely—was grimy again, too, the windows dull. She sighed. More work for Molly. In this fog, scrubbing the steps was an endless job. Those Incorruptibles deserved punishment for that alone.

She let herself in, to the delicious smells of hot supper. The polished hall furniture glimmered in soft electric light. She set her things on the hall stand—WHO IS HARLEQUIN? DESPICABLE FRENCH SPYMASTER ELUDES CAPTURE AGAIN read the headline on her evening edition—and Hippocrates bounced from her bag and boinged into his corner. "Welcome home! Welcome!"

"Thank you, Hipp." He'd calmed, mercifully, but she could still hear the click and whir of overstressed cogs. An overhaul, Mr. Brigham had said. Perhaps he was right.

"You're home early, Doctor." Her housekeeper swept in,

stocky as a bulldog, her white bonnet tucked over steel-gray hair. "There's blood on your skirt. Have a pleasant day?"

"No, Mrs. Poole, it was positively disheartening." Eliza tugged off her gloves, frowning at the blood-smeared leather. "Oh, dear. These are ruined, I think. Perhaps Molly can have them cleaned."

"Your boots are filthy, too. Where have you been, mudlarking?" Mrs. Poole dusted the already spotless hall stand. "That Chief Inspector's case take a bad turn?"

"Worse," admitted Eliza. "A *dull* turn. The man's making fun of me. And please don't say 'I told you so.'"

"Never did like that Mr. Reeve. Ugly manners, stinks of cigars." A sly wink. "Your handsome army captain, now, there's a proper gentleman. Shall we be seeing him again?"

"Who?" Eliza widened her eyes.

"For certain, clever rich fellows pop into your consulting room and propose all the time. Hardly surprising he should slip your mind."

"Oh, you mean that insufferable Royal Society agent?" Eliza waved carelessly. "Decidedly an *improper* gentleman, and certainly doesn't belong to me."

"He could do. Taking your sweet time, aren't you?" Mrs. Poole bustled around, assaulting invisible dust. "Dashing officer with prospects and a fortune, pleasing to look at, knows words of more than one syllable. Even you ought to be satisfied with that. He won't wait forever."

"What a shame. Perhaps *you* should marry him."

"I might, if you dilly-dally much longer." Mrs. Poole dusted Hipp's head, eliciting an indignant squeak. "Oh, your new lodger arrived. Miss Burton. Pleasant girl, three shillings a week. I believe she'll do nicely."

Eliza's heart sank. Renting out the spare third-floor rooms was better than selling furniture or pawning her mother's jewels. But it still smacked of professional failure. And what if this Miss Burton noticed Lizzie's comings and goings? What if Lizzie . . . interfered?

She forced a smile. She needed to pay Mrs. Poole and Molly. Decision made. "Excellent. Whatever should I do without you?"

"Replace me with one of those brass monstrosities? Why, just the other day, the Bistlethwaites at number twenty-five bought a clockwork butler. Let poor Mr. Simkins go after thirty-four years. He'll never find another situation at his age."

"Poor fellow. It's awful that people are losing their jobs. Still, the technology is marvelous. One must admire progress."

A doubtful sniff. "Will you be dining early, Doctor?"

"No, thank you. I've work to do."

"Just as well. A patient's waiting in your consulting room."

Eliza gaped, stunned. "Why didn't you say something?"

"I just did." Mrs. Poole dusted on, as if the news were of no import. "Weren't you expecting anyone?"

"You know perfectly well I was not." She'd not had a patient in weeks. Not since the Chopper case, when her name had yet again made the newspapers connected with murderers and escaped lunatics. Once was tantalizing, worthy of gossip. Twice was merely bad manners. She'd devolved from dashing heroine into wicked lady of loose morals and rampant laudanum addiction, probably a poisoner and a suffragette to boot. One particularly garish publication had labeled her "Madam Murder."

Hastily, Eliza dusted her muddy skirts and shoved loose hair into its pins. "What's her name? Has she been waiting long? Oh, never mind. How do I look? Shall I impress?"

A cursory glance. "I suppose you'll do."

"A fountain of confidence, as ever." Nervously, Eliza grinned. "Wish me luck."

"Wouldn't waste it on you."

She gulped a steadying breath and opened the door.

Her consulting room was blessedly tidy. Writing desk by the window, medical books lined neatly on tall shelves. On the big rosewood table sat a vase of fresh-scented freesias. Tiny arc-lamps glowed in sconces, and a small coal fire burned. By the low sofa, a velvet-shaded lamp cast her patient into shadow.

Eliza cleared her throat. "Sorry to keep you waiting, madam . . ." Her guts heated. "Oh. I'm so terribly sorry. I was expecting . . ."

"No matter." The gentleman—fancy that!—jumped up, bowler hat in hand. A youthful fellow, blond with an upturned nose. He bowed, eyes—green or hazel?—twinkling. "Moriarty Quick, at your service or for your entertainment, whichever lasts the longer."

Despite her embarrassment, the Dubliner's lilt on that odd greeting charmed her. "Delighted, sir. Dr. Eliza Jekyll."

"I know who y'are. This is your office." An impish smile that matched his surname. Expensive bottle-green coat, black satin necktie in an elaborate knot. Not impecunious. Vain, she guessed; he had the kind of rakish aspect that had been fashionable twenty or thirty years ago, but was now considered disreputable.

"Please, sit." She took her own desk chair, confused. Dozens of physicians worked in the West End alone. Had she come recommended? "Forgive my presumption. It's only . . . a female physician tends to attract . . ."

"Only the finest clientele, I'm sure. Yours is the clever sex, and mine the humble. I submit eagerly to your expertise."

He muffled a dry cough, reminding Eliza of her own parched throat, where that new pink remedy's sweetfire flavor lingered. "Water, sir? Or tea?"

"I could murder a whiskey." Another cheeky smile. "But we've barely met. Water would be grand."

She poured two glasses, and sipped. Pink iridescence swirled from her lips, coating the water's surface like oil. "What can I do for you, Mr. Quick?"

"It's more a question of what *I* can do for *you*." He hooked the brass frames of green-tinted spectacles over his ears. They made him look faintly demented. "I'm something of a professional meself. With a certain specialty, if you take my meaning."

"I'm afraid I do not." But her heart sank, despairing. Why could no one take her seriously? After Razor Jack's sensational trial, she'd been targeted by gossip-mongers and rubber-neckers who wanted a glimpse of the infamous "lady doctor" who'd single-handedly caught the lunatic. She'd felt like a zoo exhibit, poked and prodded for public amusement.

"I'm rather busy," she added shortly. "If you're merely curious, I'd prefer you to leave now."

"But we've barely begun. Shall we take a look?" And he circled the room, examining her trinkets and poking at her papers. "Yes. I see. Hmm. Thought so." From his coat skirts— voluminous like a pickpocket's—he produced a silver tobacco case and a wad of matches. He thumbed the case open and dipped in a match, coating the head in sparkly black powder.

She jumped up. "I'd rather you didn't smoke. I say, whatever are you doing?"

He just struck his match—*ker-pop!*—and flicked it into her water glass. *Hissst!* The match sizzled out . . . but the water's surface caught alight. A tell-tale lick of strawberry flame.

That oily iridescence, washed from her lips. Finch's remedy. Unorthodox. Illegal. Dangerous.

"Oh, dear." Regretfully, Moriarty Quick shook his head . . . but above those sinister glasses, his cunning eyes gleamed. "That's alchemy, Dr. Jekyll. Whatever shall we do with you?"

THE BEST IN TOWN

• • •

WHAT'S THE MEANING OF THIS?" ELIZA DEMANDED. "Slip some noxious poison into my drink, will you, like a common cad?" Lizzie remained oddly quiescent, but still Eliza's pulse thudded, demanding she act. Scream. Run. Smash those glinting spectacles into his eyes and watch them bleed.

Quick didn't smile. Not a gloat or threat in sight. "Told ye I know who y'are."

She edged towards her desk. What was that black powder? Highlighting traces of alchemical flux in the visible spectrum? God help her if the Royal ever got their hands on that. "You make no sense, sir. We have nothing to discuss. Kindly leave my house."

"But I can help," insisted Quick. "An improvement on your present pharmaceutical arrangements. At little or no cost to you, of course. Think of me as . . . a talented friend in need."

"Oh, so I'm to agree to your ignoble demands, whatever they are, to stop you spreading malicious slander?" Eliza whipped her electric stinger from the drawer and kindled it, *zzap!* "I don't think so."

"Whoa, Nellie. Take it easy." He lifted his hands, with an injured expression. "And I was being so polite—"

"You've ambushed the wrong weak female, Mr. Quick. Were you ever stung by one of these? Not lethal current, heavens no. But the voltage is quite ridiculous. I'm told the sensation is most disagreeable. Now get out, before my mood deteriorates."

"All right, fine, don't get your garters in a tangle." Quick swept his hat on with a flourish, tipping his tinted glasses down. Like a stage actor, every movement choreographed. "Truly, I'm pained we couldn't come to terms. You're an intelligent woman, Dr. Jekyll. Think on whether it might serve ye well to oblige me."

"I'll oblige you with three thousand volts if you don't get out of my house. And don't come back. I shall be summoning the police directly."

He flipped a card onto the sofa. "In case you reconsider. I'll see meself out."

In the hall, Hippocrates *zzzp!d* indignantly at him, and flashed his red *unhappy* light. Quick tilted his hat ironically, and slammed the front door behind him.

Eliza thumbed off her stinger and ran to the window, peering out. Dusk, a sinister yellow-gray miasma. There he strode, beneath flickering arc-lamps into the fog-bound park. Hands in pockets, bowler hat at a jaunty angle, a whistle on his lips. Who was this Quick? How did he know her secret?

She scooped up the trade card he'd dropped. Stiff white paper, embossed lettering in black and gold, all the barely suppressed excitement of a fairground playbill:

PROFESSOR MORIARTY QUICK!
POTIONS! LOTIONS!
EFFICACIOUS PHARMACEUTICALS!
THE BEST IN TOWN!

and an address along the expensive end of Piccadilly.

At your service, he'd said, *or for your entertainment.*

She snorted. Professor, indeed. A circus charlatan, with his mysterious powders and flashy matchbook tricks, making a fine living charming unsuspecting ladies out of their husbands' cash for snake oil and fake fairy dust at inflated prices. Money, that's what he wanted. Gold in return for his silence.

She almost laughed. He'd picked the wrong target . . . but her stomach twisted. Madam Murder. Had he merely heard rumors, and confronted her to see what she'd do? Or did he *know* what she was?

No, he was just an opportunist. A con man. Yes. That had to be it.

Mrs. Poole poked her head around the doorframe. "Went well, did it?"

"Another sightseer, I'm afraid. Don't let him in again." A thought struck her. "What time did you say he arrived?"

"A quarter hour ago. I told him you'd be out until eight, but he said he was certain you'd be along soon and he'd wait, thank me very much. Wouldn't take tea either." A dismissive

sniff. "Bless me, Irishmen in your parlor. Next it'll be Frenchmen and Republicans." Mrs. Poole handed her the mail tray
and bustled out.

Eliza rubbed aching eyes. Quick had waited. As if he'd
known to expect her early.

Had he eavesdropped at Finch's? Was the horrid fellow
spying on her?

Ridiculous. Not everyone was plotting against her. She'd
attended deluded patients like that at Bethlem. Huddling in
corners or under the bed, imagining themselves the target of
nefarious plots and persecutions. *They're spying on me. They're
after me. It's THEM.*

But that chilly strawberry sweetness lingered on her
tongue, nagging, and she couldn't escape this creeping unease. Like a sticky rut in the road, dragging her deeper the
more she struggled.

She toe-poked Hippocrates, who awoke with a jerk. "Hipp,
pop along and wire Mr. Finch. Ask him what he knows about
a pestilent Irishman named Professor Moriarty Quick. Oh,
and same question to Inspector Griffin."

"Finch," echoed Hipp sleepily. "Griffin. Professor." She
opened the front door a crack, and he scuttled out, whistling.

Listless, she wandered back inside, flipping through the
post. An account from her book-seller, another from her
glove-maker. Always more bills.

She tore open an unmarked envelope with her fingers.
Since the business with Razor Jack, she'd avoided letter open-
ers. She didn't like to touch their smooth silver, recall that
wickedly sharp edge.

Inside lurked an antique-white invitation card.

A PRIVATE VIEWING
THE ROYAL ACADEMY OF ARTS
SUMMER EXHIBITION OF NEW WORKS
THE NATIONAL GALLERY, TRAFALGAR SQUARE

She turned it over. Confident, flyaway handwriting, but without a wasted blot of ink:

> *Dr. J,*
> *In case you change your mind.*
> *Tomorrow night?*
> *Remy*

Her smile quirked. Change her mind, indeed. The *y*'s tail curled, a cocky swirl. Insolent use of his first name. He could wish they were so familiar.

Stubbornly, she tossed the card onto her desk and sat. Notice from the dustman, advertisement for a new dress shop . . .

Trembling, she picked up the last letter.

Delivered by penny post, stamp pasted in one corner. Exquisite linen paper, the kind she wanted to smell or brush across her lips. Folded into three and sealed with crimson wax, the imprint of a tiny rose.

Her name—*Eliza Jekyll, M.D.*—and address, in narrow left-slanting letters. No sender.

But she knew the handwriting, the paper, the seal. Artist, escaped lunatic, wielder of a bloody straight razor. Murderer of seventeen people; at least, seventeen that the police knew about. The newspapers called him Razor Jack, but in her thoughts—her darkened, breathless dreams—he was always and forever Mr. Todd.

Her fingers turned the letter, considering it. A faint chemical odor, memories of a wet midnight in Chelsea, and another, stormy one at Bethlem Asylum, the Chopper's awful laboratory, rich with secrets and thunder. Todd had vanished into the rain that night, gone like a frosted breath. Her lips tingled, the echo of a murderer's almost-kiss . . .

She dropped the letter as if it burned her. It landed alongside Lafayette's invitation, an unsettling unspoken question.

Suddenly her situation suffocated her. She'd no money, not without accepting Mr. Hyde's ill-gotten charity. No income, since she'd alienated Chief Inspector Reeve. Add this Moriarty Quick's inscrutable demands . . . Either she found more work, or she admitted failure—and that, she would not do.

She *needed* this new case. Even if it meant proceeding without Harley Griffin, whose career needed just as bitterly as hers to be salvaged. At least it was real police work, a case that mattered. And—she gritted her teeth on stung pride— lest she attract the Royal's ire, she needed to keep on safe terms with Remy Lafayette.

So he'd proposed. The dreaded M-word. What of it? He'd no right to pressure her into an answer. A husband—whoever he might be—would take her property, her income, her right to make business decisions. Everything but trinkets and the clothes she wore. English common law at its finest. She wouldn't surrender her independence lightly.

So why not take the case? Maintain a professional relationship. If Lafayette had it in mind to flirt—and when didn't he?—she was more than fit for the challenge.

As for Mr. Todd . . .

Glowing coals guttered in the grate, beckoning. *Burn it,* hissed Lizzie, a red-lit demon in the shadows. *Burn it unopened.*

Compelled, Eliza slipped a hooked key from her pocket and unsnapped a hidden drawer in her writing desk.

A pile of newspaper clippings stared up at her. She fingered through the headlines, discomfited. Rumors, sightings, deaths of a specific and bloody kind. Nothing confirmed, nothing concrete . . . but she knew better.

Todd was alive. And Todd was killing. The two were inextricable.

THREADNEEDLE STREET SLASHING
BANKER FOUND DEAD

A money-lender, officious, bad-mannered. Had he annoyed Todd? Refused him credit? Worn the wrong color coat?

TALES OF CHELSEA HAUNTINGS SPURIOUS,
SAYS LANDLORD

That one was a laugh. Souvenir hunters had flocked to Todd's Chelsea studio, hoping to scrounge a memento, but the place had been stripped on police orders. Nothing remained of that strange, fragrant attic boudoir. Still, hardly surprising no one would rent the place.

MISSING BEADLE IMPLICATED IN PARISH
EMBEZZLEMENT SCANDAL

Her bones shuddered, and she pushed the clipping aside. The man who'd fired her from the parish workhouse, "missing" and exposed as a thief. Coincidence?

She'd told no one about her collection. Especially not Harley, who thought her obsession with Todd's case unhealthy. Harley didn't know the half of it.

Beneath the clippings lay a pile of letters. Identical crimson seals, imprinted with a rose. But these seals were broken.

Eliza shivered, sweating. She'd read his letters, alone at midnight, sleepless at her desk or huddled in her bed by candlelight. Lingered over their singular contents, word for darkly beautiful word. And wondered . . .

The night Todd had escaped—*you LET him escape, oh yes*—he'd visited her while she slept. Spied on her at her most vulnerable. She imagined him tracking the rise and fall of her breath, brushing her hair aside, fingering the pulsing vein in her throat . . .

If Mr. Todd wanted to kill her—and heaven knew he had cause—then why hadn't he?

She cursed. Harley was right. She should inform the police. They'd watch her house, track her mail deliveries. Set a trap.

But her nerves wriggled, worms from salt. If he was caught, he'd be hanged. That wasn't justice. She was a doctor, not an executioner, and Todd was ill. Not criminally responsible. The surgeon's "therapy" regime at Bethlem had been anything but civilized. She'd researched other options. Aversion training. Drugs to aid memory of repressed trauma. Hypnotism, if you believed in that sort of thing. Her professional curiosity itched at the prospect of a challenge. Science could solve any problem. Surely, with proper treatment . . .

A scratching at the front door dragged her back to sense. Flustered, she hurried to open it, and Hippocrates bounded in. "Telegraph. Success!"

"Good boy." She dropped the latch and walked back to her desk. Her gaze jumped from letter to invitation and back again . . .

This was ridiculous. She didn't care *what* Todd wanted. Let him write her, if it fed his fantasies. She needn't respond. He wasn't her responsibility. Right?

Then burn his god-rotted letters! Lizzie, fighting to be heard? Or just Eliza's own common sense? *Toss 'em on the fire and be done. What's stopping you?*

Eliza put the new letter with the others, turned the key, and with a sigh, pulled from her bag the pile of papers Lafayette had taken from Sir Dalziel's office. She flipped through them. Just dull correspondence from bankers, brokers, the Academy Hanging Committee.

Sketches, too, mostly of beautiful ladies in flowing dresses. Exquisite faces and forms with expressions that seemed alive, lips on the brink of speech or smile. One pair of dark eyes in particular arrested her, beautiful but bitter with self-knowledge. Landscapes, too: an inky moonlit sky, a hunting scene, the penciled skyline of London in a storm. Dalziel had an excellent eye for light and shadow.

Here was the dinner guest list, in the butler Brigham's careful hand:

Dr. Silberman, Lord & Lady Havisham,
Lord Montrose, Sir Wm Thorne, Hon.
Mr. Cartwright MP, Revd and Mrs. Mortimer,

Hon. Miss Mary Wallace, Miss Watt,
Lt Lestrange, Mr. Zanotti, Mr. Hunt,
Mr. Lightwood . . .

She recognized none of them. She'd need Lafayette's help. Wearily, she put the list aside and reached for a book. *On the Origin of Species,* a fascinating new publication by an intrepid naturalist. The Philosopher himself had recommended it as revolutionary. She tried to lose herself in tortoises, water birds, the faraway Galápagos Isles.

But like a magnet drawn to iron, her gaze kept sliding to her desk. The white card. That locked drawer.

What was stopping her, indeed?

Resolved, she retrieved Lafayette's invitation and set it on the mantel. "Mrs. Poole?" she called into the hallway. "To-morrow morning, have Molly fetch out my best dress, if you please. I'll be going out in the evening."

And then, with pounding heart, she locked her consulting room door. Slipped that rose-sealed letter from the secret drawer—was something slim folded within?—and settled by the dying fire to read.

> Precious Eliza,
>
> I'm no poet, I fear; my words are clumsy studies in charcoal for a glory I'll one day paint in color— but I'm compelled to write again, even though you can't (or won't) reply. This morning, I colored my new Lot's Wife—such rapture!—coaxing forth her moment of temptation and decision!—and eagerly my thoughts ran to you.

If I may abandon a gentleman's modesty—
I think I might?—the scene is delightful. I should
like very much to show it to you. How ardently I
crave your kind opinion—

But enough. You deserve abject truth. I'm
tortured by purer desires than vanity, Eliza,
creatures not so patient, nor so gentle. Night and
day, I thirst: that awakening; the absolute truth of
that sibilant slice; that elusive alpha and omega,
bled out in endless crimson by those other, brighter
tools of my art, which inspire in you such—well,
I can only call it hesitation, Eliza, though I can't
imagine why. You wield such cruel power over me
that, at your whim, I should meekly breathe my
last. You laugh—how golden, your laughter!—you
laugh, but it's true.

Yet the memory of your pulse teasing my
fingertip, your breath quivering on my lips—

Forgive these fragments. You torment me. Can
this be your intention? Without you, I languish in
darkness, shackled as brutally as ever you saw me,
and the Shadow is hungry.

I cannot bear it. Help me, sweet lady, lest I fade
into that nightfall forever.

Your innocent friend
M.

NOBODY'S DULLNESS
BUT MY OWN

•••

A T NINE O'CLOCK THE NEXT EVENING, ELIZA'S CAB
rattled to a stop at the stone steps of the National
Gallery. Trafalgar Square's gaslights shed watery
halos, stretching like jack-o'-lanterns into the fog. Carriages
flitted in silhouette towards Whitehall and the square edi-
fices of Horse Guards and Scotland Yard. Eerie pink sunset
stained the foggy twilight, and the Gallery's tall Greek pillars
loomed, half obscured in the gloom.

Tucking her best silken skirts out of the dirt, Eliza jumped
down and paid the driver. Strange eagerness quickened her
pulse, the warm air tingling her skin alive. At the top of the
steps, she showed her invitation to the obsequious doorman,
who admitted her into the cavernous entry hall.

"Private viewing" apparently meant "no poor people,"
rather than any limitation on numbers. On the red-carpeted
stone staircase, ladies tittered in the latest finery: skirts in
turquoise and bottle green, lace and gold trimmings, feather-
edged fans, their hair pinned in elaborately artless curls.
Fashionable gentlemen preened like peacocks, satiny lapels

and sweep-cut coattails, intricately knotted ties, scarves in expensive shades of purple and gold. Glasses tinkled, snatches of laughter and conversation drifting above the hubbub. The bloody murder of society's pre-eminent art critic certainly hadn't dampened the crowd's enthusiasm for showing off. All subtly jostling for position, the perfect space to be seen.

Eliza shouldered through into the brightly lit gallery, and gaped in amazement. Art covered every inch of the vast walls. Gilt and iron frames were crammed together like jigsaw pieces, from the floor to the coveted eye-level positions "on the rail" to the painted architrave. Space at the Exhibition was in high demand, with most submissions rejected by the Academy's all-powerful Hanging Committee.

Glass-globed arc-lights hung suspended on overhead wires, their crackling electrostatic auras lifting the hair on her arms. The more intrepid art enthusiasts rode hovering alloy plat-forms, twenty feet above the floor. Tiny aetheric engines puffed them from painting to painting, amidst burps of white smoke and the smell of thunder.

A young woman in a loud silver crinoline peered through a huge magnifying glass at a painting of a dying auburn-haired beauty. "I say," she drawled, "this is fabulous. Herbert, dear, what do you call one of these?"

Herbert squinted through a monocle, twirling epic mus-taches. "I believe that's an 'oil painting,' Lady Alice. Quite the fashion this year."

"How quaint," offered Lady Alice, apparently unable to think of anything else to say. Her gaze caught on Eliza—neatly pinned hair, subdued gown, plain white gloves—and she sniffed, as if she'd detected a foul smell.

"Well screw you, too," retorted spectral Lizzie, popping into view in a whiff of gin-scented breeze. Eliza stifled a groan. Ruby satin, frills up to here and cleavage down to there, and to hell with 'em all if they didn't approve. The pink remedy must be wearing off.

"Don't you dare embarrass me tonight," she hissed. "We're here to find out who wanted Sir Dalziel dead, and that's all."

"Right. 'Cause you ain't prettied up to impress." Lizzie twirled, ghostly red skirts bouncing.

Defensively, Eliza smoothed her own pale golden skirts. The Dress, with all its redolent memories, her long-dead mother's diamond necklace heavy at her throat. Her best evening outfit—her only one, the kind Mr. Hyde liked her to wear, with a father's gruff fondness. But the silk whispering about her ankles ignited fiery memories of an artist's attic boudoir in Chelsea. Glittering green eyes, wild blood-red hair, the cold sharp kiss of steel . . .

Her fingers crept nervously to the necklace, and angrily, she yanked them away. No one deemed her worthy of notice, so why did she feel stared at from all sides? Weighed up, found wanting?

Impatiently, she teetered on tiptoes, searching for a flash of scarlet uniform. She spied Lady Lovelace, silver skirts gleaming, her jointed iron arm draped in lace. The countess's cold eyes cataloged the crowd, storing every detail, and Eliza sidled warily out of her sight. Lafayette was late, curse him. If he'd changed his mind . . .

"All look the same, don't they?"

"Eh?" Eliza turned, but Lizzie had vanished. "Beg pardon?"

A young lady smiled at her. Startlingly pretty, in a slim black mourning gown and jet choker. "Gentlemen, I mean. Frightfully dull fellows, nothing to choose between them. Until they open their mouths, whereupon you invariably wish they hadn't."

Eliza grinned. "I find one or two clever enough to be tolerable."

"Really? You *must* introduce me." Laughing, the girl offered a black-gloved hand. Her glossy auburn curls flowed loose like Lizzie's. Her ribboned neckline revealed a broad creamy expanse, her waist tight-laced. Either courageous or foolish in this company, who, from the glares they fired in her direction—the ladies, not the gentlemen, whose regard burned far more honestly—clearly thought her a prostitute. But they all seemed to know her.

"Penny Watt, struggling artist and shameless gossip," the girl said. "Are you buying or selling?"

"Hmm? Oh. Neither. Just attending with a friend. Dr. Eliza Jekyll." She shook hands, curious. Miss Watt. From Brigham's list of Sir Dalziel's dinner guests. "An artist, no less. Are there many female academicians?"

"Are there many female doctors at the College of Physicians?" Penny lit a cigarette, an elegant opium-roughened puff, and tossed the match away. "Ladies don't *paint*. What unspeakable scandal that would be. Next we'll run around *thinking*, and before you know it, we'll all wear blue stockings and refuse to have babies, all while we're lining up to vote. Society will crumble!"

"Heaven forbid. Have you work on display?"

Penny squinted towards the ceiling. "You might just spy

me with a telescope. Old Dalziel put in a good word with the Hanging Committee, otherwise I'd have no chance. I had to adopt a male pseudonym, of course." She crossed her eyes ironically. "Whereas all the properly successful brown-nosers are right on the rail. Thrust before your eyes, so you can't help but notice. Like Sheridan there. Story of his life, the loathsome little worm." She pointed to a large gilded frame hanging at eye level.

Nelson at Trafalgar, meticulously executed. Painted whitecaps frothed, and wind puffed the ships' sails. Beyond the theater of battle, a hellish storm threatened. The French ships held a sinister aspect, their hungry figureheads grinning, foreshadowing the evil sorcery that had plagued the Continent since the latest *coup d'état.* Admiral Lord Nelson lay bleeding on the quarterdeck of *HMS Victory,* his vitality drained, just one shuddering breath from death.

Eliza shivered. In this nightmarish vision, valiant Nelson had sacrificed in vain. Still, the painting wore a satirical smirk, as if the artist mocked his own message. Which was the greater danger: sorcery, or the indefatigable storm of British imperialism, obliterating the spirit of revolution?

She squinted at the hook-lettered signature. "Sheridan Lightwood?"

"The late Sir Dalziel's favorite *protégé.* Is his name not familiar? Heavens, don't tell him that. His sneer will kill you at twenty paces. I'll introduce you, but be warned: he's utterly intolerable." Penny waved towards a young fellow a few yards away in the crowd.

He wore his glossy dark hair long, in the bohemian fashion. Languidly, he sipped plum-red wine, a cigarette burning between two fingers, and murmured to the wide-eyed debutante at his side. The girl blushed to match her rose-madder skirts, and Lightwood gave a bored smile. He looked vaguely familiar. Where had Eliza seen him?

Ghostly Lizzie sauntered up, peering into his face. "Cocky little toad, ain't he?"

Eliza's guts clenched . . . but of course, no one reacted. No one could see Lizzie but she.

"Good God. You're truly merciless, aren't you?"

She whirled, startled. "Eh?"

Remy Lafayette flashed a brilliant smile. Arc-light crackled his chestnut curls with azure fire. "Knew you couldn't resist. Victory to me, I think."

"Well, you know. Nothing better to do this evening." But her heart flipped, unprepared. He wasn't wearing his dashing scarlet-and-gold uniform. No, she'd grown almost immune to that spectacle. So, of course, he'd turned up in civilian dress—as elegant as any of them, midnight coat and immaculate white tie—and the sight was . . .

Behind him, Lizzie tumbled, a theatrical swoon. Inwardly, Eliza rolled her eyes. "I say, what do you mean, 'merciless'?"

"You arrive looking like that, and pretend you harbor one meager ounce of pity?"

"Is that truly your best effort at a compliment? Because if it is . . ."

He kissed her gloved hand, drawing her close. "You look ravishing, madam," he whispered, a sudden glory of sky-blue warmth. "I'm lost for words. Melting at your feet. Pledging my undying admiration. Is that better?"

She laughed. "It'll do. If overly operatic."

Lafayette grinned, releasing her. "What, no razor-sharp reproach? Immediately I suspect a trap. Won't you introduce me to your friend?"

"Of course. Miss Penny Watt, Captain Remy Lafayette. Miss Watt is an artist."

Penny wrinkled her nose in a smile. "A Frenchman, no less. I'm smitten."

"*Sans vouloir vous décevoir, mademoiselle,* but I'm mind-numbingly English, I'm afraid. Are you a painter? Fascinating."

"We were just discussing Sheridan Lightwood, Sir Dalziel's *protégé,* and his *Nelson.*" Eliza indicated the corpse-strewn deck of HMS *Victory.* "What do you think?"

Lafayette studied it with a frown. "Brutally effective. Still, someone really ought to tell Mr. Lightwood we *won* at Trafalgar."

Penny giggled. "You, sir, can stay. It's tolerable, certainly, but no *Eve and the Serpent.* Without Dalziel, the vulgar little snake is back to being a lowly watch-maker's apprentice. Not that anyone's sorry."

Lafayette eyed Eliza meaningfully. "Did you know Sir Dalziel well, Miss Watt? My condolences."

"Everyone knew Dalziel, darling. Terrible business. We're all in mourning, like Lady Fleet." Penny struck a tragic pose, hand dramatically to forehead.

"Do tell," exclaimed Eliza. "We love juicy gossip."

"Well, you know. Indiscreet affairs are all the rage, and Lady Fleet's nothing if not fashionable. They say Dalziel encouraged handsome young talents to ravish his wife, so he wouldn't have to." Penny grew solemn. "In truth, I shall miss the old sweetie. He got me commissions, even if I did have to lie about my sex. Our careers are just as murdered, you know, especially Sheridan's. Some say they must have been more than friends," she added in a loud whisper, a wicked glint in her eyes, "or Dalziel wouldn't have lauded him as he did. Utter bollocks, of course."

Eliza laughed. "Indeed?"

"Trust me: old Dalziel was a miserable prude. Much as I detest Mr. Lightwood, I declare, it's frightfully unfair the way people gossip. A pretty lad can't pick up a paintbrush without some jealous Academy fool shouting 'sodomy!' and 'blackmail!'"

Lafayette cocked an eyebrow. "Protesting too much, are they?"

"I should say. Look at him, stalking that star-struck heir-ess. Field mouse, meet hawk." Penny mimed sticking a finger down her throat. "He's about as effeminate as the Duke of Wellington's stallion, and I have it on good authority that the drugs he's taking both prolong and fortify the performance, if you get my drift. Sheridan, I mean, not the duke's horse."

Lizzie chortled, slapping her thighs. Too late, Eliza clapped a hand over her own mouth.

Penny widened her eyes. "What?"

"Ahem. Nothing. You remind me of a friend, that's all."

"So if half a dozen people within earshot could outpaint Sheridan in a heartbeat," remarked Lafayette, "and no black-mail was involved, then why did Dalziel think the world of him?"

"Quite clever for a man, aren't you?" Penny gave a conde-scending smile. "Some say Sheridan laid a hex on him. Traded his soul to the Devil, don't you know, for Dalziel's patronage. Or was it for a few added inches to his male member?"

Eliza laughed. "And how, pray, did he forge this diabolical pact?"

"Summoning rituals, bathing in the blood of virgins, the usual." Penny chuckled. "Apparently London's positively *riddled* with evil covens holding *séances* in the dead of night, where they smoke delightful substances and copulate frantically in groups while imagining their lovers to be Satan. Why am *I* never invited to these occult debaucheries? That's what I'd like to know."

"I confess, I heard something about how Sir Dalziel died. People are whispering about rituals."

Penny puffed smoke rings. "Stabbed in the neck with Jesus Christ himself, they say. Face torn right off. More original than anything he ever painted, for sure. I must have posed for a dozen shepherdesses and 'fallen women.' But if he enjoyed orgies and black sabbats, he certainly hid it well. We all attended his party at Grosvenor Square that night, and I'm sorry to say it was excruciatingly dull. Not a scandal in sight. I really must get in with the right people."

Eliza cleared her throat. "If you don't mind my asking . . . where were you at ten to four that morning?"

Mischief lit Penny's eyes. "My word, you're some kind of investigator! How wonderfully cunning. I assure you, I was *desperately* oblivious."

Eliza exchanged glances with Lafayette. Mentioning the Royal seemed unwise, with Penny in such voluble mood. "I work for the police, yes."

"Then I'm at your service— Wait. I remember you! The famous physician who caught that Razor Jack fellow! And the other one, with the severed legs?"

The Chopper. Eliza sighed. Madam Murder.

Penny finished her cigarette, licking her lips. "An artist, wasn't he? Razor Jack, I mean. What was he like?"

"I didn't have much to do with him."

"That's not what the papers said when he escaped."

Eliza made a show of laughter. "Married him, didn't I, and flitted off to Constantinople? Or was it Rangoon?"

"Bolivia," put in Lafayette. "That's what I read. But it didn't say you were married."

Penny winced. "I sympathize. My gentlemen colleagues make the press, and it's all about art. Any publicity *I* get is about my figure and the cut of my gown." She made a rude face as she lit a fresh cigarette. "Now, let's see. We all endured Dalziel's dinner. Everyone arguing politics, frightfully dull. I'm afraid we left rather early, about half past one." Penny sighed. "I'd simply *love* to tell you that Sheridan lurked behind and bumped Dalziel off in a fit of smug insufferableness, but it isn't true. He and I rode a cab to the coffee house."

"I thought you didn't like Mr. Lightwood."

"Positively loathe the greasy-nosed runt. Doesn't mean he can't pay for my cab. Carmine was there, too, playing cards. Carmine Zanotti, I mean, of *Eve and the Serpent*. Have you seen it? It's simply wonderful. What a surprising new talent. We didn't shamble home until the sun crept up."

"And home is?"

"Here, of course. The Academy has student rooms."

"Which coffee house?"

Penny frowned, vague. "You know. The place we go. In Soho." She waved across the way. "I say," she called, "Sheridan, you disgusting little toad, we were just discussing your *poor* bartered soul."

Lightwood sauntered over. A picturesque fellow, his long locks tied in a ribbon. He wore an antique long-fronted waistcoat in rainbow colors beneath his tapered black coat. "A bad bargain, as it turned out," he said. "I've waved my magic wand a dozen times and you still won't drop dead."

"What do they all see in you?" muttered Penny. "It certainly isn't talent."

Sheridan smirked. "Charm, fame, and good looks? More than your *talented* friend Carmine has to offer."

"I wouldn't join that measuring contest, if I were you." Penny grinned like a hyena. "Are you done with this evening's petty conquest? I hear Lady Fleet's newly available."

He narrowed dark eyes at her. "Forgive me if my heart's not quite in it this evening."

"Oh, dear. Have you been blubbering over Dalziel again? Poor thing, your face is positively bloated."

"What do you want, Watt? The sight of you's already making me queasy."

"This lady's asking about the murder. I thought you might like to help, as you were *such* good friends."

Lightwood studied Lafayette, and then Eliza, unfocused, as if he looked through her. Short-sighted? Bad news for a watch-maker's apprentice who wanted to be an artist. The victim of a perennial sick headache? Hmm. What odds he was chasing the dragon? Pale, bad-tempered, that elusive, faraway cast to his gaze . . . but somehow, not so vague as he seemed.

Observant, perhaps memorizing details for some future sketch. Once again, sly fingers tickled her memory . . . but she couldn't place him.

"Forgive Miss Watt, madam," he said. "She's far too worthless a degenerate to properly introduce us."

"For heaven's sake." Penny waved her cigarette. "Dr. Jekyll and Captain Lafayette, meet rude, drunken gutter-snipe who thinks he's God's gift to ladies and art lovers both. Sheridan, meet eminently sensible professional who's so clearly out of your league that I'm tempted to watch you try, and the fellow who'll thrash your lights out if you do."

"That about covers it," murmured Lafayette with a cold smile.

Sharply, Lightwood bowed. As he bent over her hand, Eliza's senses prickled. His mingled scents drifted: claret, yes, he was halfway drunk, but also a sickly-sweet fruity smell that burned her palate.

She wished for her optical. *Chinese opium, or some such?* Magical, by that acid-sugar odor. Some artists used fey hallucinogens for the dreamlike, psychedelic state they induced, but they were horribly addictive, playing sly games with the body's chemistry until without them you shivered and sweated, horrors creeping under your skin. Could it be the same intoxicant she and Finch had found in Dalziel's tobacco?

"My condolences," she offered, watching him closely. "Sir Dalziel was a great man."

Lightwood's jaw tightened. "Yes, he was. I shall miss his insight."

"And his money," drawled Penny. "I was just explaining about the coffee house. What's the god-awful place called?"

Lightwood wiped his nose. "The Rising Sun, I believe. Fabulous tobacco, appalling coffee. I think someone relieved themselves in the brew jug."

"Probably it was you," Penny remarked. "You were intoxicated enough."

"A categorical denial would be difficult," admitted Lightwood coolly. "Not that you ceased fornicating with that pox-ridden sailor and his screeching bloody parrot for long enough to notice. Seriously, a parrot? Teach you a few maritime positions, did he?"

Penny arched dark brows. "Kiss my backside, Sheridan. You're only jealous it wasn't you."

Lightwood grinned, no doubt relishing a caustic rejoinder . . . and abruptly walked off. Had he spotted someone he didn't wish to see?

"Toadface," muttered Penny. Then she brightened, waving. "Here comes Carmine. You simply *must* meet him. Carmine!"

Eliza studied him, curious. A young fellow, short brown hair and evasive long-lashed eyes. Stubble darkened his chin, even though he'd shaved. Pleasant-looking, but somehow incongruous. As if, like her, he didn't belong.

Curiosity jabbed her ribs. Pale-skinned and useless were the gentry's defining characteristics. This Carmine looked more like a man Lizzie might flirt with at the Cockatrice. As if he worked for a living—heaven forbid!—or had crawled into white tie and tails from the gambling tent at a traveling carnival.

"Has he gone?" Good English, a ripple of Neapolitan vowels. "Protect me, *signorina*. Sherry means to sting me with his thorny West End wit."

"The coast is clear." Penny kissed his cheek, glowing. "In any case, I shouldn't worry. You got the better of him the other night."

Zanotti rubbed bruised knuckles. "He has not the advantage of my upbringing. Penny, we must talk—"

"Meet Eliza Jekyll, she's frightfully clever." Penny pushed him towards Eliza. "A police physician, don't you know? And her friend Captain Lafayette."

"I look forward to viewing your painting, sir," said Lafayette. "I've heard it well praised."

Zanotti reddened. Humble, or merely shy? "I suppose Penny tells you wild tales about me? None of them are true."

"Frightfully dull for a tortured genius," Penny declared. "Not a broken heart nor vanished muse in sight. Dr. Jekyll is investigating Dalziel's murder, isn't that fascinating?"

Eliza smiled encouragingly. "Did you know the baronet well?"

"Many times he examined my work."

"May I ask what time you left his dinner party?"

"Twelve, something like that. I didn't go down afterwards. The political discussion, it was not to my taste." A defensive gloss coated his tone.

"Too many bloodsucking Tories?" suggested Lafayette.

"Too many . . . how do you say it? Republicans with the bleeding hearts." He glanced at *Nelson at Trafalgar*. "I have experience with republics, Captain. Liberty and equality, they soon grow less compulsory."

"So I've heard," murmured Lafayette. "Did you leave the dinner alone?"

Zanotti's expression froze over. "I must account for every moment? I met Penny and Sheridan later, at the coffee house. They will tell you."

Penny rolled her eyes. "You'd make a terrible criminal. I vote for a steamy tryst with a mysterious high-born lady to account for your missing hours."

Zanotti grinned tightly. "Why did I not think of this? Immediately I shall seduce a duchess to lie for me."

"Or a baronet's wife," murmured Penny with a cruel smile. "I say, there's Mr. Paxton from the North-Western Railway. Carmine, you *must* convince him to look at my *Abélard and Héloïse*. Excuse us, won't you?" And she steered hapless Zanotti away.

"Well," said Eliza expectantly. "That was interesting."

Lafayette brushed a fleck of Penny's cigarette ash from his sleeve. "Astonish me with your insight, then."

Eliza considered. "Penny, voluble but genuine. Her confidence seemed honest. I rather envy her. Carmine, refreshingly shy but a bad liar. Sheridan, drunk and rude, but grieving. Desperately jealous of Carmine."

"Of his talent, surely, but of his success? Where Dalziel leads, society follows. Sheridan was set up for life."

"Then a better artist passed over might find motive for murder?"

"If Carmine's guilty, I'd have expected a better alibi. Still, I gather those two came to blows. Our scorned genius has a problem with his temper."

"Conveniently self-incriminating, but we don't know who started it. Perhaps Lightwood provoked him."

Lafayette laughed. "Do you think so? Handsome, rich, famous, no more talented than the next man? Allow me to illuminate the jealous male mind: no one's more annoying than a mediocrity who gets more girls than you. I assure you, Lightwood provokes merely by existing."

"How prehistoric," she remarked. "Is that why gentlemen don't like you?"

A wink. "And to think I still haven't won the lady I want."

"Still, it doesn't prove either of them killed Dalziel. We yet have no clear motive. Despite that odd remark of Penny's about Carmine and Lady Fleet. Perhaps he does have an alibi, but he can't reveal it."

"See, I knew you'd want this case. It's better than an opera. We must interrogate this slighted swain at once, before the fun wears off." Lafayette laughed more. Sweat glistened in his hair, and his eyes glittered, overly bright.

Eliza smiled, uneasy. He was behaving oddly. Recklessly, as if he'd abandoned caution. Could the approaching full moon be affecting him?

"Speaking of theater," he added, still laughing to himself, "have you observed Lady Fleet's little melodrama?"

"I could hardly miss it." The widow wore black satin fishtail skirts and dabbed a handkerchief prettily at her face. An entourage of fashionable young things fawned around her. "How tragic. All those gentlemen, dying to offer their condolences. The woman's a force of nature."

"Wealthy fellows, all. Viscount what's-his-name, Sir William something-or-other. That fat one's an earl's son, if I recall. Mean anything to you?"

Lord and Lady Havisham, Lord Montrose, Sir Wm Thorne . . . "I don't suppose we're looking at the guest list for Dalziel's infamous party?"

"Applause all round." Lafayette watched the scene dryly. "For a lady who killed her husband, she's certainly thick with his friends. I'd introduce you, but I doubt their lordships would remember me."

She smiled sweetly. "How deflating for you."

"*Au contraire,*" said Lafayette cheerfully. "An advantage of the badge and the uniform: no one looks closely at my face. This white tie is a strangely impenetrable disguise. My brother knows these sort of people," he added, careless. "You could ask him for an introduction. If you ever agree to meet him, that is. François is half convinced I've invented you to irritate our mother."

Eliza snickered . . . and a flash of crimson stole her breath.

A man, half hidden in the crowd. Dark suit, red necktie . . . and a glimpse of bright hair the color of blood.

Her heart thudded. That hair belonged only to one man.

"Excuse me, I must speak with someone." Before Lafayette could object, she darted into the crowd, shoving through a forest of elbows and skirts.

Where was he? Gone. Melted into the crush. Curse it. Her soft-slippered toe slammed into a table leg. "Ow! Damn it." She hopped, unladylike, and limped faster. If Mr. Todd were here . . .

Finally, she reached the room's perimeter. Overhead, a floating viewing platform puffed aether smoke, drenching her in thundery scent. Freshly varnished canvases covered every inch of the wall, surrounded by eager viewers. Dying Moses in the desert; Roundheads in orange sashes firing flintlocks at dissolute Cavaliers; a loch in some fog-bound Scottish highland . . . but the man she'd glimpsed was gone.

Breathless, she searched the crowd on tiptoes, but her heart somersaulted. "You imagined 'im," accused Lizzie, who slouched beside her, puffing on a cigarette. "Going nuts, you is."

"I am not . . ." Scintillating oil paints danced before Eliza's eyes, and her vision telescoped.

The Garden of Eden. A naked beauty, wandering in a glade, silvery hair trailing on whispering breeze. The birds and small creatures seemed alive. She could practically hear birdsong, rustling foliage, the silvery bubble of a waterfall, a rabbit's whicker as it munched grass . . . and the slither of scaly muscle, wrapping a forked tree.

Eve and the Serpent.

Eliza's mouth watered. How she longed to *touch* this miniature universe, brush those cool leaves against her cheek. Taste the water, inhale that sweet garden air. Climb into the picture, sprawl on that lush green meadow, and bask in sinless sunlight . . .

But her forehead knotted. The colors looked *wrong*. The grass was *too* green, the sky's daytime blue hurting her eyes, that bird's yellow plumage a sensory assault. The shadows beneath the Tree of Life swallowed her alive, sucking her down into seething darkness.

Eliza's blood burned. She'd know those startling colors anywhere. This hadn't been painted by any Carmine Zanotti. She'd seen this before. At midnight, in a candlelit attic in Chelsea.

She rubbed aching eyes. The serpent's lecherous gaze

flickered, cunning. Its crimson-slashed tongue oozed like blood. Eve's face shone, radiant with curiosity, a fair-haired angel with hope-filled storm-gray eyes . . .

Eve was unmistakably *her*.

Oh, my.

Her muscles watered, a treacherous swoon. That glistening, leathery serpent eyed her boldly, grinning mouth agape. Daring her to flinch . . . or edge closer.

Dizzy urges swamped her, a bloodstained tide. Fingers clawing for a throat, teeth clashing, the sweet *thwock!* of sharp steel into flesh, blood's iron taint in her mouth, *our* mouth, *my* mouth . . . and we SCREAM . . .

My ears clang, bats in the belfry. What's happening? I'm yelling, it's my voice, me, Lizzie Hyde—but it's *not* my voice. Her corset's crushing my ribs, I can't breathe, I scrabble for our laces but my hands are *her* hands and I'm clumsy, I can't undo. Our skin crawls. Jesus, is this *my* face I'm wearing? *Her* face? Something monstrous in between?

Hot tears block my nose. We're weeping, shouting, cackling like twin witches mocking each other. I rake my hair, claw at the edge of my face. I want to peel off this hideous mask and be FREE . . .

Deep in Eliza's skull, something snapped.

Bang! She reeled, flesh writhing inside. What had just happened? Had Lizzie burst free, in front of all these people? What if Lady Lovelace was watching? God help her, had she *changed*?

Frantic, she scrabbled in her dress pocket for Finch's shimmering pink-purple ooze. Fumbled with the stopper, and tipped a big splash into her mouth.

Icy fire roared up the back of her nose. Blinding sensation, gin and laudanum and sparkling fey intoxicants, caresses, sighs. Her skin rippled . . . but no, it's *our* skin, *my* skin, *my* ears filled with whispers of rage and hunger . . .

Strong hands shook her shoulders and a warm touch—*a kiss?*—sparkled on the corner of her mouth. She dragged in a sharp breath . . .

The storm-scent of aether flooded in, blessedly real. Artworks blossomed into focus, a rainbow of delicate colors. The crowd closed in, swirling skirts and starched collars and dizzy drunken laughter.

"Eliza?" Lafayette, warm and real, intense with concern. Not a dream. She exhaled, a wash of delirious relief.

Lizzie didn't stir.

The pink potion frothed angrily in her guts. *One drop only,* Finch had insisted. Too late to worry about that now. But the remedy bottle seared her palm like frostbite, and hurriedly she slipped it away. "Uh. Yes. Did you just kiss me?"

Sheepishly, he released her. "I apologize. But I said your name four times. You weren't there."

"I'm fine," she insisted mechanically. But the urge to hide clawed her flesh. She recalled Zanotti's edgy gaze. Shy, she'd thought . . . but what if he'd recognized her from *Eve*? Surely, someone would notice. Point at her, exclaim *aren't you that girl? Carmine, you must introduce us to your model* . . .

Her head pounded, a mess of conflicting compulsions that ate her vision like acid. A horrid itch under her skin threatened to erupt. Her courage faltered. Lizzie could burst out again at any moment.

She had to leave. Now.

"I suppose I'm a little off-color," she lied. "Do you mind if I go?"

"Of course not. I'll see you home."

Her stomach clenched. Certainly, he *knew*. That didn't mean she wanted him to *see*. And Lizzie and he had . . . an understanding. Could she trust Lizzie not to betray her? "That's not necessary—"

"I'm afraid it is. This fog will be teeming with footpads. It's not safe."

"I can mind myself, sir. Besides, you've no weapons."

"None that you can see." He warded off her protests. "Please, I insist. I fear for my safety, alone in the dark."

Despite herself, she laughed. "Very well, I shall protect you."

"I believe you would."

They picked their way towards the exit. Beneath the marble archway, and down the steps into blessedly cool Trafalgar Square. The fog had thickened, a gritty brown pall that made her cough. Nelson's Column loomed, his statue disappearing into the gloom.

Lafayette hailed an electric cab, and it clacked up on six brass feet. Eliza grabbed his hand and clambered into the cold leather seat. He jumped up opposite her, and the cab rattled off.

An electric lamp flickered inside, its filament nearly spent. Lafayette fidgeted, animated, gloved fingers tapping one knee. His eyes shone, luminous in dim purple light. "We can argue about the case, if it'll cheer you up," he offered. "I say Carmine Zanotti. The old man passed him over, so he killed him, in a highly picturesque fit of rage."

"Better than that, you'll be glad to hear. *Eve and the Serpent*? Zanotti didn't paint it."

"What?"

"That painting was in Razor Jack's studio, the night we caught him." She swallowed, warm with dread. "The girl in it, Eve . . . she's me."

Lafayette blinked. "Are you sure?"

"I've never been more so. My skin is crawling. That painting is Todd's."

"Which makes our Mr. Zanotti . . ."

"A fraud, and probably a thief, too. Harley ordered all Todd's work locked away to thwart unscrupulous souvenir hunters. Zanotti—or someone in league with him—must have stolen it weeks ago. Now he's passing *Eve* off as his own."

The perfect crime. Mr. Todd was hardly in a position to complain. But why hadn't Harley told her the paintings were stolen? Was he so concerned about her fixation on Todd's case? She'd telegraph, discover what had happened . . .

But she shivered, recalling those ominous headlines. Zanotti had better sleep with the light on. Or get some throat armor.

Lafayette grinned, enjoying himself. "This is wonderful. I knew this case would be fun. So Dalziel discovers he's a fraud, and Zanotti kills him to keep it quiet?"

"But that doesn't explain the mutilations." Her gloves were sweat-damp. She didn't dare peel them off. "Why not just kill him and flee? We've plenty of suspects to confuse. That long-suffering butler. Lady Fleet and her boorish footman. Even Reeve's famous burglar."

"Sheridan Lightwood's name is linked with Satanism," suggested Lafayette. "Joke or not, perhaps Zanotti tried to frame him, get back at a rival. One murder, two victims. Tidy."

"Or ruin Dalziel's reputation, by implicating *him* in black magic."

"Isn't killing him enough? Why risk leaving clues?"

"I've no idea," she admitted, frustrated. "But your point remains. A man who peels off his victim's face isn't merely covering his tracks. No, the motive is desecration. Revenge and ruin."

"So who wanted revenge on Sir Dalziel, and why? Is it wrong that I'm tantalized?" Lafayette sighed, and stretched immodestly, arching his back. It was quite a sight, and with a start, she realized he *enjoyed* his wolf, at least in this stage of its emergence. The same secret, guilty pleasure with which she sometimes relished Lizzie's outlandish freedoms.

"For shame," she scolded, though her own pulse quickened, too, "this is serious."

"Don't pretend you're not enjoying it."

"I merely present the facts." But a smile teased her lips. The pink remedy had worked. Lizzie was quiescent, dormant like a wound-down clockwork. And Lafayette was easy, relaxed, not threatening at all. Even if he was acting a little . . . *wolfish*. Unexpectedly—and not a little unspeakably—she found it charming.

Good lord. Eliza Jekyll was having *fun*.

How dreadfully vexing . . . and potentially dangerous.

HER STARRY SHADE
OF LONELINESS

•••

ELIZA AND REMY ARGUE THE CASE ALL THE WAY home, motive and evidence and wild conjecture what sets 'em both laughing like children. They're friends. This is good. She's easier with him, her suspicions fading like mist at sunrise.

But as we rattle and sway over broken cobbles, his exotic scent maddens me. I'm squirming like worms stuffed into a can. His curling golden lashes, the crisp purple-lit glory of his hair, that beguiling twitch of smile. I want him to smile at *me,* but he sees only *her.*

Damn it. This is mine. *He's* mine.

Our skirts rub against his knee in the cramped cab, with its lingering smells of leather and flowers. He shifts, a flex of muscled thigh. Our mouth still sparkles with his brief, chaste kiss. Christ, I want to climb onto his lap, crack open his shell, and devour the tender, passionate meat inside.

But she's strangling me. I'm trapped, my substance rinsed thin. Those vile stink-sweet drops of Finch's drain my strength, and I'm bruised and alone and can't break free.

God's bleeding innards. I *know* he likes me. I knew it that night in Regent's Park, his palms pressing against my back. We took our pleasure, and I felt his desperation when he whispered my name . . .

But how much of sweet stuff-all that means now.

Jealous green bile bubbles up my throat, and I can't spit it out. God rot her to mud. *She's* smart, pretty, desperately proper, everything a clever gentleman wants. Me? I'm just half a person, and the dark and dirty half at that. A thing to be used and discarded. Fuck me and forget me.

They share a laugh, leaning perilously close. Our gaze brushes his, for a breathless moment, and I see *caution* in those brilliant eyes. Remy's a clever soldier. He knows threat for what it is. This witty, laughing Eliza? She could break his heart. A power Miss Lizzie won't never possess.

My rage screeches, thrashing in rusted chains. She's spoiling *everything*. It ain't just that she still thinks he's a dirty Royal spy out to burn her. Ain't even that it's *she* he's courting, even though it were *me* he kissed and *me* he lay with and he can't pretend he never delighted in every sizzling second of *that*.

She thinks she's more worthy than Lizzie to be alive.

It ain't right. Just 'cause she were here first. I deserve my own life. And Remy—his strange wolfish heat tingling our skin, his fingers and ours quivering inches apart, drawn together like magnets—Remy is *mine*.

The cab rattles to a halt outside our town house, drenched in dirty mist. I can't see across the street, just gaslights along the park side, glowing streaks fading into fog. A ghost of what lurks, waiting.

Remy helps her down. Our skirts brush his side. His gloved hand lingers on our waist. And sweet madness fires my blood.

I can be subtle, aye. I can creep and hide and whisper. Too faint to be noticed, too demanding to ignore. We've charms enough between us. She's clever, I'm crafty. She's the waif, I'm the seductress. She's a challenge, I'm a restless memory of delirium. Perfect combination to trap a man.

I grin, thirsty for satisfaction. We'll have him, she and I . . . and when he's at our mercy? We'll see who's worthy to live, Eliza Jekyll.

Aye, we most certainly will.

———◆———

A light burned beneath Eliza's porch, shedding a pale golden pall. She swallowed, self-conscious. Such a pleasant drive home. So why did she feel edgy, lost, confused? *Lizzie,* she begged, *help me.* But Lizzie was distant, fogged over like the dim-lit street.

"It seems this matter remains to be settled," she offered, trying to keep it light. "I suppose we ought to inform Chief Inspector Reeve."

"Absolutely." Lafayette sniffed the damp air with relish. "That's the thing to do, I'm sure of it."

"Are you suggesting we take matters into our own hands?"

His gaze twinkled. "Dr. Jekyll, you insubordinate ruffian. The thought never crossed my mind."

"Well, if the Royal Society insists . . . let's corner Zanotti tomorrow and question him, in true Reeve style."

"I can hardly wait. Shall I call early?"

"Do. He mustn't escape before we can thrash him into confessing." She smoothed guilty golden skirts. "Tomorrow, then . . ."

"Stay a moment. Please." He touched her forearm, a gentle challenge. "I didn't yet beg your forgiveness for the way I acted tonight."

"Didn't you? I recall a species of bumbling apology."

"For my presumption, not for kissing you in front of half the town. Assuming you noticed," he added carelessly. "Shocking. Whatever will people say?"

Her courage wavered. If ever she'd heard an invitation . . . Ignore it? Slap him? Run indoors?

She laughed. "Don't pretend you care one whit what 'people' say. Besides, they were a tough crowd. All manner of poorly veiled debauchery. I doubt anyone noticed us. Anyway, I'd hardly call *that* a kiss."

Was it Lizzie talking? Or was she, Eliza, provoking him? What on earth for?

He cocked one eyebrow. "Excuse me, but I believe your lips touched mine. I'm certain of it, in fact. The sensation is forever scorched into my soul."

"Is it? Poor you."

"Not the word I'd have chosen." A charming smile. "I'm forgiven, then?"

"I'd forgive you in an instant, if I believed you to be sorry."

"Not a whisker, sadly. I meant what I said. You look magnificent." He brushed his thumb down the side of her bodice. "This is gorgeous. But I'd want to kiss you again no matter what you were wearing. And I desperately want to kiss you again, Eliza Jekyll."

Suddenly the fog cocooned them, intimate. A secret space. A *small* space. Her skin prickled, wary yet warm. How close he was. His strange body heat, alluring like a fire on a winter's night. She couldn't peel her gaze from the perfect curve of his mouth, and questions brewed tempting alchemy in her blood. What would it feel like . . . ?

He traced her jaw with a gloved fingertip. Tilted her chin up, a frank invitation. Hmm . . . but was it Lizzie's or her own, this quickening of pulse, that edginess of breath? Could she tell?

Did she care?

Let's see, then . . . She stretched onto her toes and captured his mouth with hers.

His lips were warm, sweet with surprise. Her nerves zinged shock and illicit pleasure. *Oh, my.* Her hand tightened on his shoulder. Seeing what it felt like was one thing, but . . . Compelled, she let the kiss linger. Tested her resolve.

He barely moved. Just let her kiss him, and when she pulled back, his smile curled. "Um," he murmured hoarsely. "That was . . ."

Her pulse throbbed, too fast. She felt giddy. Like panic, only her thoughts were too sharp, her senses too vivid. *We kissed him. We kissed Remy Lafayette. Good God, I've turned into an idiot.*

Shakily, she laughed. "Unexpected? Foolish? A terrible idea?"

"I was about to say 'insufficient.' I'm afraid I must insist on another." And he took it, and this time *he* was kissing *her*, and he slid warm fingers in her hair and eased her head back to deepen the kiss and suddenly it didn't feel so safe or clever. More like temporary insanity. What was that, sparkling all the way to her fingertips? He tasted like starlight, fresh and mysterious and frustratingly out of reach. His lips teased hers, never quite enough, inviting her to press closer, surrender.

Her experience of kissing was limited, but apparently he was rather good at it. She wanted to drag his mouth down to her throat, break open her bodice, feel his lips on her most private skin . . .

"Mmm." She extricated herself, arranging her skirts. Her lips still tingled with that startling flavor. How badly she longed to kiss him again. Take it further, find out what it was like to lose herself in shared heat. Do what Lizzie had done, and to hell with the consequences. "Well. I say. Um . . ."

His eyes glittered wildly. "Eliza, can't we please talk about it?"

First names. Gosh. He only pulled *that* out as a last resort.

Breathless, she pushed up her spectacles. "Ahem. I believe the last twenty seconds spoke eloquently for themselves, did they not?"

Twenty seconds? It could have been twenty minutes, or an hour. A light breeze had risen, and thinning fog swirled around her skirts. Perhaps they'd been kissing all night.

"I don't mean that. I mean whatever's wrong."

"I say, it's late. I really should—"

"It's just that I'm utterly confused." He tugged a chestnut curl over his ear. "I asked you to marry me and you didn't slap me or throw your cup of tea in my face. That was encouraging. But instead of simply telling me no—which would be more than distressing, if you must know, but eminently understandable—you're avoiding me."

"I'm not avoiding you."

"Oh, I'm afraid you are. We've barely spoken in weeks. I had to bribe you with a juicy murder scene so you'd even acknowledge I existed . . ." His grin sparked, infectious. "And what a delightful sentence that was. No wonder I'm smitten. But"—and he was serious again—"now we finally meet, and we end the evening like *that*. So, as I say: you baffle me, madam. Won't you tell me what's on your mind?"

His gentle accusations stung, all the harder for truth. Not unreasonable of him to seek explanation. She'd ventured where a woman of proper manners didn't go. Should she feel scandalized? Guilty?

Unfaithful? It bubbled up, unbidden. Ridiculous. Unfaithful to whom? But she couldn't unthink it, any more than she could un-kiss Remy.

How desperately inconvenient.

Her thoughts stumbled over rock piles. What to do? No one could see her, not in this fog-bound dark. Her reputation—what was left of it, after those lurid newspaper reports—remained intact. And she was a physician: she knew what happened between men and women. Besides, Lizzie's memories of making love to Remy Lafayette had featured garishly in more than one unwanted fever dream.

Unwanted, certainly. Unpleasant?

Eliza flushed. No point denying it. He was attractive; she was interested. (*Are you?* A lithe whisper licked her ear. *Or do you just want what Lizzie wants?*) She wasn't frightened . . . well, maybe a little. Nothing she couldn't handle. And she could list a dozen rational, mathematical, mutually beneficial reasons why marrying him was a sensible idea.

So what was the problem?

Aargh. She wanted to punch something. How dare some stupid *sensation* cloud her judgment? It was an assault on rational thought. It was the way Lizzie lived, seeking gratification at any cost. Not sensible Eliza.

But she shivered, troubled by the spectral echo of another occasion when uninvited, unwanted emotion had melted her reason. *Eve and the Serpent.* Excitement and terror. Passion and death. God help her, she was losing her wits.

"There's nothing on my mind," she insisted, defensive. "I'm just . . . it's all happened rather quickly. Marriage was never part of my plan, don't you see? It's an adjustment for me."

"Fair enough. Take as long as you like. I understand."

"Do you? Forgive me if I feel it's all a little easier for you. You're a man. You won't cease to exist." Her tone clipped, and immediately she regretted it.

"You could never cease to exist for me." He squeezed her hand. The barrier of two gloves lay safely between them, but his warmth still invaded her space. "Is it the legal nonsense that bothers you? We'll talk to your lawyers, draw up a pre-contract. You could keep your house, the business, the money. Everything. I'll sign whatever you like."

"I know," she said desperately. "I know you would—"

"Is it me, then? Still think I'll spill your secrets to the Royal?" A searching glance for the moon, and a low chuckle. "I assure you, we're far beyond that."

How she wanted to believe him. "It's not that. I just . . ."

"You don't have to say it." He sighed. "It's Lizzie and me, isn't it?"

And there it sparkled, unveiled between them like a malicious magic trick—but for a moment, she felt only giddy relief that he hadn't said something else. Something involving a homicidal artist and the ghastly letters locked in her drawer.

But whatever could she say? *You're ridiculously perfect, Remy, but I can't possibly marry you, because I'm being courted by a crimson-haired razor murderer who wants to ravish me in a ménage à trois with his imaginary friend. Isn't it horrid weather we're having?*

"I can't apologize for that," Lafayette added when she didn't reply. "I can't disrespect Lizzie—or you—by pretending it was an accident. Full moon or not, I was *there*. That'll never go away. But I promise you, Eliza: she and I are done. Over. It's you I want."

She twisted her hands. "I appreciate that. But . . . you and I barely know each other."

"What do you want to know? Ask me whatever you like."

How very like a man. "I don't mean . . ." She sighed, and relented. "I know it's frightfully poor manners, but I simply haven't made up my mind. Can you bear with me?"

He just kissed her hand, his steadfast gaze never letting her go.

Her heart ached. She searched for anything to say that would help. But nothing would—except yes or no. And for that she hadn't yet mustered the courage. What a cruel, selfish woman she was. "Tomorrow, then?"

A flintlock flash of smile. "Wouldn't miss it. Good night, Doctor."

"Good night." And she fled, sick.

A DISGUSTFUL CURIOSITY

∙•∙

HER CHILLY HALL LAY SILENT, A SINGLE LIGHT BURN-ing. In the vestibule hung a woman's long double-breasted coat in black. Not hers. Her lodger, Miss Burton's? They hadn't yet crossed paths.

Sleep crooked its bony finger, beckoning. She blinked gritty eyes, longing for her warm bed, the illusion of safety. But if she surrendered to sleep . . .

Her teeth chattered. Need for the elixir cavorted through her flesh, a dizzy dance of thirst. Stubbornly, she bit her lip, the sting shocking her back to reality. Lizzie had made trouble enough today. As for Finch's sweet-purple remedy . . . No, she must stay awake. Keep Lizzie at bay.

Listless, she wandered into her consulting room. No fire burned. She was economizing on household expenses. She huddled in her shawl and lit the lamp by the blotter. Electric light licked the edge of Moriarty Quick's trade card. *Potions! Lotions!* it sniggered. *The best in town!*

She scowled and flipped it over. "Silence," she ordered.

It didn't reply.

Beside it curled a telegraph ticker tape.

NIL INFO RE: PROF QUICK. WILL KEEP LOOKING. HG.

A new letter gleamed, too, Marcellus Finch's usually neat handwriting scribbled in haste.

Do NOT engage with that man. <u>Promise me.</u>

She'd no intention of engaging with him. But her nerves wriggled. So that rat Quick *did* know his alchemy. Finch could have elucidated. Tomorrow, she'd press him, discover what he knew . . .

Unbidden, her fingers crawled to the locked drawer, and turned the key.

Mr. Todd's letters glistened in the lamplight. Fascinated, Eliza stroked the paper. Always so pleasant to touch. That chemical scent, recalling his crimson hair. Eve strolling in the garden, oblivious, while behind her, the serpent wrapped lazy knots around a tree and grinned.

As if Eve were tempted, without even knowing the darkness was there.

Lizzie squirmed inside her, an angry black shadow. Still there. Still yearning for freedom.

So where was Mr. Todd now? Perhaps he'd already slipped into comfortable homicidal habits. Murders happened by the fistful in London every night. A few more would raise no notice. In her mind, he stalked his prey in foggy twilight, stealing over dark-lit cobbles. *Ker-ping!* Steel on ivory, a shriek, a hot crimson splash . . .

The letter tilted in her fingers, and out dropped the card she'd found inside.

MR. ODYSSEUS SHARP

Crazy laughter waltzed up her throat. The night they'd met, he'd shown her his startling portfolio. His *Odysseus and the Sirens* showed a man struggling in agony, roped to the mast, ears stuffed with wax. Leave him, and he'd die from want. Release him, and he'd leap overboard to his doom.

On the back, in Todd's delicate left-slanted hand, an address on Fleet Street.

Was this her salvation? Tell Harley Griffin, have Todd arrested. This time, so-called insanity wouldn't spare him a hanging. He'd kill no more. Lives would be saved, likely hers included.

Simple.

Unless it was a trap.

Her thoughts rattled, pebbles in a tin. Why would he reveal his new name and whereabouts to her? Already, she'd failed to dispatch Mr. Todd when offered the chance. Then, at his trial, she'd testified he wasn't responsible for his crimes. Left him rotting in Bethlem Asylum, at the mercy of electroshock and ice baths, when a sane man would have swung on a rope at Newgate and good riddance.

And then, he'd escaped Bethlem because of her.

Guilt splashed burning wax over her heart. She believed in fair treatment for lunatics who broke the law. But was Todd insane? Or just a beast in human guise, a dark-hearted demon who delighted in death?

She bit her lip, torn. Honestly? Yes, Todd had charmed her into forgetting he'd slit the throats of seventeen people. He was an intelligent, witty, charismatic man. A tragic romantic with talent to burn. Who wouldn't be a tiny bit smitten?

But Todd was damaged, vulnerable, deserving of pity and help. She'd acted reprehensibly. Instead of ignoring his flirtations as a professional should . . .

Cold sweat chilled her. Was she no better than those corrupt asylum keepers of legend, who took advantage of their dim-witted charges, slobbering over them in the dark where no one would see?

But her soul still tingled with the memory of that night at Bethlem when Todd had escaped. The Chopper's awful laboratory bathed in eerie lightning, that terrifying almost-kiss on the brink of death. A maniac Mr. Todd might be, but certainly no fool. He'd used her weakness for him to fashion his escape. Calculated her confusion to the last trembling fraction of an inch.

If he now imagined himself obsessed with her—his fragile mind twisting along bizarre, broken pathways—she'd only herself to blame.

Not her responsibility, she'd thought. It made her laugh sickly. A coward's lie. His every crime was her responsibility. Especially if he was killing to get her attention.

She had to fix this. No one else could.

Resolute, she pulled out a slip of writing paper and dipped her pen.

Mr. Sharp,

Her hand shook, ink splashing. She forced it steady.

Thank you for taking the time to write, and for
your flattering sentiments. I viewed the Exhibition
this evening—such a delight! What I saw was
surprising, to say the least.

She chewed the pen's tip, worried. What if someone was
reading his mail? She must be careful . . .

The world is not as one might wish. You must
know we cannot meet. But I should like for us to
remain friends—and I hope the memory of my
fond regard will comfort you, when your dreams
take that darker turn. When you are troubled, I beg
you, think of me, and have pause. It would make
me most happy.
    Yours is a unique and precious talent, Mr. Sharp.
With each stroke of your brush, the world becomes
more beautiful—and I trust with all my heart that
the satisfaction you earn from your art can provide
all necessary solace for your distress.

I remain, sir,
your honored friend
E.

Her skin crawled. She was taking a wild, reckless chance. Concealing vital evidence that could help apprehend a multiple murderer. If it backfired . . .

"No." Disgusted, she shook her head. Her squeamishness was insufferably selfish. If she hadn't let Todd escape, he'd be safe in an asylum right now, with medical staff taking care of him. Not at large, putting lives at risk.

His treatment—dare she say "cure"?—was her responsibility now. If she had to write all night, every night? That's exactly what she'd do.

She sealed the letter and, with a sigh, set it aside to be posted. Her bleary eyes stung, and fatigue tugged her hand, urging her upstairs to sleep. Tomorrow they'd question Carmine Zanotti. She ought to get a good night's rest.

But Lizzie pulled in her blood, too, a dark undertow, dragging her inexorably towards that secret cabinet, where the elixir waited . . .

Her mouth watered. Always warm, that elixir. Possessed of a wicked life of its own. That strangely bitter flavor, fiery in her gullet. Her senses exploding, shudders racking her blood, limbs twisting, muscles shrieking, bones crackling fit to snap. Ecstasy and horror throbbing as one . . .

Eliza had halfway risen before she realized she'd moved.

Her vision wobbled, flawed glass. Her corset crushed her breath away. Gasping, she fumbled for her buttons and popped the top clip. Air rushed in, blessedly fresh, and she panted, her chemise soaked in sweat. *Not tonight, Lizzie. Go away.*

She plonked onto the sofa, grabbing a book. The room was chilly, the lamp overly bright. The spidery text made her squint. *Treatise on Dissociative States and Disorders of the Nervous Mind.* Borrowed from Marcellus. Perhaps something in it could help Mr. Todd. But the letters scrambled like foreign script, indecipherable. Her attention crawled away, wrapping cold tentacles around darker concepts. Remy's scent, the hot sweep of his lips on hers, his wolfish growl of desire . . .

She shook herself, and began the page again. The mantel clock ticked ever more slowly, each second stretching, seemingly eternal. Would morning never come?

Her head throbbed. Stubbornly, she wiped her spectacles. She wouldn't sleep. Wouldn't dream . . .

The light lured and flickered, an electric will-o'-the-wisp, and as minutes dragged into an hour, the book dropped into her silk-clad lap, and she slept.

A SOUL WRAPT IN STEEL

•••

AT LAST.

I suck in sweet air, wriggling like a skinned eel. Muscles scream, joints twist, bones judder and crack. In her sleep, Eliza drowns, struggling for the surface. I writhe and shriek, and my hair springs free, not blond but luxuriant dark mahogany. Our body swells and changes shape to fit me, a sniggering dark fairy twisting her face into mine.

Pop! Out I lurch. I stagger on the carpet, a ghost from a bottle, panting and sweating and finally *whole*.

In the mantel mirror, *my* reflection leers, caught like a guilty moment. I wink. Hello, Miss Lizzie. My chin's sharper than Eliza's, my cheekbones better defined. Pins spit from my crackling curls. My eyes glitter and darkle. My fingers curl to throttle Eliza, but I'm laughing, too, laughing like her crimson-haired loon under the moon, because I'm free.

Mischief springs my grin crooked. I kick a delighted jig. To hell with that glacial pink brew. FREE.

Not a moment to lose neither. Too long since she popped my shackles and let me play. I've catching up to do. An hour or more we've pissed away, and Remy's long gone. Eliza's golden dress squeezes my curves, too tight. I'm bursting out. I've places to see, things to go, people to do . . . and between you and me? I'm dying for a drink.

What's that? Shut it with your god-rotted preaching. A woman's gotta have a vice, and Miss Lizzie needs dirty habits enough to sate us both.

I toss her spectacles aside, glassy edges leaping sharper. I grab her dumb-arse letter—Odysseus Sharp, Christ, even his *name* wriggles my guts cold—and sneak into the hall. Shadows cling to her expensive rosewood furnishings. It's a fine house, but I hate it. I hate its shiny façades, these grim middle-class walls trapping me in like a dungeon's. I yearn to set it alight and screech like a harpy while the flames leap higher.

Her brass idiot crouches by the hall stand, his lights flickering with dim electric dreams. He mutters sleepy nonsense. "*Rattus rattus* . . . Make greater speed . . . Ratty-rat-rat . . ."

No one's awake to spy me. Mrs. Poole and Molly the housemaid . . . well, maybe they knows and maybe they doesn't. Close-mouthed, those two, like as twin peas. But Eliza gave 'em the evening. As if she knew she'd be doing bad things tonight.

I chuckle. Brittle Eliza, pretending she don't count the hours. Tell me you don't relish it, you lying girl, tell me you ain't lurking like a ringworm beneath Lizzie's skin, savoring every laugh and gasp and sweet-bitter swallow.

Crick! Creak! I hasten to the shadowy second floor, an awful hurry gnawing my bones what won't let me rest. *Now,* it whispers, *right now, this minute, I'm hungry, Lizzie, so very HUNGRY, why d'you make me wait?* Eliza's bedroom, her

curtained bed a black shape in the dark. It smells of un-
burned coal and the lavender she uses to wash her hair. A
good smell of home . . . but it itches my lungs, too, a poison-
ous arsenic rash. I won't never belong. Just an impostor,
thieving her life away.

I skid across the rug to the cold hearth. *Crunch!* Yank the
hinged sconce above the mantel, and my secret cabinet
swings open.

I pop the arc-light, and it sheds a reddish glow. The shady
half of Eliza's library, forbidden books on alchemy, experimental medicine, unorthodox science. Further in, my wardrobe, stuffed with bright colors. None of her dull grays for me.

A flick of silken ribbon, and her golden gown pools at my
feet, a pile of guilty memory. I pop her tiny corset—damn,
who knew air tasted so good?—and pull on *mine,* what shows
off my womanly advantages, instead of pounding 'em flat like
oatcakes. I push my twin beauties up and yank the laces tight.

What can I say? A girl fights with the weapons to hand. I
ain't got no ladylike façade to make 'em think twice. A second
or two of distraction's all I need.

Hmm. Red, red, or red? I choose a flirty piece in dark
scarlet velveteen, skirts flounced up to show my ankles.
Ooh-er, we're dressing to impress tonight. I fondle our mother's diamond necklace—I do adore how he sparkles so wild—
but reluctantly I toss him onto the bed and clip on my glossy
jet choker. Where I'm bound, folk aplenty'd cosh me senseless
for sixpence. No sense dying for a flashy bauble.

On with my boots, buckle and button and pointed heels. I
keep her pretty stockings—her best for her fancy tryst tonight, for all the good they done her. I grab a little red top hat

and knot my bouncing hair. Toss on a flimsy red shawl—it's damp and raw out—and I'm ready.

I blow the mirror a kiss. Miss Lizzie, you're looking saucy tonight. Who could resist you? Certainly not the wolfish bloke we've got in mind.

In the cupboard by my feet, the elixir whispers, its black bottle glowing with eerie inner light. Only one left. I stuff it into my pocket, for Eliza's found me out: I swig it when I feel I'm fading, when I don't yet want to be dragged back into my shackled nightmare. Hell, she started this medicinal war. She can't complain if I carry it on.

My sweet steel sister murmurs, too, a four-inch stiletto with a blackwood handle. I poke her down between my bosoms. She nestles, muttering warm discontent.

Hush, sister. We'll find games for you yet.

Down the hidden back stairs I hop, a song on my lips. Along the dusty lane and out onto Southampton Street, where fog marches by, a parade of wispy ghosts. I tip my hat. "Evening, gents. Lovely night for a haunting."

Hello, Miss Lizzie, they whisper. They lick at my ankles, twist between my outstretched fingers. They're my friends. They *see* me. And that's more than most.

I skip towards the distant river. Moonlight strains through the fog, a piss-yellow gleam. She's nearly full, this greedy moon, which accounts for Remy's temper, if not for his crackbrained notions. *She and I are done. It's you I want.*

We'll see about that, my fine captain. You might *think* you want Eliza, her quicksilver wits and modest manners, a civilized wife for a civilized man. But close your eyes in the dark and listen to your moonstruck heart. Ask the wolf what *he* wants . . .

My vengeful muscles shudder, and my rage whispers murder. Think I weren't watching, Eliza? Think I'd never notice
when you kissed him and *liked* it? He's mine, and you can
bloody well let it alone . . .

A thought rattles, and I groan. Shit. Forgot her letter,
didn't I, to the red-haired loon. Left it on her writing desk,
instead of pissing on its ashes as I'd planned. If her housekeeper *posts* the stinkin' thing . . .

Unquiet breath prickles the back of my neck.

I whirl, poised. A footstep? A rustling skirt in the tail of
my eye? I squint into blinding fog. Eliza's overwrought nerves,
is all. Delusions of persy-cootion.

A solitary coach clip-clops by. The driver hunches beneath
his lantern, his whip a black sting. A lushington staggers,
singing raucously, glassy eyes rolling in opposite directions.
*"While soft . . . the wiiind . . . blew downnn the glade . . . and
shoook the golden bar-leyyy . . ."*

A crusher in a long blue coat strolls by on his beat. Fog
licks his hat, wreaths his silver buttons.

I wave, grinning. "Top o' the evening to you, *cunt*stable."

The copper waves his truncheon. "Move along. No place
for your sort." He ignores the drunk, for clearly the fellow's
quality and can do as he please. One rule for us, another for
them.

"Screw you. How 'bout *your* sort, you poxy butt-flapper?"

"No solicitation on the street, missy. Now git."

"Ain't no lady, so I must be on the game, is that it? As if
you don't buy yerself bangtail when the fancy strikes." I flip
him a two-finger salute. "Get this up ya."

"Look 'ere, you mouthy skirt—"

"Rather not, if it's all the same. Wouldn't blow your measly pipe for a hundred quid. Ha ha!" And I run.

Boots thud after me, but I skip into a side street, and *poof!* I'm gone like a bad dream. Vanished into the wet gloom on a splash and a giggle. Ha! Don't want me another night in the Bow Street lock-up. Quaff what elixir I might, when my time runs out, I'll once more be Eliza. And then what?

In less than a quarter hour, I reach New Oxford Street. Coal-greased shop windows, brass carriages with purple electric coils crackling in the fog. Dung collectors scrape the street, plopping their noisome treasure into buckets. A buyer for everything, be it rags and bones, dead men's clothes, used dripping, or the stuff they call "pure" for the tanneries, what the rest of us know as dog turds. The penniless don't let nothing go to waste.

I fight across the thronging arc-lit street and turn down a grimy lane, what narrows into a dark alleyway, what twists down crooked steps into a pitch-black tunnel splashed with mud and shit, and between one noisome breath and the next I'm in hell.

True darkness reigns in the rookery, a forsaken maze of lanes and cesspits where sun don't never shine and even the moonbeams slant high overhead. But my eyes adjust like a cat's to the night. I skip and slip-slide over puddles and muck. The stench churns my guts, but it's invigorating, too, like air you can eat, only no one ever fought off the bloody flux by breathing.

Drunken tenements totter, threatening to crush me. Rags hang limply over shutterless casements. In a doorway, a pile of ill-clad urchins snoozes. Their little fingers is blue, faces pinched. One's got a goat's trotters for feet. Inside, a woman screams gin-soaked curses. People grunt and snore and holler. Beneath a cracked lintel, a girl's on her knees in the mud, sucking some fat bloke's prick.

A scrawny fellow wallows and wails in a piss-stained puddle. Waist-down naked, just a holey frock coat soaked in gunk, and a scaly snake's tail for legs.

I grab the sorry bastard's armpits and haul him out afore he drowns. A haze of stale gin nearly floors me, and suddenly Snake Man whiplashes and snaps for my ankles, crocodile jaws drooling black venom.

I leap away, missing his hidden trip wire by a bee's dick. The trip wire connected to a rusty spring-loaded scythe. That puddle fakement? Snake Man's catching his supper.

"You rat-fucking twerp." I slam my boot into his skinny ribs, but my idiot face burns. Jesus on a jumping bean. Hit the dirt in the last shower, did I?

I hurry on. Humph. Me and my big bleeding heart. Down here, where the *weird* lurks, you learn the rules or perish. It's riddled with blind corners, doorways leading nowhere, trapdoors to spiked pits, springs with axes poised to fall, and everyone's running a fakement, a swindle, some cruel or violent game. The Royal's brass-arse Enforcers don't dare venture here, coppers neither. The rookery keeps its own law.

Tonight, I'm headed a few blocks over from my typical haunts, across Crown Street and out of the effluent. I turn a corner, and from the foggy gloom springs a glittering rainbow heaven.

Dazzling gaslights illuminate the gay façades of flophouses, coffee dens, theaters hosting risqué burlesques. Mirror-flashed gin palaces shimmer like fairy-tale castles.

The crowd spills onto the street, bringing cigar smoke and the glorious stink of gin. Soho Square, den of the dissolute. These places was once fancy town houses for strutting rich folk. When the livelier industries moved in, the quality turned tail, but Soho still carries itself with a corrupted elegance, like a glossy apple rotting on the inside.

Music ripples from dance halls, clashing into discordant din. Drunks shamble. A shifty-eyed carnie gang parade their clockwork menagerie, snarling brass lions and a teetering metal giraffe with a concertina neck. The swell mob's out in force, too, teams of thieves square-rigged, fingers twitching into pockets and reticules, passing the loot to their accomplices before the mark kens it snaffled. I grab a wide-eyed country boy and hop a polka, jig-up, jig-up! He laughs and dances with me until I swirl away, his fumbling kiss on my lips and his pocket watch in my palm.

By a broken paling fence, a fight's started, big ugly versus bigger uglier, swinging bare-knuckled inside a ring of cheering vultures. Not all shabby folk neither. Top hats and starched white shirts mingle with ragged neckties and bare chests beneath second-hand frocks. Chinamen, dark-skinned Turks, even Irishmen is welcome, so long as they flash the readies. An enterprising book-maker in a ragged navy officer's coat is dashing to and fro, stuffing banknotes and collateral into his beat-up leather bag. His hat sports a tricolor cockade. Ain't no Union colors, I'll be bound, but a saucy bit o' treason. It's one o' life's happy accidents that the Frenchies' flag and ours be the same color.

"Two bob on the big ugly bloke!" yells I. Someone shouts an obscenity, and I flip 'em a how-do and carry on.

"Fish, tasty fi-i-ish!" A lad with drooping hound's ears clutches a clawed fistful of sardines. Now and again, he steals a bite. Brave little codger, creeping from the rookery's shadows where weird folk go unremarked into a bright and ugly world where Royal Enforcers still jump their brassy arses from corners and haul you away on a whim.

I toss him a penny and grab some *tasty fi-i-ish*. Salty rot stings my tongue, foul but delicious. A bit like this world.

I bump shoulders with a lady of the night in a ragged Regency gown, earning a curse and a painted glare. She and her sisters in sin, on the prowl for prey. Mary-Anns, too, lads dressed as ladies, for gents what likes that sort o' thing. In a stairway beside a penny-gaff theater, a brothel madam hovers, tapping a riding crop against her skirts to advertise the games her girls play. A half hour's release in a greasy room for half a crown, a quick frig against the palings for a shilling. If you're too strapped for that? Find a hungry street urchin who'll blow you on her knees for sixpence.

Don't get me wrong, it ain't my trade. But it ain't a bad life compared to dropping dead from overwork in a coal-burning plant or rotting your jaw off in a phossy match factory. Sometimes a girl lasts a good couple o' years, fed and sheltered with all the gin she can swill, and now and again she gulps the old Romany crone's sour herb drink and a glob of bleeding flesh spits from her insides and she carries on. Until she gets the clap or the pox or the flesh-crawling gripe once too often and wastes away, sores splitting her lips and a rotting itch inside what won't never heal.

Them's the lucky ones. In the shadows, darker shapes shift. Girls too old, too *weird*, or just not flash enough at the act. Starving, homeless, desperate. Any foul thing for pennies, be it banal or beastly, and when a bangtail turns up at dawnlight with her neck askew or her face battered in, it'll more often than not be one of these sad sisters.

Just things to be used, and not good for much. Old meat, tossed into the gutter when a fellow's gnawed his fill—and it ain't them fine gents getting spat at in the street and called vermin, oh no. Them girls is like Lizzie Hyde. Fun while she lasts, but shunned for a shameful secret when Eliza's done.

I ducks alongside a gin palace, where the big window shows a riot of drunken fools, dancing girls, life-or-death card games and punch-ups. My blood hisses, eager for gin's gritty pleasure. But time enough for drunken foolery when work's done.

The noise fades as I stride into a muddy yard. A plump Chinaman sits cross-legged on a mat by a hessian curtain. I toss him a silver crown. He nods gravely, speaks in his twanging language.

"*Ni-how*," agrees I, and skips by into the den.

Smoke unfurls at eye level, a fug of uneasy dreams. Tasseled cushions pile the dirt floor. A square-rigged cove lies a-faint on a couch, entranced by spirits only he can see, a pipe dangling from limp fingers. From his pocket drops a gold watch, and a tiny girl snatches it with webbed hands. A woman sprawls face-down, drooling into the dirt. Maybe sleeping. Maybe dead.

A crooked wicker door beckons. I rattle it. "Open up, rat-brain!"

A sniggering green face with rodent teeth pokes out. "You again. He said to say he ain't here."

"Brilliant, you is." I shove the green door-keeper aside. Inside, a fire pit stains the room bloody. Fearsome heat dizzies me, only a tiny hole kicked in one wall letting out the dream-smoke. A bearded cove in a dented top hat giggles, gnawing stubby fingers to the bone.

And here's Remy Lafayette. Out of twig in a dirty brown coat, and deep in whispered palaver with a trio of shady coves at a wooden table. Pewter cups, a platter of suspicious-looking stew, a bottle holding a scant inch of emerald absinthe. I twist my ears but can't make 'em out . . . then one laughs, his voice lifts, and it's a language I recognize but don't understand.

My palms itch. Holding court with dirty Froggies? All banished from London, so I heard, a pointless exercise seeing as only the law-abiding ones will obey.

A plump coin purse squats on the table. One fat Froggie with a purple beetroot mark across his face tests its weight, makes it disappear, and the three mooch away, hats pulled low. Business—whatever it be—is done.

Remy devours what's left of the food, like he's not eaten for a month. Polishes off the absinthe, neat. Ouch. Then slouches into a corner, alone.

A cauldron bubbles over the fire, tended by a shirtless raw-ribbed lad. Fleshy abortions of wings flop down his back. He stirs the pot, tentacled fingers wrapping twice around his wooden stick. He dips in a straw, thumbs the end, and splashes a drop of evil-eye green into the packed bulb of a tobacco pipe.

I choke, swamped by black memories of the night I over-indulged on some ugly-arse fey brew and about got *eaten* for my trouble. They cook it from tears and heartache and darkfire dreams, and it'll rot your wits and warp your wants to moldy horror. Malicious magic, no mistake.

Remy's lounging on a tattered red velvet couch, now, pipe in hand. Dusty coat shrugged off, shirt open in the heat. Firelight gilds his skin, jewels of sweat glittering in his hair.

He draws smoke, ash flaring. Lets his head fall back, and exhales. Green smoke hisses upwards, a tricksy demon.

I knew it. He still ain't given it up, not these three weeks. Can't, for want of aught else to fight his affliction. I want to punch his handsome face. But my jaded throat parches. He's mesmerizing, a dangerous fallen prince from a dark fairy-tale.

Which is why, ten seconds later, I'm still staring like a gob-struck idiot when Remy's bloodshot glance trips up on my face.

Our gazes lock, unspoken words of loss.

He resumes his ceiling study. "Go away, Lizzie."

I march up and twist the pipe from his hand, just as he's sucked in another lungful. Remy just exhales, evilsweet smoke tingling my face. I toss the pipe away, though that smoke waters my mouth with want. I yank him up, expecting a fight, but he lets me drag him out, and stumbles only a little as we march by the fat Chinaman and into the dark-lit street.

My arms prickle in the chill. But I'm too busy hurling Remy against the wall to care. "Bleeding Christ. It's been what, an hour? Two? And already you're up to your gills in it."

"Told you before. S'medicinal." Furtively, he searches the sky for any hint of moonglow. "I'm starving. Are you hungry? Let's eat."

I go right ahead and pretend the way that damp shirt licks his body—the way his lip quivers, for God's sake, on the brink of wild beauty—ain't of no interest to me. "Think you can *cure* your curse with a pipe of green? You're crazier than I thought." *Cure* comes out bitter as dead fish. He loathes his creature. What does that make me?

"Nothing else works." A shadow of his stunning grin. "I can't hold it in. I don't sleep for days when it's like this. The pipe, well . . . it calms *the thing*, for a while. I learned that in India, when it first started." Crazy laughter, as if the very notion of *calm* is lunacy. "She kissed me, Lizzie. It's three days early and she kissed me and *it woke up*."

The thing. As if it ain't part of him, and if he could, he'd wield a blade and carve it out, like the spoiled portion of a joint.

I try to stuff my indignation back down. There's things more important than my bruised pride. I've seen what happens to him. It's beautiful, the way a wild beast is beautiful. But it's also hungry, bristling with blind animal rage. It *bleeds*. What if he starts *changing* without the moon?

But I can't help it. "Are you even listening to the tripe you're spouting? How can you *lie* to her?"

It's out before I understand my own words. Not *lie to me*. He's keeping secrets from Eliza. And that hurts, a keen ache in my heart that won't ease.

For sure, I keep secrets from Eliza, too. When she wakes, she won't recall what I done tonight, and if she does, she'll laugh it off as a frightful dream.

But Lizzie's *supposed* to be the bad egg in this sordid little pie. I'm *meant* to lie, to snigger with satisfaction at my despicable deeds.

He ain't.

God's bleeding innards. It's *me* what knows the truth. Me what *sees* him, in all his tragic splendor. And still he wants *her*.

My skin stings green like poison ivy. It ain't fair. Fuck me, if I could cut *her* out . . .

Remy shakes his head, mutinous. "This affliction? It's not her world. She doesn't belong here."

I want to rake bloodied nails down my cheeks. *I'm a person, too! Why can't you SEE me?* "So that's all I am? An *affliction?*"

"You know I don't mean that. Please, Lizzie, go. It's not safe here."

"Oh, aye? Why's you here, then? Thought them Froggies was kicked out o' London like plague dogs."

Fog swirls, parting. Light from that swaggering moon slants silver onto his face. His hands shake, not so much you'd notice, but I'm standing right close, close enough to feel he's trembling, feverish, losing control. I can taste that green absinthe fairy dancing on his breath. The air around us shimmers, a bubble about to pop.

"It's official business," he mutters. "Nothing I can share with either of you."

Oho. My cunning twinkles bright. Wheedle it out of him, so we will. "Secret-squirrel tricks for the Royal, then? That metal-arsed countess got you trawling the pubs for sorcerers and runaway fey folk?"

"Lizzie, don't ask questions. Please. I can't answer them."

"But—"

"It's for your protection." He cuts me off, flat and final. "I've already failed to save one woman I cared for. I shan't fail again."

My stomach hollows. Ouch. He means his wife. The dead one. At his own unwitting hand. Exit Lizzie, stage left.

But he don't edge away. Don't cease *looking* at me, even as his monster growls for my blood.

What would happen if his wolf erupted right now? Compelled by some dark magnetic force, I touch his jaw with one fingertip. His throat, that tender pulse. Find his collarbone, slip inside his open shirt . . .

He pulls my hand away. But his fingers crush mine, demented with wolf-fever, the drug, that greedy moon.

Guilt stings me, needle-sharp. I'm taking advantage . . . but hell, that ain't never held me back before. "Remy, this is crackers. Why are we pretending? I want you, and I ain't afraid."

"I've noticed." An intoxicated chuckle. "Believe me."

"Then let me in." Let me taste that wolf on your tongue, feel his dark jolt in my bones. Let's put our unwanted halves together and make *one*.

His glower darkens. "I can't."

"What, because I ain't no fancy lady?"

"Don't be ridiculous. You're a smart and beautiful woman, Lizzie, and I'm proud to know you."

A damn fool grin pastes itself across my face like a wet pancake. I can't help it. His golden brilliance pierces my soul, and all my vaunted wiles make like piss-scared rabbits and scarper.

He's stripped me bare, sure as if he'd shredded my gown and left me standing naked. I can't lie. I can't joke. I can't even flirt like a two-penny whore, not with this man. I can only be me.

So I sink my hands into that glorious chestnut hair, and

kiss him. Like I've wanted to for weeks. His mouth is hot, he tastes of smoke and tears and delicious dark dreams . . .

He shoves me away, and for a second, his teeth flash bright, an instinctive snarl of *fuck off.*

I stumble, numb. I can't feel my fingers, my skin. As if my vitality's been sucked away.

"Lizzie. Good God. Forgive me." Remy swipes a hand across his mouth, muffling a curse. His eyes gleam, an edge of wild wolfish gold that stirs dark mischief in my blood. His wolf-eyes was always blue, till tonight. Lucid. Human.

Now should I be afraid?

"Don't want your 'sorry,'" I blurt out. "Just tell me why." But I'm already cowering inside. Christ, I want to hit the dirt and beg. I'll go. I'll stay. I'll do whatever you ask. Just leave it unsaid, my heart unflayed.

But he's steadfast, without a flinch. Nary a crack in his ironclad courage. He don't even need to speak it.

You're not her.

My stupid ears ring as if he's punched me in the skull. The world shudders and *grows,* lurching into the yonder, and like Lizzie in fucking Wonderland, I'm three inches tall.

So pitilessly honest with me, as if he don't know no other way. And yet he'll lie to *her.* Kick his precious principles to the dust in an instant, if it means *she'll* be safe. For *her,* he'll sacrifice his own self.

But not for me.

God's bleeding innards. I stare at my hands, my skirts, my muddied boots. I half expect me to be transparent. Fading, a ghost searching in vain for its long-decayed corpse.

Never really here at all.

"I mean it, Lizzie. I'm proud to know you." He's quiet. Gentle. Brutal as they come. "But I gave her my word, and it's a promise I must keep."

And how in God's green hell do I argue with that?

My vision blurs, and a raw and rotting ache chews my heart. It'd hurt less, if I didn't believe him. If I thought he were brushing me off for a lark, 'cause his habit's to love girls and leave 'em.

If his god-rotted *decency* weren't the reason I like him, for fuck's sake.

I wipe a bland smile over my pain, and stumble away.

TINCTURA THEBAICA

•••

I N THE STREET, THE CROWD SWALLOWS THE MARVELOUS
Invisible Lizzie without a burp. Remy don't follow. I don't
look back. Wouldn't see a damn thing anyhow, not
through these tears. God rot it, I never cry.

I trip over unseen feet, and pick meself up. Someone
shoves me, a black-coated blur. I shove him back, spitting a
curse, and then we're swept asunder by the crush, evil swirling melodies, the stink of sex and drugged breath, and all the
fun other folks is having.

I wipe my face, fury and shame smearing like rank sweat.
Remy's rejection rips me raw. He's just a man. Why'd I give a
pigeon's runny poop what he thinks? I've always been the
lesser half, wallowing in dirt and decadence while Eliza keeps
pure . . . but now a poxy itch plagues my flesh, this diseased
notion that no, Miss Lizzie, you *ain't* half a person after all.

You're no person.

A shadow. An empty cipher. A figment of some ugly dream
she's having while tucked safely in bed. Come morning, she'll
recall fragments—my voice, liquor's dark flavor, the starlit

shock of a caress—and a shiver will rack her spine . . . then she'll turn her face to the sun, and forget me.

And I'll vanish. Ashes on the breeze. Like that shit-spitting letter to Todd what I stupidly forgot to burn.

Devil's moldy guts, *I'm part of her.* Why does she HATE me so much?

Bodies bump me, I lurch left and right, stumble into a doorstep, and grab it to keep from falling. I'm tearing my hair in hanks. I'm wheezing, a gritty groaning sound that hacks my lungs to bleeding. Fuck me, I need a drink. A disgusting burnt coffee smell scratches my nose, and on its fur-spiked back rides another, deeply luscious aroma what waters my mouth: that sly seducer named *gin.*

I screw hot palms into my eyes, and when I let go, a sign lurches from fading stars: a yellow-painted sun on a black horizon.

THE RISING SUN.

Now, where'd I hear that before?

Ding-ding! The boxing bell rings in my head. Curiosity versus self-pity, a swift but brutal to-do that leaves self-pity groaning on the floor in a pile of bloody teeth. So this night never turned out as I planned? Don't mean I have to pissfart about, weeping into my porridge like a jilted dolly.

I dust off my skirts, light a saucy twinkle in my eye, and stride in.

Promptly, I trip over a chair, and by a scant inch miss braining myself on the bar. All class, me.

Undeterred, I shakes meself off. Christ, is this really the joint them posh artists frequent? Talk about rough trade. I can barely move in here. Dark, smoky, tables jammed tight.

Greasy low-lifes hunch over steaming bowls of that loath-some coffee. From shadowy corners ooze grunts, sighs, drunken moans. A few bolder ones is actually going at it where all can behold. "Jesus," I mutter, "put that thing away."

A fuck-ugly cuckoo clock on the wall goes off like a chirpy bomb and chimes eleven. Wrong, you witless crank. Must be way past midnight already. I collide with some liquor-reeking cove, and career into the zinc-topped bar. "Your pardon, miss," he mumbles. Then he spies my chest, and does a drunken double-take.

Minus the gin, so do I.

Long chocolaty hair in a ribbon, ice-carven chin, dark eyes a-shimmer with much drink and little sleep. His rainbow waistcoat's a mite crumpled, his necktie charmingly crooked.

Oho. Seems Remy ain't the only one seeking solace after a rough night in a monkey suit, clambering over piles of money and kissing the wrong girl. This is Sheridan Lightwood. Eli-za's artist. The gang's all here.

I cast a critical eye. A looker, some girls might say, but sommat's up I don't like. He's too slick. Too glossy, a painted icon not quite real . . . and still he's goggling at my chest, as if he ain't never seen boobs before.

My crafty self cackles, a witch crooking her finger. Come into my gingerbread house, little boy. What say I ferret some good oil on Eliza's murder case? Perhaps a certain uppity Royal Society captain might be interested.

A grin swaggers onto my lips and crouches there. Not that I'm undermining poor Eliza, oh no. Not that I'd steal Remy from her in a heartbeat, if only I could figure how.

For shame. Ain't that at all.

I dip this Sheridan a wink, fingering my velvet skirts as if he makes me want to *touch*. "I say, sir," I purr, "ain't you that artist?"

He's got the grace to laugh. Tipsy and pleasant, or a man accustomed to harmless fakement. "Astonishing, how far my fame has spread these last few days." His tones are pure West End, a gentleman's gentleman, but with a bitter, cynical edge.

I play with my hair. "Could you paint me? I'd like that." His eyes are shot, his face puffy. I'd bet gold he's been weeping tonight. The working girls' glances slide over him, seeking trade elsewhere. Hmm. Too proud, is he? Or just more trouble than he pays for?

"Miss, I'd strip you bare and paint you until you screamed my name, if I weren't so drunk I'm about to topple." He frowns. "Or be sick. Just so you're fully informed."

His eyes are glazing. Swiftly, I ease him around to face the bar, in case he does either. Seems only the direct approach will profit. "What's you so sad about, then? Your dog die?"

He sucks smoke from a pipe. "My pitiful life is over, that's what. For what it was worth."

"Oh. Well, least you're still breathing," I offer, cheerful-like. "Word is, one of your lot got bumped off. Could be worse, eh? Unless you done it, I suppose."

A sidelong glance. "And what if I did?"

I signal to the snaggle-toothed house keeper for gin. He brings coffee. I glare up his pox-rotted nose in disgust. "Could be to your profit, is all."

"Ah." Sheridan offers me his pipe. "The part where you swindle me. Sell it, then, whatever it is. I'm all ears."

I suck in a twist of smoke, a shady opium dream. I exhale,

hoarse, and pass the pipe back. "What'd you say your name was?"

A sharp smile. "Not so famous after all. Sheridan, to you."

"Well, *Sheridan,* what if we was to go somewhere together?" I flash an ankle and a cheeky wink. "If I thought you could be dangerous, I'd be all wet and breathless, wouldn't I? Maybe you'll cut me up, or squeeze my throat till I choke a little." I chew a speculative fingertip. "A girl might enjoy that."

He clicks his tongue, mock outrage. "The whims of modern young ladies."

"I hate being bored. You arty coves? Bloody crooks, the lot o' you. Wouldn't shock me one inch if you was a killer. Or a thief, neither. D'you know that *Eve and the Snake*? I heard that Italian never painted it at all. Stole it and wrote his name on it."

Sheridan chuckles, but his face goes dark. Not surprised. More like angry. "Seek no further for your homicidal excitement, then. Clearly the talentless runt is a born criminal."

"Your murdered friend what's-'is-name? A sorcerer, s'what I heard. Ooga booga round a bonfire, black cats on broomsticks, rogering the Devil up the arse, or some such."

"Stupid rumors." He swallows more smoke. "That man made me famous. He'd have made me rich, too, if he'd lived. I owed him more than any man should owe another." A cracked laugh. "I just wanted to be good at something. Is that so much to ask?"

That loony cuckoo clock goes off again, clucking like a moonstruck hen. Four o'clock this time. Jesus, the cursed thing's only got one job. "As it happens, I were jawing 'bout the murder with a girl called Penny—"

"What a curious coincidence. I knew that pretty doctor had to be a plant. Friend of yours?"

"—and Penny said them coppers reckoned *she* must've done for 'im."

"Not that it's your concern"—another drag on the pipe—"but that isn't true. The Watt bitch was indulging her disgusting pleasures in this fine establishment that night." He drinks his coffee, pulling a face. "Bertie, this is fabulously grotesque. Even filthier than usual. I congratulate you. Oh," he added, "be a good fellow and tell me where I was, night before last."

Hunchbacked Bertie leers, his snaggle tooth shining. "In 'ere from two till dawn. You an' that bronze-haired floozy, what went upstairs with that stinkin' sailor and 'is parrot."

I snicker. "And he'd know what bloody time it was, with that crack-brained cuckoo sounding off as it pleases. You're a watch-maker, ain't you? Fix it."

Sheridan just scowls.

"If I recalls right," Bertie adds, "you whiled away the hours beneath a pair o' local ladies yerself."

"I see. That explains the sorry state of my trousers. Business must truly have been desperate. I heard a rumor that I pissed in the coffee. Any truth?"

A cackle. "Tasted no worse if you done so."

"There you are, then," says Sheridan loftily. "Gambling, whores, intoxicated oblivion. Sorry to disappoint." A quizzical frown. "Do I really look like a man who'd strangle you for a lark?"

"Everyone's a killer, sweetheart. Most folks is just too scared to act on it." I smile, crooked. Maybe he'll keep talking, if I play him right. "Are you?"

He critiques me with an ungentlemanly eye. "What I am is tired, miserable, and too damned drunk to play games. Shall we cut to the chase?"

"Suits me."

"I've two observations. The first is that if you're a police informer, they've definitely raised their standards for nosy lying tarts." He cuts me that edged smile. "But I didn't do it, and that sick whore Penny didn't do it, so go fuck yourself."

"Fair's fair," agrees I. "And the second?"

"The second is that yours is far and away the most spectacular attire I've witnessed this evening, and I've been squinting at rich bitches' finery since six o'clock." He drains his coffee and slides a sovereign onto the counter. Deft fingers, stained with red paint. "This appears to have your name on it. I won't be gentle, but I pay accordingly. Yes or no?"

His redshot gaze meets mine. Such weary, defeated eyes, for a youngster, and sharp sympathy needles my heart. Smart, handsome, career on the rise. Yet he drinks and whores to forget. Dives willingly into his darkest places, because drowning slowly down there is easier to bear than the glaring light of day . . . and I halt my fingers in the sordid treachery of creeping towards that coin, if only to cheer the tragic bastard up for an hour or two.

I swallow hot bile. I always swore no man'll use me like that. Not Lizzie Hyde. I ain't no bloody pet, without purpose but to please whatever master should stagger by.

So what the fuck *is* my purpose, then?

"Keep your gold, sir," I mutter, and stalk out.

Outside, the crowd carries me along, sweeping me almost off my feet in the crush. Music clangs, rough-tuned and raucous like my thoughts. I'm aimless, barely watching where I'm headed.

It should bother me. Inattention's a killer around here. But I'm too damned angry at myself for the mess I've made tonight. Is this Carmine really the killer? Or is Sheridan winding me up? Eliza'd figure it in an instant, o' course. God rot her. *She's* smart enough to pick it when a man's lying through his teeth.

Just one more reason she's better than me.

The party sounds of Soho fade, and I melt back into the rookery, dissolving like an evil spirit into hell. Naked green-haired children splat about playing catch-me in the muck, and fairy fire flickers at my feet. Ahh. Already, I'm relaxing into myself, relief groaning through muscle and bone.

My stiletto thrums between my breasts, singing edgy harmony. Even my skin fits better, not someone else's baggy flesh-suit but *mine,* taut and succulent as it ought to be. Down here, in the mud-strewn alleys and broken streets, no one can spy me . . . but it's a good, welcoming hide.

I'm home.

Screw it. I ain't Eliza, and thank bleeding Christ for that. It's the Cockatrice for Lizzie Hyde, gin and laughter and illicit good times. And if Eliza don't like it—if she whines and belly-aches, her skull pounding jealously with what it's like to be unfettered and free?

She deserves it. I don't give a fuck.

On the Broad Street corner, the usual crowd of drunkards and fools carouse merry hell in torchlight, a faded rainbow of second-hand rigs. Shouts and laughter clang. A lump-shouldered dwarf fumbles at my skirts, but he's too damned drunk to pick my pocket, and trips face-first into a dung pile.

"Serve you right," I mutter. Shorty just pisses himself. At least it's warm.

The Cockatrice looms from the fog, a tall narrow lurk jammed between a rotting tenement and a brick-walled brewery. Firelight bleeds from cracked shutters. Already I smell gin, rich and treacherous as a lover's promise, and that warm creature inside me murmurs, eager for oblivion.

I blow a kiss to the namesake figurine winking at me from the lintel, lion's head and scaly dragon's body. "How do, you handsome cad?" Then giddy heat rinses me, smoke and sweat and every sweet flavor of sin.

The fire's bright, stoked afresh with coal and refuse. Crooked card games, drinking, guffaws and snatches of bellowed song. From darker corners, sighs and muffled squeals. The night's no longer young, and men already slump snoring on the floor, lucky to keep their duds in this den of thieves and scoundrels, what rings with the patter flash.

Boingg! A screeching thing slaps me in the face.

I stumble back, pulse a-gallop . . . and curse at mad Jacky Spring-Heels, the stringy lice-haired cove in the dirty white union suit what just leapt out at me from behind a barrel. He capers triumphantly. "Lizzie git! Lizzie git!"

"Christ, Jacky, you frightened me tripe out." I swat his scrawny buttoned backside. Jacky just giggles, cross-eyed, and stuffs the ends of ragged white hair into his mouth.

The Cockatrice is a flash house, the haunt of dippers and cracksmen and prigs of all shades, swapping contacts, putting up lays, and getting roaring drunk and screwed. Forgers on the game, too, faking banknotes, doctoring letters of credit, a few telling alterations on a deed from time immemorial indistinguishable from the original. Violent men for sale, too, rampsmen and garroters and toe-cutting thugs who'll commit any bloodsoaked deed for the price of a night's lodging and a whore. And fey-struck regulars like Jacky Spring-Heels, who don't fit no place else, and like as not'd be starved or hanged by now if left to their own odd devices.

At a table, here's Tom o' Nine Lives, a fetching mobsman square-rigged, sporting a lecher's juicy black eye. He's matching gins with Strangeface Willy, a rotund red-coated Yorkshireman with a face like a dropped pie. Willy handles stolen treasure, silver plate, the kind of pogue a cracksman swipes from a town-house pull, and at some sad juncture he got beat near to death with the ugly stick. His cauliflower noggin and bulging eyes belie a fellow so sweet-natured he almost can't bear to screw you over.

I wave. "Willy, you handsome devil. Heard some tinny bastard lifted the Queen's oiler. Got 'er Majesty stuffed up yer arse?"

Willy giggles, drunk. "Fook, no. Wild Johnny 'imself couldn't christen that streak of shite."

"Don't let Johnny hear you say that."

Willy blows me a kiss, gold a-glimmer on his podgy fingers. A showy cove, is Willy, with an English lord's manners and a French pirate's wicked tongue—so I'm reliably informed—on account o' which pretty girls trip over their petticoats for that ugly twist-lipped smile.

Simpering by Willy's side is buxom Three-Tot Polly—so called because she'll do anything for two gins, and God help you if she manages three. I wave at her, too. At the next table slouches King Carlos, a skinny cattle thief with warts and a lisping Spanish lilt, dealing a hand of loo with swarthy Philo Horsecock from the pawnshop, what needs no further introduction.

Others I recognize, too, alongside faces new that make me glance sidelong. A girl's gotta take care. Can't never tell who's a snout, a police informer—or worse, a spy for the god-rotted Royal, telling tales about who's trading unorthodox gear, who's spouting radical nonsense, or who's just plain *weird*. Whisper the wrong sweet nothings, and by sunrise you'll be screaming for mercy in a stinking electrified hole in the Tower—if they'll only listen you'll tell 'em all you know and invent more when you run out. But them clockwork bastards don't know pity, nor compassion neither.

Think no one in this flash house would spot for that crackpot Philosopher? Think again. Everyone's got a weakness—be it liquor, gold, or worse—and the Royal ain't afraid to play it dirty.

Which puts me in mind of Remy Lafayette, who could've shopped us a dozen times if he felt like it. I conjure him at the Tower, stripping skin from some screaming fey bleeder while he smiles that sunshine smile, and I'm maudlin and dark-tempered all over again.

The landlord—a friend of mine, so he is—waves at me from behind the copper-topped bar. I shoulder through a gang of grotty Welsh navvies, who rain me with what I ken to be curses in their soup-thick dialect. One leers and flings gin over my skirts. I kick him, and he vomits on his boots. Christ, Welshmen really do eat anything.

I hike my skirts knee-high to step over, and at my side, some bloke whistles in admiration. "Jesus, Mary, and Joseph, that ought t'be criminal."

I don't look. I just ram my elbow to where his smart-arse whistling guts should be.

But he grabs it, strong fingers pinching. And all of a moment, I'm stumbling into a fire-dark corner. "Get off me, you pinchdick slapper!"

He winks as he lets me go, tipping tinted specs. Flashy, like a sideshow magician or a seller of snake oil. Long green coat, bowler hat, blond curls.

Moriarty Quick.

What in hell is *he* doing here? How'd he find me? Were it he I heard, dogging our every footstep in the fog outside Eliza's house? Look at that innocent, lost-puppy face. I'll warrant it gets him petted by all manner of unsuspecting misses. *It followed me home, Mama, can I keep it?* But I can smell his night's entertainment on his breath

(*I could murder a whiskey*)

and his eyes—green or hazel?—are disturbingly glassy in the firelight. Unblinking, like Mr. Todd's serpent.

Quick sucks in a juicy eyeful of my cleavage and licks those cupid's-bow lips. "This is a sweet change, Dr. Jekyll. I dreamed of what you'd be like inside"—he sniggers at his own joke—"but I never imagined this."

My nerves seethe, rats in a bag, and my steely sister thrums against my ribs, hungry for blood. *He KNOWS. Kill him now . . .*

"Up here, maggot." I slap his chin to shift his attention.

"You've mistook me for somebody else. Now clear off, before I chew your balls into pie meat."

"Told y'I know who y'are." That Dubliner's sing-song is stronger now he's drunk. "C'mon, let's talk. You've not even asked what I want."

"Did I never?" I frown. "Oh, right. I don't *give* a rat's arse. Now piss off." Roughly, I push by.

But Quick shoulders the wall, cornering me. "I can help you, Lizzie Hyde. Didn't y'ever long for your own life?"

He knows my name. He *KNOWS*.

My fingers twitch, darkly eager. Stab his scrawny neck. Lick his blood from my palms. End his meddling . . . But my mouth waters, too, bittersweet, and curse it if I don't hesitate like a coward.

"I know a thing or three about forbidden pharmaceuticals," Quick adds, inspired seeing as I ain't yet killed him. "Shall we say, the *shadowy* side of chemistry? And I know that *you*"—he prods a drunken forefinger into my bare shoulder—"could use your own preparation. To favor you over the other, if you catch me meaning." His fingertip lingers. Drifts lower.

I catch his meaning, all right.

My own elixir. My own *life,* to do what *I* want, and to hell with Eliza's restraints. Jesus, my legs are shaking. I *want* it.

"Fuck off, you glocky sot." I swat his hand away, but he darts in, that serpent a-strike. Now my elbow's smarting again in his grip, and I inhale his strange flavor, whiskey and acid and dark alchemical threat.

Ugh. I've rarely wanted less to touch a man. He ain't a dead loss in the looks department, and I'm partial as the next girl to that canny Irish lilt. But the feel of his skin—scaly and cold-blooded, somehow, though it ain't—makes me wriggle, a chilly whisper of *beware*.

Something's *wrong* with Moriarty Quick. Something evil.

A knowing wink. "Did y'ask Finch about me? What'd he say?"

"Don't know what you're jawing about." But I falter, spooked. *Do NOT engage with that man,* Finch's scrawl implored. I'm beginning to wish I'd listened.

That's it. I go for my stiletto, but he just twists my arm harder. We collide, I'm back to the wall, he's right in my *face*, and damn, for a weedy Fenian fuckball, he's *strong*.

"Don't imagine I won't be the end o' you," he hisses. "Tell Marcellus that Moriarty Quick sends his salutations. Tell him I haven't forgotten. Ask him if it might serve ye better to oblige me—"

Smash! Glass shatters, stinging my cheek. Quick slumps, and I'm free.

A SLAVE OF MY APPETITE

•••

WILD JOHNNY—FOR IT'S HE, MY OLDEST FRIEND
and the Cockatrice's new landlord since he won
the place in a game of loo a few weeks back, or so
he tells it, and maybe it's even true—Johnny drops his broken
bottle and fetches good Professor Quick a long-legged kick in
his scrawny ribs. Quick don't twitch. Already out cold.

What did he mean, he hasn't forgotten? Forgotten what?
Then again, who gives a moldy flog? A pair of heavies drag
Quick's skinny carcass to the door and heave him into the
street. Splash, thud, see you later. Humph. That'll be the
back o' him. "And piss in his hat while you're at it," I yell out
to the heavies.

Johnny makes a rakish bow, and 'pon my word, a prettier
thing this side of Soho you ain't likely to see. He's built lean
like a racing dog, with wild black hair and a tomcat's grin.
Firelight spices his lopsided black eyes. An odd, fey-struck
sort of gent.

His glaring fuchsia frock coat stings my eyes, and I snort
laughter. Where in hell does he find these rigs? "Brave Sir

Lancelot, you rescued me! Hurry, flip me over the bolster and have your wicked way."

"Lizzie, my princess," announces Johnny drunkenly, "why d'you tease me so? End my lovesick misery and be my wedded wife."

"Ha! Not while you're wearing that fucking coat. You look like a fairy-arse strawberry."

"Bloody handsome one, but." Johnny grins, and hands me to the bar as if I'm some mincing duchess at a ball. No one's giving me shite now, is they? He might act the drunken dimwit, but Johnny ain't never so drunk—nor so dim—as he makes out. His name, like his self, is larger than life. Even the lushingtons edge out of his way.

Once, Johnny were a swell dipper—his spindly three-knuckled fingers are the best asset in Seven Dials, for more reasons than one—before the crushers learned his face. Then he started christening the loot at a fat profit. Now a venerable old cove of twenty-one, he's turned publican, and everyone who's anyone comes to Johnny's Cockatrice to drink and screw and arrange their seedy to-dos. And if now and again, he sells one out to the coppers for a pile o' cash? Cost of doing business, lads. So sorry. When your stretch in the Steel is done, come see me and I'll put you right.

At least, that's how a few jealous arsebrains claim. Don't credit it, meself. Johnny's many things the lazy side of genteel, but I'd swear with hand on heart he ain't no crusher's snout. Even a fairy-arse strawberry's got his pride.

Johnny splashes gin into twin pewter cups. "Fresh liquor, my lovely. Special for you."

"Don't mind if I do." We clink and sink. Hellfire explodes

in my mouth, molten gold rolling down my throat. I gasp, heart pounding afresh. "Sweet Jesus. Where'd you steal this?"

Gaily, he pours us another. "I'll have you know I came by this uppity distillation fair and square. Ain't my fault it fell from some lackwit's cart down at Saint Katherine's dock."

"Just as you was strutting by? I'm all a-bloody-stonishment."

He winks, cock-eyed. "I play the cards life deals, sweet ruby Lizzie."

"Aces up your sleeve, more like." We drink again, and it slides down rich and smooth. Consider my cockles warmed, lads. Already my cares mooch off into the distance, not half so hurtful no more. I let out a happy burp. "Good to see you, Johnny."

And I mean it. Now I'm here, I've missed him, in all my angry pursuit of something other. Those prodigious fingers, curling further around that cup than they've any right. That witchy glamourshine dancing about his eyes. Johnny's got fairy ancestry, an elusive glimmer in his blood, and once you've seen him by the light of the Rats' Castle, where the *weird* sparkles in giddy rainbows, you don't never forget.

"Place is looking fine." I salute the mayhem with my cup. By the gin barrels, one bloke decks another with a king hit. A skinny girl in a tall hat saws a tipsy Scottish jig from her fiddle, and Jacky Spring-Heels hoots and bounces on his skinny haunches in time. No sign of Moriarty Quick. Good friggin' riddance.

"Finer with you in it." Johnny don't lower his voice, but that were just for me.

I laugh, torn between *oh, hell* and *screw it, yes please*. We've not exactly kept our distance, though he's a lying snitch for my father and I'm a prick-teasing tart what can't never be his, not while Eliza lurks in me. Still, it's eggshells between us, since . . . well, since I made some shitty mistakes, on account of which I hit him for my hurt, when it weren't his fault at all.

Still, Johnny's *my* friend, not Eliza's. Johnny *sees* me. And that's better than some I could mention.

But no time for regrets now. I slap a handful of sovereigns onto the bar.

"On the house, my darlin'."

"Not for the gin."

He makes the coins disappear, a silvery flash of *nothing-to-see*. "Say on."

"Someone lifted Razor Jack's paintings from the crushers' stash. Passing 'em off."

A loose shrug. "Never seen the loot. Heard whispers. Out-of-town putter-up, on the hush. A hardened crew."

Hmm. Seems Carmine could be worth a question or two. "Guess I'll try Willy—"

"Weren't Willy neither." Johnny blinks, a cock-eyed smile that melts my heart, even as I wonder what he'll tell Eddie Hyde about me later. "This is my house, my scrumptious cherry truffle, and Willy's gear is *my* gear. Would I lie to you?"

"Hell, yes, if it were worth your while."

He mimes blood spurting from his chest. "Cruel jade, your poisoned barbs pierce me to the heart."

I laugh. The liquor's lazy heat makes me reckless. Fondly, Johnny flicks a curl from my cheek. His crooked black gaze settles on mine, and my thoughts wander along irresponsible paths. His shredded-velvet hair, his sugar-sweet heat, that clever tongue curling behind his teeth . . .

Aye. I edge away, stretching those tempting inches between us into a respectable space. This be enemy territory,
and here she slinks, a dusky thief with a shock of beaded
braids and a jealous smile.

I salute her with my dripping cup. "Top o' the midnight,
Becky Pearce."

Johnny's new lady nods, civil for the now. A well-favored
lass, sixteen years old and a clever pickpocket, too, making her
living stealing purses and pocket watches long before Johnny
happened to her. Daughter of an escaped slave, they say, though
there's free-born folk of every color and screw anyone who likes
different. A better sort than Johnny's previous squeeze, what
for all her sad circumstances were a dim-witted dolly.

Beck kisses him, and I can't help but watch. Her hips flare
sweetly in tight trousers, and she wears stays and waistcoat
over a man's shirt, just to make you look while she fleeces you
of everything you own. Right now she's easing Johnny's palm
onto her breast and licking her tongue into his mouth while
her other hand waltzes lightly towards his coat pocket.

But Johnny's no mark. He grabs those naughty fingers, and
smartly slaps her heart-shaped rear. "Enough, saucy witch."

She grins, and whispers against his smile, *Ain't never
enough.*

I bite my lip. Younger, prettier, cleverer. Johnny ain't my
fancy man. Don't mean he can have his own goddamn life.

"Drink with us?" I force a smile. Politeness costs naught
but pride.

"Thanks, but I need to see a man about a nag." Becky
slides a purse onto the counter. Didn't see no lump in her
slinky rig. Hiding that up her arse?

Johnny makes it vanish. "Pleasure's all mine."

"There'll be more. Come by later?"

"You'd better." He steals another kiss. He means it, I see that. How his thumb strokes her cheek, how his gaze follows her when she takes her leave. But Johnny means everything he says. If only at the moment he's saying it.

"She's a rum cove," I offer, filling an awkward pause.

"The best." Johnny tosses Becky's gold watch in his palm. Shadows ripple, and it disappears. "Well, maybe second best."

I snort. "Don't fuck it up, then. She's good for you."

"That she is." But his gaze shifts, and inside, the hungry shark of my envy grins.

I swig from the bottle. "Empty, by God. What sort of land-lord you call yourself?"

He vaults the bar, a pink velvet swish, and sloshes me an-other tot. "My guest, madam."

"Johnny, you dirty flirt. Ply me with booze, will you, to get my skirts up?"

A dangerously charming smile. "My darlin', I'm practically a married man. The torments of hell await, should I stray one step from my righteous path."

"Christ in a cathouse, where'd you learn that? Guess y'always did claim your old man to be clergy." Which would make Johnny a gentleman, what he decidedly ain't, for all his fancy talk.

"He were an arsehole," agrees Johnny. "The two ain't shit and sugar. But my point remains: I am immune to your charms, you bold Delilah."

The challenge in his crooked eyes makes me purr. Care-ful, sweetheart. This game, I always win.

"Well, fuck it, then." I drain my cup, thirsty for pleasure and liquor-soaked oblivion. "If there ain't no harm to be done? Let's misbehave."

An hour later, in a shadowy corner, I'm astride Johnny's lap in a pile of guilty red velvet, and our treacherous rat-fink mouths is stuck together like wet paper.

He's drunk, o' course, and tastes of gin and bitter loneliness. Damn, the lad kisses like an angel. My corset's half loosened, and my flesh aches sweetly from the marks of his mouth. I wrap his hair around my fists, kiss him more, make him want me.

Hell, he were mine the moment I waltzed in. You're a bad woman, Lizzie Hyde, or breaking this giddy boy's heart wouldn't feel so goddamned good.

Defeated, Johnny groans, and sucks on my tongue. "Lizzie, this is fucked. We're fucked."

Anyone could spy us. I don't care. I'm red and angry inside, the memory of that look in Remy's eyes like a bloody gut-punch, and the black-toothed creature what long ago ate my conscience is laughing like a loon.

I nuzzle Johnny's throat, seeking that uncanny scent. I search beneath my skirts, and giggle. Mmm. Not so plastered as all that. "It don't mean nothing," I urge, undoing his trousers. "Becky ain't thinking you'll be faithful, is she? A man with your name?"

"Not precisely, but— Ah!" He bites my lip, gasping. "Jesus, woman. Ain't convinced you count as harmless fun . . . Shit, don't do that."

Too late. I handle his naked skin and he drags my skirt up and touches *me,* such clever long fingers he has. Our teeth clash, the copper-penny tinge of blood. I want to get on my knees, take him in my mouth in front of everyone. But I want him inside me more. I want to carve my name into his soul and watch it bleed.

This is madness. Eliza will hate me. Becky will hate me. Johnny will hate me.

But Johnny *sees* me. And I'm sick to my guts of being ignored.

Fuck it. Quickly, now, before I recall that this iron-cruel heart of mine is exactly why Eliza truly *is* the better half.

I suck my salty slickness from his thumb. "Take me, Johnny."

"Oh, hell," is all he says. We're fumbling clothing from between us, he feels hot and so smooth, I'm guiding him, he's whispering sommat about *I can't* and *we shouldn't* but still he's helping me, and holy God, this ain't gunna take very long.

I move, sighing. "Ah, that's good. Knew there were a reason I liked you."

He grips my hips, eyes squeezed shut. "Lizzie, stop it."

"You serious?"

"Yes. No. Shit."

"Thought not. Kiss me." I give him my tongue again, and he's lost. He folds those uncanny fingers around my waist, and as I ride him he gasps the secrets of his heart into my mouth, so alone and helpless, so damn beautiful, Johnny . . .

"You poxy bangtail." A body slams my shoulder. I somersault to the floor, an undignified flurry of skirts and damp thighs.

It's Becky. Her braids spark with rage like the fur on a

witch's cat. But her eyes gape, empty. As if she don't rightly get what she's seeing.

He promised her. And she *believed* him.

And now it laughs, this cruel child I've birthed, and remorse claws my soul. So good, a moment ago, that sweet sigh of victory. Now I just want to spew.

I scramble away, bracing for a right slating at best. I'm strangely eager for the pain, the grunts, the crack of bone. I deserve it.

But it ain't me Becky lays into.

Wham! Johnny's teeth crunch. Becky curses to shame a master's mate, and hits him again, a bristle of fists and wild hair. He don't fight back. Just takes it. Christ, he's practically begging her for more.

"Take it easy, Becky," I rasp. "'Twere my fault. He never wanted to, but I made him."

Becky just spits into my face, and stalks out.

Fumbling, I clip my corset, swipe my cheek dry. Johnny don't speak. Just lets his head fall against the wall, eyes shut. Blood oozes on his lip. He don't wipe it away.

He never wanted to. But I made him.

"I'm sorry." My voice sounds a thousand miles away. "Don't know what came over me . . . Oh, fuck this." Determined, I stumble for the door.

I can't let her walk out on him. I'm the devil here, that cunning serpent, flickering my forked tongue. Johnny ain't a bad man. He's just a man, lustful and easy to lead, and old habits die hard. I'll make Becky see that. Fix what I've broken, before the pieces are lost for good.

If they ain't already.

The pub's still half full, but no one dares guffaw or catcall. These greasy old coves was likely watching us, fiddling their wrinkled members under the table. "God rot your pricks to mush," I mutter, and run outside.

The hour's late, that misshapen moon sunken behind chimneys and ramshackle roofs. The slanting shadows recall Remy, and I wonder where he is, what he's about . . . then I recall what *I've* been about, and I feel sick and don't think of him no more.

The crowd's thinning, drifting into the dark. I spare a glance into the drain, half hoping to spy Moriarty Quick, tormented by a gang of lunatic sodomites clutching barbed wire. No such luck.

I've dropped my shawl, somewhere between the bar and Johnny's lap. Daren't go back. I rub goose-pimpled arms, looking left and right. Where's Becky? Shit. My heart thumps, guilty. She's gone . . .

Beaded braids flash, swinging around the corner in hazy lamplight.

"Becky, wait!" I grab damp skirts, and sprint after.

———◄•►———

I stumble around the drunks and refuse clogging the Seven Dials—a seven-way crossroads, and who knows what unquiet spirits lurk?—and slip-slide into a muddy lane off Little Earl Street.

Darkness creeps after me, smothering all. I can barely see Becky, a lithe shadow slipping between blacker shadows ahead. Greenish fey-light sparkles in her wake. I can hear mud sloshing, a blistering curse or two. She's weeping. Not watching where she's headed.

A toothless ancient gapes from a doorway. I skip from his groping hands. Fuck. Should've brought a light. These streets are riddled with footpads, press gangs, drunken boors on the mooch for a wriggling bit of skirt they needn't pay for.

Where the hell's she headed? She's a canny shadower, I'll give her that. Now you see her, now you don't. I scramble to keep up, shoving aside a starved three-legged cat, and hurdle a harmless-looking broken board lying in the mud. Step on that, you'll be sorry—a deadfall trap, a stinking pit lined with scrap metal and shit. A slow, horrible end, with slobbering, cross-eyed folks a-waiting in the dark to butcher you for pork and pies. Don't bother 'em if you ain't quite dead neither. Pigs cost to feed, but fools is free.

In a casement, a dim tallow candle puffs fatty black smoke. A low lodging house, jammed with chickens and snarling dogs and folk piled in on the floor, tight as a slave ship. Somewhere, a pair of 'em at least are going at it, grunting in the dark. A few sleep against the wall, rope strung under their armpits to stop 'em falling. One snoring bloke hangs, doubled over two bits of rag strung from the ceiling. Ain't luxury, but it's cheap.

I toss a penny to a claw-fingered match girl, and grab a fistful. They strike poorly, but a weak golden halo bobs as I follow Becky around the corner.

A wooden-fenced courtyard, plastered with muck. Stinks like a cesspit, which is what it is. My light barely stains the rotting walls. Overhead, a wonky plank sags between two up-stairs windows. Below, a forbidding tunnel yawns beneath a stone lintel. And here's Becky, splashed with mud, braids knotted over her shoulder.

Huzzah. Sooner we do this, sooner I can wallow in guilty gin. I'm still hot and aching inside, and it sickens me. No, I ain't finished abusing myself tonight. Maybe I'll slink back to Soho, hunt out that Sheridan Lightwood, see how bad he meant it . . .

In the shadows, a man-shape moves.

I halt. Becky's trading fierce whispers with it, displeased. I glimpse a tall hat, a swish of scarlet-lined cape like a melodrama villain . . . and then my light gutters and dies.

Seeing a man about a nag. Some flash putter-up, cutting Johnny out of the lay? So much for true love. Not on my watch, sister.

But as I fumble for more matches, my mind itches, dissatisfied. Why now, at this unflattering juncture? Arranged meeting or coincidence?

I don't care. My business with Becky can't wait. But rustles and rough breathing eke from the blackness. He's got men lurking there. I grope for my stiletto, just to be safe . . .

Shit and fuck the nanny goat. Gone, ain't she? Dropped at the Cockatrice. Never thought o' *that* when Johnny were stuffing his face down my corset.

Screw it, then. Now or never.

I step into view, and strike a handful of matches. *Pop!* Light flares, a wisp of phossy smoke. "Becky, it's me. Listen—"

Becky staggers, grabbing her guts.

A dark patch spreads, dripping over her hands. Blood. Gouts of it, copper-smelling, the tell-tale stink of ordure. Becky retches and gasps, but there's only gore.

The caped gent oozes from the shadows. His dagger glints, a bright crimson slash.

She falls. Her face slaps the mud. I wait for her to curse
and scramble afoot . . . but the only thing moving is her leaking blood.

My muscles clench, tight as a frog's arsehole.

She's dead. Gut-stabbed, chilly as you like. And here I
stand, dumb and cheery in a red dress, holding a god-rotted
light.

Jesus fucking Christ.

Red Cape glances up. My pulse thunders. *I never seen you.*
Never seen your face . . . but that singular visage sears like
red-hot iron into my memory. Hooked nose, slashing brows,
eyes dark as the devil's heart.

He wipes her blood from his hands, and gives a rueful
headshake. "I rather wish you hadn't seen that."

STRUNG TO THE PITCH
OF MURDER

•••

I DROP THE MATCHES, AND RUN.

I slip-slide in treacherous mud, my heart's pounding, I can't see, can't think. Behind, those unseen rustles deepen into grunts, and heavy boots splash after me. The killer's henchmen. At least two, maybe more.

Baby Jesus on a bonfire. I'm a witness. A loose end. I ain't escaping alive.

Around the corner I skid, past the lodging house and the match girl, who scarpers with a screech. Smart girl. Smarter than I, what should've turned the blind eye as soon as I seen Becky doing business on the sly. Clever Becky, blinded by betrayal, wits askew with rage. She never seen it coming. She died in a cesspit with her guts in her hands because of me.

Footsteps lurch up behind, *squick! squock!* My legs weigh down like logs. My lungs burn fit to burst. The henchman paws for my skirts, missing by an inch. "Come 'ere, you dopey quim!" He yanks me backwards, fuck, I'm falling . . .

I stub my toe on a slab of rotting wood, and instinctively I jump. *Crack!* The trap breaks under the henchman's tread.

He falls, screaming. A guttural giggle, and the scream slices to silence.

Splat! On my face in stinking mud. I scrabble up, on, away from henchman-soon-to-be-pie and poor dead Becky and the devil in the red-lined cape. I glimpse the second henchman behind me, a leering giant waving a rusty-nicked knife . . . but I'm a local and soon I've lost him in tangling lanes. I don't stop running till I spy the murky green lights of Great Earl Street, and swear to God, drunks and thieves and grinning fools ain't never looked so fine.

I lurch up the Cockatrice's steps, where that figurehead guffaws its half-dragon arse off at me, gasping Miss Lizzie with her sassy red dress soaked in shit. Miss Lizzie the idiot. Miss Lizzie the murderer.

The door slams. I fall against the wall, numb with relief. That legless bloke on the trolley drags his stunted self by with bulging arms. Jacky Spring-Heels eats the lice from his hair. People drink, curse, sing rude songs. Business as normal.

But restless seeps chill into my bones, and the once-delicious smells and sights are alien to me. Unsafe. Over and again, I glance behind. If Red Cape finds me, I'm a dead woman.

For once, I want to blend in. At my feet, a droopy-nosed bloke retches and drools. I drag off his rat-chewed coat. It reaches my knees, drowning me in sour spew smell. I bunch my scarlet skirts out of sight. Filch his shovel hat, too, jam it over my eyes.

Not a classy fakement. It'll have to serve, till I can get out of here.

But that square-rigged bastard's face—vicious nose, high-boned forehead with dark hair swept back—scorches un-dimmed into my brain, as if I stared too long at the sun.

Hmm. Gent in fancy new-tailored duds, putting up lays with thieves? Ain't exactly inconspicuous, is he?

See, cracksmen are a vain bunch. They talk 'emselves up, the lays they scoped, the deadlurks they fleeced of jewels and gold. They sell stories, especially to a man I know with a big name.

Grimly, my determination sparkles. I'll winkle Red Cape out, mark my words. Avenge poor Becky's murder, or I ain't Lizzie Hyde. For all the profit it'll win Becky now.

But I cringe like a whipped dog at the idea of facing Johnny after what I done. Strangeface Willy, then? A fence'll know his competition. Or maybe Tom o' Nine Lives hears whisperings. Someone haunting this flash joint must know sommat . . .

I groan as I scan the crowd. Tom's gone. Willy and Three-Tot Polly, too.

My guts burn. I don't want to. Let me slink into unholy darkness and die. But I make myself look for him. Not just for Becky's sake. For me.

By the bar, a strawberry velvet slash. Drunker now, a glazed fug over his eyes. His hair's still tousled from my hands, a reddish bruise staining his lip.

Stiff like a clockwork servant, I march up. Johnny takes in my muddy face, my stinking coat. "Lizzie, what . . . ?"

"Becky's murdered." My throat strangles, surely as if that killer squeezed my windpipe.

Johnny's crooked gaze don't slip.

Faltering, I explain. The cesspit, Red Cape, the blood-splashed dagger. My flight through mud-choked streets. Henchmen. Deadfall trap.

Johnny swallows, eyes a-shimmer, and reaches for the gin. My heart aches. I touch his sleeve, expecting a stinging rebuke. He can punch my lights out, for all I care.

He just offers me the bottle. Hardly a ringing invitation, just a listless one-fingered push. But bitter acid eats at my heart.

I did this. Me, Miss Lizzie. Lured him when I know he can't say no, and now a clever girl's croaked believing he don't love her. And Johnny still won't punish me. Won't say, *get the fuck out of my place, you conniving twat, before I have your sorry carcass fleeced to the bone.* Hell, he don't even *blame* me.

My brains boil. I kick the bar, hard, a hot bullet into my ankle. Ain't enough. Slam my skull into the sawdust, Johnny, kick me until I piss red. Watch while your dumb-faced thugs do with me as they please and heave me into the mud when they're sated, because Becky's dead and I'm alive and there ain't no justice in this black and ugly world.

Johnny, it ain't your fault. I'll make amends. I'll end the bastard who did this, so help me.

It ain't your fault.

But muddy guilt clogs my throat silent.

Blindly, I stagger into the dark street. A turbaned Turk jostles me, calls me an ugly name. I just huddle into my stolen coat, let my stumbles drag me where they will.

Beneath a broken archway, across a courtyard, down a twisting lane that reeks of rot. The night chill slides an icy sword deep inside my bones. My fingers was blue and stinging, now they're white and numb, just a distant ache. People lose limbs that way.

Don't care. Just keep sloshing through the mud. A starving dog gnaws a corpse. Livid flesh, purple and black. I want to lie in its stinking embrace, wallow in decay. Let my living warmth seep away.

My vision swims. My mouth bubbles sourly, foul rat stew. Eliza's vile pink juice repeating on me at last. I don't want to go back. Not to my dungeon, her respectable shell where it's safe and tidy and no one knows what I am.

Icy rain needles my face. Don't care. Leave me be, Eliza. Dirty your precious hands in my affairs, will you? You've your own murderer to chase, your own smug justice to uphold, in your sheltered black-and-white world where criminals and killers is other people, *bad* people. Keep your disgust, Eliza. I've enough of my own.

I fumble the elixir from my knotted skirts. The neck's broken where I fell, and the hellbrew's leaked away to soak my dress. I suck out the last of it anyway. Splintered glass cuts my lips. Cruel and bitter, fire swirling in my guts.

Let him find me, that gentleman killer. Gut me with that crimson-splashed dagger, spill my soul into the shit where Becky lies. Let him lather his hands in my worthless blood and laugh.

ELIMINATING THE IMPOSSIBLE

•••

THE NEXT MORNING, ELIZA AND CAPTAIN LAFAYETTE regarded the bloodied mess in the tiny attic room with dismay. "Gruesome," she offered at last. "I doubt even Reeve could claim *this* as a burglary gone wrong."

Acidic yellow fog seeped in through a slanted clerestory, blotting out the straining sun. It coiled around her skirts, making them damp and itchy. The room contained little but an empty easel, a wooden chest, a half-made bed. But fresh blood soaked the wooden floor and splashed the dusty walls, and a meaty, metallic stink nauseated her.

The thing tied to an overturned chair by wrists and ankles didn't look much like Carmine Zanotti anymore.

They'd come to question him. But too late. His face was beaten, his dark hair soaked in gore. Welts and burns criss-crossed his naked torso. A slashed pentacle dripped on his breast, and below his sternum, ragged flesh dangled from a fist-sized hole.

On a table, in a puddle of blood, sat the mangled remains of his heart. An eyeball, trailing clotted veins. And his severed tongue.

"I suppose we can scratch Carmine as a suspect." Lafayette was back in uniform, saber and pistol polished, spurs glistening. Just like her, his armor back in place. Probably just as well. But he wrinkled his sensitive nose, fidgeting in the smell of blood. Today was Wednesday. On Friday night . . .

Hippocrates ran mad laps, spattering Eliza's skirts with red. "Witness examination! Opportunity missed! Make greater speed!"

"A fine help," she muttered. But guilty memory swirled, of her own handwritten letter, a foolish throwaway line. Posted, of course, by the ever-helpful Mrs. Poole. *I viewed the Exhibition this evening. What I saw was surprising, to say the least.*

Eliza had told Mr. Todd about *Eve and the Serpent.* And now Carmine Zanotti was dead.

Her guts chilled. Surely, such carnage wasn't Todd's style? Could he even have received her letter in time? The penny post stuck to a meticulous schedule, delivering until late at night . . .

"Doctor?" Lafayette nudged her. "Are you ill?"

"I feel responsible, that's all," she improvised. "We retired early last night on my account. If we'd arrested Carmine on suspicion, he'd still be alive."

"He might. And another might be dead. You can't save everyone."

No, she thought dizzily. But it'd be nice if I could save someone.

She dragged her gaze from all that mutilated flesh. Hipp trotted about, snuffling at the dead man's things. Outside, sickly fog hung between tall houses, carrying the shrieks of terrified animals from a nearby slaughterhouse. What a charming neighborhood.

Eliza had woken before dawn, huddled in a Covent Garden doorway, wrapped in a mud-splattered coat and dangerously numb with cold. Her mouth had stung bitter, gin and elixir and half-forgotten remorse. She'd hurried home, squirming under the scrutiny of passers-by. Probably they'd thought her a disobedient servant after an illicit night out.

But like this mist-shrouded morning, Lizzie's memories proved elusive. A crowded street of gaslights, a smoke-wreathed room. Tobacco, gin, berry-pink kisses . . . a bright squelch of blood in creeping shadows . . . but pervading all, the flesh-crawling ache of guilt.

Lizzie? What did you do?

But Lizzie shuddered, and wouldn't speak.

That bottle of chilly pink remedy dragged Eliza's pocket down, as if it weighed ten pounds. She'd risked a few more drops this morning, and the sickly-sweet taste still bubbled up in her gullet.

"A little late to arrest poor Carmine for fraud," said Lafayette. Cheerful as usual, but his eyes were reddened. As if he, too, hadn't slept well. "Still, this is good news. If we needed further proof that this pentacle-carving lunatic is a habitual killer."

"Your enthusiasm disturbs me, sir. How is that *good* news?"

"Multiple murderers do seem to follow you around, Doctor. I'm gratified that I've chosen the best woman for the job."

"Thank you. I think." But her mouth twisted. Yes, she'd caught the Chopper, but only by accident. As for Razor Jack . . . Determined, she jammed on her optical. If Todd hadn't done this, she'd prove it. "Shall we proceed? Looks as if Carmine was a real painter after all, or at least a forger." She indicated a couple of rolled canvases on a shelf, tied with string, paint on the outside. Next to them, a clutter of paint pots, brushes, oils and solvents.

"Another ransacking," said Lafayette, poking at papers and books that scattered the bloodstained floor. Candles lay overturned, wax splashed white. "Hardly an efficacious cover-up, given the carnage."

"Agreed." On that gruesome table, beside those unfortunate parts, sat tools: a ghastly pair of pliers, an oil-painting knife, a wooden-handled scalpel. All smeared with blood.

Unnecessary mess. None of Todd's chilling elegance at all.

She laid fingers on Carmine's dead flesh, anticipating that cold waxy texture . . . "He's still warm," she exclaimed. "Limbs pliable, no rigor. I'd say he's been dead an hour. Since dawn, at the very earliest."

Lafayette examined the corpse's mangled chest. "Forgive my ignorance, but for a man with his heart torn out, there doesn't appear to be an obvious cause of death."

"I'm afraid there is." She popped on the tiny brass-cased electric light on her waist chain, then wiped sticky blood from the corpse's chest onto a slide and added a few drops of solution. Slipping a spectroscopical lens into her optical, she pulled the brass concertina to focus. The blood cells crawled, separating into tell-tale spectral lines. "As I thought. He's experienced massive shock. All this"—she indicated the lacerations—"happened while he was conscious. His sensory system attempted to shut down."

"A natural painkiller." Lafayette's expression was grim. "Tortured to death."

Carefully, she turned the eyeball. "Look at those burst capillaries. This was forcibly extracted, probably with a finger. And the tongue's torn, not sliced." She picked up the pliers, checking the pincers with her magnifying glass. "The killer shoved these into his mouth and yanked."

Lafayette poked the heart. "Aren't there supposed to be four chambers?"

"Indeed there are. Part is missing . . . Oh, my." Her stomach cramped, sick. "It's been *chewed*."

"Good God. You mean an animal?"

"Animal," muttered Hipp, skulking under the bed.

"I'm afraid not." Stiffly, Eliza pulled out her ruler to measure the teeth marks. A man's, most likely. Surely, this couldn't be Mr. Todd's work. Death, not pain, aroused him. And as for eating the victim's heart . . .

Her courage quailed. At least with Todd she knew what she was dealing with. But whoever did this was either utterly inhuman or irretrievably insane. How did one catch such a creature?

"'Means, motive, and opportunity,'" she quoted shakily. "That's how Harley always starts."

Lafayette pointed at the tools. "All items you'd find in an artist's things. Only cold blood and a strong stomach required."

"A ready-made killing jar." That ragged eye socket stared at her, and she tried not to look as she inspected the corpse's graying skin with her tweezers. "Similar pentacle," she reported, "with the same mercury symbol. Half-circle, circle, cross

Left-hand knuckles smashed, three fingernails pulled. Also some burns. A cigar end?"

"*Voilà.*" Lafayette retrieved a cigar butt from the floor. "Some brutish Continental blend."

"Opium? Or that drug you smelled at Dalziel's?"

"Not a whiff, sadly for Carmine. But good for us. He must have screamed fit to split. Surely, someone heard." Lafayette cocked his ear to the screeches of dying beasts. "Then again, hardly a quiet street."

She put the stub away carefully. "Still, the killer's means are in ready supply. All our man required was evil intent. He enters, subdues Carmine enough to get his shirt off and tie him to a chair . . ."

Lafayette pointed to a heavy paperweight on the desk. "Hits him? There's blood and hair on that."

"Or he thinks he's with a friend."

"Maybe he's under a spell." Lafayette mimed swinging a watch chain before her eyes. "Abracadabra, you're very sleepy; sit down and let me burn you with my cigar."

"Brilliant. A cannibal dwarf hypnotist. Wild-flung theories, sir, will profit us none."

"They worked last time. We began with vengeful ballerinas, progressed through rogue assassins, and ended at a crazed surgeon with a wolf curse who coveted your skull. A hungry dwarf sounds positively banal."

She shivered, remembering how the Chopper had tricked her. Pretended to befriend her while all along he was sewing dead girls into grotesque homunculi. "Motive, that's the key. What does the killer want?"

"If it were Carmine alone, I'd favor a greedy criminal competitor. You don't just decide to torture someone mid-conversation for no reason." Lafayette frowned. "Unless . . . Help me move him, will you?"

She grabbed the chair and helped Lafayette roll the corpse aside. On the floor, partly obscured by gore . . .

"Another pentacle!" she exclaimed. "In white chalk, right beneath his chair. How did you know?"

He picked up a candle stub, and matched its base to a waxy blob on the floor. "Five candles, five points of the star. I've seen this before. Pain wasn't the point here. It's a summoning."

"I'm sorry, I thought you just said this was a magic spell."

"I've investigated those accused of witchcraft. It's an interest of mine. Black cats, broomsticks, magical flying ointment, the works. This pentacle business? It's to summon a familiar spirit, or dedicate a soul."

"To whom, pray?"

"Satan, of course. The Dread Forces of Evil. Last I heard, even Roman Catholics don't pray to the Blessed Virgin by eating a man's heart."

Uneasily, she recalled ironical Penny Watt. *Apparently London's positively riddled with evil covens . . . sold his soul to the Devil . . . why am I never invited to these occult orgies . . .*

"So you'd have me believe that this"—she indicated the bloody mess—"is not merely the work of some poor demented creature who enjoys butchery, but a ritual murder?"

"Two ritual murders," corrected Lafayette with a glint of grin. "You don't need to believe in magic, Doctor. The killer does. That's what matters."

"But to what purpose? Will there be more? And why these two? Were they victims, or willing disciples?"

"That is what we must discover." He winked. "Aren't you glad you came?"

"Shame on you," she scolded, but illicit excitement tingled her bones. This case was everything she'd dreamed of. Bizarre, shocking, seemingly inexplicable. An irresistible challenge.

Certainly, if Todd was the killer, she was finished. An accessory to murder, and she'd deserve everything they did to her.

But her glance drew back to the mutilated body, the chalked white pentacle, that chewed heart. She'd never seen anything like this. An important case. A worthy foe. This could make her career . . . or ruin her forever.

THE MORE DESPERATE
THE REMEDY

•••

BLACK MAGIC," TRUMPETED HIPP FROM UNDER THE bed. "Irrational! Does not compute."

"Any more irrational than senseless mutilation?" asked Lafayette. "If killing Carmine was the only aim, why not just sneak up while he slept and cut his throat? This was done for a reason, and in my experience, torturers operate for one of two."

"Depravity or insanity?"

"I was going to say information or pleasure. I further remark that tearing out the victim's tongue seems an odd interrogation technique."

Images flashed, of dark cells in the Tower where the Royal's agents tormented their captives. Screams, bloodied sweat, the stink as the victims lost control of their functions. Crunching bones, crackling voltage . . . and always in her visions, the torturer's face remained stubbornly obscured. "Not how you'd have done it?"

Lafayette's gaze frosted. "No, since you mention it. The subject's fear of pain is the primary weapon. To act on such threats is the last resort of incompetence. This"—he indicated the bloody mess—"is recreational. Or in this case, ritual."

Eliza considered. "So. First, our man stabs Dalziel with a crucifix. Carves a pentacle onto his chest, removes his face, and rips out his heart."

"Then two days later, he tortures Carmine to death," continued Lafayette, "and *munch!* takes a bite."

"I'd call that an escalation, wouldn't you? Although apparently he's lost interest in peeling faces. Whatever prompted that in Dalziel's case wasn't present here."

Lafayette examined the dead man's torn fingernails. "So either we're looking for an abruptly rapacious madman with no motive but cruelty, who happened to know both Carmine and Dalziel. Or . . ."

"Or a disciple of this mythical coven everyone insists doesn't exist," she finished. "With Carmine dead, we're left with a bunch of suspects who conveniently lack apparent motive or opportunity. I for one am growing skeptical of this 'dinner party' of Dalziel's. Perhaps they were up to darker things than dining."

"Still, that clockwork footman corroborated Mr. Brigham's tale. For that matter, so did that charming trio at the Exhibition, including poor Carmine. Everyone left before two, and Dalziel was alive at ten to four."

Vague memories stirred, a crowded bar, a cuckoo clock cackling madly. "So either they're all lying, or this crazed killer returns afterwards. Perhaps Carmine and Dalziel saw something at that party they weren't meant to see."

"Or did something that raised the killer's ire."

"So he gifted their souls to the Devil," she mused. "Vengeance . . . but for what?"

Lafayette crossed his eyes.

"It sounds ridiculous," she admitted. "Maybe the killer faked the whole thing. Made this *look* like black magic, to cover his true motive."

Her skin prickled. His true motive . . . or his usual method. A method so singular, it was burned into the memory of every police officer and thief-taker and vigilante prowler in London.

No, it didn't ring true. Hiding wasn't Mr. Todd's style. Besides, he was never caught unprepared. He'd dispatched each of his seventeen victims with an ivory-handled straight razor. Even those he hadn't strictly planned to kill.

"So far as you seen," put in Lizzie, who suddenly lounged in the corner, tossing the bloodstained pliers from hand to hand. "Who knows what mad arsepokery that loon gets up to? Remember what he told you? 'Shadow don't always behave.'"

"What's that?" Lafayette eyed Eliza strangely.

"Nothing," she lied. "Something Mr. Fairfax at Bethlem Asylum used to say about lunatics."

Lafayette was already hunting through papers on the desk. "Accounts, sketches, diaries, the usual. Some in Italian, some in English." He hefted a leather purse. "A lot of gold for a penniless artist."

"Not if he's a thief and a con man."

"Look at this." He handed her a torn scrap of paper, and she read aloud.

Your assistance in this matter is appreciated. Proceed tonight as planned, and we shall meet afterwards, when the thing is done.

DF

She frowned. "Dalziel Fleet?"

"No salutation. Seems strange. What 'thing is done'?"

She dug in her bag for the papers they'd taken from Dalziel's closet. "These might help. Could that one be a reply?"

Together, they sorted through them. "Sketches," said Lafayette, "and scraps. I don't see . . . Wait, do you smell that? Something spoiled, or . . . yes." He ferreted out a crinkled page.

Canvas 6' x 4'
Ormond's best varnish, 2qt
New liniment
Linseed oil, special
Enamel (gray)
Cochineal—not from Maw's!
Horsehair, 1 oz.
Ethyl alcohol

She eyed it dubiously. "An odiferous art supply list? How is that relevant?"

"Your confidence staggers me. Observe the initial letters of each line."

"CON LECHE," she read. "An acrostic? They did tell me you were clever for a man."

"That candle stub, if you please."

She lit the wick. He held the paper a few inches above the flame . . . and *between* the inked lines, new letters charred and smoked.

"Milk!" she exclaimed. "Cleverly unearthed, sir. I take back everything I said about you."

Lafayette grinned, satisfied. "Doctor, I present a secret letter."

I beg you do not ignore this.
We must speak in secret before tonight's
Conclave. I can not write what I know
or our Master will discover me. He is a
Traitor and Wicked beyond sense. If we
do not unmask Him everything is lost.
He will be the End of us all.

She ran her thumb over the blackened writing. "Carmine's hand? The syntax is a little stilted, as one might expect. Who is this 'master'? Does he mean an artist?"

"Or someone who murdered two men rather than be 'unmasked.'"

"The leader of their alleged black magic hocus-pocus?" she scoffed. "Please."

"Give me a better explanation for that." He pointed to the savaged body. "Magic is a capital crime. If someone threatened to expose you, wouldn't you take drastic steps?"

Think on whether it'd serve you well to oblige me, hissed Moriarty Quick in her mind, and behind Lafayette, Lizzie mimed wringing a scrawny Irish neck.

"Yes," admitted Eliza, "but I wouldn't torture a man to death."

"You might if you worshipped the devil."

"I suppose this could be a bad attempt at blackmail. Carmine and Dalziel threaten this 'master,' he kills them before they proceed. But it all supposes this fabled coven actually exists, and the 'master' truly has something to hide."

Lafayette shrugged, non-committal. "Time we looked more closely at that dinner guest list."

She gathered her things, glad to be leaving that ravaged corpse behind. But something Lafayette had said gnawed at the edges of her mind. *An interest of mine.* Why an interest in witchcraft? "What happened to those witches you investigated, by the way?"

"Superstition and foolishness, the lot of it." Lafayette's expression was grim as they exited the room. "But they believed it. And the Royal burned them all."

Outside, she peeled off her gloves, squinting in foggy sunshine. Zanotti's tumbledown tenement teetered among its fellows with an apologetic air. "What now? Do we call the police?"

Lafayette brushed dirt from his coattails. Muddy rats scattered away from his boots. "I suppose we must. Let Reeve make a mess of it."

Hippocrates scuttled beneath the wooden steps, pouncing on a squirming rat. "Mess," he echoed gleefully. "Evidence inconclusive. Information please."

They sloshed towards Upper Thames Street and Black-friars Bridge. "We labor under no dearth of suspects," admitted Eliza, whisking her skirts from the mud. "Any of the twenty dinner-party guests could have done it. If it truly was only a dinner."

"Everyone at the house said so." Lafayette hopped across a wide puddle, offering his hand.

She took it and jumped, boots sinking into the gloop on the other side. "That's what disturbs me."

"Disturbed!" yelled Hipp, splashing up and down in the noisome gutter. "Disturb-urb-urb . . ."

"Well, conjecture never solved a case. I must collect more samples, perform my analyses." She gritted her teeth. "Assuming Reeve will let me see Dalziel's cadaver, which he won't."

"Oh, the body isn't at the police morgue." Lafayette grinned. "The weeping widow wouldn't allow it, and Reeve didn't dare insist. It's at an undertaker's near Regent's Park, for embalming. Not that you'd be interested."

"Embalming!" trumpeted a mud-spattered Hipp. "Data destroyed! Make greater speed!"

Eliza groaned. "Why does no one understand about preserving evidence? It's hardly multi-dimensional physics. We must examine the body before it's too late." She adjusted her bag over her shoulder. "Well, shall we risk Scotland Yard's awe-inspiring displeasure?"

"You go ahead. I've a report to make. Ritual magic, ahoy! Lady Lovelace will adore me forever."

Just the mention of that name bristled Eliza's hackles. "How nice for you," she said coolly.

Lafayette laughed. "Not really. After the way that Chopper business ended—you might recall wolves were involved?— I had to invent a lot of stories. Convincing her I'm playing for her team is hard work. Being utterly merciless with a murdering Satanist ought to earn me a few points."

"You could tell her about my elixir," suggested Eliza, half joking. "That'd win her over." But she squirmed, all too aware that it wasn't funny. He'd everything to gain from betraying her.

"Now you're being ridiculous."

"Just what she needs, isn't it, to heal those dying half-flesh abortions of hers?"

Lafayette stopped walking.

"Did Lizzie visit you last night?" She wanted to slap a hand over her mouth, but the question had already bolted.

"Yes." He didn't flinch from the truth. Never did.

"Why didn't you tell me?"

"You didn't ask." His eyes narrowed. "Don't you remember?"

Dream shards whirled, colliding. A midnight street, a snake man snapping rotted fangs. A fat Chinaman's sidelong smile. *Is that what I am, an AFFLICTION?* Crisp hair in her fists, the bright shock of a kiss, smoke and blood and carnal pleasure . . . and a flash of bloodsoaked steel.

Lizzie's guilt swamped her, a rising tide. "Something terrible happened," she spluttered. "What did Lizzie do? Tell me!"

"I don't know," insisted Lafayette. "We spoke, that's all. Argued about you, if you must know. Then she left."

The pink remedy frothed up in her throat, aggressively sweet, and with it bubbled unnatural suspicion. Her fingers clenched stubbornly. "Is that all?"

He laughed. "Would you like me to say we met for some illicit lovers' tryst?"

"Yes, if it's true. I remember . . ." Her face burned, surely the color of beetroot. "Lizzie was with someone. Was it you?"

"No." Not a flicker. "I don't want secrets between us. Do you truly believe I'd lie?"

"Of course not. I just . . . Where did she find you? What were you doing in that place?" A dark den writhing with green smoke, strangers whispering in French, absinthe's licorice lure. Not a classy establishment.

"I'm working for my brother. Official business. I'm afraid I can't tell you."

"Involving un-deported enemies of the state? Hardly likely to endear you to Lady Lovelace."

Lafayette didn't drop his gaze. "If it were my choice, I'd tell you everything, but the secrecy's for your protection. And before you ask, I didn't tell Lizzie either."

Now she couldn't meet his eyes. It was *she* who was keeping secrets. How she longed to scream them to the sky, heave this horrid weight from her heart and be free. *Yes, I wrote to Malachi Todd. Yes, I begged him not to kill anyone else, because he imagines himself in love with me and I thought he'd listen, but it didn't work. He kills to get my attention. He's the reason I can't marry you. Now tell me I'm a weak, irrational, unprincipled woman and leave me be!*

But her throat swelled tight, and she couldn't speak.

With a sigh, Lafayette ruffled his hair. "I realize this is difficult. But if Lizzie's a separate person, with affairs of her own, then what right have I to discuss her behind her back? And if she isn't, then . . . well, the mind boggles."

She gave a half-laugh, half-shrug. "I don't know. I'm sorry. I just . . ."

"You just what? Don't trust her?" Surprised laughter. "Won't you please tell me what's bothering you?"

She squared her shoulders. "What bothers me, Captain, is that I know so little about you. Specifically, your job for the Royal *bothers* me. What exactly do you *do*?"

A puzzled frown. "I investigate. I reach conclusions. I report, with varying levels of honesty. Oh, and I try to stop Lady Lovelace learning my secret and burning me to death. That rather fills up my day."

His discomfort—nay, *resentment*—stung her heart. How she longed to turn the conversation to happier things. But doubt ate at her, a hungry parasite that wouldn't be sated by less than abject, painful truth. "Have you ever burned anyone?"

"I've questioned people who went on to be executed," he admitted, "but no, not personally. Please tell me what this is really about—"

"Have you ever tortured anyone?"

He swallowed. "I'm a soldier, not a brute. I don't hurt people. My job—and I'm good at it—is to extract information and confessions."

"How?"

"Do you really want—"

"I must know the kind of man you are," she said simply. "Don't you see? That's all that matters."

He sighed, dark. "First, I ask nicely. I say, 'just a chat between friends, tell me everything and we can all go home for tea.' If that doesn't work, I frighten, then offer safety. 'Enforcers aren't renowned for mercy. Suggest you confess while you're still talking to a human being.' Next, I appeal to reason. 'Think we don't know what your friends are plotting? Whom do you think you're protecting? Confess now, and this can all just go away.' Finally—and I don't often get this far—I threaten."

"With what?"

"Eliza, please. You're talking about a systematic process of eroding a person's desire to remain silent. I consider it my purpose at the Royal to get results in a civilized manner. It's unpleasant, but surely it's better I do it than some cross-eyed idiot who *wants* to watch people bleed."

Her fists clenched, guilty. So *reasonable*. Why couldn't she accept it? "And what if someone calls your bluff, and won't talk? Or hadn't you thought of that?"

Lafayette gave her a bruised look. "Is this your way of calling me a liar? Because it seems to me you're searching rather desperately for a reason to despise me so you won't have to face the truth, whatever it is. Forgive me, madam, but your failure of courage surprises me."

Her heart stung, poisoned. "So sorry to disappoint," she retorted. "I believe we're done here. I'll let you know what my analysis shows. Good day, Captain."

She hurried away, blinking smarting eyes. Hipp galloped after, but she barely noticed. Emotions clashed, using her body as a battleground. How she longed to lie down and sleep, lose herself in Lizzie's nightmare world.

Forget that Lafayette had called her a coward.

Her guts watered. He was right. She could invent all the reasons in the world, but it didn't alter the truth: she was afraid.

Of Todd. Of Lafayette. Of her own duplicitous heart.

Determined, she shook it off. The facts were plain: Captain Lafayette had everything to gain by betraying her to the Royal, and—his frankly unlikely marriage proposal notwithstanding—not much to lose. She daren't take a chance. He'd never made any secret of his allegiance. So why was she disappointed?

She stalked along the paved Embankment, where beyond the stone barrier, smoke-stacked barges inched on pallid gray water, engines coughing in the fog. Her boot heels clacked, stinging like her temper. This unprincipled anger was liberating. Fine. She'd investigate the case without him.

"Oh, aye?" Lizzie shoved her in the back, sending her stumbling towards the barrier and the stinking Thames. "How'll you pull that off? This is his case, remember? Since you bollocksed it up with Chief Inspector Prat-face, you ain't even working for the crushers no more. Ha ha! Think yourself so smart. Can't even get that right!"

Eliza's vision doubled alarmingly. She wasn't herself, not since that pink-purple remedy. How could Lizzie *push* her? Lizzie wasn't REAL. "Shut up and leave me alone! I don't want you here."

Lizzie pirouetted, red satin flouncing. "I've 'ad a gutful of you telling me 'do this, don't do that.' This is my body, too. It's my *life*."

"It is *not* your life! Stop pretending you're real, because you're not. You're just a . . . a shadow in the mirror. You're a bad dream!"

A snide chuckle. "I'm real enough for Remy. He told me what he's about in Soho, y'know. He just don't want to tell *you*."

"Rubbish. I don't believe you."

"What if I told you he and I spent last night together?" Lizzie skipped backwards in Eliza's path, mocking, just out of reach. "You remember, don't you? We lay together naked, I *took* him from you, and ain't nothing you can do. Ha ha!"

"Don't be horrid," snapped Eliza. "He's better than that. Why must you drag him with you into the gutter?"

"Better, is he? I were good enough for him once. I know how to give a man what he needs. Think he'd want you when he can have me?"

"That's it. I'm not letting you out again until you promise to behave." And Eliza whipped out her pink remedy, and took a defiant strawberry swig. It boiled in her stomach, ice hissing in fire. She burped, unladylike. "Now stay there."

"Try and make me . . ." Lizzie twirled away along the Embankment, fading, until nothing remained but the cruel ghost of her laughter.

Eliza kicked the ground, scattering frustrated pebbles. Irrational emotions scratched inside her, a pink-stained fever of doubt and suspicion that tormented her beyond reason. *Delusions of persy-cootion.* Couldn't be real . . .

She shook her woozy head. No, she wasn't going mad. Lizzie must be right. Lafayette's "secret business" was all a plot to trap her, Eliza. The memory of his open, honest face

when he *lied* to her—she knew a lie when she saw one, oh
yes—knotted her guts into an inextricable snarl. And that
duplicitous pink remedy only murmured sly encouragement.

He and Lizzie were keeping secrets. Both of them. The
thought of it chewed her knuckles raw, rats at a corpse. If
Lafayette lied about that . . . what else was just a sham?

She jammed the bottle back in her bag and strode off. Her
mutinous mind rattled, plotting and scheming. She'd find
them out, mark her words. And *both* would be sorry they'd
crossed her. Yes, they surely would . . .

Oof! She collided with a warm shoulder, hard enough to
knock her sideways. Rich fabric, an unsettlingly familiar
antique-paper scent.

A man's gloved hand gripped hers. At her feet, Hippocrates whirred and muttered "Oops." And with a sick thud,
Eliza's heart dropped into her guts.

"Egad," remarked the Philosopher dryly, "Dr. Jekyll. I was
only this moment thinking of you."

———◦◦◦———

Her wits lurched and scrambled. She risked a swift glance
along the Embankment . . . but Lafayette and Lizzie were
gone. She was alone.

She smoothed her skirts. "Sir Isaac. How nice to see you
again."

The Philosopher surveyed her, his ageless, unfathomable
eyes the non-color of rain. His long hair—same washed-out
hue, his characteristic style a century and a half out of date—
was tucked under a sharply modern brushed-felt hat. Charcoal
coat, silver watch chain, kid gloves, and a shiny black cane.

On his arm, her steel-gray gown gleaming, was Lady Lovelace.

Eliza blanched. The countess constructed a smile, empty as death, and the hinges in her metal jaw made a grinding sound.

Around them, the crowd parted, oblivious. Strolling ladies, harried servants on errands. A fellow pedaled madly by on an immensely tall bicycle, long ears flapping. As if this man she stood next to wasn't an impossible aberration. As if he didn't possess the power to burn her.

"You didn't answer my last letter," Sir Isaac accused. "Are we no longer friends? Alas, whatever shall I do?"

A few weeks ago—after solving the Chopper case—Eliza had agreed to inform on Mr. Hyde for the Royal. She'd had no choice. Since then, she'd stalled for time. She drummed up a weak smile. "Did you not receive my reply? I'll check my records."

"Don't trouble yourself. I've a fresh task for you." That strange gaze, dead yet alive.

"Excellent," she said briskly. "Would you mind terribly to put it in another letter? I'm afraid I'm—"

"In an awful rush, yes, so on, so forth. I shan't take up much time." He extended his cane: *walk beside me, if you please.* His empty stare: *I dare you to refuse.* Dismissively, Lady Lovelace sniffed, averting her face.

Eliza obeyed, but her skin zapped in warning. Sir Isaac's politeness—like Lafayette's?—was sugar-coated poison. People whispered that he, not Her Majesty, ruled the Empire. That the Mad Queen lived in terror of his temper, submitting meekly to his every command, like a child obeying her schoolmaster to avoid a beating. That the Prince of Wales, her drooling simpleton of an heir, was no simpleton at all, but brain-poisoned, rendered witless and obliging by the Philosopher's evil drugs.

Hipp jittered nervously beneath her skirts. She toed him aside lest she trip. Alongside them, the river burbled, coated in a patina of filth, and an evil urge gripped her to shove the Philosopher and his horrid metal countess over the side. Whipping children and poisoning addled princes seemed just the kind of things these two would enjoy.

"What can I do for you, sir?" Her voice strangled. Mr. Finch's incriminating pink remedy bubbled up in her throat all over again. Couldn't the Philosopher smell the alchemy clinging to her clothing? Her skin bulged like a stretched rubber ball, hidden serpents wriggling to be free . . .

"I want to talk to your King of Rats." He tapped his cane on the cobbles, a hint of old-fashioned swagger.

"Mr. Hyde? I can't do that."

"Your enthusiasm for public service shines on undimmed." He grinned, and it made him look young again, imbued with wonder and curiosity. "Hyde and I have business. The terms of his surrender."

"Surrender?" she repeated stupidly. The second time her wits had floundered in his presence. Probably happened to everyone. No doubt he counted on it.

"Don't pretend ignorance." Impatient, sick of explaining himself to idiotic inferiors. "Everybody knows what he's up to. Civil disobedience, chaos, anarchy. I said I'd crush his wretched rebellion, and so I shall, but the Rats and the Royal might still come to terms. Once the Palace have exhausted their idiotic attempts at French *diplomacy*." He ejected the word like a rotted plum pit.

She shivered, recalling what he'd once told her of his ambition to set the world right. *When blood runs in English gutters, it shall belong to bishops and sorcerers and anyone who dares defy the truth . . .*

"Areas of mutual interest," he added. "Certain upheavals that might benefit us both. Hyde has a second option, of course. He can defy me and see what happens."

Her head ached. "You want me to broker a truce?"

"Don't bother dissembling. I know you're thick with him. In one fashion or another." A sly, utterly unendearing wink.

He knew Hyde was her guardian. Did he know about her double life, her use of Mr. Finch's potions? Heavens, was Finch in danger?

Lady Lovelace studied Eliza's face with dead eyes: one red, one black. She tilted her chin, sun flashing on silver. "Untrustworthy," she concluded, a metallic contralto that scraped Eliza's nerves like nails on slate. "Knows more than she's offering. I recommend immediate search and seizure."

Involuntarily, Eliza backed off, clutching her bag. "You can't do that. I've done nothing wrong—"

"Come, that won't be necessary." The Philosopher patted Lady Lovelace's hand, placating, but his gaze didn't let Eliza go. "Or will it? I once hunted counterfeiters, did you know? Caught them, too, forced them to give up their overlords. Traitors, the lot of them. They all cooperated, Doctor, and so will you. Or I'm afraid I'll have to allow my colleague . . . shall we say, her *over-zealous* way?"

Lady Lovelace flexed steel fingers, and laughed. A broken, corroded noise, *rrrk! rrrk!*

Eliza's skin shrank, cold. She longed to cover her ears, block out that rusted mirth. *The subject's fear is the primary weapon.* Lafayette's statement resounded in the primitive lizard part of her brain. Words threatened to spill from her mouth. Any words. Just to make Lady Lovelace stop *staring,* with that terrifying, burning eye . . .

An animal urge clawed her—Lizzie's?—to inform on Moriarty Quick. *Here's an alchemist for you! Strap him to the stake and stoke the fire!* Memory made her head swirl. Whiskey-rich breath, tinted spectacles, a man's finger toying with a mahogany curl on her shoulder. *Shall we say, the shadowy side of chemistry?*

She gulped down crazed giggles. Good lord, she *was* going mad. Imagining the whole thing. The Philosopher and Lovelace knew nothing of Finch, or the elixir. Hyde interested them, not she. She was merely the means to their end. Right?

Sir Isaac sighed. "Pros and cons, ifs and buts. Shall we get on?"

She mustered her courage. "Very well, sir. If I've no choice—"

"At last! We approach the point." He inclined his head. "My compliments to your *King.* Tell him I wish to see him. In person. Soon."

She almost guffawed. Edward Hyde and the Philosopher. The murderer and the megalomaniac. "And if he refuses?"

"You're a scientist, Dr. Jekyll. Make sure he sees reason."

Now that she'd spoken her assent aloud, her treachery stabbed her heart cold. Hyde was her *father*, for heaven's sake. He'd only ever wanted the best for her.

Sir Isaac stared, pale like death. "Oh, and might I expect the pleasure of your company at my skyship launch later this week? The new Skyborne Fleet's flagship, fabulous scientific work. I named her *Invincible*." A brittle smile. "One's permitted the occasional whimsy."

"It does sound fascinating." Her first honest words for this entire conversation.

"Doesn't it? I assure you, the launch will be quite something. I venture London's never seen the like." The Philosopher tipped his hat, and he and Lady Lovelace vanished into the crowd.

AN ABIDING UGLINESS

•••

ELIZA'S NERVES STILL SMARTED LATER THAT AFTER-
noon as she approached the undertaker's shop across
from Regent's Park. HARE'S FUNERALS, the sign murmured discreetly, above broad bay windows somberly draped
in black.

"Bloody murder in Blackfriars! Escaped lunatic strikes
again! Razor Jack's back!" A boy in a red cap jumped onto his
stack of newspapers, brandishing his latest edition:

"PENTACLE KILLER" CLAIMS SECOND VICTIM

The police had found Carmine, then. The papers loved to
blame anything gruesome on Todd. He wasn't responsible, she
was sure of it . . . but her sweating skin chilled when she recalled
that missing beadle. If Todd wanted her attention, he'd gotten it.
Help me, sweet lady, lest I fade into that nightfall forever . . .

No bell tinkled as she entered the shop. Elaborate black
drapes and a vase of white lilies enforced an overtly funereal
atmosphere. Dried lavender sprigs lined the room, an effort to
obscure the inevitable stink of chemicals and death.

"May I help you?" A man in an ill-fitting suit studied her rudely above wire-rimmed spectacles. Snotty, with emphasis on the *help. Shall I HELP you, madam, or shall I KICK you out onto the STREET?* Blue-black hair greased his skull, smelling strongly of hair dye. Unlikely it was his wife he wanted to impress.

She flashed her best smile. "Dr. Eliza Jekyll, police physician. I've been sent to examine one of your deceased. Sir Dalziel Fleet?"

The clerk sniffed. "Even if you're truly a doctor, madam—which I doubt *very* much—the grieving widow has declined permission. No police. The late baronet is not to be disturbed. Good day."

Inwardly, she screwed up her face. Good thing her pink remedy was still in effect, or Lizzie would have throttled this idiot on the spot.

From the depths of her bag, Hipp whirred, mocking the clerk's prissy voice. "Good day. No police. Good day."

Surreptitiously, Eliza whacked him with her elbow. "Oh, dear. Can't you help me, sir? It's my first day on the job, you see." She dropped her gaze modestly, and worked up a maidenly flush. "My Chief Inspector sent me—*such* an impressive man, you know—and he'll be so dreadfully cross with me if I don't report back."

"No police," the clerk repeated, pointedly flipping his ledger open.

Eliza laid her hand on the counter, three glinting sovereigns half-hidden beneath. "What a pity we can't come to some arrangement."

Temptation and fear warred across his brow. "I'm afraid I can't possibly . . ."

"I've gone to such lengths, you see, to get this job." She smiled, suggestive. "I'd be so very grateful, sir."

The clerk's damp hand covered hers. "I'll see what I can do. Shall we?"

"Work before play," she simpered, ignoring Hipp's electric snort, and withdrew her hand, leaving her hard-earned bribe. As much as this horrid clerk likely earned in a month. Sympathy stung, and ruthlessly she plucked it out. She still wanted to punch his condescending face.

"Very well," he grumbled, clearly put out. "We've half an hour before Mr. Hare returns. The embalming room's through the parlor." Greedily he watched her skirts sway as she walked. "Don't be long."

"Can't wait." Out of sight, she dropped her fake smile with a shudder. His speculative gaze had greased her skin. She felt dirty, a deceiver, committing some vile sin.

Bollocks, whispered Lizzie, just a faraway echo. *Ain't your fault he's up for it, the lousy cheating sod.*

"That doesn't make it right to sink to his level."

Hell, it don't. Screw him for a dirty dog. Think he'd spare a drop of piss if you was on fire?

This parlor also served as a chapel, firmly Anglican in its lack of gaudy trimmings. No popish fripperies here, thank you very much. Dark cloth masked the windows, and soft gaslights burned in the scent of fresh lilies and brassy chemical undertones.

She closed the frosted glass door of the embalmer's room. A row of high tables served for the cadavers. A wooden trolley held make-up pots, sturdy needles, and thick black thread. On another, a range of autopsy tools, clamps, a staple gun, an electric cauterizer. Barrels of preserving chemicals, wads of cotton packing for sunken cheeks and chests, coils of copper wire.

The place was spotless. She'd seen much worse, in the dank police morgue, or filthy makeshift dead houses set up in pubs and drawing rooms. Here, death was all business, the sanitization of horror. Paint them, stitch them, put them in the ground, so we don't have to remember that one day, it'll be us. And pervading all was that cold meaty whiff that never completely left her nostrils or washed out of her clothes: the beckoning scent of death.

Such was the career she'd chosen. What was it, this fascination with *ending*? *Alpha and omega, that sibilant slice* . . .

She tugged on her white crime scene gloves. There was only one body, covered by a sheet. Hipp leapt from her bag and capered beneath the table, springs boinging. "Samples," he yammered. "Sample-ample-ample . . ."

"Take dictation, there's a good boy. And do try to stay in one piece." She pulled the sheet away.

"Sir Dalziel Fleet," she reported, and Hipp's cogs chattered as he recorded her voice. "Mid-fifties, looks every minute of it. Why did I have the idea he was younger? Excess body fat, skin yellowed. I'd say he both ate and drank too much. Face has been peeled away. Numerous old scars on his torso." She prodded one. "Not smallpox. Neat cuts, deep. Perhaps some quack applied leeches. Hooray for the nineteenth century."

She settled her optical on her forehead, and the body loomed, magnified. "Apparent cause of death is a gaping throat wound, made by a bronze crucifix now missing. A large star-shaped entry point, consistent with a blunt stabbing . . . Wait."

Her pulse quickened. "That's not an entry point. I see a slice with a small neat puncture. Same on the right side . . ."

She blinked. Frowned. "These are knife wounds. Same as the carved pentacle. Our killer didn't stab. He slashed, one way and then the other. From behind, presumably, while large quantities of blood squirted. Do you know what this means, Hipp?"

"Squirt," he burbled. "Squirt-squirt-squirt . . ."

"It means, you gruesome little beast, that our crucifix was *not* the murder weapon." She straightened, perplexed. No answers. Only more questions. "Why kill a man with a knife, then shove a crucifix into the wound?"

She checked the forearms. "No defense wounds. The victim didn't fight back. Consistent with attack from behind. Or maybe too drunk."

She recalled that ashtray, the strange hallucinogen. *Chinese opium, or some such.* Glancing swiftly over her shoulder, lest that lustful clerk be lurking, she slipped an iridescent alchemical filter into her optical. *Zing!* The world shimmered, luminous, and she probed the throat wound with her tweezers.

"I say, Hipp! The flesh inside his esophagus is scintillating. He didn't inhale this drug. He swallowed it. Was he poisoned?" She sniffed the wound. "No scent I can detect. What a pity Captain Lafayette isn't here. Remind me to press Mr. Finch for an analysis." She sliced off a chunk of glittering flesh and popped it into a phial. "Look, something's balled up in his throat."

She tugged. *Pop!* Out it came in a spatter of blood. "Someone—the killer—has stuffed in a wad of canvas. What on earth is that about?"

Carefully, she unfolded it, shaking away stained fluid, and pushed up her optical. "Well, well. It's Dalziel himself. Sharp-looking gent, in his younger days. A fragment, sliced from a larger portrait." She brightened. "What if this is from the ru-ined picture that hid Dalziel's wall safe? I must check if this piece matches. Certainly such desecration would support our revenge motive." She rolled the canvas carefully into a test tube. "So if the painted face is stuffed down his throat, where's the *real* face?"

"Real face," snorted Hipp, on his back with legs kicking. "Realfacerealfacerealface . . ."

On the wooden tray, a scalpel winked, tempting. She still had a few minutes. Perhaps she could get stomach contents. Eagerly, she turned for her instruments.

The grinning clerk grabbed her.

She backed into the cadaver's table. "Unhand me, buffoon!"

"Hands off! Hands off!" squeaked Hipp.

The clerk advanced. "You've had long enough. Shall we get to it?"

Enraged, Eliza shoved him backwards, hard. At his stupid, shocked expression—what absurdity, a woman *fighting back*—her blood boiled over. Not Lizzie's fury this time, but her own. At this stupid, inequitable world and the fools like this who ran it.

Wildly, she slapped him, kicked his shins, clawed for his eyes. "You arrogant fool. Did you imagine I'd trade *favors*? You think far too much of yourself!"

Lizzie cheered. *Huzzah! About time. Now let me strangle the limpdick rat.* Eliza's hands flexed hungrily. Her flesh tin-gled, heating. How she burned to end him . . .

"You lying hussy," he snarled. Already his face blossomed red where she'd hit him. "I'll make you sorry."

"Don't take that tone with me, you witless runt." With a supreme effort, she controlled her breath. She swept her optical into its case, ripped off her gloves, and made for the door. "I have all I require. Keep the money. Call it a consolation prize. Zap him, Hipp, there's a good boy."

Hipp popped out his crackling copper coil and jabbed the clerk's thigh. *Zzzap!*

The fellow cursed, hopping, and slapped ineffectually at Hipp. "Stop it, you brassy fiend." *Zzzap!* "Don't think I won't report this to your inspector, you evil tart!" *Zzzap!*

She halted, one hand on the swinging door. "By all means, sir. Don't think I won't report *you* to Lady Fleet. Defying her instructions, just to get your sticky hands on a bit of skirt? Your Mr. Hare will surely hear of it, and you'll be dismissed on the spot. Think on that, before you open your vulgar mouth." She smiled sweetly. "Now go home and beg your wife's forgiveness, you despicable man. You don't deserve her. Good day."

Satisfied, she strutted out into the street, and collided with a stocky body.

She stared, heart pounding. "Hello, Mr. Brigham. Didn't expect to see you here."

It was Brigham, for sure, lush black curls and youthful face. No more bruises, naturally. Captain Lafayette's genial threats had done their work. Out of butler's costume—

instead, a rough brown coat and trousers. He clutched a bulging canvas bag by wicker handles.

"Ma'am." He touched his cap, trying to sidle by.

She blocked his path, a casual swish of skirts. "Not at work this afternoon?"

"Come to pay respects." His East End tones were stronger, as if reinforced by his clothing.

"To a master who beat you? Isn't that odd?"

"Got nuffing to say to you . . . Oi!"

Hippocrates barreled from Hare's and launched at Brigham. *Doinng!* The boy stumbled, dropping his bag, and its contents tumbled into the dirt.

A clockwork servant's head, knobbly neck bolts unscrewed. A disassembled logical processor, sprouting dusty wires. Spanners, probes, a rusted electrical meter with a cracked casing.

Hipp scrabbled at the brass head. "Clockwork overstressed! Logic unit failure! Maintenance imperative!"

"You'll bust it, you rotter. Get off." Hastily, Brigham stuffed the head back into his bag. Papers spilled, circuit diagrams and notes in Brigham's painstaking hand.

Starlit memory sparkled. That same writing, listing the guests at Sir Dalziel's dinner. Lady Fleet's obsequious entourage. *Dr. Silberman, Lord and Lady Havisham, Lord Montrose, Sir Wm Thorne . . .* She frowned. "Wait. Why did you write Dr. Silberman's name first?"

"Beg pardon?"

"On that guest list. In order of precedence, wasn't it? Except you put Dr. Silberman first. Why does a lowly physician take precedence over a viscount? Unless he or she is some-how the most important."

Brigham's dark eyes shifted. "Thought of him first, is all." Again, he tried to push by.

"Are you taking that clockwork for maintenance?" She grabbed his elbow. "Don't you do that yourself? Keep the mon-sters in good repair, you said. So why was it malfunctioning?"

Brigham shrugged her off. "Daft things break down all the time."

"No, they don't," she retorted, inspired by splintered mem-ories of a broken cuckoo clock. "Where did you learn to repair clockworks? Not from Mr. Lightwood, by chance?"

Another shrug.

"You sabotaged that machine, didn't you? So it would lie to us about that night. What really happened at that dinner? Was this Silberman in charge?"

"Don't know what you're gobbing about."

"Come, Mr. Brigham, you're a better liar than even Cap-tain Lafayette gave you credit for." She watched his expres-sion, triumphant. "Aha! That still gets a blush. We imagined you'd no reason to protect Sir Dalziel, but we were wrong. Tell me the truth and there'll be no more unpleasantness." *And we can all go home for tea,* she almost added.

Brigham scowled. "Vicious old codger gave me a job, didn't he? Could've replaced me wiv a clockwork, but he never. I can take a slap or two if it keeps me in a situation."

Clearly he accepted such abuse as a way of life. "I'm sorry he mistreated you. Couldn't you protest?"

Brigham laughed. "Right. Keep your sorry, lady. Never swallowed your pride to get your way? Hell, I done whatever he asked. His students took it harder than I ever did. And now he's croaked, and at last that screeching crow's got her way and put me out on the street. Crueled me right and proper. Think I'll find a new place as high?" His chin trembled. "To think I lied for her all this time. Mary Mother of God, if I told half of what goes on in that filthy house . . ."

"Take care, sir, lest your curses betray your sympathies. Do you mean black magic? Is this Silberman the ringleader?"

His face drained. "Never said that."

She dragged him into the bay window's niche, out of the noisy crowd. Time for a dose of Lafayette's methods. "Don't waste my time with more lies. Sir Dalziel was murdered for plotting to expose this Silberman. Now Carmine Zanotti's dead, and he might not be the last."

A shrug. "Ain't my problem."

Incensed, she slapped his cheek. "Shame on your chilly heart," she hissed. "It'll be your problem, when I tell the police you tampered with those clockworks to falsify evidence. Fancy a stretch in Coldbath Fields? I hear the convicts reserve special treatment for pretty papist lads such as yourself."

"Piss on you," muttered Brigham, but his sullen gaze shifted.

"Whatever floats your boat, sir. Who else knew about this?"

He fidgeted. "Lady Fleet'll know I told."

"We'll keep you safe," she promised, far from sure it was true. "Captain Lafayette has powerful friends. Who can just as easily implicate you as protect you, if you don't prove your worth. Does Lady Fleet deserve your silence so well?"

Defeated, Brigham yanked his cap off to rake his black hair. "All of 'em stayed until three," he admitted. "Lady Fleet never went down to the country. She wouldn't miss their naff-arse rituals. Blood sacrifices, demon summoning, the usual bollocks. There's a secret basement where they all go at it. Old Dalziel were nutty as a fruitcake. Thought he'd live for-ever." He flushed. "I've already crowed too much. I 'ave to go."

Briskly, she grabbed his coat and shoved him against the window. "Don't imagine I'm too ladylike to thrash sense into you," she lied. "Where can I find this Silberman?"

Brigham's eyes lit. "Joking, ain't you? That's just what he calls himself. No fixed abode. A bad egg, no mistake."

She relinquished her grip, only half satisfied. "Do you mean a murderer?"

"Lady, there's worse things than dying." Casually, he yanked his coat straight, but his brow gleamed with sweat. "Look, I don't know who done it. I lied about the dinner 'cause I wanted to keep my job, that's all. I never talked to you, all right? Swear to Christ, if you come looking, I'll make you sorry." He stuffed his bag under his arm, the electric head poking out. "Get your pet looked to, madam," he added po-litely, as Hipp capered at his ankles, yelling nonsense. "Leave him much longer, he'll pop."

"Please—"

But Brigham was already swallowed by the teeming rush-hour crowd.

A DYING SCREAM

•••

HIPP," ANNOUNCED ELIZA, HER MOOD ONCE AGAIN buoyant, "we have a suspect."

Hipp bounced in agreement. "Investigate," he yammered. "Information please. Information-mation-mation . . ."

"Do try to calm down," she added, exasperated. She'd more important things to do than tinker with Hipp. Witnesses to re-examine, a case to build. Who was this elusive Dr. Silberman? Everyone at that Exhibition had lied, and she intended to extract the truth.

Beside her, Lizzie laughed, a bright phantom in red skirts. "Oh, aye. You and whose army?"

Eliza rolled her eyes. "For heaven's sake, don't *you* start."

"You ain't the police," persisted ghost-Lizzie. "If they's all in on it, like Brigham claims, think they'll talk to you? Not without a certain scarlet-coated Royal agent to strike fear into 'em."

"Indeed. Did it escape your notice that the captain and I disagreed?"

"Well, you'd best agree again, missy, or for you this case is over." Jauntily, Lizzie tossed bouncing curls. This time, she wore a crooked top hat and a huge monocle, one eye looming impossibly large. She seemed scarily real. Almost opaque.

"Nonsense. I don't need him. I'll return to the Fleet house, ascertain if this secret basement is real . . ."

Lizzie just laughed.

Stubbornly, Eliza pursed her lips. "I don't *need* anyone. Especially not you."

She hailed an electric omnibus, waving at the driver through the raucous crowd. The thundery aether scent brought to mind that stormy night at Bethlem, when the Chopper tried to bring a stitched-up corpse to life.

Mr. Todd had offered bizarre insights into the Chopper case. What would Todd say about this pentacle-carving, heart-eating killer? Perhaps she could mail him her case notes. She wouldn't need Captain Lafayette for that. *Dear Mr. Todd, why did the crazy person do this?*

She squeezed onto the crowded omnibus, thanking a gaunt fellow in black with a rolling glass eye who offered her his seat. He clambered up the spiral steps onto the roof, and the omnibus rattled away, leaving Lizzie standing on the sidewalk.

Eliza grinned, and waved. *Ha! See you later.*

Hipp bounded into her lap. "Bus! Bus! Bus-bus-bus . . ."

Her vision wobbled, lurching vertigo, and the pale-haired governess sitting opposite suddenly seemed to wear Lizzie's face.

"Aye," the apparition taunted, "stand on your stupid pride, until this pentacle-brain loon kills someone else. Face it, missy. You NEED Remy."

The cramped omnibus suddenly trapped Eliza, the thick

air choking her. Surely everyone was staring. What she *needed* was a tonic and a good lie-down . . .

The Lizzie-thing practically purred. "Pox on your precious independence. Would it be so dreadful to spend another day in his company? Or is you scared *he* don't want to see *you*, after you accused him of torturing folks for fun?"

Bang! The omnibus jerked to a halt at the corner of Southampton Row, and Lizzie smirked and vanished. The governess returned Eliza's stare with suspicious eyes.

Heavens, she was losing her mind.

Hurriedly, Eliza paid her threepence and jumped down with Hipp under one arm. The gaunt glass-eyed man tipped his hat to her, and her spine crackled cold. Hadn't she seen him before? He put her in mind of Lizzie skipping along a dark street, a weaving drunkard who bellowed a song. *While soft the wind blew down the glade . . .*

Good God. Was the whole town spying on her?

"Fine," she snapped, to no one in particular. "Hipp, if you please, telegraph Captain Lafayette. Tell him I've a development in the Pentacle Killer case, and I'll come by tomorrow morning, if he doesn't mind terribly. If he's not too busy, that is."

"Busy," yelled Hipp happily, galloping away. "Inner Temple, ten o'clock . . ."

Niggled by dumb animal guilt—what had her harsh words with Lafayette even been about?—Eliza headed reluctantly for home. Birds twittered in the leafy park, irritatingly cheerful. Shoppers strolled and laughed. Smiling couples flirted. Children frolicked on verdant grass. How infuriatingly domestic.

She stomped onwards, peeved. If Lafayette thought she'd forgiven him—"For what," yelled Lizzie from a passing carriage window, "making you face the truth?"—he could think again. In the meantime, she must do the Philosopher's bidding. Unless she fancied a rusty electrified dungeon in the Tower.

And that meant the elixir. Lizzie would fare better by far in the Rats' Castle than she . . . and as always, since her guardian's identity had been revealed, Eliza felt a strange mixture of reluctance and girlish eagerness at the prospect of seeing Mr. Hyde.

But the Philosopher's coercion maddened her. Always subject to another's orders, following another's plans. Never acting of her own volition.

"Not so nice, is it?" called Lizzie gaily, swinging lace-gartered legs atop the spiked park fence. "Ha ha! How'd you like *them* apples?"

"I like 'them apples' perfectly well, thank you." Eliza crossed the street, dodging a blue-skirted young lady swerving along on an electric velocipede, and stomped up her front steps. "What does that mean, anyway? Where are these 'apples' you're forever on about? Why do you have to be so picturesque?"

"Picture-who?" Now Lizzie lurked beneath the porch, spitting on a dirty handkerchief and polishing Eliza's shingle.

"You know that word. You can display perfectly respectable manners when you feel like it, but insist on acting like a circus clown. No one likes following the rules, Lizzie. I can behave myself. Why can't you?" Eliza slammed the door, her breath short.

Was she truly going mad at last? Or just that sweet-pink remedy, playing tricks?

She dropped her bag on the consulting-room desk. Now Lizzie was fighting in her guts again, punching her insides black and blue. "Stop it! You're not squirming out while I'm sleeping this time. I need to remember, not wake up half drunk in a doorway with mud up my skirts. It's the elixir, or nothing. And you'll come straight back when you're finished, young lady," she added, half-hidden memory scorching her cheeks. "No messing about with your seedy gentlemen friends. Kindly salvage a whisker of self-respect."

"Ha!" Lizzie's grin poked from between the drapes. "At least I'm honest about it, instead of making out my turds don't stink. Forever pretending to be sommat you ain't, just to impress a man. Call that self-respect? Arse-licking, more like."

"Call it what you please," snapped Eliza, flinging herself into her chair. "Just don't expect sympathy from me when you contract some horrible disease."

"Don't matter if I do, eh? I just *change,* and everything's healed! Ha! How'd you like *them* apples . . . ?"

Mrs. Poole bustled in, brandishing a vase of fresh freesias. "Everything all right, Doctor? I heard voices."

Confused, Eliza glanced left and right. Lizzie had vanished. "Er . . . quite. Thank you. Uh . . . I'll retire early tonight, if you please. I'm rather tired."

Mrs. Poole bossed the flowers into order. "Quite an evening last night, was it?"

Eliza covered a fake yawn. "Home by eleven, if you must know. I barely stayed awake."

"You poor thing. How unbearable, swanning about in a fancy gown with that handsome captain on your arm. Took you long enough to come inside, didn't it? Anyone would think something salacious was going on."

"Is that what happened? I hardly recall. Might you fetch me milk and a sandwich, please? I'm not very hungry."

"Humph. Something amiss with my suppers, is there?"

"You have me. All these years, I've been pampering your feelings. I'm afraid you can't cook to save yourself."

"All that fine food wasted," grumbled Mrs. Poole. "I suppose I can rustle up something."

"A jewel, as always. Whatever should I do without you?" Eliza started upstairs.

"Starve and work yourself to death, like your father?" called Mrs. Poole after her.

"In a matter of days. I've little doubt."

The sunset had faded, staining her bedroom's white drapes with watery blood. She lit the electric light, *pop!* Her skin jittered, a poor fit, and her palms itched, begging her to scratch them raw. How she longed for Lizzie's devil-may-care confidence. Yank that well-oiled sconce, dive into the secret chamber, fill her mouth with that bitter delight . . .

Mrs. Poole arrived with supper. Eliza ate it, barely tasting. She sat at her writing desk and tried to read—Herr Gross's text on the identification and preservation of crime scene fluid samples—but her concentration scattered like marbles. She paced up and down. Loosened her clips, pulled hairpins loose in readiness. Fetched her elixir from the cabinet. The glass felt warm and greasy in her hand. Pulsing, like a living creature, eager to be free.

Grimly, she stared at it. It stared back. Waiting. Yearning.

The mantel clock struck eight.

THE ART OF MAKING A POINT

•••

I SMACK MY LIPS, ELIXIR ROLLING IN MY BELLY LIKE molten gold.

About time.

I ditch the empty bottle. Stretch my hungry muscles, pop my neck, *crack!* I feel . . . odd, as if my skin don't fit proper. That shiny pink hellbrew is playing merry bugfuck with me, my friends, and I won't stand for it.

My dresses beckon from my closet, tempting red devils . . . but I let 'em be. Becky's killer might still be a-hunting, and if he is, he's wanting a saucy-eyed dolly in a red dress, not a prim schoolmarmish lady. Out of twig, no less! Ha ha!

I pop a few corset clips, and my chest swells, grateful. Her shoes are too damn sensible, ugly, too, but they'll serve. No stiletto—my sweet steel sister's lost—so I grab Eliza's stinger and test the button. *Bzz-ZAP!* Current forks blue between twin metal prongs. Well enough. I tuck him into a pocket.

I knot my crackling dark hair, and check my reflection, *sans* spectacles. Christ, we looks a sight. This dull gray dress makes me out like a ghost, corpse-pale face and shadow-ringed eyes. I giggle. I feel like them ladies of the night from

Soho, putting on a fancy fakement. *Sir, you make me blush. Be gentle!*

Or maybe the particular sort. I pout, and crack an imaginary whip, *ka-chishh! You're a bad boy, Gerald. I shall spank your skinny arse with this handy riding crop until you repent.* Ha ha! Plenty o' cringing weasels in Soho would pay good coin for a whuppin' from Dr. Eliza. Missed her calling, that's what.

Giggling, I creep down the back stairs. In the alley, chilly air hangs damp, them promised warm nights of summer stubbornly unarrived. Fog haunts the streets, shrouding the almost-full moon. When I reach New Oxford Street, thick clouds streak. By the time I stomp down the twisting lane with the cracked blue-lit doorway, it's raining, her stupid dress is soggy to my skin, and I'm gripped by a right foul mood. On the broken wall by the entrance, someone's scrawled this season's revolutionary claptrap.

INCORRUPTIBLE

I salute it, mocking. Vicious crop of bomb-happy madmen, if you ask me, though Eddie Hyde seems to enjoy their antics. Shoot Her Crazy Majesty down, lads, and her god-rotted Philosopher with 'er. Suits me.

Chilly rainwater drips from my hair, seeping down into my bodice. I knock. The beady-eyed door-keeper's head pokes out. "What?"

I leer. "The watchword's *let me the fuck in, snotface.*"

He grunts and oozes aside, for he recognizes me. The boss's daughter, Princess Lizzie of the Rats' Castle, second only to King Eddie hisself.

Don't work like that, o' course. No jeweled tiara, none o' that shit. Only that Eddie cares for me, and they say you mess with Eddie's cares at your peril. Right. Tell it to Becky's red-caped killer.

I sashay down the pitch-black corridor in the musty sweetness of fairy dust. Push aside a creaking leather curtain and I'm in.

My eyes boggle. Magic ripples over my skin, creeping beneath my clothes to pleasure me. The noise smothers, voices and laughter and music of all sorts, endlessly layered and reflected. So loud it judders nails into my bones.

In here, your perception *stretches,* drunken yet alert. Most of the Rats' Castle lies underground, bigger than you'd think possible from outside. A vast atrium, gallery stacked upon gallery, down and forever till I can't see no bottom. Giddy plank walkways criss-cross, lurching above nothing. Rat-nosed boys, squirrel-tailed urchins, and odder chimeras caper and swing, whooping with the thrill.

Around the galleries, the crowd heaves and roars, a force of nature. Deformed, warped folk, half-man and half-beast, the magical and the mad. If the god-rotted Royal would burn you, this be the place for you. Hair of all colors, frilled skirts and rough-spun coats, weirder rigs of silk and brocade, from rags to the richest finery. I smell perfume, pig shit and noisome coal smoke, gin and absinthe, and the storm-rich scent of aether.

Curious fingers tug my skirts. A blueberry-faced boy thrusts a sloshing drink into my hand. Wine, sin's bloody red. I drink deep. "Hail to the King!" I yell, and a pig-snouted bloke cheers. "Incorruptible!"

The buzz is immediate, intoxicating . . . but I'm troubled. Something's off tonight. The crowd's pushy, hungry, ripe with muttered curses. They flex yellow claws, bare sharp teeth in thirsty grins. I can taste their rage, bitter and fragile like my own, the sulfur-piss tang of gunpowder. The air bristles, armed, a battle poised to erupt.

But I lets 'em sweep me along, down ladders and across bridges, beneath archways and down drainpipes, always down, to where Eddie's carnival dances its tipsy waltz. His carousel, wacky plaster creatures draped in electric lights, bobbing in that eerie organ melody. Men on stilts, acrobats flipping, fire-eaters and blade-swallowers and sultry belly dancers with naked breasts soaked in gin. All roads lead to Eddie.

Here's a card game, deep in some dim-lit corner of a forgotten gallery. A fire pit glows red, and the table's heaped with strange collateral. Coins, clothing, a hedgehog in a wicker cage. A broken piece of Enforcer, two brass forearm bones and a jointed hand. A coil of green hair tied in a stained love knot. A pot of congealing blood. Is that a kidney in a box? Here, you really can bet your life.

My father's slouched in a winged chair, dented top hat askew. Empty bottles litter the floor. He points with his cigar, a wave of foul smoke, and laughs his fucking head off.

Drunk, Marcellus Finch might say, as a skunk. Excy-llent.

I glance around for Johnny the rat-fink traitor, thicker with my father than he dared, for ten years, to let on. Don't see him. Good. I'm still too heartsore and guilty to face Johnny now.

I strut up behind Eddie, clap fingers over his eyes. Inhale him, booze and sadness and darksweet alchemy. "Gin," I announce. "Game's mine."

"Eliza?" Weary, alight with hope.

Fuck him. I drop a kiss on his forehead. "Try again."

A grin erupts. "Lizzie, m'darling. Thought you was some-one else." He jumps up, flinging his cards aside—his hand were rubbish anyway, a pair o' tens is all—and knocking the hedgehog to the floor. The cage smashes, and the creature's spiny arse scuttles away. A furry-faced cove sprints after it, snuffling with a long agile nose. Mayhap the hedgehog's his lady friend.

"Your Majesty." I spread Eliza's prim skirts, a proper lady.

"How do?" My father flips me a bow. He ain't tall—his shoulder's sort of hunched, if you must know, and he lurches about lopsided like a cross-eyed tortoise—but somehow he's graceful, too, vigorous as a man half his age.

"Not too shabby. We need to talk."

"Good day, I trust you're well, how quaint, good golly gosh, is that the time?" He thumps me again with that rakish Eddie grin, what must've spelled doom for so many enrap-tured ladies in its day. Hell, today's still its day, because I want to be sore at him for loving Eliza best—doesn't every-one, God rot their eyes?—but suddenly I ain't.

I ain't. He gives me those big, mad eyes—storm-gray, like hers and Henry's, but glimmering like thunder clouds with the *weird*—and I want to grab him and dance. Laugh like jackals to the stars, dive into madness together and die.

He twirls me on one hand, flaring my skirts. Tough hands, roughened like no gentleman's should be. "Holy goat's balls. Don't know 'bout the rest of these giddy bastards, but I'm in *love*."

This is Eddie's idea of charm.

"Piss off," mutters I as we go to the gallery's rail to survey his domain. "I'm out of twig, all right?"

"What for? You in trouble?" Those storm clouds blacken, ominous. A muscle jumps in his cheek, and his once-handsome mouth twists into something cruel and ever-hungry.

This, my friends, is how murder looks. Unless you're a red-haired loon with a razor, but that's a knottier sack of eels. And even as my guts recoil, my stupid girlish heart overflows.

So easy, what with Eddie's wild romantic soul, to forget what he is. The rascal what spat Henry Jekyll's good intentions to the dust, what took the good doctor's wife to bed on the sly, and produced *us*—and then hurled her down the stairs when she wouldn't have him no more.

The devil what gave Eliza her elixir, and cursed me to this nether-life forever.

"Ain't nothing." A drunken funeral cortege staggers through the carnival, black crepe and lacquered coffin. A fat tattooed dwarf howls a dirge, accompanied by groaning organ pipes. "Setting a trap, is all. A toff square-rigged, stabbed a girl in Seven Dials. Hooked nose, wears a red-lined cape."

Hyde's expression clears. "You might try Mrs. Fletcher's in Soho. The girls there cater to his sort."

I wonder what "his sort" means. "Rich and ugly?"

A wicked-sweet grin. "Been there myself. 'Cept I always act the perfect gent." Emphasis on the *act*.

I grin, too, but I'm squirming like a wet worm. What the hell do you say to your father, when he starts on about whore-houses? *Ho ho, good one, Papa, go and get your rocks off?*

But it's worse than daughterly embarrassment. His brutal smile unnerves me. I've heard the sin-black whispers. God help the sorry lady of pleasure who lucks into Eddie for a customer.

"Where's the Queen of Tarts tonight? Powdering her pig?" His lady, green-skinned and lithe and nutty as a Yuletide pudding.

His grin don't fade. "She disappointed me."

And I eyes that severed green lovelock on the card table, and wish I never asked.

I get to business. "Have I got a deal for you," says I, and tell of the Philosopher stopping Eliza in the street. A truce, Royal and Rats. Cease fucking fire. "Talk is, you've got new friends," I add. "Those boom-happy Incorruptibles and their Mr. Nemo. I dunno, Eddie. Them new Enforcers, half human . . . there's a bloody lot of 'em. Maybe some arrangement?"

Eddie laughs.

Raucous, reckless laughter. The fire pit flares, and far above, fireworks shower green and golden. When Eddie Hyde laughs, lights shine brighter. It's contagious. The card-table folk are guffawing, tears streaking pockmarked cheeks. Everyone's lost it, an outbreak of mirth fever with no cure.

I start, too. I can't help it. Hoarse, belly-splitting howls. It feels good.

At last, it subsides. We wipe away tears. God forgive me, Eddie, but I love you. And you won't never love me back. Not the way you love *her,* all hopeful and starry-eyed. I'm forever the embarrassing stepchild, and deep in the rotted bilges of my soul, I burn to *KILL* her for it.

"Arrangement," sputters King Eddie, still chortling like the loon he is. "You're fucking joking."

And that's all that need be said.

———◆◇◆———

An hour later, the parlor of Mrs. Fletcher's high-class whore-house in Soho. Brocade drapes, lacquered white furniture, and a girl named Rose in silk stockings and a French maid's outfit. Sixteen if she's a day, pert boobs and a heart-stoppingly high bottom.

Rose chews a candied apple, pigtails bobbing. "Depends. You a snout?"

I point at Eliza's drab skirts. "Do I look like a copper's whore?"

"Fucking copper's wife, more like. Aye, I knows 'im. Or should I say," she adds, dropping into a fancy accent and tittering girlishly, "yes, most definitely, I'm acquainted with this fine fellow. What you might call a most singular visage. Heh heh! How awfully quaint."

She's startled me, I confess. Didn't think she'd talk so easy. "He got a name?"

"Milord." Back into bored Soho drawl. "As in, 'Certainly, milord, I'd be honored to suck you off,' or, 'God, yes, milord, jam it up my arse, please!'"

Snicker. "Is he a lord, then?"

"He never said he ain't. I figure he's in the Commons at least. Forever on about committees and petitions and the like."

I scrunch my nose, recalling Eliza's snotty insults. *Have some self-respect.* The whores, I get. But why would some Parliament-minded cove hoof it down to Seven Dials and slaughter Becky Pearce? Don't make no sense.

Rose rouges plump cheeks. "Anyway, your red-caped gent's rich. Flashes gold as if it ain't nothing."

"How much does he pay?"

She names the figure.

"Jesus wept. What d'you do that's worth that?"

She lips her lolly. "Pay and I'll show you."

I smirk. "Likes it exotic, then?"

Rose blanches, just a little. "He's all right. Talks fancy, likes a game. Harmless once you get your hand on it. It's his gang of roughs what's the trouble. They ain't gents, not especially the bigger one. Tips extra if you fake it while he bites your titties."

Charming. My erstwhile pursuer, stuffed into sausages as we speak? Or—more likely—his still-breathing mate with the rusty nicked knife?

"But I ain't 'is regular," Rose adds. "The red-caped bloke, I mean."

And now we gets to it. I flick her a pair of crowns.

She checks for clipping with an experienced eye. "Saucy May," says she. "We rents upstairs rooms to streetwalkers. She's one. Skinny chit, yellow hair."

"Thanks." I halt, inspired by some impulse I don't comprehend. "Last thing. You know a cove with a parrot?"

Rose sucks her lolly. "Sure. Pirate Ship Gino. Raw-boned lag with three gold earrings and the clap." Smirking, she waggles her little finger. "Likely got it fucking that bloody bird, if you get my meaning."

In Soho's stinking rainbow streets, I'm asking for Saucy May.

I've coin, so it's quick work. A fat, sloppy cove shrugs, a flower girl shakes her lice-cropped head. But a half-drunk

Turk sloshes gin on my skirts and waves me towards Crown
Street—sixpence—and then a skinny Creole boy with a
furred growth on his face points me towards a side lane. Tup-
pence, thanks very much, and cheap at the price.

This lane looks dark and noisome, hell of a place for a
working girl. I slosh through puddles towards it, to look for
Saucy May . . . but a flash of multi-colored waistcoat swings
my head.

Upturned like a bad shilling, it's Sheridan Lightwood.

In a gin palace doorway, reflected in gleaming mirrors to
infinity. Disheveled, that glossy hair loose, holding nasty palaver with stormy-faced Penny Watt. Penny's tricked out like
a Covent Garden "lady," her tight-laced ivory bodice showing
acres of skin, and she's snapping at Sheridan like a shark.

I sidle into the shadows, peel my ears back.

"I didn't *ask* you to . . . I don't care!" The rest's drowned
out. And then, louder. "You can't keep doing this, Sherry.
Leave me be. You're not my responsibility anymore!"

Sherry snaps something back, a cruel glint in his eye. She
slaps him, *pow!* He recoils, and arcs up to hit her back, but
cries off at the last second. She smirks and struts away, a
shimmer of auburn curls and satin-black satisfaction.

Sherry curses and kicks the mud. Grabs up his bag—a big
one with a buckled top—and storms off.

In my direction.

I slip deeper into the shadows, and trip on something in
the slosh. A dead bird stares up at me, his yellow plumage
grot-soaked. Neck twisted backwards, like a dog snapped it.
A parrot.

Heh. Chin up, Gino my lad, wherever you are. Skanky fowl had the clap anyhow, I heard.

Sheridan storms by, muttering with discontent. I wait until he's all but swallowed by the gloom, and sneak after.

He knocks at the door of a creaking two-story house. What's this place? No sign outside. Candlelight leaks from a cracked shutter above. Door opens, Sherry enters . . . and inside, I spy a hooked nose, slashing dark brows, a flurry of satiny scarlet.

Holy shitwallop. Red Cape.

A man of particular politics, Rose said. Lurking in a flophouse? I'm thinking this ain't no law-abiding Tory establishment. Money's changing hands, Sherry's pulling a dark cylindrical shape from his bag . . . I can't hear their jawing. Frustrated, I inch closer, into the finger of candlelight.

A heavy grip bruises my arm, yanks me about. "If it isn't the same nosy tart."

Big body, squashed head, pale eyes hard like a starved dog's. Red Cape's henchman, the hulking brute what bites titties. An extra tip if you fake it.

Shit.

I struggle, ripping free. He just grabs me tighter. I kick. He dodges. I bite. He slaps me across the forehead. *Boinng!* My vision bounces, my ears ring, and when I fetch back my senses, he's dragging me into a crack between two decaying buildings.

"Let me go, you rot-crotch son of a louse!" I fight, rage, kick up mud. No one pays me mind. Another yowling dolly ain't no front-page news. I fumble for Eliza's stinger, but he knocks it to the mud, and voltage cracks harmlessly and snaps out.

He hurls me against a wall and rummages in his trousers. "Shut it, twat. I'll teach you to spy where you're not wanted."

"Would you, sir? I'd be ever so grateful." I fly at him, biting, clawing, jabbing my knee for his balls. If he's hard, so much the better.

But his lips stretch into a whack-job cannibal's grin, and it ain't his cock he pulls out.

It's that jagged, rusty blade.

He slashes. *Rrrp!* My skirts tear. I scream, shock rather than pain. He covers my lips, slamming me back against the splintery wall. Not a happy place, Miss Lizzie. My heart's thumping, so fierce I can't hear a goddamn thing, not his lustful panting, not his giggles, nor that blunt notched blade hacking for my flesh . . .

Wet warmth splashes my face, blinding me.

His hulking frame jerks. His grip falters . . . and he's gone.

I stagger, gasping. Paw the wet stuff from my eyes.

The henchman flops in the mud, blood spurting from his neatly slashed throat. His fingers jiggle. The spurt dwindles to a trickle, and he's still.

Silver flashes in the dark, a crimson-licked blade. Drip, drop, you're dead. And a shifting shadow by the wall coalesces into a man.

A man with luminous eyes, green like fairyshine and just as mad.

Mr. Todd bows. "Excuse me, madam. Was this fellow bothering you?"

A MURDERER'S AUTOGRAPH

• • •

W-WELL," STAMMERS I, "THIS IS UNEXPECTED."
Mr. Todd tips his hat, that razor still dripping in his left hand. Black tailcoat, red necktie with a gold-and-diamond pin. The perfect deadly gent. "Forgive me, we've not been properly introduced—"

"I know who you are." My sweaty fingers clench. My stinger's lost, buried in the mud. And I can't get past him. This forsaken dead-end alley's too narrow. Brilliant. The murderer what covets Eliza's blood just saved my life, and I'm cornered. Weaponless, too, but for a flirty smile and a pair of juicy thighs, and I wouldn't wager a bunch on those to distract *this* death-loving loon.

Still, I can't help but stare. He and I ain't never met in the flesh. He's a lean man, is Mr. Todd, but striking for all that, sharp chin and cheekbones and inquisitive nose. In the gloom, that candlelight seeks him out like a cheating sweetheart, abandoning all else to darkness.

"Of course you do," he agrees. His hair's dyed blue-black, covering that improbable, tell-tale crimson. Clipped short, too, instead of bouncing all over the joint like a fey-struck ruffian's. "There, Miss Hyde, catch your breath, I shan't kill you just yet. You and I need to talk."

"Ain't got nothing to say to you— Oi!" I jerk like a shit-scared rabbit, ready to run.

But he's only holding out a handkerchief. Shaking, I take it. Wipe my face and neck, blot my bloodsoaked neckline. God rot him, I ain't afraid of much. Not wolf-men, not red-caped assassins.

"I do apologize for the mess. I'd never leave a lady in so disheveled a state, but the timing was somewhat awkward." Meticulously, Todd polishes his razor with another cloth. Wrist-flicks the blade into the ivory handle, *zing!,* and slips the lot into his waistcoat pocket, tidy as you like. He frowns at a gore-specked cuff. "I say. Anyone would imagine me a common footpad."

I toss his ruined handkerchief away. My pulse still thrums, a startled bird's. Yet I long to smile. *Eliza* longs to smile. "What do you want, Todd? Following me, is you?"

"Only taking the air, madam, a pleasant midnight jaunt. Fortunate for you that I happened by. One never knows what's lurking in the dark. Unsavory characters, boorish manners, tragic fashion sense. It's positively alarming."

"Crack-brained weasels like you, you mean."

"Now, that's not nice. I merely offer a gentleman's assistance." He plucks my stinger from the mud and offers it to me, handle first. "Did you drop something?"

I grab for it.

But he whisks it away, with that indecent scarlet smile that always addles Eliza's wits. "Weren't planning to kill me with it, by chance? It's most undignified. Electrocution, I mean. I've endured enough of it in Mr. Fairfax's revolting excuse for a hospital to know. All that tedious messing about with muscle cramps and soiling myself and blood coming out my nose, and for what? Anyone would think he was trying to drive me mad."

He offers the stinger again, and this time I snatches it. But he don't let go, and suddenly he's inches away. So close, I can smell him, that horribly lickable scent of roses and murder. "Don't think I don't know that's Eliza's dress, by the way," he murmurs. "You look quite peculiar. Kindly don't wear it again." And he releases me.

I back off, eyeballing that narrow escape route between him and the wall. "Last I looked, numbskull, you ain't in charge of my wardrobe."

He lifts regretful hands. "Forgive me. I find it incongruous. The effect is all wrong. You're much more aesthetic in rufescent shades. Try a cherry, or double-white vermilion? I confess I miss Eliza's eyes." He smiles, starry, and damn it if he don't look like a fool in love. "Her particular shades have no name, you know. They're poorly approximated by ordinary grays. One must mix ultramarine and ivory black. The proportions are . . ." He licks his lips, and it makes me stare. "Quite astonishing."

"Did you mistake me for someone who gives a turd? Because I really must be going—"

Swiftly, he blocks my path. "But we've only just begun."

I sidestep. He follows. I sidestep back. He follows again. "Out of my way, nutbag."

Todd wrinkles his nose, considering. Shakes his head.

"Eliza ain't here, all right? So sorry. Spew your loony love poetry in her ear some other time."

"And as much as I'd like to"—a delicately hungry grin—"it's you I've come to see. We need to talk. You've been meddling in our affairs, Miss Hyde, and I won't have it."

I edge away. "Don't know what you're on about."

"But I think you do. There's no other explanation. She wrote me the most disturbing letter, did you know? I can hardly bear to repeat what it said. I couldn't believe my eyes, and if I may say so, my eyes are somewhat notorious for attention to detail." His chin tightens. "Her rejection hurt me, Miss Hyde. Honestly, it did. I can only imagine her coldness to be because of *you*."

"Ha! Hate to spoil your wedding, Romeo, but that was all Eliza. She thinks you're offing folks to get her attention." *Thinks she can save you,* I almost add, and swallow a guffaw. Like hell. "That Zanotti, for one, what stole your painting?"

A bewildered arch of brows. "Why on earth would she imagine me responsible for *that*? The newspapers described all manner of bizarre disorder. Savaged hearts, indeed. Most displeasing. A lunatic, I daresay." He smiles slyly. "Or a cunning fox with a desperate need. Searching for something, I'll warrant, and not only revenge. I shouldn't be surprised if all sorts of dirty secrets wash out in *that* river of blood."

"That missing beadle, then. The fat fool what dismissed her from the workhouse."

"Ah." Sadly, he shakes his head. "*Mea culpa.* An accident, all the same. Shadow lost his temper."

"Who the hell's Shadow?"

"Hardly a question I'd have expected from you."

I can't help but laugh. "''Tweren't me, I swear! My imaginary friend done it!' You keep telling yourself that. Own your bleedin' sins, Todd. Renouncing what you done don't make it disappear."

But doubt pops blisters in my blood. What if it's true? Is he hiding his own Lizzie, some chortling black-hearted rascal what pops out to dispatch the ugly and ill-mannered while his attention is elsewhere?

Aye. And it weren't me what fucked Johnny and got Becky stabbed in the guts neither.

Todd gives me a puzzled look. "You shan't distract me with feeble riddles. I must ask that you cease your interference immediately. As a gentleman to a lady, you understand. A matter of good manners."

I cock hands on hips. "And if I says 'go to hell'?"

"Then I'm afraid I shall have to *make* you stop, and there'll be much distasteful nonsense with screaming and sweating and bad smells, not to mention all that blood soaking the carpet. Who'll clean that up?" He clicks his tongue in disapproval. "No one wants a mess like that. Least of all I."

"That's the shabbiest threat I ever heard. Kill me, and she dies, too. You do realize that, you piss-brained half-wit?"

Cruel glitter fires his stare. "Your ill manners make my head ache, Miss Hyde. Who said anything about *death*?"

I laugh to bolster my courage, but screw me raw, I've never longed harder for my stiletto. Stab him in the throat, send him howling back to hell. "Think you frighten me, Odysseus

Sharp, Esquire? I could grass on you to the coppers this very night and they'd hang you in a heartbeat."

"Would they? What will you tell them?" Todd folds his arms, crosses one ankle before the other. Eyes the henchman's corpse with distaste. "Beastly fellow. Look at the abominable rat-fur shade of his coat. Deserved to die choking for his fashion sense alone. I fancy Mr. Sharp is quite the hero."

"You want gratitude? I don't owe you a pink spit. And Inspector Griffin would know your pointy mug anywhere." I almost guffaw. Me, taking a copper's part. Next I'll be swearing off gin.

Todd grimaces. "Ah. You have me there. *Dear* Harley. I know where he lives, you know," he adds airily. "That desperately middle-class town house he really can't afford. I'd visit him—his pretty wife expired, did you hear, it's *such* a tear-jerker—but I'm afraid he's never been very good at listening to what I have to say. Frustrating chap. Unhinged, I should think. I'm sorry to say our next meeting could well turn violent."

"Captain Lafayette, then," I retort. And then I wish I hadn't.

A dark, jealous chuckle that makes me cringe. "The Royal Society lapdog? Please. You don't scare me."

"You don't know me yet." Christ, am I threatening a thrill killer? With what, a smart-arse smirk?

"I could say the same, Miss Hyde. Which strikes me as a shame, seeing as Eliza and I . . ." He smiles, enraptured. "Well, there's only one ending to that story, isn't there?"

"I'm disappointed in you, Todd. Thought you had higher concerns." I sigh. "Fine. You want to bed her, go right ahead. Just warn me out, so I won't be there when it happens."

His mouth twists in faint disgust. "You mistake me, madam. Honestly, do you take me for a common man?"

And the truth I only suspected until now punches me in the face.

I'm safe as a rug bunny with this loon. Because it ain't *me* he wants to hurt.

My flesh crawls. Get rid of him, Lizzie. Now. Before he seduces Eliza with his tragic bleeding-heart fakement and slices her apart to bathe in our blood.

I'm sweating. I'm shaking. My heartbeat's rattling like a runaway diligence. Deep in my pocket, Eliza's stinger beckons. Shove it in his ear and shock him to death, before he twigs what I'm at and lunges in for the cut—but I'll need to get close enough to touch.

Bloody Christ, I don't want to. Not his murdering skin, not his hair, not even his clothes, warmed by that vile Todd-flavored fever.

But I must. Or he'll kill her, the second he lays hands.

Or will he dishonor her, despite his high-minded talk? Does he play with his prey, when the fancy takes?

Jesus, I don't *want* to know.

I smile, sultry-like. "Look, I were hasty. We oughta try to get along."

"Are we not? I was so enjoying our chat. One meets so few truly interesting people in my line of work."

"This Shadow thing . . . It's a lonely life, aye?" I toy with my hair. Step over the corpse, closing in. "We ain't so different. So rare to find a man what understands."

Mr. Todd backs away, a glitter-green warning. His fingers twitch, an edgy razor gunslinger's. "Don't touch me."

Aha! A weakness, no less. Steeling myself, I touch his hand. My pulse skitters. He's warm, fragrant, terrifyingly human. "Don't be shy, sweetheart. You might like it— Ow!"

He grabs a fistful of my hair, and *twists*. "Don't be disgusting," he hisses, holding me at arm's length. "Do you imagine me such an easy mark? Think your *flesh* is something I *covet?*"

He flings me away, and fastidiously tidies his cuffs. His red mouth is tight. Dismayed, as if he never touched a woman that sordid way, and never wants to, and fears what might happen if he does.

My palms itch. Jump him while he's distracted and vulnerable. Shove that stinger into his throat and fry him like a fish . . . but I can't.

Eliza won't let me move.

Her paralyzing venom oozes into my veins. Stupidly, I long to comfort him. She's dreaming of his touch, the sting of steel under her chin, and that awful pink remedy makes me weak. It's as if our places is reversed. *She's* the breath on the back of *my* neck, the ghostly shiver beneath *my* skin, imploring me, *no, please, don't hurt him* . . .

God rot her. I don't GET it. Does she want him, is it that simple, the aching thirst of any woman for a man? God knows, we don't get to choose who lights our fire.

Or is it a darker, more unspeakable craving? Eliza's memories addle my senses. I can't think. Like this, he swindled her into helping him, one stormy evening in his solitary cell at Bethlem. Befuddling her wits with his strange charm, secretly slipping a pin from her hair, the same pin he'll later use to pick his cuffs and escape. *Kill me,* she whispers, drenched in wild lightning. And he says, *thank you* . . .

My nerves snarl like a cornered beast. Get out of my way, woman. How can I protect us if *YOU WON'T LET ME*?

Todd gives me that mad, tragic smile, same as he gave Eliza in that wintry courtroom when he tricked her into letting him live . . . and he beckons me closer. Imperious, just the way she wants it. Clever Eliza, begging at a madman's whim.

I edge nearer. Powerless in her grip. An automaton with a broken, bleeding heart.

But he's quite calm. "Do you see my difficulty, Miss Hyde? I'm a rational man. But Shadow doesn't think before he acts. If you attempt to thwart me again, I can't answer for what might befall you." His whisper kisses my ear. "And then at least two of the four of us"—he licks his lips, that tiny hypnotic sound—*"will be very disappointed."*

His rosy scent drenches me, a half-remembered nightmare of beauty. I burn to act, flee, kill. But I can't move.

I've failed her. Failed us both.

"You're a monster," I croak. When what she wants me to say is *kill me now. Take me. Show me how you love me.*

Trembling, I close our eyes, and wait for the end.

In a breath of poison-sweet roses, he's gone.

EQUAL AND
INDIFFERENT JUSTICE

• • •

IN FOG-STRAINED MORNING SUNSHINE, HIPPOCRATES lay prostrate on Eliza's desk blotter with his legs in the air. "Be still," she scolded, waving a screwdriver. "This won't hurt."

Hipp wriggled like an upturned turtle. "Evidence insufficient. Conclusion spurious. Recompute."

She blinked gritty eyes. She was stumbling in mind and body, exhausted by Lizzie's intrigue and her own rose-scented nightmares of Mr. Todd. *If you attempt to thwart me again* . . .

Not to mention Lizzie's palaver with Edward Hyde. Eliza had already scribbled a note to the Philosopher. She hardly dared imagine the response. Hyde was befuddled. Mad. Flirting with catastrophe.

Did that same disintegration threaten her future, if she couldn't keep Lizzie under control?

Carefully, she loosened Hipp's propulsion spring. *WHIRRR!* Hipp's legs jerked, and flopped limp.

She pried up his brass casing, blowing dust from the clockwork, and squinted through her magnifier. A pair of notched cylinders, his voice recorder. His data store, a stack of tiny crosshatched wafers. His power generator, a kernel of light emitting the faint whiff of burned aether . . .

Clink! Her tweezers hit an unexpected bump.

She poked it. The size of a pea, it seemed *attached,* by a network of fine wires. She pulled harder. *Pop!* Off it snapped, and bounced onto the blotter. Tiny octopus-like limbs writhed from a silvery metal body. A filament unwrapped itself, turning inquisitively like a snail's stalked eye. The horrid thing's wire tentacles flexed, a hungry parasite searching for a host.

She trapped it under an upturned beaker, wrinkling her nose in distaste. She'd built Hipp. She knew what was meant to be there. She flipped a thicker lens into her magnifier, peering closer . . .

An hour later, nervy and breathless, she tapped the knocker on Captain Lafayette's door near Inner Temple Gardens.

Across the wide boulevard, steam barges putted on the Thames, alongside paddle-driven rafts and bobbing coracles. The dirty fog had thinned, and sunshine jeweled the water, painting golden ribbons along the iron-railed Embankment and the stately granite arches of Waterloo Bridge. The trees lining the bank shed a rich summer-blossom scent.

She fidgeted on the flower-lined garden path, waiting. Maybe Lafayette wasn't home. He hadn't yet responded to her telegram from yesterday. Was *he* avoiding *her,* now? She'd all but accused him of betraying her to the Royal. Called him a torturer . . .

But the thing had to be faced. The issue of his proposal remained to be settled. And she'd left Hipp at home in pieces.

As if it weren't death to a lady's reputation to call on a gentleman alone. Good God, this was insane. Mortified, she turned to scuttle away.

"Leaving already?"

She halted, flushing. In the doorway, Lafayette smiled at her, ingenuous. Coatless, his shirt blinding white. Sun-glare ricocheted off the river to kiss his chestnut hair with gold.

"Er . . . no. Good morning." She'd come to apologize for her foolishness, start afresh . . . but some stubborn diamond of fearful caution still glittered in her heart. She despaired. Would she ever get over this? Did it matter? Even Lafayette's epic patience must have limits.

He ushered her in, with a swift glance left and right along the street. Searching for ordinary prying eyes? Or Lady Lovelace, that steel-hearted spy?

The hall was bare, ancient wood panels well oiled. Just a table and mirror. Only recently moved in? No ornaments or pictures. The place felt . . . empty. Soulless. Nothing of the man himself.

He took her cape, and she glanced around, curious. "Don't you keep anyone?"

"Not here. I need a place to be alone."

She forced a smile. "I hope you don't mind my dropping by. I've a development in the case—"

"I've something to show you. Come." He offered his hand. As if he hadn't been listening.

Swallowing, she took it. He led her to the back stairs, where a weak electric light flickered and buzzed. "After you, Doctor. Dusty, I'm afraid. I haven't had the chance to clean up."

Nonplussed, she peered down into the gloom. "Am I to be

interred alive, like poor Fortunato? Do you belong to the secret coven, too? Or is it just your own personal dungeon?"

He handed her a lit candle. "Don't despair, I shan't shackle
you to the wall and starve information out of you. At least not
this morning."

"How comforting." She descended, brushing away an arc
of cobweb, to find a long wooden room where a frosted basement window admitted grudging light. Once a servants' hall,
empty now.

Except for an iron cage. Six feet square of two-inch bars,
bolted to the scratched floor. Twin fat padlocks dangled from
bolts as thick as her thumbs.

"For dogs," he explained. "I bought this place from ratters."

Eliza covered her mouth. The awful thing made her shudder. Dungeons, torture, all the terrible things she'd accused
him of. The bars looked unbreakable. But Lafayette's monster
was no ordinary animal. "Oh, Captain. You can't . . ."

"I must." Dark, final. No choice. "Tomorrow night will be
the first test. It has to be better than Regent's Park Zoo. At
least I'll be out of sight."

Her own selfishness mocked her, a witch's cruel laughter.
She'd troubled him with such irrational suspicions, when he
was preparing to endure *this*. She faced him. "I owe you an
apology."

"That isn't necessary—"

"I'm afraid it is. You've given me no reason not to trust you.
And your work is your business." She twisted her gloved
hands. "It's only that I hate this! I can't bear not knowing
what Lizzie said, or where she's been. I'm scared she'll . . .
I don't want her to spoil things."

Lafayette just watched, unfathomable.

"But I see she already has. Or rather, I have." Her stomach hollowed, desolate. "Well, it was kind of you to see me. I shan't trouble you further—"

"Don't go." He touched her shoulder to halt her. "Madam, I apologize for yesterday from the bottom of my heart. I was perfectly rude. I should have told you about meeting Lizzie, and as for the other . . ."

"The fault was mine." Her throat tightened. Impossible man, to warp her selfish jealousies into *his* failing. "I spoke cruelly, and you reacted, and that's that. I believe we've endured sufficient apologies for one day."

"Truce, then?" A blue twinkle that made her laugh inwardly. Honestly, the man was unreasonably charming.

"Cease-fire, at the very least." Briskly, she dusted her skirts. "While you walk me home, and we discuss your murder case. You'll never guess whom I ran into outside the undertaker's." As they returned upstairs, she told him about Brigham's confession. "Apparently, this Dr. Silberman is the brains behind the whole thing."

Lafayette grabbed his hat and scarlet coat. "So that pretty rascal *was* lying. Well done him. Cleverer than I credited."

She shrugged into her cape. "Don't despair. The poor fellow's still languishing in love. I told him you'd protect him and he practically swooned at my feet."

"Perhaps I'll torment him further, then. Could use a strapping lad to clean up after me. Likes dogs, does he?"

"That really isn't funny." She arched her brows as he buckled on his pistol. "Are we expecting a fight?"

"Always." Lafayette fastened the front door—triple locks, no chances—and they strolled onto the sunny Embankment. Crows squawked in green leafy branches. A light breeze wafted, bringing the first clear day for a week. A skinny fellow pedaled by on a reclining aerocycle, lurching along unsteadily on flapping canvas wings.

Self-conscious, she slipped her hand into Lafayette's elbow. His sleeve felt smooth, overwarm.

He glanced down, a flicker of surprise. A damp curl licked to his cheek beside his ear. "Immediately I wonder from what you're distracting me."

"I might ask the same, sir. You're running a fever. I trust you're not ill."

He smiled, tolerant. "As much as I relish the prospect of your medical ministrations? No. Just a little expectant."

"Oh." Dizzy laughter threatened to unbalance her. That special time of the month.

"So what's next? Track down this mysterious Silberman?"

"Indeed. I checked at the College of Physicians. No Silberman is a member. If he truly is a doctor, he's not from London. I telegraphed Edinburgh and await their reply."

They turned onto the Strand, leaving the river behind. The traffic thickened, rattling wheels and the *boom-bang!* of engines impeding conversation, and she was glad. How she wanted to relish this. Forget the case, Mr. Todd, Moriarty Quick. Savor the simple pleasure of walking in the sun with a man she liked.

But as they passed the grassy corner of Lincoln's Inn Fields, where law students caroused and painted ladies prowled, she couldn't put it off any longer.

Reluctantly, she pulled from her bag the tiny metal creature, which she'd forced into a jar. It batted the glass angrily with its wire filaments, a thwarted spider. "I tried to fix Hipp this morning, and in his works, I found this."

Lafayette held it to the light. "A recording node. I've heard of these. Amazing. So tiny. Whatever will they think of next?"

"Fascinating, to be sure. But it means I'm under surveillance." She squirmed. Would he make her ask?

But he just shrugged. "I almost wish I could ease your mind, but this isn't mine. Which begs the question: Who put it there, and why?"

She lowered her voice. "Could it be Lady Lovelace? What if she's watching us? Watching you?"

"Wasting her time if she is. What would she learn? You work too hard, Hipp's an idiot, and I'm irretrievably besotted with you?" He grinned, offhanded. "Hardly requires a secret surveillance system."

"That obvious, are you?"

"Madam, I positively bleed infatuation. Hadn't you noticed?"

"How quaint. I thought you were just playing the village idiot." As they approached Russell Square, a costermonger called out his wares, offering roasted chestnuts in paper cones. Their dark scent watered her mouth. She hadn't breakfasted. Perhaps Captain Lafayette could join her. Tea and toast, just half an hour of relaxation . . .

She sighed. Ignoring her problems wouldn't make them vanish. "It could be Mr. Finch she's after."

"Then wouldn't she watch his shop? No, I fear this is someone else's work entirely."

"But who'd want to spy on me? I'm just a police physician..."
Her voice trailed off. A team of brutish fellows in shirtsleeves
were carrying furniture from a doorway and piling it in the
street.

"I say," remarked Lafayette, "isn't that your house?"

———◦◦◦———

Bewildered, Eliza picked up her skirts and ran, leaving Lafayette behind. She leapt up her steps, shoving the men aside. In
the hallway, Mrs. Poole steamed indignantly, hands on stocky
hips. "Doctor, thank heavens. These ruffians shoved me aside
like a sack of suet. Imagine it! A frail old woman like me."

"Don't worry, Mrs. Poole, everything's fine." Eliza rounded
on a pear-shaped fellow in a disreputably dusty coat who loitered on the steps. "What's the meaning of this?"

He tipped his crumpled hat. "Bailiffs, madam. Are you ..."
He checked his paperwork. "Dr. Eliza Jekyll?"

"I most certainly am, sir."

The bailiff flourished an official-looking form. "You owe
fifty-six pounds seven shillings and threepence to a Professor
Moriarty Quick."

A horrid sensation of falling.

"That little rat," she burst out. "I've never done business
with him in my life. It's a malicious lie!"

Unperturbed, the bailiff shrugged. "That's for a court to
decide."

Her thoughts scrambled. Quick must have bribed the bailiffs, falsified the documents. His laughing Irish lilt capered in
dim Lizzie-colored memory. *A preparation that'll favor you over
the other. Think on whether it'd serve you better to oblige me.*

Her stomach sank. Fifty-six pounds. More than she earned in months. She could challenge the claim in debtors' court, of course. Take it to Chancery, even, plead that Quick's claim was concocted. But those exorbitant lawyers' fees . . .

Illicit rage curdled her blood. The vermin was clever. The law dealt harshly with debtors: if she couldn't pay, she'd be thrown in prison until she did.

Prison. With Lizzie popping out at will. God help her.

Agony knifed her belly, and she stifled a gasp. Her spectacles misted, a flush of fever. Evil cackles echoed left and right, and her vision doubled and refocused. Indigestion? Dropsy? Had she eaten something rotten?

This wasn't just Lizzie fighting. Something was terribly wrong.

"Leave my things be, sir," she demanded shakily. "I've a week to settle from service of claim. You should know that."

The bailiff just ignored her while his men carried her gleaming hall table into the street. Outside, spectral Lizzie popped into view, shaking the wrought-iron fence. "You rank little squeeze-arses, I'll chew your skins off and spit 'em out!"

Vexed, Eliza yanked the bailiff's arm. Close up, his skin held a greenish cast, his forefingers over-sized and wet like a frog's. "Didn't you hear me? It's all a mistake. You can't take my belongings without due process!"

"Madam, I've heard that every day for fifteen years. Take it up with the sheriff's office."

"Don't be so damned impertinent, sir. You know perfectly well the lady's correct." Lafayette had caught up at last, and roasted the bailiff on an electric glare. Behind him, Lizzie cheered and waved.

At the sight of Lafayette—scarlet uniform, Royal Society badge—the froggy fellow blanched, and seemed to shrink three sizes, as if he'd washed himself in too-hot water. "Only doing my job, Captain," he muttered.

A twinge of sympathy surprised her. Lafayette hadn't said the word "fey." Hadn't glanced at the clear fluid oozing from the bailiff's misshapen hands. He didn't need to. The fellow knew too well the danger he was in.

"Then do it better," said Lafayette. "Replace those items immediately, or I'll have you investigated for taking bribes in public office."

The bailiff's green jowls wobbled, hidden gills bubbling wet. "I'm fully invested—"

"Oh, are you an idiot? My apologies. I'll translate into smaller words." In a purple-crackled blur, Lafayette leveled his pistol at the man's eyeball. "Belay my lady's things, or I'll shoot all three of you for the dirty thieves you are."

Crash! The lackeys dropped her table and backed off. Passers-by stopped to watch.

Humph. Gratifying, to be sure, but the nasty amphibian fellow had *ignored* her. Whereas because Lafayette was an officer . . . and a Royal Society agent . . . and a *man* . . .

"Who cares?" crowed Lizzie, a flash of red skirts beneath the steps. "Getting us what we want, ain't he? Caught in a lie, you fat fuck. Sheriff's office, my arse."

Lafayette flicked a glance at her door. "Go on, back to where you found it. Good lads. Not a scratch, mind."

"You heard him." The bailiff sounded resigned.

His men obeyed, and triumphantly, Eliza snatched the paperwork away. "I'll get to the bottom of this. You can tell your *friend* Professor Quick"—she salted the name with sarcasm—"that I'll see him in court."

"In a dark alley, more like," muttered Lizzie. The bailiff and his men shambled away, and she spat after them, cursing. "Hope that crackbrain Todd really *is* watching us. He'll slit your pudgy throat, frog man. And Moriarty friggin' Quick's, and all . . ."

For once, Eliza's respect for due process seemed foolish and naive. Her lovely furniture knocked about by idiots. Ugly boots trampling her carpets. Her housekeeper *manhandled*. That thieving Irishman deserved harsher justice. Didn't he?

Oblivious, Lafayette powered down his pistol, *hiss-flick!* "That was unpleasant."

"Thank you for your help, Captain. What despicable fellows. I'm sure I can take it from here." Eliza kept her voice light. He meant well. But the idea of needing his help—his very presence, forever popping up at her side whenever she felt vulnerable—bristled her hackles. "My lady," he'd said. As if he *claimed* her.

"So who's this Professor Quick?" Concern lit his face. It looked genuine. What expression of his didn't?

She sighed, and explained about Quick's harassment. "I expect I'm the victim of a scam," she finished. "But what can I do, other than fight it in court?"

"Did he threaten you?" Matter-of-fact, grim. "Physically, I mean. You could report him for assault."

"Not exactly." Memory flickered, a blurred cinematograph of Quick at the Cockatrice. He'd grabbed Lizzie, laughed . . .

"Could he be responsible for sabotaging your pet? Likely that's some misdemeanor they could arrest him for."

"I hadn't thought of that," she admitted, recalling poor Hipp lying in pieces upstairs. "He claimed to be an old acquaintance of Mr. Finch's, and to know something of my, er, medicines."

"Ah." Lafayette grimaced in sympathy. "A pity. Anything I can do?"

Her belly heated. How tempting, to set the Royal on Moriarty Quick . . . But this didn't add up. If Quick merely wanted money, why falsify such a large claim, so easily challenged? He could simply have blackmailed her in private, risk-free.

No, Quick didn't want money. He wanted attention. He wanted not to be ignored.

At her side, Lizzie grinned like a hungry eel. "Why, then, we'll give 'im just that. Only he won't enjoy my attention so much as he thinks."

Eliza managed a smile. "I believe I can deal with it."

"I'm sure you can," said Lafayette, "but—"

"Peace, Captain. You can't imprison everyone who looks at me the wrong way." *Or murder them,* she nearly added. *No, that's Mr. Todd's job.*

Lafayette grinned. "Actually, I can. Perquisite of the badge."

And now she couldn't meet his eye.

"Well," he added, "I'm sure your affairs are in perfect order. If ever you should need a loan, I can put you in touch."

She flushed. He meant a gift. A second son, to be sure, but he'd made his own fortune in India. Fifty-six pounds would be nothing. But the air twanged taut like wire with what he *hadn't* said.

Quick's vexatious lawsuit, her dearth of employment, her refusal to share in Mr. Hyde's ill-gotten gains. All her financial worries would vanish—*if* she agreed to be Lafayette's wife.

Her courage quailed. How easy, to reject responsibility and ambition. To allow oneself to be taken care of, like a child . . . or a pet. But the very idea stung her teeth hollow. "You're very kind, but I'm sure I can solve my own problems. Did I tell you I found Dalziel's face? The painted version, I mean, from that picture torn down from the safe. The killer cut the face out and stuffed it down Dalziel's throat."

"You don't say. What on earth for?"

"I intend to find out. We must re-examine the dinner guests, find this Dr. Silberman. Any one of them could be next."

"Silberman it is." Lafayette studied his fingernails. "I've business with my brother this afternoon. Sure you wouldn't care to meet him?"

Invisible walls closed in around her. Meeting his family made it *real*. How close were the brothers? Did this François know about Remy's curse? About *her*? "I couldn't possibly impose—"

"He asks after you, you know. He's dubbed you my Mythical Mistress of Mystery. Which," Lafayette added airily, "rather paints me into a corner where denials are concerned. If I say, 'Don't be ridiculous, François, she isn't mythical,' then *he* says—"

"Yes," she cut in coolly, "I see the potential for your feeble schoolboy hilarities. But not today, I'm afraid. I must seek Mr. Finch's advice. Perhaps this Quick can be dissuaded with common sense."

The falsehood clanged, harsh discord. Lizzie's rash eagerness to act boiled Eliza's blood, made her reckless in turn. Lafayette was no fool. Surely, he'd call her on her lies, ask what she was truly planning.

But he just made an elegant bow. "Another time, then. I'll call this evening if I'm able. Good day, Doctor."

"Good day, Captain." She watched him go, perplexed. His generous resourcefulness impressed and maddened her at the same time. She needed to fight her own battles. If she wedded, it'd be because she *wanted* to. Not because it was expedient or cheap. And certainly not on a girlish whim.

Besides, in the dark depths of her heart, she'd a niggling idea about exactly how to deal with Moriarty Quick.

Aye, we most certainly do.

A DANGEROUS FELONY

• • •

I DID WARN YOU, DEAR GIRL," REMARKED MARCELLUS Finch sadly, tipping powder into the silver hopper of his pill machine. Midday sun glared, and the coal fire glowed, overheating the pharmacy to sweating.

"He approached *me*," Eliza protested. "Twice. Then this morning, he takes my furniture! Those odious bailiffs wouldn't listen to a word. It was only fortunate that Captain Lafayette happened to pass by." Impatiently, she wiped perspiration from her cheek. She'd wanted to quiz Finch about that angry pink remedy, but it hardly seemed the time. "This Professor Quick. Is he a colleague of yours?"

Zealously, Finch yanked the machine's handle, stamping a new row of pills in a cloud of funny-smelling dust. "Pah! Quick's no professor. Haven't seen the sneaky charlatan for years. Bad circus act, I've always said so. Snake oil, flim-flam, blue-sky concoctions. As likely to kill you as cure."

"He told me he specializes in unorthodox pharmaceuticals."

"Dark alchemy, he means. Nose-poking where noses shouldn't poke, say what?"

"Like that exploding hallucinogen?" She'd sent to Finch by courier those tissue samples from Dalziel's corpse, to help identify the substance. So far, no luck. "I thought alchemy didn't differentiate between good and evil."

"It doesn't. But the flow of life force is directional, eh? The Worshipful Company of Alchemists—long since disbanded, and good thing, too, the persnickety old fools. Honestly, all that trouble about galvanism and homicidal body-snatchers and the proper Latin word for 'electric shock.' Anyhow, back in the day, the guild mandated rules." Finch popped a misshapen pill into his mouth and crunched. "Oh, that's foul. A pinch more caterpillar brains. Hand me that nutcracker, would you? Like any science," he continued, bashing a pile of dried grubs to dust, "we've basic laws that can't be fooled with. Up versus down, light versus its absence. Subvert those, it gets messy, doesn't it? Can open, worms wriggling all over the joint, say what?"

On the wall, the obligatory portrait of the Philosopher—imperious and arrogant, at the height of his near-miraculous powers—glared down in tacit disapproval. She resisted a bright urge to tear it down and stamp on it.

"But how did Quick find out about me?"

Finch poked a finger into his mouth. Withdrew it stained blue, and frowned at it, cross-eyed. "Trust me, dear girl: you don't want to know. Quick has loathsome ways."

Her rebellious flesh crawled, and she squirmed, overheating. *Shut up, Lizzie. Keep out of this. We're doing it my way.* She pulled out her remedy—that gleaming pink poison—and gulped. Her heart rate jumped, her vision swimming. It didn't help. She swallowed more, gasping at the chill in her gullet.

"I say, don't gobble that! I said one drop only."

Unnatural suspicion slithered in her veins. "Why? What does it do? To whom else have you given this?"

His gaze shifted, sullen. "No one."

"Marcellus," she warned.

"Hereditary afflictions," he muttered. "Same blood, same medicine. Worth a try."

She gaped. "You made this for Edward Hyde?"

"It was supposed to help," protested Finch. "He was raving. Eddie's no longer two people, remember. He's only *him*. I thought a dualistic stimulus might calm him down."

"You tried to *cure* my father? What kind of hare-brained idea was that?" Her palms itched to strangle Finch. Already, the strange pink drug sprinted laps in her skull, whooping and turning cartwheels like an over-eager village idiot.

"Experimental, dear girl. Cutting edge, final frontier, all that. Worked about as well as you're thinking, too," he added glumly. "Still, science is never wasted."

"But . . ." She clenched shaking fists. Finch's loyalty had always been to Hyde first, to everything else second. "We'll discuss this later. Quick said I should tell you he 'hasn't forgotten.' What did he mean?"

Feverishly, Finch hammered his caterpillars. "Who knows? He's a maniac! Off his rocker. Marbles reported missing. A spanner short of the toolbox, say what?"

"Marcellus, tell me what's going on, or I shall tickle you into a shivering heap."

"You wouldn't dare."

Eliza arched her brows, waiting.

He sighed, and from a drawer he pulled a faded sepia photograph.

Her heart sank. A dusty laboratory, men in old-fashioned stiff-necked suits. "Another of my father's shady colleagues? I swear, Mr. Finch, one day I shall tie you to a chair with a pen in your hand, and you shall write me an essay entitled 'Mad Scientists Who Worked with Henry Jekyll,' just to ensure there will be no more surprises."

She recognized most of the men by name. Henry, of course, beside a bright-eyed and boyish Finch. Arrogant Mr. Fairfax, the late surgeon of Bethlem. Victor Frankenstein, the eccentric from Geneva with his macabre electrical machines. And poor Mr. Faraday, so admired by Lady Lovelace and burned for defying the Philosopher's rules.

She frowned. "But I know nearly all these people. Quick isn't here."

"Isn't supposed to be in it, that's why. Perilous experiments, widely ill thought of. Volatile chemicals, incantations, hocus-pocus. Henry ejected him from the cabal, you know, which considering what Henry got up to . . . well, even Victor denounced Quick for a madman." He pointed to a fuzzy shape in the background. A man bending over, fiddling with a retort, half hidden amongst lab equipment. "There's Quick, sneaking about like a spider. Lab assistant, pah! Meddler, more like."

"So what happened?"

Ruefully, Finch scratched his head. "I told you I was once investigated by the Royal? Quick's fault, naturally. Wise Marcellus talked his way out of it." He tapped a sly finger beside his nose. "For Moriarty, fourteen years in Van Diemen's Land.

Chain gangs, cannibals, floggings before tea, and desperately unfashionable arrows on your clothes, eh?"

"Transported? Don't the Royal execute alchemists?"

"Ah, but the magistrate interfered, didn't he, and a deal was done. A matter of missing persons. Strange cuts of meat roasting in Quick's kitchen. Horrid stench, neighbors complaining. Only escaped a hanging because no one could prove he actually killed anyone."

"So you two are enemies? What does he hope to gain from tormenting me? Revenge on you? Hardly seems reasonable."

"Reason, sadly, is not Moriarty's defining characteristic."

I'm a rational man, whispered Mr. Todd in her ear. She shivered. What did "rational" mean to a murderer?

She eyed Finch sternly. "Fabulous. I'm so pleased you didn't mention all this earlier."

"Eh? Don't mumble, dear girl. Can't understand a word you're saying." Finch blinked vaguely at the bailiff's summons. "Fifty-six pounds? Gadzooks. Paying the odious fellow off would be easiest. Don't suppose your young man's got the pocket change?"

"More," she admitted. "But I can't accept such an enormous gift, and I certainly shan't marry him for it."

"Wise, dear girl, very wise. Besides, if you pay up this time, what's to stop Quick coming back?"

Me, muttered Lizzie, roiling in brackish depths. *Just let me at 'im with a carving knife and we'll see who comes out second best . . .*

"Can't we just have him re-arrested?" Eliza cut in hastily. "You said he's a convicted felon."

"Double jeopardy, eh? Can't transport a man twice. No, I fear it's Chancery for us." Finch sniffed gloomily. "I suppose we ought to discuss lawyers. Miserly space-wasters, the lot of them. Bottom of the Thames, say what?"

———◄•►———

Interminable hours later—was it only three o'clock?—Eliza closed her front door, exhausted after an afternoon at Finch's, discussing counsel, applications, hearings. Her mind boggled in protest, and Lizzie thrashed beneath her skin, demanding to be free. *Who cares about god-rotted lawyers? Put this arse-hole Quick in a box and be done.*

Eliza's head throbbed. She wasn't a murderer. She didn't take justice into her own hands. She'd see to Quick the legal, civilized way. But her vision doubled repeatedly, edged with glaring rainbows, as if she viewed the world through two sets of eyes: one in ordinary colors and the other . . .

Mrs. Poole emerged, dusting floury hands. "Back at last? What was all that fuss this morning?"

Invisible centipedes crawled all over Eliza's body, pincers nipping at her skin. She wanted to slap them, force her thrashing flesh still. "What? Oh. Just a silly misunderstanding. I really must go—"

"Lucky that handsome captain of yours showed up. Flashy fellow, isn't he? Fancies himself, for certain."

"Couldn't agree more." Her chest bulged, a creature inside writhing to escape. Lizzie would burst out, and Mrs. Poole wouldn't be able to pretend anymore. The lie they'd enjoyed all these years—the pleasant fiction that she wasn't thrusting

the dear woman into terrible danger, every day of her life—
would be over.

"Quite the show-off," added Mrs. Poole blandly. "Anyone
would think him desperate to impress you—"

"Forgive me, I've much work to do." Eliza scooted into her
consulting room, slammed the door, and doubled over, clutching her guts. Oh, God, it *hurts*. Our lungs burn, a hot autopsy
knife levering our ribs apart. Our chest bursts like ripe fruit,
and *pop!*, out I splurt, screaming bloody vengeance.

My reflection looms in the mantel mirror, pale-faced and
glitter-eyed like a consumptive. My itching hair hangs in a
madwoman's hanks. I fumble for our corset, the damned buttons won't open, I scrabble until the dress tears and I let out
a raw-throated yell.

Fuck me, I'm so furious it's shredding my insides. Why
can't she ever do what's best for us? *Civilized way*, my arse. *I'll*
put that weasel Quick right, and it won't be Miss Lizzie coming off second best.

I hurl Eliza's spectacles away. She's got mail, a folded note.
A visiting card drops out.

Miss Penelope Watt

I grab a pen and scribble *THE LIAR!* after her name.

Dr. Jekyll,

We met only briefly, but I feel I can trust
you implicitly. I must speak with you in

*strictest confidence. Might I call this
evening for an appointment?*

*Your friend,
PW*

I snort. Whatever you say, you tight-laced hussy. Here's a telegraph ticker tape, too.

PROF QUICK: DANGEROUS FELON.
AVOID AT ALL COSTS. HG.

Well, thank you, Inspector Obvious. I toss it aside, and find what I'm seeking.

PROFESSOR MORIARTY QUICK!
POTIONS! LOTIONS!
EFFICACIOUS PHARMACEUTICALS!
THE BEST IN TOWN!

My damp fingers crush the pasteboard. *Best in town,* indeed. Time for palaver, Professor Dangerous Felon.

But I can't go undefended. The memory of Mr. Todd's breath still creeps over my skin, a hungry rose-scented spider. I ain't safe. *We* ain't.

I raid the drawers for a weapon, any weapon. And unseen, I slip out.

THE ONLY THING WORTH HAVING

...

IBLINK IN WARM SUNLIGHT AT THE GRAND THREE-STORY shops along Piccadilly. Shoppers stroll, trailing parcel-toting metal servants. A lady's carriage halts, and her clockwork footman dashes into a dress shop to fetch the proprietor so she needn't alight and dirty her fine shoes.

The smell of fresh-cut grass wafts across the road from Green Park. In a gap in the trees, a canvas banner flutters.

HAIL THE ENLIGHTENED BRITISH EMPIRE!
HMS *INVINCIBLE*
FLAGSHIP OF THE ROYAL NAVY'S SKYBORNE FLEET
BY ORDER OF THE PRESIDENT OF THE ROYAL SOCIETY
HIS GRACE THE LORD HIGH ADMIRAL
AND
HER GRACIOUS MAJESTY QUEEN VICTORIA

In that order of precedence, I'm betting. Acres of linen screen puff in the breeze, hiding the skyship's silvery bulk from prying eyes. They say the Mad Queen herself will appear at the launch. Ha! The Philosopher cutting her leash, after all these years? I'll believe it when I see her podgy face in the sun.

I stroll, peering into each window, looking for Quick's pharmacy. Dress shop. Hat shop. Dress shop. Jeweler's . . .

I pause at an etched bay window. Advertising boards are bedded in white lace.

MAGNETIC ROCK WATER DEW FROM THE SAHARA DESERT!
ARMENIAN LIQUID FOR REMOVING WRINKLES!

A particularly fancy one reads

THE ROYAL ARABIAN TOILET OF BEAUTY
ENAMELING—20 GUINEAS PER ANNUM
BEAUTIFUL FOR EVER

accompanied by a drawing of a mad-eyed lady with a stiff china-doll face. Twenty guineas to clog your skin like a circus clown's? Do they really think gents *like* that? Or are they just taught to loathe their own faces?

The shop's insides are hidden by bell-fringed saffron drapes. No apothecary's serpent symbol, no brass shingle reading M. QUICK, LSA, or PROFESSOR QUICK M.D., or even MORIARTY QUICK, DEMENTED FENIAN ABOUT TOWN, BUY YOUR SNAKE OIL HERE! The placard above the door just says

MADAME RACHEL
PURVEYOR OF BEAUTY

Oho. Quick's shop isn't an apothecary. It's a beauty parlor. Beneath, in smaller letters:

BY APPOINTMENT HM THE EMPRESS OF AUSTRIA

Not anymore, sunshine. I believe that lucky lady's bleeding head dropped into a basket when the revolution hit. But who's arguing?

Squeak! No bell rings as I enter. Inside, it's decorated as an Oriental boudoir, with saffron and white drapes, a sofa or two, cascades of fresh flowers. Sultry sandalwood perfume makes me sneeze, but a bad fairy drifts beneath, a sinister echo of misfortune and mishap. As if last night, in the dark, evil happened here.

Wrapped parcels pile on the counter, awaiting the courier. I pick one up. LADY GRAY'S FAMOUS PARISIAN ENAMEL. That twenty-guinea gear? The parcel smells chalky, sour. I pocket it. Let's see what quackery Quick's peddling. He ain't the only one what might indulge in a spot of blackmail.

Fragrant steam puffs from behind a lacy screen. Bathwater splashes, some fancy lady having a Royal Arabian Toilet of Bullshit. Like as not, he takes coin from sweaty old gents to spy on the bathing beauties through a peephole. A line of 'em back there, fiddling with 'emselves while they wait their turn.

I shiver, despite the heat. The shop's not empty, but it feels deserted. Forsaken. Damned.

"Professor?" I puts on a prissy voice. "I say, is anyone in attendance, I'd rather like an Arabian Toilet . . . Oik!"

I whirl, the back of my neck prickling.

Moriarty Quick sniggers like a mad mudlark. Same snot-green coat, that louche blond hair curling. "Good morning to ye. Get your attention at last, did I?"

Shit. I heave a breath. "Let's get this over with, before the sight of you makes me puke. What d'you want from us?"

"You're the one who snuck into my shop like a criminal." His crazy eyes twinkle. "Perhaps I just want me money."

"Bollocks. She don't owe you one fart-arsed penny."

"Aren't you the smart one? I only want to help, Lizzie Hyde." His accent makes my name sound like *Hoyd*. "I can see that sharing a body's not workin' for ye. I can make that problem disappear. Pewf!" He flutters his fingers.

My mouth waters. Make Eliza disappear. Not just lurking about beneath my skin, sneering at me. Gone. So she can't wriggle and evade, like she done last night with the red-haired loon at our mercy.

Can't drag me back from what needs doing.

"Temporarily, o' course," adds Quick. "Only for long enough."

I fake a bored yawn. "Long enough for what?"

A snaky Quick grin. "I imagine you'll think o' somethin'."

God rot him. He knows I crave what he's offering. But I trust this grubby snotgroper as far as I can spit him, which considering his size ain't very far. "And why would a poxy blackmailing rat-squeezer like you want to help me?"

He winks, and I wish he hadn't. "Call it professional curiosity. The potion's experimental, y'see. Lend a hand, and we can talk about settling that debt. A shame, if *both* o' ye should rot in the compter over a trifle."

All my instincts scream, and a clearer message I've rarely heard. *He's up to no good. Fallen out of his tree. Madder than a shithouse rat. Walk away, Lizzie, and don't look back . . .*

"You call fifty-six quid a trifle? Screw your eyes, ratbrain. For quaffing your stinking brew on spec, I want more than you ceasing your lies."

"Such as?"

Screw me suspicious, but I don't entirely trust Finch's story, with his god-rotted loyalty to Eddie Hyde above all. "Tell me about you and Marcellus."

Quick licks his teeth. "It's complicated."

Already I'm cursing myself for a fool. "Poor you. It's that or nothing."

"Very well. I tell you about Marcellus, you test my potion, we forget the fifty-six quid and walk away smiling." He offers his hand. "Agreed?"

Guilt stings, a thousand angry wasps. I can't betray her like this. Even if Quick's telling me true, which he likely ain't.

But a lifetime of black resentment bubbles up to choke me. She'd do it to me. She hates me. Wants me gone. Wants Remy all to herself, and as for the red-haired loon . . .

It's either Todd or us. And I can't get rid of Todd while Eliza's still here. Miss Lizzie needs to take control. Or poor innocent Eliza will get us *both* killed.

I suck in a breath, and for the first time in my sordid half-dead existence, I step across the line.

I shake his scaly-smooth hand. Jesus in a jam jar, I'm a bloody idiot.

Quick lights a cigarette, puffing brown smoke. "'Twere a long time ago. We worked together, Marcellus and I and Henry Jekyll. You know the sort of lines they crossed?"

"Murdering my mother? Bringing corpses back from the dead?"

"Right. So Henry had the nerve to call *my* experiments 'uncanny.'" Quick waves his cigarette, deepening his voice in mockery of the good doctor. "'Moriarty, some things we're just not meant to know. Things only the lord God can control.' Nice talk, for a bloody Protestant."

"Witchcraft, you mean? That black magic hocus-pocus?" My feet itch. Sommat about his tale smells rotten.

Quick blows smoke rings. "Witchcraft is bollocks. My work's solid alchemy and I won't hear a word to the contrary. But back to Marcellus. He and I fell out over a young lady." A melodramatic eye roll. "The love of his life. Wasting away, poor thing, and try as he might, Marcellus couldn't treat her. In despair, he came to me."

And that crafty old Finch-bean told Eliza he'd never been in love. "And?"

"It didn't work out. At least, not for him."

"Is that what this is about? You stole Finch's lady friend?"

That sly namesake grin. "You can't fight true love, Miss Hyde. Marcellus couldn't see that. He tried to come between us. It got ugly."

"I should say. Fourteen years on the wave?"

"Well, there was that. But the past is past. I'm not the man holdin' a grudge." Quick stubs the cigarette out. A glass-stoppered bottle appears in his hand, and with a bad stage magician's flourish, he offers it to me. "I believe it's your turn."

I hold the bottle to the light. Slimy pewter-colored goo slides inside, like the oozings from a cooked snail. Sparkles drift in the liquid, dreamlike, as if it's sleeping . . . or dying. "How much do I take?"

"Up to you. No charge," he adds airily. "Just tell me what happens. I'll know if you lie."

I slam him against the bar, and jam my blade under his pointy chin. "And what's to stop me from killing you right now? Put an end to your sneaky lawsuit for good, that's what."

He giggles. "Easy, darlin'. We've barely met. And I've made arrangements. A package to be mailed to the Philosopher himself in the event of my untimely demise. About you, Dr. Jekyll, Marcellus. Everything."

"Don't believe you."

Quick's breathing hard, eyes glazed. He *likes* this. "That essence is experimental, y'know. Might not work . . . or it might work too well. Who's to know? Can you trust Marcellus to clean up the mess?"

"Shut up." I shove his chin higher, and his necktie loosens, shirt pulling from his shoulder. He's got a design inked there, a tiny tattoo.

Half-circle, circle, cross. Mercury.

"Well, lookie here," accuses I. "Witchcraft's bollocks, is it? What's this mark mean?"

"I've got more." He wheezes laughter. "Want to see 'em?"

"What d'you know about two dead artists and a chewed-up heart?"

He laughs still harder. "Sweetie, you're making no sense. Now, will you do me, or must I satisfy meself?"

My blade slices, a slim crimson kiss that warms my cockles. I want to lick it. Press harder, slit the blackmailing bastard a fresh-bleeding grin . . .

Excuse me, madam, whispers ghostly Todd, *was this fellow bothering you?*

No. I ain't delighting in death. This is self-defense. Not the same thing . . . but we made a god-rotted deal, Quick and I, and screw me for a simpleton, but Miss Lizzie keeps her word.

Disgusted, I hurl Quick to the floor. "If you've tricked me, you addle-brained worm eater, I'll come for you, and you won't get off on what comes with me."

He cackles. "Wouldn't bet on that."

I pluck the bottle's glass marble stopper. Thumb the neck, and upturn it. A slick pewter drop oozes, and a rusty smell assaults me, some rotted, corrupt stench that oils my nostrils.

Fuck it. I shove my wet thumb into my mouth.

My tongue burns, gritty slime spreading. I inhale, and metallic fumes water my eyes. My heart jumps a few beats faster, and stays there. And a strange knot in my belly I didn't realize was there . . . *loosens*.

That's all.

On the floor, Moriarty Quick wipes his bleeding throat and licks his fingers, sniggering. "Enjoy."

I kick him, just for fun, and stride out.

Warm Piccadilly sun kisses my skin awake. That oily taste is fading, leaving a contented glow. Compelled, I sip a little more. It slides down nice, murmuring like a dream lover, eager to please. I flex experimental muscles. I'm strong, relaxed, untroubled by doubt. The chortling little facteroo that Moriarty Quick might have more'n his share to do with that black-magic malarkey makes no nevermind to me. I feel *good*.

I'm twenty yards up the street before I tumble to what were nagging me.

Henry Jekyll's near twenty years gone. Which makes Marcellus Finch quite the youngster, back in the day when he brewed Henry's potion. Now, Finch is white-haired, frail, misplacing his marbles. Practically an old man.

But Quick—the PURVEYOR OF BEAUTY—Quick's skin is smooth. Good teeth, bright yellow hair. Looks twenty-five at worst, even after fourteen hard-bitten years in Van Diemen's Land, which by all accounts is on the far side of the world and the Empire's blackest hell.

Potions, lotions, efficacious pharmaceuticals. The best in town.

Half-circle, circle, cross. Mercury.

Unsettled, I glance back at Quick's window. That pamphlet, wreathed in white lace. BEAUTIFUL FOR EVER.

Hmm.

THE SHIPWRECK OF MY REASON

• • •

I BARELY REACH ELIZA'S HOUSE IN TIME. BECAUSE AS I blunder in the front—I have to, don't I? my cabinet's locked from the inside—when I creep in, muttering to myself like a nut-crazed squirrel, Penny Watt's waiting in Eliza's consulting room.

Shit. I'd forgotten. The murder case, those alibis. Penny the liar. And now Moriarty Quick, with that tell-tale symbol inked into his skin.

"Hello," says she, pleasant-like. "I'm waiting for Dr. Jekyll. Is she available?" Still wearing mourning black, her skin improbably flawless. That twenty-quid enamel? Waist not so tight-laced today, curls neatly pinned. Daytime Penny, fit for public consumption.

Like the Eliza version of me.

"Um. For certain. I'll just fetch her. You, er, wait right there."

Cursing, I duck upstairs to Eliza's study. Her brass pet's still in forlorn pieces on the desk. I grab a paper scrap, scribble a message, stuff it down our bodice where she'll find it. I breathe deeply, relax. Let Eliza out.

She don't come.

I try again. Soften my muscles, ease in a breath . . .

I rub stinging eyes. My head's swirling, dark storm water down a drain. Come, Eliza, don't ignore me now . . .

Nothing.

Quick's potion. Only a sip. Just a whisper on my tongue.

It works.

Perverse sunshine warms my soul. I giggle and whirl, arms outstretched. *It works.* I'm FREE, God rot her, this body is MINE and I can do as I please . . . and I took only a drop! Imagine if I scarfed the *whole thing* . . .

But abruptly, I subside. Jesus up a drainpipe. Not *now.* I need her.

Ain't irony a killer?

Swiftly, I stuff Quick's greasy bottle under the sofa cushions and fumble in her bag for Finch's sugar-pink poison. Eddie's Patented Calm Juice, eh? How'd that work for you, Marcellus?

I quaff, nearly draining it in haste. Unbearable chilly sweetness, obliterating the gritty oil of Quick's hellbrew. The stuff splashes into my stomach, a starburst of cold *sick,* and too late it occurs to me that we never asked Finch what this gear actually *did* to Eddie.

My guts thrash like salted snakes, and Eliza stirs. Yes. Come, girl. No danger here. I breathe, wriggle, stretch . . .

Spoinngg! Eliza gasped, fighting misshapen lungs. Her skin stung, overstretched, and her scalp tingled with newly blond hair shrinking tight. A horrid oily taste coated her throat. She felt as if she'd been dragged headfirst through a laundry mangle.

She fumbled for her spare spectacles, fastened her loosened buttons . . . and paper crackled under her fingertips. She pulled it from her bodice, smearing fresh ink.

Lizzie's handwriting, stark and black. *QUICK*, it said, and a symbol. Half-circle, circle, cross.

Mercury.

Dizzy images floated. Saffron curtains, frothing lace, a fine crimson-dripped slice. BEAUTIFUL FOR EVER. What deal had Lizzie done with Moriarty Quick?

Baffled, Eliza pocketed the note and hurried down to her consulting room. "Miss Watt, so pleased you dropped by."

Heartily, the girl shook her hand. "Please, it's Penny. May I call you Eliza?"

"Of course. Tea?" she offered belatedly, noticing Mrs. Poole hovering meaningfully in the doorway. "I'm afraid I've nothing stronger."

"Tea would be lovely." Penny arranged her skirts as Mrs. Poole poured. A pair of corkscrew curls hung starkly against her ultra-pale cheeks, and a stiff jet choker forced her chin high. A doll, pretty and pliable, but her eyes were puffy from weeping. "Did you hear the dreadful news about Carmine? I'm beside myself. If I'd only done the decent thing and taken the poor boy home that night, he might still be alive."

As Mrs. Poole exited, Eliza played with her cup, wishing for Harley Griffin's talent for detecting lies. Penny's distress *sounded* genuine. "Do you mind if I ask . . ."

"Not at all. One must face these things head-on." Penny sipped delicately. "Do I know anyone who'd want Carmine dead? Dozens, darling. We're all frightfully jealous. Including me, sadly. I'd give anything for a fraction of his talent."

Eliza's indignation flared. The man was a common thief. "Was Mr. Lightwood jealous, too?"

"Especially Sherry. Are you establishing alibis? How exciting." Penny's gaze shone. "That evening, I visited Soho again. More gruesome all-night debauchery, I'm afraid. Sheridan, too. I suppose it pleases the little monster to sneer at me."

Liar! Lizzie's yell echoed from afar. *I seen Sherry that night at the Rising Sun. But* she *weren't there.*

"Well, that's strange," countered Eliza, "because I've since heard a different story about what happened at Sir Dalziel's the night he died."

Penny laughed. "From whom, pray? They must be lying."

"Did you really leave before two?"

"Of course."

"Wasn't something other than dinner happening?"

"I'm sure I don't—"

"Carmine didn't paint *Eve and the Serpent,* did he?" Change-of-subject ambush, Lafayette style.

Tea splashed Penny's hand. "What? Nonsense. You must be mistaken."

"No. I happen to know the true artist. Carmine stole *Eve* and passed her off as his own."

"You don't say." Penny's face greened. Eliza had envied her brash confidence. But she didn't look confident now. Just scared and vulnerable.

Firmly, Eliza crushed her sympathy. This was no time to go easy. "Oh, I do say, Miss Watt. Hard to believe his closest friends knew nothing. I daresay the police will be interested in your version of the story. Or would you prefer to tell me?"

Penny set her tea aside, saucer rattling. "After Dalziel was

killed, we suspected what had happened, but I was afraid. I
didn't know what to do! But now Carmine's dead, too." Her
eyes shimmered. "We should have spoken up. It's all my fault."

"You can't blame yourself." *Yes, you should.* The uncharita-
ble thought splattered like blood. Just like Lizzie, acting up
and crying about it later. What had Penny expected? Actions
had consequences, even for celebrated art models and society
butterflies. "Tell me everything, and maybe we can fix this."

Penny cleared her throat. "I'm afraid we've been dishonest
with you. Sheridan and I, that is. That night, after Dalziel's
party . . . we were together. A scandalous liaison. It went
badly for him, and he's frightfully vain. I . . . I didn't want to
tell anyone. So we lied about where we were. But Dalziel was
alive when we left the party." She shuddered. "I can only de-
duce what happened, but . . ."

Eliza recalled her suspicion that Carmine had hidden his
true whereabouts. She'd picked the wrong liar. "Tell me about
the coven meetings," she prompted. "We found letters suggesting that Carmine and Sir Dalziel were threatening to expose
someone they called the 'master,' for practicing black magic."

"Then they were fools. He always knows everything."

Eliza leaned forwards. "Who? The culprit won't go unpun-
ished. You have my word."

Penny toyed with her choker. "The *séances* were fun, the
first few times. Incantations, sex magic, pretending to raise
the spirits of the dead. A change from dry political talk. And
you needed a secret invitation to get in. All very cloak-and-
dagger. But it was only in fun. There was absinthe, opium,
arsenic. All manner of debauchery."

"So the magic wasn't real?"

"I didn't say that. Crazy old Dalziel was convinced he'd made a pact with a devil he called 'the gray man.' He claimed he sketched for this gray man, and in return the gray man gave him eternal life."

Nutty as a fruitcake, Brigham had said. *He thought he'd live forever.* Uneasily, Eliza recalled the Philosopher's ageless eyes and translucent skin, all his vitality drained. A living husk. What had Sir Isaac sacrificed for his immortality? "The gray man? Did he mean this Dr. Silberman?"

Penny hesitated. "Have you ever experienced mesmerism?"

Eliza winced. She preferred to keep an open mind. Once she'd attended one of those popular entertainments where people spoke in garbled tongues or flapped their arms like a chicken's wings, supposedly under a hypnotist's influence. Oddly, she'd remained unaffected. The Royal Society insisted mind control was rubbish. For once, she agreed. "I don't believe it has scientific basis."

"That's what I thought. But I tell you, I *saw* those 'demons' he pretended to conjure. I was drawn in utterly. Mass hypnotism is very real, Doctor. Eagerly, I agreed to everything he wanted. You can imagine the sort of thing. Disgusting."

"Who?"

"The master. The man with the tattoo. His power is terrifying. Everyone becomes his slave."

"You mean Silberman?"

Penny shivered, nodding. "That isn't his real name. Sheridan and I sneaked a look at his things once. I found a card."

"Yes?" Eliza held her breath. In her pocket, Lizzie's note rustled, ominous. Quick. Mercury. Quicksilver. And the German word for "silver" was . . .

Scritch-scratch! Something rubbed against the door.

Abruptly, Penny shrank back into her seat. Frustrated, Eliza jumped up and flung open the door. "What?"

At her feet, a pile of blue skirts cursed, and from it scrambled a young lady, her plum-red lips pursed in an expression of chagrin. Not remorse. Just disappointment she'd been caught.

It was the girl Hipp had knocked over in Finch's shop. Who'd ridden a velocipede past Eliza's house yesterday afternoon, almost knocking Eliza over in turn. Same blue velvet dress, round face, pretty brown eyes.

Swiftly, Eliza leveled her stinger. "Who are you? How did you get in? Answer, or I'll have you arrested."

"I'm sorry," said the intruder. "I can explain . . ."

"Miss Burton, there you are!" Mrs. Poole bustled into the hall. "Oh, have you two finally met? About time."

The girl bobbed a defiant curtsy. Miss Burton. Her boarder. Eliza spluttered. "How dare you eavesdrop on my private conversations?"

"I say," put in Penny, emerging from the consulting room, "how frightfully droll. Do carry on, ladies."

"Humph." Mrs. Poole folded indignant arms. "Spy, is it? We'll have you out on the street, you little ingrate. I've a mind to report you to the police."

"I wouldn't recommend that." Miss Burton held out a polished iron badge, engraved with the words NULLIUS IN VERBA.

A Royal Society agent.

Flee, Eliza's muscles hissed urgently. *The game's up. Run!* Delusions of persy-cootion, indeed. She'd been right all along.

But guilty waters swirled over her head. She'd invited the spy into her *house*. Asked no questions. What a fool she'd been. "Are you spying for Lady Lovelace? Did you put that listening device in my pet, you brazen jade?"

Miss Burton slipped her badge away. "A spy, as you say, but I didn't touch your pet. And I don't work for Lady Lovelace."

"Then who . . . ?" Eliza's voice withered. "Oh, my. He sent you to watch me, didn't he?"

"As I said, I can explain—"

"He put you in my *house*. And all the time, I . . . Heavens, I must be the daftest woman in London . . ."

Crack!

She recoiled, flailing. What now?

The front door's mail slot snapped, dropping a tri-folded letter at her feet. A crimson seal winked up at her, the imprint of a tiny rose.

Breathless, she feigned disinterest. "Well, this is a fine snake pit of deception, isn't it? Miss Burton, you'll leave my house the minute you've somewhere fit to go. Miss Watt, thank you for your information. I'll follow up in due course. Might I see you out?"

The moment she was alone, she tore the letter open. Mr. Todd's handwriting looked bolder, messier. As if he'd written in a frenzy.

> My princess,
>
> It's so piquant to write to you, knowing you have read my letters and misunderstand me so utterly,

it hurts. Your reply opened my eyes. Some days,
I see more clearly, and I know now that I see
what you are to me in shifting shades.

Yes—I'm laughing as I write this!—it's true.
Something wonderful has happened to me—to <u>us</u>?
I no longer know the word. Was it in that frightful
asylum, those wires stabbing hellfire into my skull,
all those hours spent screaming into the dark? I
only know that I'm no longer myself. Or am I
myself at last? Ha ha!

As for your offer of distraction and solace, I'm
afraid it won't do. The world must be put in order.
It's merely a matter of <u>time</u>. Oh! I can barely
contain my excitement. You and I will be special
together, Eliza. I crave that so deeply. If you saw
how I imagine us—well, you'd blush. I know I do.

So, shall we begin? I left you a gift, at that
desperately somber establishment you visited
yesterday. As you know, I can't abide rudeness.
Messy, I'm afraid, but I'm out of practice.

I hope you enjoy it.

I did.

> Your eager slave,
> Odysseus Sharp

P.S. That thieving Italian deserved to die. Pity
someone got there before me. Ha ha! Did you see
Eve, my princess? She has your face. But are you
the lady, or the serpent?

Chilled, she dropped the letter. It bore no stamp. Hand-delivered. Had he visited in broad daylight? *A gift. At that establishment you visited yesterday . . .*

All the air sucked from her chest, and she grabbed her skirts and ran.

She sprinted all the way, stumbling over gutters and in front of speeding carriages, shoving aside startled pedestrians. On Tottenham Court Road, a crossing sweeper cursed at her, kicking scattered horse dung. She dodged, nearly upsetting a clockwork valet, who clacked and screeched, "Stop! Thief!"

At last, she skidded to a halt at Hare's Funerals.

Bloody sunset splashed the dusty shop windows. A small crowd jostled and muttered. "Down in front!" "God spare us, I've never seen anything like . . ." Eliza shoved to the front, fighting for breath.

A police constable with mutton-chop whiskers stood on duty, silver buttons brightly polished on his long dark blue coat. "Sorry, madam. Shop's closed. Police business."

Frantic, she teetered on tiptoe, trying to see, but the black drapes were drawn. "What's happened? Is everyone all right?"

But she knew. That rude clerk had *handled* her. Made ill-mannered remarks about women in unsuitable professions. Certainly hadn't treated her like a lady.

Her head whirled like Mr. Hyde's carousel, sickening her. Her knees buckled, and she gripped the constable's shoulder. *Oh, God . . .*

He steadied her. "Move along, madam. Nothing to see."

She trailed away listlessly. Dusk had crept in, and a man with a tall matchlock lit glass-boxed gaslights atop wrought-iron posts, *pop! pop!*

Mr. Todd had killed the clerk. Slashed his throat, drained his life. She knew it, the way she knew two and two equaled four.

But as she slowly headed for home along Great Russell Street, dodging commuters and rattling carts, her heart protested, a swift bitter ache. Todd wrote strange letters, but always poetic. Brimming with romance and wide-eyed wonder.

This latest one was wild. Scribbled in a fever.

Eerie giggles burst out. A bewildered gentleman tipped his hat, and Eliza only laughed more. A fever of what? Lunacy? Todd was *mad*. She'd gambled, and she'd lost. She dreaded the next morning's paper, the headlines. *Messy, I'm afraid . . .*

"No point wailing about it now," retorted Lizzie, slinging her arm around Eliza's shoulder. "The greasy lecher had it coming. But what are we gunna do about it? And who'll be next? That's the question."

Eliza shoved her away. "Have you no compassion? That man likely had a family who depended on him."

Lizzie tweaked Eliza's nose. "None too bright, are you? Don't you see what it means? Todd's following us about! Prob'ly lurking in the shadows right now with a hard-on, sniggering at us."

Eliza whirled, heart racing. Was that a footstep? A snatch of dark laughter?

No one. Just the usual domestic comings and goings.

She walked on, a guilty itch in her veins. Her boots drummed accusations on the muddy sidewalk. *It's my fault. My fault. My fault.* People upset and insulted her every day. If all were in danger . . .

Her guts watered. What if Todd had watched her kiss Remy Lafayette?

"Oho," crowed Lizzie, "now we're getting to it!"

Stubbornly, Eliza shook her head. "Todd must protect his new identity. He wouldn't attack people connected with his old life. Besides, he's been free for weeks. What's he waiting for?"

"Your bloody letter, that's what." Lizzie swung upside down from a lamppost, flashing her scarlet garters. "Acting up for your attention, ain't he? He's off his rocker. You won't never find no sense in it."

Eliza shuddered, disturbed. Cocky, handsome Captain Lafayette, who irritated other gentlemen merely by existing. Todd had nicknamed him "lapdog." Few managed the last word in conversation with Remy. Hostility had bristled between them from the moment they'd met at Bethlem.

Then again, indirectly, Lafayette had helped Todd escape. A favor for a favor?

Despairing, she halted, where the British Museum's lofty columns smothered her in thick reddish shadows, and rubbed her aching eyes. What to do? She'd no time for this. Already she'd one crafty killer to apprehend. And lest she forget, Lafayette had planted a *spy* in her house. He wasn't the friend he'd pretended to be.

Should she act as if nothing had happened? Write to thank Todd for his gift? Scold him, she was most displeased and would he mind terribly not doing this again?

Inevitability clanged, an executioner's death bell in her bones. She'd swum far out of her depth. Time she abandoned her squeamish half-measures. Either adopt the courage of her convictions, and *treat* the man, or turn him in to the police . . .

"Are you even listening?" Lizzie prodded Eliza in the chest. "It's too late. We need to get Todd before he gets *us*. Let's kill him and be done."

"Don't be ridiculous. We're not murderers. We don't take justice into our own hands . . . Wait." Her nose twitched, and spidery feet clattered up her spine. "What's that?"

Lizzie frowned. "D'you smell smoke?"

Eliza shoved her way out into Oxford Street, dodging drunks and night carts and hurtling velocipedes. A coach and pair swerved around her, their liveried driver cursing. In the midst of noisy traffic, she searched the cloud-streaked sky.

The moon lurked below the horizon, splashing leaden rain clouds with silver. But a malicious red stain flushed the horizon. The gritty air rang with shouts and distant gunfire. Acrid ash coated her tongue, and above rooftops and chimney pots, beyond the pointed silhouette of St. Giles's steeple, an evil smoky specter clawed the sky.

Seven Dials was burning.

Lizzie wailed, and gripped Eliza's throat with invisible hands, and with an excruciating *crack!* of bone and sinew, she *changed*.

ULTIMA RATIO REGUM

..

BY THE TIME I GET THERE, GREAT EARL STREET IS full of Enforcers.

Dozens of 'em, brass limbs and white masks reflecting the growling flames . . . but flesh glistens, too, grafted with wire and rivets, sweat-slick and mottled with impending decay. Bloodshot eyeballs, human limbs with bolted steel joints, half a face stretched over an angular metal skull.

The new models, part man, part machine. They think quicker, move faster . . . but they're all under the command of one massive full-brass monster, all machine and no remorse. And behind it, strutting to and fro with gunmetal skirts gleaming, is Lady Lovelace. She surveys the carnage, thin lips eagerly parting . . . and damn it if she don't fix that filthy red eye on me, and *smile*.

Zzzap! Zzzop! The Enforcers fire electric pistols, arc-flash blinding blue. People fall. Charcoal dust clogs the air. Smoke billows from the bonfire that once were the brewery, amidst broken iron struts and crumbled brick and the thundery stink of aether.

This is what you get for defying the Philosopher. I want to claw my eyes, scream at Eddie till my lungs bleed raw that I told him so . . . but I want to scream with laughter, too. This fight's been coming a long time.

At the seven-way crossroads, a wailing gaggle of *weird* folk drags an Enforcer to its knees. It takes ten of 'em, but they rip the pistol from its hand and shoot it in the face. *Crrack!* Blue lightning explodes down its brass frame into the earth.

It don't scream. Ain't designed to make sound. The stretched skin of its face melts and bubbles, exposing cogs and a glinting quartz crystal. A whistle crescendos, and *boom!*, the thing explodes, taking five or six blokes with it. Brass splinters and fleshy gobbets fly . . . and beyond lurks the tall silhouette of a man in uniform.

Dusted in ash, sword and pistol drawn. He's got more brass machines with him, little four-legged ones running in a pack like hounds. They're herding folks away from the fire, making them wail and holler and scarper into the dark.

"Remy!" I stagger up, panting, for I'm wearing Eliza's dress and I can't breathe right.

He wipes his smudged face with a forearm. "Lizzie, go home. This will only get messier."

Across the way, Lady Lovelace orders a fresh barrage of Enforcers into the fray. Folk scream and scuttle every which way. I grab Remy's red-coated arm. I can smell him, gunpowder and steel and dark wolfish fever. "She can't just burn everything. Stop her!"

"I can't," he yells, over the thunder of a building falling in the next street. His pack of brass dogs scatter and wheel.

"This is what I do, Lizzie. I play the Royal's games. I save whom I can."

"But not us." My throat squeezes tight. We always knew his loyalty's divided, forced down a forked path by the monster inside him. He ain't never made it no secret. And his best intentions don't hide the fact that he's our enemy.

He's everyone's enemy.

Fatigue bruises Remy's eyes. Sweat slicks his face, drenches his dirty hair. His exhaustion glows, that wolfish fever eating him from inside. Tomorrow's full moon's already dragging him under. "I can't defy her openly. If she finds out about me . . ."

My body burns. I want to scratch bloody ruts into his skin and sign my name.

But I can't. Because I know what he means. And the fear lurking in his raw blue gaze slashes at my heart.

If Lady Lovelace finds out about *him* . . . why, then she'll find out about *us,* too.

Remy knows the Royal's dungeons better than most. He knows what they'll do to him to make him betray his precious Eliza. And he knows he can't withstand it. No one can.

This—the carnage, the bonfires, the screams that rip the sky ragged—this is how far he'll go to protect her.

"Would you do it for me?" My voice is hoarse with smoky dread. "If it were only me, would you . . ."

Remy pushes knotted hair from my eyes, with the hand holding his pistol. Hot metal stings my cheek, exquisite, so wishful I ache. "Go home, Lizzie," says he, and leans in to kiss my forehead.

Before he can land it—before my fickle woman's heart can forgive him for loving her and not me—I turn and run.

Across Great Earl Street, the Cockatrice is burning. Flame licks up the walls, the windowsills, the eaves. Heat blows my hair back. The brick wall next door crumbles, crushing part of the pub's roof . . . and whoever were standing beneath it.

I charge, leaving Remy and his brutal world behind.

The riot's impenetrable, thrashing elbows and punching fists. Rocks fly, old-fashioned iron bullets sing. An electric pistol crackles next to my ear, standing my hair on end. Burning yeast clogs my lungs, my bladder aches, I need to piss . . . *Doinng!* Something pointy clocks me in the temple, but there ain't no room to fall. The staring fellow squashing my shoulder is dead, neck broken, body held upright by the crush.

At last, still reeling, I reach the flame-stuffed door. That grinning figurehead's just a charred lump. I shield my eyes, but the heat drives me back. "Johnny, for God's sake . . ."

Long fingers wrap my elbow. "Lizzie. Here."

Dizzy, I fall into his arms. He smells so good, sweetness and light, and my bruised heart aches. For all I mistreat him, I'd miss the fairy-arse tosser like breathing. "Bugger me dead," I pant, "thought you was . . ."

"And leave you for all them other unworthy rapscallions? Never." Johnny's all sooty, his strawberry coat singed, but still pretty as they come. "Jesus, what the hell are you wearing?"

I shove him. "You can bloody talk."

"Arseholes burned down my pub," he adds, as if I might've missed it. "Right bollocksed up my drinking time, and all."

Three-Tot Polly and Strangeface Willy hold hands, coughing. Willy's cabbage head is bruised, his claret-colored coat burned ragged. At their feet, that little legless bloke has peeked up his last skirt. He sprawls flat on his trolley, limp fingers begging.

Weeping Jacky Spring-Heels is bounding about in his dirty unmentionables, flailing skinny elbows like a grasshopper gone mad. Johnny shushes him with an absent cuddle. "Peace, Jacky. Hush, now."

Jacky moans, raking his snot-plastered hair, and I want to moan along with him. Fetch water . . . but from where? No point, with the roof on fire and flames roaring from the upstairs windows.

Guilt stabs me. I could've stopped this. Should've tried harder to convince Eddie to hear the Philosopher's bargain. Would've . . . but secretly, part of me *wanted* this fight. And why? For no better reason than to laugh at others' misery.

Funny thing is—and who knew?—it ain't all about *me*.

Johnny's staring at the hellfire ruins of his flash house, perplexed. Folks is dead, everything he's got is burning. Still, he raises a smile for me, and it lights his wonky face like starshine. Screw me raw, but I want to beg his forgiveness, promise now and forever that his precious heart is safe with me.

Somewhere, my selfish soul howls like a banshee at the injustice. *It ain't fair. He ain't my problem. I never asked him to love me.*

But I've made him my problem, with my careless games. He's my responsibility, sure as Todd is Eliza's. I've always scoffed at her wanting to *help* that red-haired loon, but if I thought a compulsive throat-slitter were my fault—if I knew it, the way I know Becky's murder is on me—would I just wander off and forget it?

Or would I try to fix it, no matter how hopeless it seemed?

I swallow, fearful. "Listen. About Becky . . ."

Whooping laughter cuts me off. Eddie Hyde, clambering atop a pile of smoking rubble. Hat missing, half his coat burned. An Enforcer's pistol's alight in each hand, and he's shooting at anything that shimmers. *Blam!* He fires at Lady Lovelace. Misses, apparently, because he curses and fires again with t'other hand. "Die, you blackguards! Burn the Enforcers! Rip their stinking brass legs off!"

His wild stormlight gaze settles on me. "Lizzie, how do?" he cries. "Come give your papa a kiss. Ha ha ha!" And now what he's yelling don't make no sense. Not a foreign tongue. Just gibberish.

Part of me aches to be up there with him, set fire to my enemies, burn this ugly world to ash . . . but at the sight of him prancing and hooting, no better than one of Eliza's witless patients in Bethlem, my guts curdle. Like Finch said: he ain't two people no more. He's only Eddie, the bad half of a once good man. Finch's frosty pink poison? It ain't curing him.

And it won't cure me.

If I suppress Eliza, will my brains rot, too? Will I lose my reason and end in some shit-stinking asylum, eating lice from my hair and imagining I'm the Queen?

Johnny cocks a brace of gunpowder pistols, and offers one to me. "To hell with it. Already drunk all the good gin anyways."

The pistol grip's warmth is bitter comfort. Finality settles over me, a weighty cloak of doom. I ain't a praying girl—never thought much of them what blames their problems on others—but I whispers one now. *Don't let me rot inside like Hyde. Let me die first. Amen.*

Distant thunder rumbles, and I flash Johnny a reckless grin. "Well, I never. You and me, dying dressed and sober. Who'da thunk?"

"My darlin', the night is but young." Johnny plants a kiss on me, fierce and breathless—because Johnny *sees* me, bless his fairy arse, and maybe now, I see him, too—and we sprint howling into the fight.

ULTRA VIRES

• • •

CERTAINLY NOT. HAVE YOU BOTH LOST YOUR WITS?" snapped Chief Inspector Reeve the next afternoon, in his cramped office at Scotland Yard, where weak sunlight dribbled in the high, soaped window. Letters and scribbled notes piled his desk, and stacks of boxed files teetered. Evidently, Reeve wasn't much for paperwork.

From the chair beside her, Captain Lafayette shot Eliza a "what-did-you-expect?" glance. A vicious headache thinned her patience. She'd had no sleep, and she hurt all over, as if she'd run twenty miles last night. Likely, she had. Overnight rain had reduced the fires in Seven Dials to smoldering black ruins, for the most part, but the city's scars would take a long time to heal. She'd come to, abruptly, staggering on her feet in some noisome alley, her dress smeared with blood and gunpowder. Her hair still smelled of smoke and uncanny sweetness.

She'd hurried to Quick's parlor on Piccadilly, intending to confront him with Penny Watt's tale . . . only to find the place much changed. Customers milling, the staff of polite young ladies administering lotions and beauty treatments, selling tonics and hair cream. The proprietor, one exotically made-up

Madame Rachel, had arched manicured brows in perfect bewilderment when Eliza asked for Moriarty Quick.

Round one to him. Perhaps he wasn't even real. She'd imagined his very existence, a drug-addled dream.

But when she'd returned home, hoping for a hot meal and a bath while she agonized over what to do next, she'd found a gilt-edged card dropped through the mail slot onto the hall floor.

Nothing printed on it. Just a scribbled signature and an address:

Silberman, M.D.
Le Caveau des Oubliettes, Covent Garden

A secret invitation. The implications—that dark, twisted lettering—made her shiver. Had Penny Watt left it? She didn't know. But unless she wanted to wait for Quick's bailiffs to toss her in the compter until she could miraculously conjure fifty-six pounds, it was her only lead.

"As I said," she began again, showing Reeve the card, "I believe 'Dr. Silberman' is the alias for a confirmed villain and transported felon named Moriarty Quick. I've a witness who'll testify—"

"I don't care if she testifies he's Attila the Hun." Reeve rocked back in his chair, chewing a fresh cigar. Same ugly brown suit, shirt creased and collar stained. Perhaps he was sleeping in his office to avoid his overbearing wife. "This magic business is rubbish. A ritual killer? It's a burglar, I tell you, who's not right in the head. This Watt floozy is just crying wolf."

Lafayette gave an ironic smile. "Miss Watt did describe illicit suggestions made under the influence of drugs. That's attempted indecent assault at the very least. Worth a few questions, isn't it?"

Reeve snorted. "More likely this Quick fellow bedded her, and she wants revenge. Maybe in your ivory tower, Royal Society, you've time to listen to wild tales of ravishment from witless chits too drunk to realize they were being duped by the oldest parlor trick in London. Spirits of the dead, indeed. At the Yard, we've real police work to do." Pointedly, he returned to his letter-writing. "I forbid it. Now clear off, I'm busy."

Eliza gritted her teeth, only thankful that Lizzie wasn't jumping out to throttle him. Fine. She'd investigate without permission, then.

She rose, Lafayette with her. "Thank you for your time."

"Not a bit. Oh," Reeve added, snatching the gilded invitation, "I'll take that. In case you take it into your head to pretend this meeting didn't happen."

"But that's mine," she protested. "I'll never . . ."

"Never get in without it?" Reeve grinned. "Last I looked, missy, you worked for me. Don't think I won't nick you for disobeying orders. What's more, I'll have you struck from the register of physicians for malpractice, and you'll never work a day in this town again. Clear?"

"Crystalline," she snapped. "*So* glad I tried to help. Good day, sir." She stalked out, and halted on the landing. "Oh, I almost forgot. Hippocrates? Fetch, there's a good boy."

Hipp dashed back into Reeve's office. *Clunk! Clatter!* "Oi!" roared Reeve. "Give that back!" *Zzap!* Hipp's electric coil flashed. "Aargh! You little brass bastard, I'll rip your springs out."

"Oi!" taunted Hipp, and galloped after Eliza, the invitation spiked on one brass forefoot.

"Thank you, Hipp." Eliza snatched the card and swept downstairs, a swirl of gray skirts and temper. She didn't check to see if Lafayette followed.

Outside in Whitehall, War Office errand boys ran in and out of Horse Guards bearing document cases and dispatches. Hippocrates gamboled happily in the warm sun, snuffling at horses' hooves and the brassy feet of clockwork servants. She'd reassembled him, *sans* that parasitic surveillance device, and immediately his behavior had improved.

She yanked angry skirts, hard enough to pop a stitch. A pity Reeve couldn't be *improved* so easily. Above the Horse Guards archway frowned a stern clock face, with a black splotch marking a quarter past two, the hour when, two centuries gone, Parliament had executed its own willfully incompetent king out of sheer exasperation. She sympathized.

Lafayette matched her stride, resplendent in the sun. "Did you expect better?"

"No, but being right doesn't make me happy." The sunshine didn't cheer her up. It only made her head throb harder, and for once, she wished she carried a parasol. Her right hand ached, too, the dim legacy of clutching a pistol. Lizzie's exertions were bleeding over into Eliza's body.

On the corner, an ink-stained paper-seller yelled, in competition with a ballad-singer and a turbaned Sikh plucking a sitar. "Bodies pile up in St. Giles! French spies arrested! Fire still smoldering!"

"French spies, indeed," muttered Eliza. As if the Royal hadn't been responsible. She didn't dare ask Lafayette how *his* evening had ended. "Thank you for backing me up, Captain," she added, an afterthought. "You needn't have gone out of your way."

"I take it you're planning to attend Le Caveau des Oubliettes in spite of Reeve?"

Triumphantly, she waved the purloined invitation.

"I wish you wouldn't. Quick already has it in for you, and a man who calls his place of business 'the dungeon vault' doesn't strike me as easily reasoned with. If he truly has slaughtered two men for threatening him, do you imagine him thinking twice about hurting you?"

"Captain, I'm surprised at you. They told me you were some kind of outrageously daring war hero."

"Flattered, I'm sure, but one thing I've learned from a dozen bungled campaigns is that there's nothing wrong with a tactical retreat." Lafayette fiddled with his cuff, uncharacteristically hesitant. Good lord, was that a *fidget*? "And you know I can't come. Not tonight."

She flushed, mortified. The full moon. His *cage*. In her obsession with the case, and Quick, and Todd, she'd half forgotten. "But how can I *not* investigate, when I know he's guilty? What if someone else was party to the blackmail, and he kills them, too, while I prevaricate? It's a matter of justice. I'll just have to go by myself."

Aye, said Lizzie sarcastically. *Same reason you refuse to turn in that crack-brained redhead. All about justice, you.*

Lafayette sidled past a tiny boy pulling a cartload of unskinned rabbits. "Is that wise? Reeve isn't making empty threats, you know. He'll have you struck off if he finds out. Is this really worth your career?"

"Pish. I'm not afraid of Reeve."

"And as ever, my admiration for your energy undoes me. But might not a moment of pause be a survival strategy?"

Hot flushes swamped her, making her sweat and shiver, a sweetberry quagmire of conflicting suspicions. "Indeed it might," she snapped. "Like burning Seven Dials in lieu of defying your precious overseer?"

Immediately, she regretted it. His chagrined expression punched her in the guts. "Fair enough," he said mildly. "But know this: if Lady Lovelace decides to put me to the question, I won't be the only one in danger."

Flashes of rusty cells beneath the Tower, sparking electrodes, blood oozing into rubber tubes. "I appreciate that, but I can't stop doing my job merely because it inconveniences me. Justice *is* inconvenient. That's the point."

"I'm merely trying to—"

"Protect me? I suppose planting a spy in my house was for my protection, too." Heavens, she'd intended to ask more politely. But his attitude hacked at her nerves, all the more maddening because her upset was perverse. He only wanted to help . . . didn't he?

Not a flicker. "Absolutely."

Her jaw dropped. "You're not even *denying* it. Were you planning to tell me, or just let me bumble on oblivious?"

"You would have said no. I needed to do something. I'm on the trail of some bad people who aren't above hurting you to threaten me." He didn't flinch. Didn't look away. "Miss Burton's more experienced than she looks. Her father is an ex-

plorer. She's braved darkest Arabia since she was twelve. I
need her, to watch over you when I can't."

Eliza's throat parched. Was her indignation unreasonable?
Were his intentions honest? Almost certainly. But it didn't
cure the glitter-ugly ache in her heart. "I respect that you're
trying to help, but do you know how patronizing that sounds?
I can take care of myself, you know. I needn't be minded like
a . . . a child."

Like some weak female, she'd almost said. Her head whirled,
overheating, that familiar sickly sweetness muddling her wits
into a pink mist. She'd thought him different. Special. But if
this was how he truly regarded her . . .

"I don't intend any disrespect." Softly, as if he knew any
answer to be futile.

Her blood boiled, a cocktail of remorse and unnatural
rage. "Don't you? That's all right, then. My mistake. Stop putting me on a pedestal, Remy. We're not married, in case you'd
forgotten. And I'm not your dead wife."

Silence.

Finally, Lafayette sighed, and his abrupt distance shocked
her. Cold, like a stranger. "Forgive me, Doctor. You must do
what you feel is right. It's none of my concern."

Her chest constricted, a warm, salty sickness. Her words
seemed unforgivably selfish and cruel. But she couldn't unsay
them. And before she could apologize—or say something
even more horrible—he bowed, and vanished into the crowd.

Such a little thing, that lost moment. Gone. Maybe forever.

She was being stupid. Unreasonable. Unscientific. All the
things that drove her crazy . . . but she couldn't shed this maddening resentment, as if the world and everyone in it were

against her, and she had to fight back. She barely knew Lafayette. This episode only proved that. Why should she even care . . . no matter that he was . . . just because they'd . . .

Oh, to hell with it.

She stalked away, swallowing a Lizzie-rich curse. The sun peeked between fluffy clouds, and a bird chirped joyfully overhead. She wanted to wring its neck. The bright-natured gleam of passing traffic, the happy hiss of pistons: *everything* infuriated her. Her tongue tingled, a sinister strawberry spritz that murmured sweet chaos . . . and black certainty blotted out the light.

This pink remedy, her elixir, Moriarty Quick's tricks. They were rotting her wits. Tormenting her with the same burning rage that plagued Lizzie . . . and Eddie Hyde. All these ugly chemicals—this unshakable, impossible duality—would be the death of her.

But the alternative—to cease her medication altogether—was just as unthinkable.

Eagerly, Hippocrates flung himself at her skirts. "Doctor! Doctor! Doc-doc-doc . . ."

"Will you shut *up*?" She shoved him, hard.

Clunk! Hipp bounced onto his head on the cobbles, brassy feet waving like an upturned beetle's. "Sorry," he yammered. "Does not compute. Sorry . . ."

"Oh, Hipp." Remorseful, she dusted him off, setting him on his feet. "I didn't mean it. Forgive me."

But he just cowered, making himself small and blinking his red *unhappy* light.

Her mood blackened. Had she made a terrible mistake? Truth was, she'd very few friends she could trust. A pang of dread stung her bones. Lafayette had trusted *her*. Let her into his solitary refuge. Asked for her help, though she'd been too stubborn to admit it. Tonight, he'd be at his most vulnerable. And she'd rejected him, precisely when he needed her most . . .

But her rebellious suspicions rattled, a clockwork with a broken cog. Lafayette had *spied* on her. In her own *house,* for heaven's sake. How could she meekly accept that? All he'd needed to do was ask first. Was she some frail creature, the weaker sex, to have such decisions made for her by a man?

"For sure." Lizzie stalked beside her again, relentless. "Ain't scared you might like it, or nothing."

"Shut up," snapped Eliza. "I'm perfectly capable of investigating this ominous Caveau des Oubliettes on my own. I don't need anyone's help, least of all Captain Lafayette's. And certainly not yours."

Determined, she marched towards the snarl of carts and carriages clogging Charing Cross, Hipp trotting resentfully at her heels. The fact that she *wanted* Lafayette's help—that she *liked* him, as if that were relevant to anything—was all the more reason to refuse.

LE CAVEAU DES OUBLIETTES

．••．

AT FRAGRANT SUMMER'S DUSK, ELIZA EMERGED from the coal-stained Electric Underground into Covent Garden. The cobbled flower market bustled with basket-clutching servants, ladies perusing freesias and roses, gardeners unloading wooden carts heaped with blooms. Soon the moon would rise, but for now, sunset reigned, and above rooftops and smoke-stacks, the sky was painted a glorious shade of purplish red. *A cherry, or a double-white vermilion?* Mr. Todd would know the color.

Clutching her invitation, Eliza pushed her way through theater-goers and shoppers, match-sellers and pickpockets. Arc-lights crackled purplish glitter over coiffured ladies twirling lacy parasols, gentlemen in tailored coats dipping freshly brushed opera hats. Acrobats flipped, their ribboned hair tumbling, and a stilt-walker dressed as a Green Man teetered above, soft foliage dangling from his costume. Cigar smoke and perfume enriched the air, and somewhere, a fiddler pedaling a unicycle belted out a merry three-step tune.

The humidity made her sweat, but she didn't dare shrug off her mantle. Lizzie nestled in Eliza's chest, fighting her for breath, an oyster stuffed into an under-sized shell. Furtively, Eliza fiddled with the laces behind her back. Lizzie's dress felt strange, conspicuous, a cherry velvet creation with ruffled skirts. She'd figured the class of people who attended these gatherings wouldn't wear drab colors, and besides, she didn't want Quick recognizing her easily from afar.

She'd examined her reflection in her bedroom mirror with trepidation and excitement. Her pale hair had glistened golden, her skin imbued with a strange glow. Her black hat was tilted to dip a veil over her bespectacled eyes. She looked . . . bold. Provocative. Would Remy like it? she wondered. Would Mr. Todd?

You still walk like a prissy schoolmarm, muttered Lizzie as Eliza searched for the correct address amongst shops and theaters. *A trussed-up ham, that's what you look like.*

"Helpful as ever . . . ah, here we are." Eliza approached a little annex attached to a stately brick dwelling. Its windows glinted in the sultry sunset, drapes drawn. The big black door with its silver knocker loomed, forbidding. A plaque on the lintel proclaimed it to be PRIVATE.

Nervously, she gripped her reticule. Inside nestled her stinger, fully charged, next to a phial of pink remedy and other medicinal odds and sods. She'd even brought elixir, lest she need in a hurry to *change.* She'd come prepared, even if she'd been forced to come alone.

Hipp had protested, but she'd left him behind, and without him, she felt oddly naked and unprotected. She spared a thought for Captain Lafayette, surely by now readying himself for a torrid night of confusion and chaos. Flesh shuddering, twisting . . . *changing.* She shivered. That awful cage . . .

But she'd her own problems now. Steeling herself, she knocked.

The door edged ajar. No greeting. Just a narrow black challenge.

She offered the signed invitation. An unseen hand snatched it, and after a moment, the door creaked open.

Inside, darkness smothered her. The door clunked shut, stranding her in utter blackness, with a dizzying scent like overripe wine . . . and then a candle flared, revealing dark green drapes and polished floors. That unseen someone thrust a white lorgnette mask in her hand.

She peered through the carven eyeholes. The person was gone. The place seemed deserted, just twin rows of candles beckoning her down a velvet-draped corridor.

Already, her head swam in heat-shimmered perfume. Her vision's edges smeared, telescoping, and from beyond, snag-toothed devils whispered to her, promising delights both exquisite and frightful. Breath seducing her skin, multiple mouths in her hair, unseen drums throbbing, louder, faster . . .

She staggered, unbalanced. Candles flickered, laughing at her. She felt drunk, irresponsible. Wild, to go with Lizzie's spectacular dress. A slow smile parted her lips. Do your worst, Moriarty Quick. If any black magic lurked here, she'd definitely give it a try . . .

Her heartbeat throbbed, a sluggish warning. *The air's drugged, you idiot!* hissed Lizzie. *Poisoned! This place is a fakement. Get the hell out of here!*

"Eh?" Sleepily, Eliza pawed inside her reticule, fighting the temptation to inhale further. Elixir, warm. Pink remedy, frigid . . . At last, her fingers closed around a tiny glass phial.

Mr. Finch's invisible prophylactic against poison gas.

She thumbed the cork away—a tiny *hfff!* like a spectral laugh—and tipped the phial onto the inside of her mask . . . and just in time remembered that Finch had drained the substance *upwards*. Lighter than air. Fumbling, she swapped positions of mask and bottle, hoping she hadn't already wasted it.

She replaced the mask over her face, and inhaled, a faint scent of oranges. Another breath, and her fuzzy vision began to clear. *Doubles as a hangover cure and kills ants!* She stifled crazy laughter. She'd have to tell Finch his pet project worked . . . But for now—thanks to Lizzie's presence of mind, not her own—she was forearmed.

She crept further into warm dark. Shadows shifted, voices murmured. Red-gold firelight flared, and she headed towards it.

A vast room yawned, dizzily endless . . . but now that she'd sobered, she could make out dusty carpets, rotted red drapes, a once-ornate plaster ceiling with crumbling painted lunettes. A dingy theater, with a cracked wooden stage and tiered galleries . . . and a crowded audience of richly dressed gentlemen and ladies, all wearing the same white masks.

They luxuriated on moth-eaten couches, all in various states of undress. Discarded gloves and stockings littered the filthy carpet. Shirts loosened, corsets unlaced to expose glistening skin.

One plump fellow's face nudged her memory, and with a start she recognized the fat lord from Lady Fleet's entourage at the Exhibition. *Lord Montrose, Sir Wm Thorne* . . . Was this Sir Dalziel's infamous coven, then? All guzzled thick, meaty red wine from cracked goblets smeared with dust. Their mouths and chins were stained purple, the color of rotten berries, and as they drank, they laughed.

In the pit below the stage, a fire roared, and . . . well, darker pastimes than drinking were being indulged. Noises slithered from the depths, moans and grunts, wet slobbers, the rending sound of tearing meat. Eliza couldn't resist a glance down . . . and shuddered, averting her gaze from writhing flesh, bitten skin, naked limbs contorted in agony.

Upstage, on a stool, in shirtsleeves and waistcoat, crouched Moriarty Quick.

He tended a glowing crucible that bubbled and spat over a hissing flame burner. That foul-smelling poison gas billowed, a noxious black smoke cloud that shimmered and dissolved to air.

Her mind raced. An unorthodox hallucinogen. Could it be the one she'd found in Dalziel's ashtray? Had Quick somehow made himself immune?

He tipped in a scoop of powder, releasing another cloud of gas. His yellow hair slicked his cheeks. His dissolute lips pursed, a singular expression. He didn't look manic or intoxicated.

He looked *bored*. As if this whole scam were far too easy.

But what *was* the scam, exactly? Clearly, these people hallucinated, the "hypnotism" of which Penny Watt had spoken. Illusory splendors, false pleasures. Fabricated horrors, also, those ethereal devils in hissing battle for their souls . . . but in the greasy shadows lurked creatures equally horrid, but *real*.

A dirty menagerie of monstrous folk, fey and fell, demented and deformed, with matted hair and sallow, warty skin. They shambled along aisles and sneaked under seats, filching trinkets from dropped coats and purses, wriggling beneath skirts, invading loosened clothing with misshapen fingers and thirsty tongues.

On one chaise swooned a lady in green, and a hooting hare-lipped fellow unhooked her diamond necklace and licked it greedily, eyes empty but for hunger. A dwarf with some awful rotting skin disease wriggled into a man's discarded clothes, laughing as he disappeared inside. At that foul pit's edge, a lizard-skinned thing with grinning jaws peeled a young lady's drawers off. It writhed its spiked tongue over her soft thighs as it dragged her down . . .

Nauseated, Eliza gripped her mask tightly with sweating fingers. What a disgusting spectacle these pitiable creatures made. Likely their victims would be too embarrassed tomorrow to demand restitution, if they remembered anything at all. Quick and his freak-show carnival would escape scot-free.

No summoning, no deals with Satan. His "black magic" was just a cruel alchemist's trick.

Ignoble and humiliating, to be sure—but it hardly seemed worth killing for. Carmine's letter blurred in Eliza's memory, a candlelit scrawl without meaning. *He is a Traitor and Wicked beyond sense.* Wicked, certainly. But a traitor? *If we do not unmask Him everything is lost.* Over a few stolen jewels? It made no sense.

Ha! Some detective you turned out. Lizzie's gleeful whisper taunted her. *Everything you thought you figured out so canny? Rubbish, the bleedin' lot of it. Not so clever now, is you?*

But if Quick didn't kill Carmine and Dalziel, who did? And why?

Still, this dirty scam ought to be stopped, and Quick brought to justice. That much was clear. And those poor malformed creatures should be in a hospital, not treated like circus animals for Quick's twisted entertainment.

She discarded her mask, gripped her stinger, and edged closer to the stage. Quick kept stirring his crucible, his back to her, singing in his smoke-roughened tenor.

"I wept, and kissed her cold clay corpse . . . then rushed o'er vale and valley . . ." He splashed rotting black goo into the mixture and stirred, rolling the crucible with long iron tongs whose tips glowed red hot.

Stealthily, she climbed onto the stage. Inside, Lizzie stirred, flexing spectral fingers, and Eliza's fingers flexed, too. *Yesss. This is going to feel goood . . .*

"My vengeance on my foe to wreak . . . while soft wind shakes the barley," hummed Quick, flicking sweat from his hair.

Eliza stole up behind him. One step, another. Any moment, a floorboard would creak and give her away . . .

She dived. *Slam!* They collided, and hit the stage, jarring.

"Ha! Dr. Jekyll. I've been waiting for you." He twisted on top of her like a snake, stinking of whiskey and those foul, decaying ingredients.

She struggled. He fought with a cornered rat's ferocity, grabbing her arms, kneeing for her guts, forcing her to the floor . . . and all the while, he laughed.

But Lizzie snarled bitter fury and *swelled,* filling Eliza's muscles with renewed strength.

She wrapped her legs around Quick, hurling him onto his back in a billow of red velvet. Jumped astride him, grabbed his hair, and jammed her stinger under his chin. "Fiend," she spat, in a shaking voice not wholly her own, "give me one reason I shouldn't kill you right now."

Quick's eyes glittered balefully. He wriggled one arm free, scrabbling for his tongs and the red-hot crucible. Her thumb tightened on the stinger's switch . . .

Bang! Electric lights popped on.

Eliza's skin wriggled. Her hair sprang loose and darkened, flesh crawling and *stretching*. Boots pounded down the aisles, bringing listless screams from Quick's wretched victims. Her head splits, *our* head, our eyes boggle and swell as if we're both seeing double. Half blind, we squint up together . . . into the grinning mustachioed mug of Chief Inspector Reeve.

Suddenly crushers close in, truncheons bristling, a net of blue-coated wrath. Between our thighs, Moriarty Quick chortles like a half-brained magpie. "Now here's a pretty problem."

Eliza and I fight over breath, and I win. Quick ain't wrong. Bad enough that Reeve's arrested me on no evidence before. Fact is, the Royal could nail his arse to the wall for employing a heretic. If *she* pops out o' me, and he learns what he's unwittingly harbored? We'll never get out of whatever stink-mud hellhole he tosses us in.

"'Ello, 'ello," cries I, "if it ain't Chief Inspector Nitwit!"

Reeve kicks Quick in the face. "Lads," orders he, "arrest this skinny Irish idiot for murder. Knew that evidence of mine would be watertight."

Eliza splutters in my chest. *I was wrong about Quick, you idiot. It won't stick! The real killer is still at large. You're making a terrible mistake!*

I laugh at Reeve, mocking. Stealing our hard-earned evidence. Taking her credit, just as he done to Harley Griffin—but we had it arse-about. He's got the wrong man. Serves the thieving little rat turd right.

"And arrest this mouthy skirt, too," adds Reeve, his triumphant grin setting my teeth a-tingle, "for disturbing the Queen's peace. That Royal Society prat's dirty bit of quim, eh? Don't think I've forgotten you, missy."

Quick's laughing gaze meets ours, conspiratorial. He's bleeding, a tooth broken, happy as a drunken clam. Utterly off his rocker.

And with a snaky whiplash, he grabs his glowing tongs, and flings 'em.

Spoingg! I go flying across the stage. Reeve swears. Constables yell and scatter. The spinning tongs hit a crusher in the face. *Ssss!* He screeches, clutching his raw-burned cheek.

Quick springs up, and upends the crucible, a river of molten red. Blinding black smoke chokes the room. The stage catches fire, flames chewing up the dry-rotted wood. The half-witted circus creatures screech and caper. The air fills with screams as half-clothed ladies and gents bang drunkenly into furniture or fall into the pit where scaly things munch and writhe.

Triumphantly, Quick bolts, but a pack of roaring coppers crash-tackle him to the stage, slamming his face into hot floorboards. *Crunch!* Blood splashes. Ow, did that hurt? So sad.

My vision splits and shudders, twin glassy worlds a-clash. Someone's hacked me in two like a half-rotted ham, for it's *my* flesh what crawls, *my* guts knotting like slithering snakes, but I'm also some dark-mirrored reflection of *her* . . . and it feels strangely good.

Together but at odds, we scramble up, and leg it into the smoke.

Reeve hollers, and constables thump after me. Great. Now we're doing a runner from the law. Like he needed sommat more to nick us for. Rotting curtains slap my face, trailing sticky spiderwebs. My eyes sting in devilsmoke. I rip off her spectacles, but it don't help. Still, the crushers can't see neither, cursing and blundering every which way.

Blam! My forehead hits a wooden beam. I stagger, blood splashing. A crusher stumbles closer. "Here she is, lads!"

And that's when someone grabs my wrist, and pulls me into the dark.

Not the coppers. Someone else.

I struggle, too canny to yell, but my stomach slicks cold. Is it the scaly pit thing, dragging me to an unsavory fate? Or is it Remy, stalking us in the moonlit night, his hungry wolfish instinct afire? My hat falls, hair tumbling. An unseen door clicks. Night air rinses my face, blessedly clean. All of a moment, I'm blinking at reddish moonlight in a shadowy alley, alone.

Then, the shadows move.

And Miss Lizzie splatters in fright, a dripping orange hurled against the wall . . . and *dissolves.*

Mr. Todd tipped his hat, and gave Eliza an impish smile. "You received my invitation, I see."

A THING THAT CRIES TO HEAVEN

•••

ELIZA STAGGERED, HER BODY TINGLING, RE-
forming, *changing*. Flesh contracted, her bones
creaking in sharp protest. Blood trickled into her
eyes, the cut on her forehead knitting with a squelch.

Todd watched her, a splash of color in the dark. Overhead,
storm clouds threatened, streaked with bloodied moonlight.
His black-dyed hair gleamed—what a travesty, to cover that
crimson—his scarlet necktie like a razor's slash . . . and his
glittering fairy-green gaze riveted her to the spot.

For a moment, she couldn't breathe.

Stars swirled, mocking her addled wits. She'd rehearsed
this meeting, what she'd say, how she'd behave . . . but all had
melted to delicious rose-scented mush at a tweak of his
wicked smile. How utterly unscientific.

"The card . . . th-that was you?" *Say anything. Stall for
time. Escape . . .*

"Naturally. And you're dressed for the occasion, too. The
eyes exult, my love. Not your usual subtle tones, but . . ." Todd
licked indecent red lips. "Well, you know me and shades of

crimson. I shall need to paint all night to get *that* out of my mind."

Instinctively, her fingers scuttled to her pockets. Empty. She'd dropped her stinger and reticule in the scuffle with Quick. She'd nothing to defend herself.

Lizzie! You were right. I need you. Help me!

But only bleak silence answered.

Eliza trembled. Lizzie had fled. There was only her, and *him* . . . and that traitorous fire in her blood. Easy to be rational, wasn't it, until she and Todd stood face-to-face. God, what a pointless contrivance two feet of empty space was. If he *touched* her, she'd probably wilt at the knees.

Todd flicked ash from his cuff, a twinkle of diamond. "What did you think of the professor's ghastly little games? He's quite mad, you know. Someone really ought to lock the fellow up, bathe him in ice every few days, jam electrified wires into his brain, that sort of thing. It's for his own good. Worked wonders for me."

Had he loitered in Quick's dungeon the whole time, watching her? "We oughtn't meet like this," she improvised. "It isn't safe."

"Of course it isn't safe, madam. It's positively perilous, and who'd want it otherwise? Since when was 'dull' a precondition for our intoxicating little chats? Did you receive my gift, by the way? I'm not ordinarily so forward, but . . ." He frowned at the moon. "Since you wrote me, I confess I haven't felt quite myself."

Or am I myself at last? hissed his most recent letter's author in her ear. *Ha ha!*

She'd promised she'd fix this. "You asked for my help. I'd be delighted. I've already researched some innovative therapies we can try."

"Eliza, you needn't pretend with me." He took her hands. Long fingers, overly smooth and febrile. As if he burned inside.

She swallowed, steeling herself. "Don't be afraid. I believe I can make you well."

Todd's face drained, ghostly. "Do you truly think so little of me?"

"I didn't mean—"

"Do you remember what I told you, the night we first met?"

Oh, she remembered, all right. *You're very pretty, Eliza. Would you like to dance with my shadow? Let me show you how I love you.* "W-we said many things—"

"I told you I like you just the way you are. I've only ever displayed faultless respect for you. I can't think what I've done to deserve such disdain. Your letter hurt me, Eliza." Utter incomprehension darkened his face. "And I can't bear the pain. It's . . . most odd."

That gaze—luminous, lost—pierced her heart. "I meant only that I understand how difficult it is. My medications don't always work well enough to suppress her. Lizzie, I mean."

Todd frowned. "Why on earth should you want that? Might as well amputate your own limbs. Inconvenient as well as painful, and only so many you can cut off before you run out of hands."

Agitated, he released her, leaving her hands chilled and bereft. Moonbeams danced over him, kissing his cheekbones, stroking his slim black coat, licking bloodied stains into his sooty hair.

Suddenly touching him seemed more important than breathing.

"Conditions such as ours can be treated," she insisted shakily. She felt drunk and reckless, as if she'd guzzled too much of Lizzie's gin. Caress his cheek, smell his hair, forget all the blood and death and secrets . . . "Come with me to Mr. Finch's. We can experiment, see what works."

"But that's impossible. Shadow is my friend. I can't just cut him out like a stinky glob of gangrene. It'd be disrespectful. Come, let's start afresh. We've so much to talk about."

Her head swirled. "But that undertaker's clerk. The beadle. All the people Shadow kills . . ."

Todd laughed, chilling. "Oh, Eliza. You're such an innocent."

Suddenly the alley walls shuddered inwards, threatening. She edged away . . . and bumped against the bricks. Her heart pounded. Nowhere to run.

"Leaving already, princess?" *Ping!* Steel flashed, and an exquisite, burning edge kissed her cheek. "Dance with my shadow, will you? You know you're my weakness. I can refuse you nothing."

Her nerves wailed. Fight, kick and scream, do anything but stand here and let him cut her. But she didn't dare move. His scent suffused her, redolent with frost-fire memory.

What would Lizzie do? "Sir, I beg you . . ."

"If you must, but I'd be disappointed. I never like it when they grovel. It's predictable and undignified." His bright gaze lingered over her loosened hair. "Yes, I killed your beadle.

Why not? He was rude and dishonest. So much blood in him, I stood there for a good four or five minutes before he finished leaking . . . no, don't avert your pretty face. I killed your revolting clerk, too." He lifted his razor to the light, admiring the moonbeams that danced along the whetted edge. "What else could I do? You wouldn't answer my letters, and when you did you weren't in your right mind."

"I meant every word," she whispered.

"You can't be serious."

"I've never been more so. This is your second chance. You can't keep doing this! Don't you understand?"

"No, and frankly, I'm astonished. I don't want to be half of me. I *can't* be half of me." His knuckles whitened on the pearly handle. "Is this going to be a problem for us? I thought we had an understanding. Was I wrong?"

Clouds scudded in front of the moon, and suddenly the light that loved him seemed menacing, the glitter in his eyes a sinister threat.

Ice crackled deep in her bones. How arrogant, imagining she could *save* him. He didn't *want* to be saved. Didn't understand why he should be. He liked it just the way he was.

Her mind stumbled, searching desperately for an escape. A team of police officers searched for Lizzie nearby, Reeve included. Eliza needed only to scream, and by morning Todd would be locked safely in Newgate. Justice would be served. She'd be free of him forever.

Her throat parched. Inhale. Scream. Such a simple thing.

"You'll be caught," she whispered. Threat, or warning?

"I don't think so. Especially not when you're being so obligingly quiet. Anyone would think you wanted me to kill you."

Delicately, he traced her jaw with his razor's edge—such precision, not to cut—and watched her flinch.

The bricks rasped against her loosened hair. Idiot emotion made her shake and sweat. Jammed against a wall in the dark, no room to recoil. Paralyzed by her own indecision. What a stupid, pointless way to die.

She raised her chin, defiant. "I know where you live. I could turn you in anytime."

"But you haven't. Why is that, do you think?" A cruel smile. As if he'd enjoyed his little game . . . but now it was over.

Her heart sickened. She felt betrayed. Tricked. Exposed as the dupe she was. "I could ask you the same," she snapped. "You vex me exceedingly. If you're planning to slit my throat, then proceed, sir. This charade grows tiresome."

Sting! A hot trickle on her jawbone. Was his hand shaking? "Are you baiting me, Eliza? I wouldn't recommend it. Not the way I feel for you. Not when you've upset me so." Todd caught her blood on one fingertip, admiring it as if it were a sparkling ruby. "Mmm. Shadow says you'd disappoint. That you'd fade just like the others, but it isn't true. You could never be like the others to me."

To think she'd trembled at his touch for a different reason. "A dozen constables are searching for me within earshot. All I need do is scream."

In a blur, he yanked her close, crushing her hair in his fist. "Be my guest," he hissed, an inch away. "Do you think they'll arrive before you bleed out?"

"Want to find out?" she spat, incensed. "Do it, then. Bathe in my blood if it makes you feel good. I was wrong about you,

Malachi Todd. All your pretty words were lies. You're not special. You're just a beast like all the rest. Go on, cut me. I *dare*
you. Will it be worth dying for?"

A heartbeat of silence.

He released her and stumbled back. Shaking, pale, eyes
a-shimmer with fairy-green tears.

Trembling, Eliza grabbed her skirts, and fled.

———◄•►———

By the time she reached Waterloo Bridge, it was four in the
morning. The mist had died, and the wet street glared, edged
with harsh gaslights. Exhaustion withered her muscles, her
nerves stretched too tight. Lizzie was still strangely absent,
just a grating echo beneath her skin, and Eliza's bones ached,
a feverish reminder that she'd made a horrendous mistake.

Todd wasn't sick. His brain wasn't addled by disease she
could *cure*. He knew perfectly well that his compulsion for
blood was unconscionable and evil.

He just didn't care.

And the worst of it was that Lizzie was right. In her head,
Eliza had always known. Her vain, foolish heart had simply
refused to believe.

Wildly, she kicked at pebbles in the road, scattering them.
So much for her precious zeal for justice, her physician's in-
stinct to heal. She'd betrayed them both . . . and for what?
Girlish fascination with rebellion. Sympathy for a murderer.
What an irretrievable idiot she'd been.

Which brought her back to Captain Lafayette. His allegiance to the hated Royal—no matter his reasons—still

crawled cold fleshworms under her skin. Could she work with a man whose loyalties were so divided?

Could she marry one?

Guilt swamped her as she ran up the steps to his darkened house. Her idiotic sensibilities didn't matter. She'd abandoned him when he most needed a friend.

She knocked, dismal, barely expecting an answer.

The door creaked open.

Her heartbeat drummed, so loud the world could surely hear. Was the wolf sleeping? Sated? Quietly, she slipped into the cold hall. Moonlight stabbed the window, hurled accusations at the floorboards, ricocheted off the mirror like bullets.

"Captain Lafayette?" She peered into the drawing room, craned her neck in the stairwell.

Silence. Darkness. Chill. And that faint flash of hope— that this month he'd been spared—flickered out.

She descended, rigid with trepidation. In the basement, a single electric light burned.

The cage sat empty. Open. Locks mangled, torn asunder by vicious claws. In the torn straw lay a single hank of golden fur, splashed with blood—and a white candle, wax splattered over straw-strewn chalk markings.

An interest of mine, he'd called it. He'd tried a spell to contain his wolf . . . and it hadn't worked.

Heavens, what had she done?

Half crippled with dread, she stumbled back to the drawing room and lit a lamp. The dying match scorched her fingertips. Just a chaise, a writing table, a few chairs. No sense of the man himself. Lafayette didn't live here. This was the

wolf's place, a safe house. And tonight, of all nights, it had
failed him.

She'd failed him. Was the terrible wolf at large? All she
knew was the deathly bitter sting of guilt.

Her strength drained, she wilted onto the chaise, hugging
a cushion to her heart. Biting her lip, she stared into the dark.
He'd be back. He'd be safe. All would be well.

It had to be.

———◆———

Sunlight skewered Eliza's eyelids, and she murmured sleepy
protest.

Her lamp smoked, burned out. Beneath her cheek, the
chaise was soft and warm. A smoky smell drifted from Lizzie's velvet skirts. A blanket cocooned her in the clean scent
of pine needles.

At the chaise's far end perched Remy Lafayette. No coat,
no gloves, freshly washed hair glistening in the sun.

She sat up, fumbling with knotted locks. "Oh. Are
you . . . ? Did the wolf . . . ? Is everything well?"

Bruises ringed his eyes, but still he managed a smile. "It is
now."

Should she ask? Did she want to know? Stiffly, she put the
blanket aside, her throat parched. "Ahem. Look, you were
right about—"

"I just wanted to say—"

They broke off together. He cleared his throat. "Ladies
first."

"You were right to warn me I was risking everything. You
tried only to protect me, and I threw it back at you. I shouldn't

have said what I said, about your wife. That was low. I'm sorry."

Lafayette dipped his head. "The fault was mine. I'm interfering with your life and it's presumptuous and utterly unforgivable. I should have told you about Miss Burton."

"No," she said firmly, "you shouldn't. Whatever you're involved in, it isn't all about me. I realize that now. I should have trusted your reasons, but I didn't, because I'm stubborn and ill-mannered and can't bear not to get my way." She swallowed. "I'm afraid that isn't likely to change."

Oddly, her eyes burned. This was the end, then. A bittersweet relief, not to exhaust herself figuring him out any longer . . . but it hurt, too, the way a missing tooth hurt, that ghostly, unaccountable yearning for a thing probably better lost.

Remy just smiled. Haunted, only a glimmer of his customary glory. But still, for a beat, it stopped her heart. "That's all right, then. For a moment, I thought you'd insist on changing your ways for me."

She gaped. "But . . . you . . . honestly, Captain. 'Impossible' doesn't even begin to cover you."

"What?" he protested. "Are you calling me a fool? Then a fool is what I am, and to hell with being sensible."

"Now listen—"

"Eliza, will you shut up and let me adore you?" He scooted closer, stopping her protests with a finger to her lips. "No, don't. Your stubbornness drives me wild. Your ill manners make me laugh. And just so you know, if given the chance I'll happily spend the rest of my days refusing to give you your way, just so you can bully me into relenting. Nothing would captivate me more."

"Oh." Bewildered, she digested what he'd said. "Well. If that's the case . . ."

He didn't speak. Just sat there, irresponsibly magnificent. Insufferable, maddening, undoubtedly dangerous. So bloody *perfect* he made her head ache.

She sniffed. "Very well. I surrender. The answer is yes."

"Excuse me?"

She rolled her eyes. "Please, tell me your wits haven't rotted in the last twenty-four hours. I said, I'll marry you."

He stared. He grinned. And this time it erupted full force, stealing her breath.

Her head swirled, like the initial stages of a fever. Was she ill? Or was this what happiness felt like? "On one condition," she added.

"Astonish me. Please."

"Promise me that one day—it needn't be today—you'll tell me everything. The Royal. Your wolf. I want it all. No secrets, Remy. Not from me."

His eyes shone, candid. "Fair enough. You have my word. If that's still good enough."

"As I hope mine is for you." She steeled herself. "That invitation to Le Caveau des Oubliettes . . . it came from Mr. Todd. He didn't hurt me," she added quickly, seeing his reaction. "Nothing like that. But I wanted . . . I thought I could cure him. I see now that I can't. I've been so very vain and foolish. Forgive me."

Heart sinking, she waited. Would *she* forgive, in his place?

"Madam, your dedication to your calling and your compassion for the lost only make you more intoxicating." Lafayette lifted her fingers to his lips. His big hands were warm, battle-scarred. Safe. "I'm drunk on you, Eliza. Utterly undone. It'd be embarrassing, if it weren't so delightful."

She laughed, dazzled by the sunshine flooding her heart. "Mannerly, I'm sure, but isn't it customary to kiss your betrothed properly at this point?"

"Thought you'd never ask." And he kissed her, until her eyes rolled back and she couldn't breathe, and he broke off with a bashful yet satisfied grin. "I believe I'm the luckiest man on this earth. Thank you."

She shoved him, still tingling all over. "You say that now. Wait until my father wants to come to the wedding."

"Christ. I hadn't thought of that."

"Ha! Too late. Shall we invite the Philosopher? They could have such a nice chat."

"By all means. Should be quite a spectacle." His laughing gaze teased her. "Speaking of relatives . . ."

She groaned. "Oh, no. Do I detect too late this cunning ambush?"

"You said 'no secrets.'" He swept her to her feet. "Luckily for you, my brother's inspecting the new Royal Navy skyship this afternoon. If you're looking for a reason to change your mind."

"That's not fair," she protested. "You know I'm simply dying to see that skyship."

"There you are, then." A shrewd wink.

"But what about the case?" She told Remy about Quick's intoxicating smoke, the wild revelry. "Reeve arrested him. Taking credit for my work, the rotten little weasel. But Quick's no sorcerer, just a charlatan alchemist. I'm afraid our investigation is at an abject dead end. We must begin again."

"Perfect. Then a few hours more won't matter, will they?"

"But . . . I'm not dressed. Look at me, I'm covered in dirt."

"Then go home and change, pretty lady. Ah," he added, forestalling her objection with a grin, "I'll have you know that my hard-won standing as a singularly disappointing second son is at stake. If you don't astound my brother in every way with your sheer magnificence, I shall never forgive you."

BLOODY WARS AND
SICKLY SEASONS

• • •

GRITTY GOLDEN SUNSHINE BATHED TALL STATELY houses, busy shops, and a noisy stream of traffic. Across Piccadilly loomed the skyship, shadows deepening beneath. That canvas banner flapped in the breeze:

HAIL THE ENLIGHTENED BRITISH EMPIRE!
HMS *INVINCIBLE*

Self-consciously, Eliza tugged her clean gray skirts, and narrowed her eyes eastwards, between strolling shoppers and rumbling carts, to Moriarty Quick's beauty parlor, where wide upstairs windows flashed gaily in the sun. Quick would have a fine view of the skyship launch and the Mad Queen's speech. When Reeve was forced to release him, that was, after the true Pentacle Killer struck again.

The idea of setting the pestilent wretch free still taunted her, a mocking carnival clown. She'd had it wrong about the murders. Didn't mean Quick wasn't guilty of something—

and she couldn't peel off the sticky suspicion that there was
more to his evil swindles than she knew.

At the corner of Green Park, hawks hovered and swerved
aloft, hunting field mice. A flower-seller in ribboned skirts
and a fat man pushing a smoking barrow shouting "Oysters!
Frrresh oysters!" fought for attention with a skinny ancient in
a stovepipe hat on a soapbox, who waved a sign announcing
THE END IS NIGH! and delivered a blistering rant about sorcerers and Frenchmen (apparently the same thing) at top volume.

At Eliza's side, Captain Lafayette—Remy, she supposed
with a bewildered laugh—looked brightly polished as ever,
uniform, weapons, and charm. So perfect, it blinded her. Already, he showed little sign of what must have been a harrow-
ing night. He handled his *changes* better than she . . . or did
he? She hadn't asked him where he'd been, or what he'd
done, and he hadn't volunteered.

But her heart sank a little as they crossed the street. Her
desperately middle-class dress itched her skin, unforgivably
plain. Even her neatly coiled hair felt insipid and unworthy.
Was she doomed forever to feel like a charity case? She could
already hear the whispers. *Why in the world did he marry
her? Must have deflowered her, poor lad, a baby on the way . . .*

Crazy laughter tickled her. *I said I'd marry him, Lizzie.
Marriage. Wedding. Wife. Am I insane?*

Remy touched her arm, soothing. "Relax. François doesn't
bite."

"Bite?" burbled Hipp hopefully, ducking from beneath her
skirts.

"Is that another wolf joke?" Exasperated, she shook her

head. "What was I thinking, taking fashion advice from you? You're *supposed* to wear the same thing every day."

"He's my brother, not the Queen's garden party. As you are is perfect."

"Easy for you to say. You're not being tested. He'll think I'm . . ." She faltered. Poor? Plain? Contemptible? "Ordinary," she finished, despondent.

Remy laughed. "A dread verdict, to be sure. Trust me: François will worship you. How could he not?"

They walked through the park gates, under the shadow of the massive skyship. Remy lifted the drapes, letting Hipp dash off across the lawn, and they entered.

She gazed upwards, and sighed joyfully. "Oh. It's fantastic."

A steel leviathan shining in the sun, forty feet high with a deck as long as three train carriages. The hull was shaped like a sailing warship's, with three gun decks, portholes bristling with cannon. A hot halo shimmered about the exhaust vents at the bulging stern, twin aetheric engines at idle. That sharp thundery scent threatened, and static lifted the hair on her arms.

An array of silvery rigging gleamed along each gunwale. The metallic sails at fore and aft thrummed in light breeze, making the vessel strain against the four thick ropes tethering it to massive iron stakes hammered into the grass.

"Amazing," she exclaimed. "I should like so very much to see it fly. Truly, science has no limit."

Remy inspected the rows of cannon with a critical soldier's eye. "If it does, it'd be gratifying if this were it. One doesn't win wars with the second-best navy."

Those horrid tales of Paris made her shudder. Ghettos, executions, ritual human sacrifice. "'Invincible,' eh? Here's hoping she lives up to it."

Far above, on the quarterdeck, a lean figure scrambled down glinting ratlines, dark coat swirling. Remy waved. The man waved back, and ran to unhook a belaying pin, and soon a knotted rope snaked down to puddle at her feet.

She eyed it dubiously, pushing up her spectacles. Glanced at the deck, thirty feet above. "You did this on purpose. You know I don't like heights."

"Nonsense. You're tougher than you imagine." Remy grabbed the rope, stuck his booted foot in the loop, and held out his hand, with a charming twinkle of eye. "Madam?"

"I rest my case." But she gripped the rope, and let him wrap his arm around her waist. He felt strong and warm. He smelled delightful, too, of pine needles and soap. It wasn't helping. "If you drop me to my death, I'll never forgive you— Oh!"

The rope jerked, hoisting them skywards. Her stomach lurched. She flung both arms around him. "Remy—"

"You're safe." His whisper warmed her cheek. "Just hold me, and don't look down."

The creaking winch reeled them in, and they soon reached the top. Remy grabbed the standing rigging, and reluctantly she let go and stepped onto the shining metal foredeck. Above, the huge central balloon groaned in the breeze, canvas luffing in the smell of steel and thunder. Below, she could see Hipp chasing butterflies in the park, brass legs flashing.

Remy jumped to the deck, red coattails flying, and helped

her alight. "Ahoy, me hearties, and pieces of eight! Or whatever you poxy pirate fellows say."

The black-coated man tied off the winch. An inch or two taller than Remy, and a lot leaner. Some years older, too, his features sharper. He wore dark glasses and no hat, and the sun lit flames in his reddish hair. "Do I look like a pirate to you?"

"You look decrepit and bewildered to me, but that's nothing new." Remy made a flashy bow, lifting Eliza's hand to show her off. "Surprise!"

Lafayette the elder removed his glasses, revealing the same brilliant eyes. If anything, they were bluer, summer-ocean indigo. "You little rat," he accused, "you could have warned me." His voice was low, roughened, precisely British. Had she expected a French accent?

Remy grinned, a tomcat licking creamy whiskers. "Dr. Eliza Jekyll, I present Captain François Lafayette, Royal Navy."

"Enchanted, madam. Finally," François added, unleashing a smile fit to stun an elephant. Good lord, that ran in the family, too. "I wondered if he'd invented you, but I see his feeble imagination would fall miserably short of reality."

Amused, she accepted a warm handshake. He smelled sweetly of brandy. "Delighted, Captain."

"François will do. Retired," he explained. "Purely a civilian nuisance these days."

Remy snorted. "A wonder you've made it this far, with the hare-brained heroics you nautical twits attempt. Think you're all Nelson at the Nile. In the army, promotion is much more civilized. We just fling money. "

"Buy yourself an entire regiment, for all I care," returned François, "I'll still outrank you. Senior service, all that."

"Keep telling yourself that. Until the Foreign Office surpasses the Royal Society for striking terror into cowardly hearts? I'll still get invited to better parties."

"Oh, I don't know," said Eliza sweetly. "I've heard you regimental fellows have a habit of arriving late to parties. Especially those hosted by the French."

François gave a throaty laugh. "Madam, I like you already. Remy, she can stay."

"You say that now. She hasn't started on you yet." A sardonic wink. "Nice skyship. I'm surprised they let a crusty old relic like you play with it."

François rolled his eyes. "Don't listen to him. Care for a tour, Doctor? I was just tinkering with a few last-minute adjustments in the engine bay."

"I'd be delighted."

They followed François aft, past coiled rope and hatches leading belowdecks. The silvery sails rippled in sunlit breeze. "Seventy-eight guns, three decks," he explained. "Cast from the new alloy, lighter and better resistant to heat. Lightweight guns, explosive shot." He tapped his gold-topped cane on the buffed metal deck. "We had to reduce the weight, or the engine space was insufficient to generate enough lift. Making the vessel bigger only reduces maneuverability."

She ran an admiring finger along the gleaming gunwale. "Were you involved with the design?"

"I chimed in here and there."

"He practically drew the blueprints," corrected Remy as they approached the brass-railed quarterdeck. "The old days of the seaborne navy might be behind us, but when they want lessons on blowing French ships to splinters, they still ask Captain François."

"Admirable," said Eliza. "Are you still serving with the War Office, then?"

"Not exactly. Remy, help me with this, will you?" The brothers heaved up a trapdoor. Warm ozone-scented air ruffled her skirts. Yards below hulked two massive cylindrical engines, all but a tiny glimpse hidden by the deck.

A control box hung open, exposing a pair of fat alloy gas conduits. François leaned down, grabbed a spanner, and wrenched a squeaking tap closed. He yanked a lever, and a tiny diode glimmered on the fuse panel. *"Voilà.* I told them the electrics were bleeding amperage." He tossed the spanner back in the box and jumped up. "What was I saying? Oh. The aether ignites, and via those conduits, the inner balloon fills with ultra-light phlogiston-rich air. We adjust the pressure of ordinary air in the outer balloon, which adds or subtracts altitude." He waved his cane at the canvas swaying above their heads.

Eliza watched, rapt. "As for a submersible craft, but designed for the air?"

"Just so." An appreciative smile. "More fuel-efficient than anything we've built before. Still coal-powered, initially, but with those sun-catching sails, when the right temperature is reached, the reaction is self-sustaining. And the waste products are non-toxic."

Eliza gazed around happily, holding on to her hat. "Marvelous."

"Isn't it? And it's the Foreign Office, mostly," François added. "A bit of this and that."

"Mostly he just flits across the Channel, smuggling cheese and champagne and trying to look mysterious." Remy skidded down-ladder, and helped her follow. The top gun deck was only six feet high, with rows of cannon and stacked shot receding into the dark.

"Steady on," said François cheerfully, ducking his head. "Official secrets, all that."

"How sinister. I do hope you're an assassin, or something equally outrageous."

"I could tell you, madam, but I'd have to do away with you, and then he'd truly be insufferable." François invited her into a cramped but well-furnished cabin with a teak dining table. Crockery and muskets bolted into racks, books and documents strapped to shelves. A map table was jammed beneath sunlit windows overlooking the stern.

"He hunts French spies," said Remy carelessly. "That ruffian Harlequin and his gang. Nice job, brother. Didn't stop them blowing that electricity generator to splinters."

"The soul of secrecy, as usual. Now I'll have to kill you both." François waved at their surroundings. "Admiral's quarters, doubles as a combat deck. That partition folds away so you can run in the guns." He indicated grooves in the floor.

Remy pulled a chair into the sun, and Eliza sat, arranging her skirts. "Have you any leads on this Harlequin miscreant?" she asked. "The papers say our home-grown republicans look like Tory reactionaries compared to him. A master of disguise, sneaking around London whipping up working-class discontent and stabbing unsuspecting Royal investigators in the back."

François wrinkled his nose. "If only the odd murder were

all. Harlequin's idea of starting a revolution is killing civilians *en masse* to frighten Her Majesty's government into enacting more draconian laws, whereupon the long-suffering populace will rebel. *Les aristocrates à la lanterne!* and all that."

"How bloodthirsty," remarked Eliza. "And a mite under-handed, don't you think?"

"Cowards," agreed Remy. "Portable bombs, indeed. It's just not cricket, old chap. What's wrong with an old-fashioned British riot?"

"That'll teach those smart Swedish fellows to invent dyna-mite, instead of forcing these terror-mongers to oblige us by blowing their own limbs off with raw nitroglycerine. Remy, while you're up, pour us some lemonade, there's a good lad." With a sigh, François took the gimbaled admiral's chair. "Still, the spy game is rather good sport for an elderly fellow such as myself. Sword fights, cunning disguises, cloak-and-dagger stuff. Much higher life expectancy than running Spanish blockades in the colonies and firing double-shot broadsides at French ships of the line. I'm saddened to admit that's a younger man's game."

Eliza laughed, aware of how deftly he'd put her at ease. "Nonsense. I can easily imagine you doing either." He looked at home in that chair. What a dashing pair the brothers La-fayette made. Did François know about Remy's curse?

"He makes it sound so heroic." Remy handed her a tall glass. "I assure you, he's a glorified civil-service snout, not the Scarlet Pimpernel."

François cocked that same single eyebrow. "You're just jealous, Royal Society. You and your tedious treason trials. No wonder you're getting fat and lazy. When did you last disguise yourself as a harlot to rescue Her Majesty's loyal spies from the Châtelet?"

"I refuse even to dignify that with the obvious retort." Remy took a chair beside her.

"I call it commendable." Eliza tasted her cool lemonade, the citrus invigorating. "Have you visited Paris recently? Is it as bad as they say?"

"Worse." François grimaced. "Just last month, the Revolutionary Guard were skinning monarchists alive in the Place Napoléon. Some frightful blood ritual. Apparently you can never have too much *salut public.*"

She shuddered, reminded of those gruesome murder scenes. If sorcerers infiltrated London, such horrors would be commonplace, or so people feared.

François relaxed, resting both hands on his cane. "So, idiot, will you give it to her, or must I do it for you?" He laughed at Remy's expression. "Don't dance around it, lad. You're only letting me meet her because she's finally said yes, so get on with it."

Remy shook his head, amused. "A true romantic. I swear, Eliza, I'd planned flowers and chocolates and breakfast by the sea, but now you must make do." He produced a tiny lacquered box, and opened it.

Sunbeams flashed on a sky-blue sapphire ring.

She gulped, sinking rapidly out of her depth. "Oh. I say. It's . . ." *Gigantic? Terrifying? Worth more than my house?*

"May I?" He eased the golden ring free, and slid it onto her finger.

She extended her hand to admire it. The weight surprised her. The stone sparkled wildly, rainbows scattering. Honestly, she'd seen smaller cherries. "It's b-beautiful," she stammered. It was. Gorgeous. Far too much.

"*You're* beautiful," whispered Remy, and she felt dizzy, overcome. Lost.

"Good God, Remy, she looks as if you just handed her the French crown jewels. Don't be alarmed, Doctor, it's comfortably *nouveau riche*. He had it unearthed last week from one of his ghastly pits in the Punjab." François sipped lemonade. "So, you're a physician. I congratulate you. That must have been more difficult for a lady." Not an insult. Merely interested.

She'd known the tests would come. "Perhaps, but I don't easily take no for an answer, sir."

"A crime scene expert, no less. That must require considerable wits and good sense."

She fidgeted. "I suppose it does."

"Yet you didn't punch my baby brother in the face when he proposed. Something wrong with you, is there?"

Startled, she laughed. "Insanity runs in my family, I'm afraid. And a lady can always use a decorative fellow with a sword, to fend off undesirables and look smart while shopping."

François guffawed, undignified. "She has your measure, *mon frère*."

Remy snickered. "My purpose in life revealed. Mother will be so pleased."

"And now he's blushing." François thumped his cane on the deck. "I insist you elope with me at once, before it's too late. You're far too good for the likes of him. I'm not as decorative, to be sure, but at shopping and swordplay, I excel."

"Perfect," Eliza declared. "Why didn't you say so before?"

Remy lifted his hands. "I surrender. In fact, I'd given up the moment you laid eyes on him. No, don't tell me. It's the same thing they all say. 'If only I'd met the elder one first.'"

"All?" She fanned herself. "Goodness, how progressive. Am I to be one of a flock?"

François's laughter deepened into coughing. Another, and another, wet hacking chokes that cramped him double. Wordlessly, Remy passed him a handkerchief. When François finally caught his breath, the cloth came away bloody.

He smiled wryly at Eliza's shocked stare. "Doesn't take a physician, I'm afraid." His whisper was hoarse. Thin, soft-spoken, that over-bright glitter in his eyes . . .

Remy fiddled with his glass, and she realized with a jolt that he knew his brother was dying.

"I'm so sorry." Her throat crisped. "How long?"

François unscrewed a pewter flask and swallowed, grimacing. She smelled brandy, a muscle relaxant. Medicinal. For what any medicine would be worth. "I'm told both lungs are quite far gone."

"They said that last year, and the year before. What do they know?" Remy picked sullenly at a thumbnail.

"Not that I've much faith in doctors," added François. "I've been cursed with too many rum-addled sawbones, killing more men than they saved. Present company excepted, naturally."

"No offense taken." Her uselessness maddened her. "If I can help in any way, anything you need . . . or your family?"

"Oh, I'm not married." François smiled faintly. "I don't imagine I could bear a grieving wife and children. Bad enough with our lady mother beside herself over the fate of our oh-so-precious fortune." He sighed. "Shall we speak of more pleasant things? Being the family disappointment is so exhausting."

Remy shrugged, careless. "I don't know. I've had the job for so much longer than you. I've rather gotten the hang of it."

But Eliza barely heard. Her mind was stuck fast, a biscuit snapped off in cold treacle.

Our oh-so-precious fortune.

The Lafayettes were wealthy. Land, cash, stocks, who knew what else. And François had no children. Remy would inherit everything.

Her stomach hollowed. *Oh, no. That's not fair, Remy. No, no, no . . .*

———◆———

The rest of the conversation passed in a blur, and before she knew it, they'd said their farewells and she stood back on the docks in brilliant sunshine, blinking and shaking herself and wondering what on earth she'd let herself in for.

The ring on her finger flashed, catching the sun, and the river glinted gaily, likewise oblivious to her turmoil. Just like the whole cursed world, expecting her to smile and carry on. Her eyes burned. Damn it.

"My lady, is everything well with you?" Remy watched her, cautious. "I suppose I should've warned you about François. It's only that I don't like to think about it. He made post captain at twenty-five, did I tell you? Always such an incorrigible hero." The ghost of a smile. "I suppose I thought he'd go on forever . . . Eliza, whatever's wrong?" He touched her cheek, where a tear rolled.

"Nothing." She wiped her face, mortified. Overly emotional, that was all. Wrung out, from the pink remedy and the murder case and Reeve's threats and Mr. Todd's . . . well, whatever that was.

Remy lifted his hand in peace. "Please, if I've somehow offended you . . ."

"No, it's all right." She attempted a smile. "I just didn't realize that when you asked me to marry you, what you really wanted was . . ."

He waited, wary. "No idea. You'll need to speak."

She swallowed. "A wife."

"Now I'm truly baffled."

"Family, Remy. Babies. To inherit your 'oh-so-precious fortune'?"

His eyes widened. "That isn't—"

"Don't you care at all about my career? Did you think for a moment about what *I* wanted?" She didn't even know if she could bear children, what with Lizzie and the *change,* her flesh always stretching and renewing. That wasn't the point.

"Of course I care," he protested. "It's *all* I care for. We can do whatever will make you happy."

She smiled, helpless. "You're precious, but it won't make me happy to strip your family of its heritage. What happens if you have no son? Everything goes to some distant cousin, I expect, whom you've likely never met."

A dark blue flicker. "Something like that."

"There you are, then. I believe in a woman's choices, but I'm not heartless. Don't you think I'd feel obliged?"

Stiffly, he bowed. "Madam, I would never insist you act out of obligation to me."

"I know that," she said desperately. "I just . . ."

"Do you know where my family's money comes from? Our name wasn't always Lafayette. My great-grandfather lost his head in the first Terror. *La guillotine.*"

"Oh. How awful. I'm sorry."

"Thank you, but don't be. The fat tyrant got what he deserved. Ever hear of an old French fortune that wasn't drenched in blood? Why do you imagine I left for India as soon as I was old enough? I don't want it. I don't want *any* of it."

She stared, guilty. He'd made his own fortune in India. Risked his life, contracted an evil monstrous curse . . . all to escape. And now here he was, whether he liked it or not. "I wish you'd told me, that's all."

A bruised look. "Well, now you know."

Aching, she touched his arm. "Remy, I'm sorry. I never meant to— What on earth?"

"Telegraph!" A clockwork messenger sprinted up, its scything brass legs nearly bowling her over. "Urgent!"

Puzzled, she took the ticker tape . . . and her heart skipped. "Oh, my."

Instantly, Remy jumped to her side. "What is it?"

"It's from Harley Griffin. There's been another murder."

LIKE COMMON EARTH

• • •

I CAN SMELL BLOOD.

Eliza's prodding me, forcing me awake. Here's Harley
Griffin, dark and impeccable, somber like the grave. His
blue-suited crushers, lighting torches in some shit-streaked
alley in the shadow of St. Giles's rickety steeple, where gore
crusts the mud and a man in a ripped russet coat lies dead.

His head's missing. Hacked off, stolen for a prize. Fleshy
gobbets dangle around a pearly knob of bone. Fingers crushed
into the ground, branded by the killer's boot heel. Shirt torn
open, and ragged, tooth-marked *things* done to his guts what
make my throat burn with bile.

Slashed into his cold, white chest is the killer's mocking
crimson calling card.

A pentacle.

I cower deeper into my cramped cell. She drags me out, an
oyster stretched in a hungry bird's beak. Don't make me look.
I belong here, deep in slithering darkness where I can't hurt
us. Todd could've finished her last night, and where was I?
Skulking under the dirt like a worm. You're a coward, Miss
Lizzie. You had your chance. You fucked it.

And now here that corpse lies, a rotting accusation I can't deny. No head, but somehow that decaying flesh wears Eliza's face. *Her* fingers, snapped like sticks under a boot. *Her* guts, spilled like offal into the mud.

The fiend what killed this poor bastard is a monster. The bad half of a bad half, with no purpose but pain. Like Todd, he don't deserve to live.

And neither do I.

———————◆◦◆———————

"Eh?"

Harley Griffin touched Eliza's sleeve, jolting her back to her senses. The sun had slunk behind the tall rooftops, stubbornly refusing to penetrate this twisting alleyway. Torchlight flickered, and St. Giles's bell chimed, dolorous. She struggled to focus, an empty hole in her chest that wouldn't fill.

Headless body, bloodied mud, pentacle. Another victim. Further testament to her failure.

Griffin stroked his mustaches. "The rector called it in an hour ago. This 'Pentacle Killer' story is all over town and we still have nothing."

"No mercury symbol this time," remarked Eliza. "Apparently he's done with framing Moriarty Quick. What would be the point? Quick's still in custody."

Remy examined the gore-trampled mud. "Belongs there, if you ask me. What a shame if unpleasantness should befall him."

"Likely it will," said Griffin. "Reeve banged him up with the drunks beneath the Yard. His noxious Irish wit will earn no sympathy there." Griffin eyed the corpse, perplexed. "But now Reeve will have to set him free."

Eliza snorted. "Serves him right. The rude little man takes credit for my evidence—which proved embarrassingly false, Harley, and you can scold me later for my rash assumptions— and arrests the wrong man. Then another victim turns up, and it's in *your* division. One almost feels sorry for him."

But as she crouched in the wavering light to inspect the severed neck, her vision swam. Why carve a pentacle at all, if not to pretend it was about black magic? A killer who left a calling card wanted to be noticed. But why?

Her wits protested, sluggish and helpless. She longed for her electric lights, her potions, her optical. Science, not blind conjecture. But she'd have to make do. This man was dead because she'd incorrectly identified the killer. No more room for error.

"I can't test for toxins here," she began, "but the cause of death seems self-evident. Stabbed in the throat, then a series of sawing blows. Not a chopping tool. Our old friend the short, sharp blade."

"A spur-of-the-moment beheading?" suggested Griffin. "Forgot his ax in the rush?"

"Or relishes taking his time. Still, nowhere near enough blood for an on-site decapitation. This man was killed elsewhere and his body dumped." She frowned. "Hmm. First a peeled face, now a missing head."

To hide his identity . . . or to hide something else? She fingered the torn coat. Rough russet. Where had she seen this before? She sniffed it. Gin, stale sweat, excrement. "New soles on his boots," she observed. "The stitching is freshly oiled. He can't have lain here very long, or they'd be gone. Anything in his pockets?"

"Stolen, if ever there was anything."

"The buttonhole's torn, a watch chain ripped away. And . . . look, his index finger has been hacked off. And a ring yanked from his middle finger." She prodded the savaged knuckle. "Enthusiastically, too. Flesh practically wrenched from bone."

Remy nudged her, and she turned with a sinking heart to see Chief Inspector Reeve marching up, thumb tucked into his braces.

"So much for your theories, missy," said Reeve. "I ought to charge you with wasting police time. Griffin, what possessed you to call her? She'll only run off on another wild-goose chase." He peered over her shoulder. "Leave your fancy gadgets in the kitchen?"

"A-ha-ha-ha." Her new sapphire ring glared, overbright in the torchlight, and hurriedly she twisted it out of sight. "If you must know, I was engaged with another matter. I didn't imagine I'd be examining a corpse this evening. I was merely observing the victim's missing rings and watch."

"Stolen, of course," said Reeve irritably. "Doesn't mean the killer filched 'em, if that's what you're thinking. Around here, a fresh stiff gets robbed in five seconds flat. Lucky he's still got his clothes."

"A lucky corpse," she remarked. "How droll. Has it occurred to you that he's still wearing a rather good pair of newly repaired boots? No common street thief has yet discovered this body."

"Which means the decapitator took his rings," put in Remy, flashing a provocative smile, "but left his clothing. Could it be that the body wasn't stripped for money?"

Griffin feigned surprise. "Why, one would almost surmise . . ."

"That the killer is concealing the victim's identity!" Eliza gasped, theatrical. "Astonishing. What do you think, Chief Inspector?"

Reeve eyed her sullenly. "That you've got a smart mouth?"

She checked a sigh. "This man is working class. No apparent connection with the other victims. Why would Pentacle take trouble to hide his identity, if it wasn't a clue? We must discover who this is! It's our only lead to the killer."

"Is it?" Smugly, Reeve shoved a note into her hand. "I got this an hour ago. Wouldn't know anything about it, would you?"

She glanced at Griffin, but he only shrugged. She unfolded the paper.

Dear Chief Inspector Moron,

Here's another for you, at the corner of St. Giles. He wriggled, so I hacked off his head. A pretty new picture in RED. Ha ha!

I hope you show the lovely lady doctor. It's the sort of thing she likes. In truth, you're just not smart enough to catch me without her.

See you SOON
Razor Jack

She covered her mouth, her stomach contents threatening to expel themselves . . .

But the inked letters glared a challenge. Unevenly spaced, with jerky hooked underswirls, and such an ugly capital "M" . . .

"This isn't Razor Jack's handwriting," she reported, breathless. "It's a fake."

Reeve eyed her as if she'd grown a second nose. "You'd know, would you?"

"The syntax is wrong, too. Todd's sentences are convoluted, not choppy. The word 'red' means nothing to him, he's most specific about colors. Nor does he say 'in truth.' It's 'honestly' or 'let me tell you something.'" Shivering, she handed the note to Griffin. "I don't know who wrote this, but it wasn't Malachi Todd."

But Todd's gloating remarks slithered in her ears, distorted echoes of madness. *So much blood in him, I stood there for a good four or five minutes. Dance with my shadow, will you?*

She shivered. No, she already had a letter from Shadow. *His* hand was identical to Todd's. *Messy, I'm afraid, but I'm out of practice . . .*

"It's a fake," she repeated firmly. "Ignore it."

"So completely off his rocker that he can't disguise his hand, is he?" Reeve snorted. "You're dumber than I thought."

Remy eyed him coldly. "Then why sign his nickname? Makes cutting off this unfortunate fellow's head a waste of effort."

Reeve chuckled. "Why the hell would this Pentacle Killer frame Razor Jack?"

Eliza sighed. "To distract us, of course. The papers already blame everything gruesome on Todd."

"Rightly so," insisted Reeve. "A crackpot like that, legging it from the nuthouse to lead a life of quiet contemplation? Not bloody likely."

"You think Jack suddenly wants to be famous?" asked Remy. "He never wrote to the police before. Why start now?"

"And what are you, Royal Society—her knight in shining armor?"

A dazzling smile. "Since you ask? I'm—"

"Also, observe the jagged edges on that vertebra," interrupted Eliza hastily, elbowing Remy and earning an amused glance. "Brutally severed. Todd's never done that before. He doesn't keep souvenirs."

"Maybe he's started," suggested Reeve. "You're the one who testified he'd lost his marbles the first time around. Hardly likely to be the picture of sanity now, is he?"

"But the pentacle," she protested. "Todd kills people who *offend* him. He doesn't even like to touch them, let alone stop to carve satanic shapes into their skin."

"He's a lunatic. Does he need a reason?" Reeve relit the last inch of his cigar, puffing smoke at her and tossing the match away. Contaminating the crime scene, just to irritate her. "Not as if you've got any better ideas, missy."

Her patience snapped. "Why are you so set on blaming Todd? Wouldn't be because you've no idea who really did it?"

"Why are you so set against it? Wouldn't be because you let him escape?"

She opened her mouth to retort . . . and shut it, flushing.

"Thought not. Ludicrous idea." Smugly, Reeve turned to address his constables. "Right, lads, let's wrap it up. Chalk this up to the Pentacle Killer. Our suspect for all three stiffs is now a mad red-headed arsehole called Razor Jack. You all know this villain, so let's get him back where he belongs. I want every inch of this district searched and everyone interviewed. Some local toe rag must've seen something. Griffin, seeing as you're here, the scene's yours. Don't bollocks it up. And if you let *her* interfere again? I'll nick you both for wasting police time." Reeve spat his cigar stub and strode away.

Griffin gave Eliza a sympathetic shrug and took charge. "You two, find a sheet and cover this body. I want it taken to the morgue right away . . ." A pair of constables grumbled and did his bidding.

Remy sighed, tugging a chestnut curl as they walked away. "For once, Reeve's plan doesn't sound an utter waste of time. Maybe someone did see something."

Frustrated, Eliza waved at the retreating cadaver. "Mr. Todd didn't do that. It's elementary. We must identify this victim!"

"And we shall. Don't let Reeve work you up—"

"A hundred people must have known both Carmine and Dalziel," she fumed. "But this victim didn't move in such exalted circles. He's the connection, don't you see? We must find that head! Or perhaps a local denizen can identify the torso, or those boots. Otherwise we've nothing to go on . . ."

Her voice trailed off, disconsolate.

Three victims, and she had nothing. Reeve was right. Some police physician she was.

Remy touched her arm. "Peace, Eliza. Are you certain you're not too close to this? Forgive me, my sweet, but thinking clearly where Todd's involved is not your strong suit."

Rosy guilt stung her blood. "That's ridiculous."

Remy smiled. "A pretty denial, but give me some credit. I saw the way you two acted the night we caught the Chopper." He warded off her indignation. "I'm not judging you. It was an excellent plan to provoke the villain. I only—"

"Todd spooked me last night," she insisted. "I'm entitled to some apprehension, aren't I? Having him following me around makes me uncomfortable. That's all."

"Is it?" A penetrating stare.

"I'm sorry, is that supposed to mean something?"

"Just an honest question. Only that I saw the look in your eyes just now, and 'uncomfortable' and 'apprehensive' didn't leap to mind."

She laughed, uneasy. "I see. And what did leap to mind?"

But he wasn't to be dissuaded. "Please, just take care. You pretend your heart is clockwork, but it isn't." He bit his lip. "Perhaps it'd be safer if you let Griffin handle this."

Not jealous, or angry. Just heartbreakingly sincere.

She squirmed, her skin burning. Remy was no fool. He hadn't quite believed her story about last night, had he, that she'd had no choice but to let Todd escape? Surely, her indecision—nay, her *duplicity*—was branded into her face, the way they used to sever thieves' noses, or burn adulterous wives on the cheek.

A pretty denial. And this time, Lizzie wasn't here to call her out.

She fidgeted. "Perhaps it would, but I can't do that. You know Reeve will arrest anyone he thinks he can pin it on. We must find the real Pentacle Killer before someone else is murdered!" She caught her breath, fighting for calm. She wanted only to catch the true murderer. What was wrong with that?

"You do agree the real killer remains unidentified?" she added. "That we have no discernible motive, and no way of identifying prospective victims?"

"I agree that Todd makes no sense for it."

"Then we must get on with it, instead of wasting time on wild speculation."

Remy surveyed the dimming skyline. "I must go, I'm afraid. Business with François tonight. Tomorrow we'll ask around, see if we can't identify that body." He helped her put on her cape, kneading her shoulder muscles lightly. "You're overwrought."

"A little. Oh, that's nice. Thank you." She wanted to lean back, let him rub the tension from her muscles.

"Eliza . . ."

"Mmm?"

"You'd say so, wouldn't you, if you knew where Todd was hiding?"

Her shoulders cramped afresh. She couldn't see his expression. "Is that an accusation?"

He kissed her hair, just a fleeting whisper of warmth gone too soon. "Just take care you don't protest too much."

And before she could retort—or flush the true color of Todd's hair—he'd gone.

Curse it.

As she stomped down the alley towards brighter-lit High Street, bumps broke out on her arms, and her insides chilled. As if some awful catastrophe were imminent, and not only the looming specter of the Pentacle Killer.

Reeve was an effective police officer when he stuck to what he was good at. Bribing witnesses, extracting confessions with beatings and threats, tracking down villains with old-fashioned legwork. And Todd—Shadow—was growing reckless. Deranged. Careless about the evidence he left.

What if Todd were caught? There'd be no trial, not a second time. No chance to prove he wasn't of sound mind. They'd simply hang him.

A hot ache stabbed her temples. Did she even care? Why was her scalp crawling, as if her hair were infested with ants?

Impatiently, she dragged back a wriggling wisp. Remy was right to question her judgment. She was too close to this. Todd was deadly dangerous. Likely she didn't know half the ghastly things he'd done.

But he wasn't the Pentacle Killer.

So who was? And when would they find the next victim?

Something about that letter—*Dear Chief Inspector Moron*—jabbed needles into her mind, some hint she wasn't latching on to. *A pretty new picture in RED. Ha ha!* The killer was gleeful, mocking. Starting to enjoy himself. *Searching for something*, whispered Mr. Todd in her ear, *and not only revenge. A cunning fox with a desperate need.*

Oh, yes. There'd be another, certain as the sun would rise. And another, until Pentacle found whatever he was looking for.

Cold grease sickened her stomach. If Todd were arrested, Reeve would close the case, and more innocents would surely be killed. And she couldn't shake the creeping irony of blaming Mr. Todd for a murder he *hadn't* committed.

She had to warn him. Now.

WANTED BITTER BAD

• • •

B Y THE TIME SHE REACHED FLEET STREET, THE DAY had turned tail like a coward on the battlefield, fleeing sinister purple twilight. Doors were barred, blinds tugged over shop windows. Even the traffic ran sparse, just a few electric cabs and a horse-drawn carriage, animals snorting in impatience for home. Chill breeze whistled, stirring coils of fog across the cobbles, *ah-ooh!*

She squinted at the conjoined buildings. Soot-stained bricks, copper storm pipes snaking down, sills spiked to deter pigeons. In one damp hand, she clutched Todd's card. *Odysseus Sharp.*

A red-painted door, almost lost in shadow. Fire and ice mingled like dark alchemy in her blood. Steeling herself, she reached for the slick copper handle.

For the first time in hours, Lizzie stirred. *Don't . . .*

Memory prickled, that wet midnight in Chelsea when she'd first laid eyes on Mr. Todd. For months, she and Harley Griffin had followed the traces he'd left, looking for patterns, trying to anticipate the killer's bafflingly motiveless moves. That night, Lizzie had deserted her, and what Todd said and

did in that strange attic studio had addled Eliza's wits ever
since. Poisoned her reason.

Time to follow her head, not her emotional heart. Last
night, Eliza admitted, disappointment at her failure had made
her lash out. She couldn't just give up on a sick man because
he'd shocked her. She owed Todd—and herself—one more
chance to learn the truth: Was he treatable, deranged by a
dark, unstoppable parasite that could be eradicated? Or just a
beast without conscience who delighted in murder?

Bitterness filled her mouth. Call herself a physician? She'd
sworn an oath. How could she refuse a patient in need just
because she was afraid? She had potions, medicines, reme-
dies. Perhaps Mr. Finch could help, they'd get rid of Mr.
Shadow forever, and . . .

. . . *and maybe I can be cured, too.*

The thought popped up like a boil. Was that why she was
so desperate to cure Todd? Not for his sake, or for justice, but
to prove *she* wasn't a lost cause?

Did she really *want* to be cured?

Her thoughts clanged, discordant bells. What on earth
could she say to him? *You have to disappear, they think you
killed someone.* Hilarious. *I can't help you, turn yourself in or
it'll be the worse for you.* Better, but useless. *I can help you. I
want to help you. Come away with me . . .*

Dim-witted all of a moment, are you? Lizzie yelled, suddenly wide-awake and chewing Eliza's innards like a trapped
rat. *Todd's bewitched you! Walk away, before he flicks that
pretty razor and slices our throat apart . . .*

Defiantly, Eliza turned the handle, and the red door
creaked open.

Inside, a dark stair twisted upwards. *Criick! Craack!* Eliza climbed, one floor, two, three. Dusty shadows crawled. The smell of oil paints thickened. Wind whistled, rattling a windowpane. At the top, a narrow curtained doorway, a crooked finger of moonlight beckoning beneath.

She pushed aside the curtain. "Mr. Sharp?"

Slanting attic windows, bare floorboards. Empty desk, easel folded in one corner. No art, no papers, no books. He'd gone.

Eliza wandered in, bereft. The last person on earth. She could feel him, a misty haunting on the back of her neck, the plaintive ghost of something beautiful lost.

She lit a candle with a broken match. A glass jug glinted on the washstand. In it stood a single blood-red rose.

Compelled, she lifted the bloom to her nose, inhaling that fragrance. Imagined his fingers sweeping the stem, brushing the soft petals across her cheek.

The jug's water was tainted, not clear. A stained towel lay tossed aside. He'd washed his hands in water, not solvent. Those stains weren't paint . . .

Sting! A hidden thorn stabbed. Blood oozed from the tender base of her thumb. Tears sprang to her eyes. It hurt unaccountably, like a paper cut.

From beneath the jug peeked a folded note. Left-slanted letters, an angry splash of ink.

You have broken my heart

She covered her mouth, sick. He'd kill her. He'd kill Remy, for God's sake. She had to stop him. Talk him out of it. Help him . . .

"Have you lost your god-rotted MIND?"

Eliza whirled in alarm. "Lizzie, for heaven's sake. You frightened me."

Lizzie grabbed her shoulders, and *shook* her. "What are you thinking? Just kill the screeching crackbrain and be done."

Eliza's brain imploded, her teeth rattling. Lizzie was *here*. Not just a specter. Flesh and blood. "You're not real. This isn't happening."

Lizzie shook her again, suffused with fury. "You can't *fix* him, Eliza. He can't *be* fixed."

"You're not *real*. Leave me alone!" Wildly, Eliza struggled free, and smacked Lizzie in the face.

Wham! Lizzie gasped, clutching her reddened cheek. "You two-timing skank."

Eliza's heart stung, and she reached out. "Oh, Lizzie. I'm sorry. I didn't mean—"

Lizzie snarled, and clawed for Eliza's eyes.

They grappled, a flurry of scratching nails, wild hair, red and gray skirts flying. Eliza went down kicking, and Lizzie dived atop her. Grabbed her throat, and squeezed.

Eliza choked, her eyeballs swelling. *No air. Can't breathe . . .* She struggled, ramming one knee in hard.

"Oof!" Lizzie gulped like a hooked eel, bending double.

Triumphant, Eliza scrambled up. Her bruised throat already ached. Her scalp trickled blood where her head had hit the floor. But her mind tumbled, rocks bouncing away. Lizzie wasn't here. Lizzie *couldn't* be here. So how did this seem so real? "Strangle me, will you? You can't kill me. This is *my* body. If I die, so do you, and good riddance."

Lizzie's eyes glittered, snakelike. "I'm dead already! What kind of life d'you call this? I'd *rather* die than live one more minute in your poxy skin."

Eliza gasped. "That's not fair—"

"You've always hated me." Lizzie's snarl twisted, feral. "Fess up: you're jealous. You want to *be* me, but you're a god-rotted coward, Eliza Jekyll, and you won't never be *free*."

Rage roasted Eliza's reason. "At least I'm not a harlot," she snapped. "Always flirting and flashing your ankles and . . . and *fornicating* where you shouldn't. And d'you know why? Because flirting and fornicating are all you've got. You're a whore, Lizzie Hyde, and it's no wonder Remy loves *me* and not *you!*"

She dragged in a breath, ready for more . . . but in a blink, Lizzie vanished.

Aghast, Eliza staggered about, searching. Checked the stairwell. Only empty floorboards, a lonesome puff of dust.

As if Lizzie had never been.

"Fine," snapped Eliza into cold silence. "Run and hide like a cur. It's what you're good at."

No answer.

Her gaze fell once more on Mr. Todd's note. If Lizzie wouldn't help her? She'd just have to deal with him herself.

She fumbled in her skirts for a pencil, a charcoal scrap, anything. Curse it, why didn't she bring her bag? Remy's ring caught on her pocket, tearing a ragged hole. Her bleeding thumb soaked a sticky red print into the fabric . . .

Inspired, she scrabbled at the wooden windowsill. Her nails stung and bled. *Crack!* A splinter snapped free.

She squeezed her pierced thumb, and blood welled. She turned Todd's letter over, dipped the splinter and wrote. By the time she'd finished, her palm was streaked with crimson.

> Please don't let him do anything.
> We can fix this, you and I.
> I beg you, meet me here at midnight.
> Forgive me.

Trembling, she tucked the note under the jug. What would she do if he came? Take him home like a lost puppy? Lock him in her basement and feed him potions until he was cured?

What if he *didn't* come?

It didn't bear thinking about. But she'd too much invested in this to give up. Too many lives were at stake.

She turned to go. She must warn Remy he was in danger. Tell him the truth. He'd understand.

"You numbskull!" yelled Lizzie. "Are you *trying* to get us killed? What if it's *us* he comes for?"

Eliza whirled. Lizzie wasn't there. "Come out where I can see you, coward!"

"You're a fool, Eliza Jekyll." Lizzie's disembodied whisper burned her ear.

Shivering, Eliza stumbled downstairs. Evil helldrums pounded in her ears. Sweat soaked her bodice. Her teeth chattered, and her eyes crawled with monstrous black silhouettes. This was it. She'd finally lost her mind.

Chilly with dread, she broke into a run.

Blam! She tripped on the first-floor landing. Her knees jolted, her palms slapped the splintery boards . . . and Lizzie's cruel, beautiful face leered into hers. Fingers grappled with Eliza's jaw, forcing her mouth open, and like a rabid snake, Lizzie whiplashed and dived down Eliza's throat.

Horror throttled her. She screamed, but no sound emerged. Scaly flesh invaded her, squirming ever deeper, and Lizzie's voice croaked nonsense from her throat, *Erk! Erk! Erk!*, the mindless grunting of a reanimated corpse.

Eliza's flesh writhed, dragged in all directions, ripping itself asunder, *we've only got one body, Eliza, and it's MINE, you won't get it killed because you're so god-rotted STUBBORN* . . .

Someone—*something*—shoved her in the back. She shrieked, tumbling down the last few steps. *Crackk!* Evil pain-teeth munched her anklebone . . . and *splat!* we hit bottom, like the stupid sack of shit we are.

Dark water shimmers overhead. We're drowning, we gasp and kick, sinking under, and the world blackens . . .

I scream, a razor scraping glass. Free. I'm real. It's me, the harlot. Lizzie Hyde.

And Eliza's gone.

———◆◆◆———

For now, at least. *Whoosh!* My lungs expand, clearing away the cobwebs. The pain in my injured foot swells, howling, louder than I can bear . . . and then it dissolves to silence. The bones crackle and heal. All good. I scramble up, renewed.

Sorry, Eliza old bean. Nothing like a *change* to heal our wounds. Part of the magic.

I don't got much time. She'll soon be wriggling her way back out, like she always does, a worm from a rotting eyeball. I turn to sprint up those stairs and burn that stupid note. Wash our hands of the whole stinkin' business, run for the hills, and never think about Todd and his bloodied steel lover again.

But I stop in mid-stride, a sly grin spreading. Leave him her letter in blood, oh yes. Let him think she's returning at midnight, and the two of 'em can piss off into the sunset. That he'll lay roses at her feet, make wild monkey love, dip his brushes in her blood and paint the Virgin Mary, or whatever unhallowed games the loon wants to play with her.

Aye, let Todd come for her at midnight . . . and Miss Lizzie'll have him right where she wants him.

I hurry into the street, where that fat grinning orb rises, just a whisker past full, to wreak sly moonlit fuckery in my blood. Ha ha! I pirouette, waving my arms in the glittery mist, and the light catches Remy's ring. My lungs scorch like acid. I want to hurl that fat jewel into the river, and wildly I tear at my finger, hacking at it with my nails.

But then I let go. I like it, my blood seeping into those tiny golden claws. It reminds me how she loathes me. How it hurt me when she said *whore*. How every time Remy favors her with that besotted smile, a piece of my heart rots bitter black.

Well, fuck her. Now his pretty jewel's mine. Ha ha!

A cab clip-clops by, a black one with a real horse. I yell for it, but the fat driver makes out he's deaf. I spit him a curse, and run on. My boots slip on fog-slick cobbles. By the time I reach Russell Square, I'm drenched in sweat, my lungs aching

with rusty-bladed fire. ELIZA JEKYLL M.D., says her shingle. I
spit at it, *plop!* Not for much longer, sister.

Catching my breath, I burst in.

Clunk! Smack-bang into someone. I stumble into the hall
stand. A vase smashes, the silver mail tray clangs to the floor.

Mrs. Poole.

I goggle at her. She goggles back. My knotted hair, my
drab gray skirts. Eliza's skirts. Shit. "Well," says I, "this is
awkward."

My fingers twitch, ready for anything. Will she attack me?
Scream? Run into the street yelling "thief"?

The old lady opens her mouth, and I clock her skull with
my elbow. *Boink!* She wilts, and I lower her softly to the floor.
Sorry, old thing, but I've no time for your idiot questions.

I run upstairs. Eliza's private study shimmers in darkness.
The mantel clock ticks, counting down the seconds until Mr.
Todd slits another throat. Until the Pentacle Killer carves up
another victim. Until Becky's red-caped murderer hunts me
out and sews my skin into shoes.

Until Eliza fights her way back.

Not a moment to waste.

The heavy drapes lie parted. Dust skates along the moonbeams, putting me in mind of long ago, when Eliza would
creep down at midnight, wrapped in pearls and her best
golden silk, to wait for Mr. Hyde. His rough-sweet voice behind the curtain, his monstrous shadow on the wall.

Such romantic notions she had. That her mysterious
guardian were an odd sort of gentleman, tender-hearted
beneath that gnarled skin. A mentor, a friend. Even a lover.

Laughter hooks my belly. Mr. Hyde turned out to be a maniac, lord of a fucked-up fairy-lit empire as sick and corrupted as the one up top. Cruel, hunchbacked, spoiled by sin . . . and her *father*, what's more, her *real* father, not the nice safe lie she'd grown up with, and how'd you like *them* apples?

But guilt stings. She can't never make friends. Not for her the whispered confidences, secrets shared. Eliza's lonely because of *me*.

Well, fuck her. *I'm* supposed to be her special friend, and she spat it back in my face like I'm nothing.

On my finger, that ring tightens and vibrates, a living reminder of affection that's hers if she dares. But does she really want Remy? Or does she just want to be *like* him, fearless in the face of his curse, courage untarnished by despair?

That old jealousy boils in my guts, searing away the last drop of sympathy.

Sorry, Eliza. You had your chance. Now you have to go, or your precious Mr. Todd will kill us all.

I fumble beneath the sofa cushions, and yank out Moriarty Quick's brew.

I pop the cork. *Squelch!* A horrid dead-slug odor wafts out. God, it don't half stink. I've swallowed some foul things in my time, elixir and rotgut gin and whatever else, but this . . .

In my head, Eliza screams, a distant flare of terror. *Lizzie, I'm begging you, don't do this!*

It's for your own good, my love. Cruel to be kind. Mayhap I'll burn in hell for this, but that's all right. Likely, I belong there.

I pinch my nose, and tip the silvery goop into my mouth.

It hits my stomach, gritty and disgusting. My eyes pour. I retch, belly cramping as if I've got the bloody flux. It's like drinking cold shit. But I clamp my teeth, and swallow until it's gone.

All of it, to the last slimy dribble.

And that knot that's twisted my guts all my life . . . loosens. Unravels. Dissolves, like a nagging ghost at dawn.

THE END OF A NIGHTMARE

·●●·

A GRIN SPLITS MY FACE. MY LIMBS WRITHE, FLING-
ing away their broken shackles, and evil-bright starlight sparkles in my blood. I'm floating, my feet have
sprouted invisible wings, and my chest swells as if I've cracked
off a steel-boned straitjacket.

I can do anything. *Feel* anything. Hate, lust, hunger and
envy, dishonesty and glee and pointless cruelty. No one to
tell me *no*. No prim Eliza to whisper *calm down, think
things through, don't be so goddamned angry*. She's gone for
good.

Rowdy mirth assails me. *A-ha-ha-harr! Keep it in, Lizzie,
this is serious!* I shout, wave my arms, whirl like a blue-assed
wasp. Blunder into the desk, knocking everything to the floor.
Specimen jars shatter, and ink spills from broken wells.

I slam my elbow into the glass-fronted bookshelf. *Crunch!*
Blood splashes my sleeve. Sweet sensation, pain or pleasure.
I rip a book in half, hurl torn pages skywards like autumn
leaves. *Treatise on Dissociative States and Disorders of the Nervous Mind*. What bollocks. I grab a pen, scrawl a dirty drawing in the margin of what's left, and toss it away.

But unslakable thirst claws my guts, God rot it, I burn to *consume*. Stuff my belly to bursting, fill me up with pleasure and delight and all the things I oughtn't have.

I grab her carafe from the wine table—why's she even got this? she never drinks—and chug. Claret sloshes down my chin, boils my stomach in a heady cocktail of *marvelous*. I roar, and hurl the empty carafe away. More. MORE. I can *fly*, God rot it. My chains are broken. I'm FREE.

My mind reels, euphoric. How long will Quick's potion last? Temporary, said he. Minutes, an hour, all night? Gotta get a plan.

Hmm. I could scour the streets for Becky's killer—aye, the hook-nosed one with the face—and make sure he can't trouble me no more. Moriarty Quick, too, that ill-begotten Irish worm . . .

Tempting. But no. Them two can wait. I believe I'll hunt me a gallant blue-eyed wolf-man, and take what I want. And if his gallant fucking sensibilities blind him to what's best for us? Why, to hell with reason. If I can't have him, sweet Eliza, I'll make damn sure you can't neither.

I'll make sure no one can.

But first, I'm plotting a darker, more delicious murder. Aye, most certainly I am.

I skip up to the bedroom, yank on the sconce. *Creeak!* My wardrobe beckons, stuffed with billowing red fabric. I wriggle into lush satin skirts the color of that claret. She's a little tight-laced—*oof!* suck 'em in—but I don't mind. This occasion's worth tarting up for.

Harlot, am I? We'll see about that. Only my best to meet my Prince Charming. Ha ha!

I tie my jet choker, clip my mahogany curls up under a black top hat. I yank our ring off and sling it on a neck chain. I want it with me, when I steal Remy from her.

I glower into the mirror, where her ghost no longer lingers in my eyes. Save yourself from me, will you? Keep him to yourself? Shouldn't have said them things about me, Eliza. Really, truly shouldn't have.

I cock one ear, listening. What's that? Nothing to say?

I never retrieved my stiletto from the Cockatrice. My saucy steel sister's dead. I wipe a tear for her—so sad—and reach deeper into that drawer. A black-lacquered cane, silver dragon's head curling on top. I grip it two-handed, and pull. Electric light licks eighteen inches of forged steel. Ooh. I shiver, and think of kisses. Long hard blade sliding into flesh, questing deeper . . .

Mmm. I test the blade's edge with my tongue. Ahh! It tingles, a subtle coppery question: How should I do Todd? A swift thrust and gurgle? Or something more rewarding? Play with my food before dining, oh yes. Miss Lizzie will dance with your shadow, Malachi Todd. Dance until you bleed . . .

My, my. Such carnal thoughts. I want to press my thighs together. Blood bubbling up his throat, his rattling gasp of surprise as I suck the gore from his dying lips . . . and Eliza's anguished scream. I hope I can hear that. I want to relish her heartbreak, as this unholy monster she's besotted with comes to a grisly end at my hand.

I laugh, cruel. Poor Eliza, for no one sees you now. See how it feels, Eliza, to be the lesser half?

I slide the blade home, *click!* Eliza can't protest. Don't even twitch . . . but from nowhere, oily conscience ripples my guts cold.

Fuck me. Can I really kill a man in cold blood?

"Shit." I kick the feeling aside, and it shrivels in the gutter and dies. Enough outta you, ugly . . . and that breathless thirst for guilty blood grins in my belly once again. A parasite what bids me do evil. My very own Shadow.

I tip my hat with the silver dragon, and tilt a sultry, crooked smile at the mirror. I'm afraid Mr. Todd has to go. Not tomorrow. Not next week. Tonight.

I skip down the back stairs and onto the street. Fleet Street ain't far, I've plenty of time afore midnight. The breeze has dropped, and electric lights twinkle through a misty shroud that licks my hair, cloaks me in sweetdark safety. No one notices me in this gritty miasma, nor smells me neither. I'll creep up on Todd's loony arse afore he gets a single whiff.

I sashay onto Southampton Row, swinging my cane and singing. *"Lizzie went a-huntin', and she did ride . . . ah-umm . . . ah-umm . . ."* That grinning moon winks like the devil through the fog. My scalp tingles, my hair alive with static. *"Lizzie went a-huntin', and she did ride . . . bloody sword-stick by her side . . . ah-umm . . . ah-umm . . ."* There's a jaunty bounce to my skirts, and in the magic-spiced air, I *glow,* shedding a darkfire halo.

Eliza's gone. I'm *me,* Lizzie Hyde. The bad half of a bad half, the monster under her skin. I spare a thought for Quick's famous experiment. *Test my potion, I can make your problem disappear.* Heh. I'll disappear you, Moriarty, my love. Into a friggin' ditch.

But I'm too damned happy to think about Quick now. King Eddie'd be proud. Ooh, now I'm blushing, imagining my papa's pride. We'll dance the waltz, swill all the gritty-shit gin in the Rats' Castle, sing at the top of our piss-ant lungs. Cackle, lie, seduce, break fingers and faces and hearts until our howling hunger is satisfied. Set a match to this black and buggered world and laugh as it screams.

Shouldering my cane, I cross New Oxford Street and head for Drury Lane, the church's tall steeple sucked into hungry fog. Hands on hips. Hmm. Across Covent Garden, to the Strand and Mr. Todd? Or turn right to Soho? It's at latest nine o'clock. Hours until our fatal rondy-voo, and I've coin in my pocket and fire in my belly. Surely a little detour can't hurt. A gin and a gentleman would go down nicely, so they would . . .

Fuck it, then. I spin on one heel and head for Leicester Square. *"She met Mr. Shadow by the hollow tree . . . ah-umm . . . ah-umm . . ."*

A drink, a tasty pipe. Maybe meet me a handsome gent who's up for some fun . . . What's that you say? Shut up with your god-rotted preaching. There's more'n enough Lizzie to go around.

"Met Mr. Shadow by the hollow tree . . . " I skip, twirling my cane. *"Said, Mr. Shadow, will you bleed for me . . . ah-umm . . . ah-umm . . ."*

Furtive fingers fasten on my purse.

Well, shit. It's that pickpocketing dwarf again. I grab the hand and, *clonk!*, clock my dragon over the bastard's noggin. He staggers, cross-eyed. I frisk him, filch the purse he's already stolen from someone else. "Can't trust no one these days."

He moans, forlorn. I kick his guts to shut him up. Whip out my blade, *schwing!*, and advance. "No second chances this time, scumbucket." He pisses himself again, watery eyes wide with fright, and I laugh and laugh . . .

And that's when I see *him*. Slinking from a doorway, half vanished in thickening fog. Tall hat, dark brows, a devil's hooked nose . . . and a flash of red-lined cape.

Becky's killer.

Well, now. I sheathe my blade again, and the piss-stinking thief scrambles up and bolts. Mr. Dragon murmurs in protest. Don't fret, sir. We'll have blood for you yet. Because deep in my secret flesh, some mad and famished thing hungers not for justice, but retribution . . . and now I know it ain't no faceless *creature*.

It's me.

Don't think. Don't argue. Just follow.

Down the darkling street my quarry goes, cape swirling in giddy mist. His footsteps echo, *click! clack!* I hurry after, a growl brewing in my throat. Towards Soho, where the theater crowds thicken, a cheerful rainbow riot. On the corner, a rakish ballad-seller bellows a love song, warring with the raucous accordion waltz spilling from an overflowing gin palace. Professional ladies prowl, painted eyes a-tilt. But Enforcers hunker and brood, and soldiers, too, in scarlet uniforms, charged arc-pistols glowing purple. Gangs of tough lads mutter and mooch, sullenly kicking the dirt. The taut air hums. Storm's a-coming.

Unfazed, Red Cape strides through. He's rich custom, but he don't stop for a drink, nor pay no mind to the ladies. I spy Rose, blond pigtails and cherry garters. I flips her a wave. Grinning, she waves back.

Likes a bit o' fantasy. My fingers clamp tight on the dragon. It hurts. I like it. Oho, Lizzie'll give him fantasy, all right. A lurid nightmare. They say you live for twenty seconds when your head's sliced off. Some Frenchie counted the blinks once, after the guillotine's blade went *schwing!* When I do for this red-caped killer, I'll tell his bleeding head, *this is for Becky Pearce, you god-rotted son of Satan. This is for ME.*

Heh. I've a flair for this. The cove deserves an ugly death. *Who are you to say what he deserves, Lizzie?* Eliza would argue. *Are you a court of justice?*

Damn right, I am. The kind of justice a small-time grifter like Becky can't never get. Besides, Mr. Rude Bastard Red Cape pissed me off. If that's good enough for Mr. Todd, it's mighty fine for me.

But my quarry's hoofing it at speed into a side street. I grab my fancy skirts, shoulder my way from the crowd, and break into a trot. The noise recedes. This rickety alley stinks of ordure and coal dust. A silvery finger of moonlight cruelly points my way.

Oi. It's Mr. Todd Alley, where that ugly henchman with the rusty blade tried to do for me. How'd that work for you, turdface? Gotta give Todd his due: he ain't afraid to announce his opinion of arseholes.

I grip my cane tightly and creep on. Red Cape heads for that same shambling shitbucket of a house. A gaunt cove in a bowler hat shakes his hand . . .

Well, hell. It's the singing bloke with the glass eye. From the omnibus, what Eliza suspected for a Royal spy. So who *is* he spying for, then?

I can't hear their furtive murmurs. I edge closer, ducking that finger of moonlight this time. Offing the two of 'em ain't no trouble. Wrong place, wrong time, Glass Eye. Jesus, I'm teary-eyed over here.

All stealth and wickedness, I slide my blade free.

The stranger behind me laughs. And wraps his arm around my throat.

Bloody hell. Not again.

I stagger back. He's choking me, I can only gurgle. I struggle, but the lucky fucker has caught me off guard, and easy as you like it, he drags me kicking into the dark. Twenty feet, thirty, out of earshot. I've dropped my cane. I've got nothing. I thrash and wriggle. Fuck me, I've no time for this. Red Cape's *getting away* . . .

Clunk! My skull hits brick, dizzying. Face-first against a wall. Steel flashes, a blade point beneath my ear. A gravelly whisper, dark with threat. "Five seconds, and I open your windpipe. Who are you?"

Trapped giggles cramp my chest. Another of Red Cape's sick-arse henchmen, is it? Good luck scaring me, lackwit. When I've had Mr. Todd's razor at my throat—his crimson vengeance splashed on my face, and me but a quiver from next—for an ambush, that's sort of hard to top.

I gulp brandy-scented air. "Fuck you. *That's* who I am."

Eyes open, I wait for the end. Will it hurt? Will I see my lifeblood, splashing over his hands? They say you live for twenty seconds. Perhaps it'll even feel good.

But another hand pulls him off me. A strong, battle-scarred hand. The first bloke curses, and in a stray flare of light I glimpse ice-cut cheekbones, reddish hair under a wide-brimmed hat . . . and eyes of glitter-sky blue.

"*François, arrête,*" hisses Remy Lafayette. "She's a friend of mine."

PEDE POENA CLAUDO

•••

THE BROTHERS LAFAYETTE STARE, KISSED BY MOON-light. Alike, yet not alike. Shadow kin, each filling in the neglected spaces of the other. Tonight, Remy's pale, agitated, his skin slick under the moon, but still he's strong and bold. Substantial, his living shadow marking the dirt. Remy takes up *room*.

François, *au contraire,* is glassy. Less real, somehow, as if once he were solid, but now he's worn through. In these clothes—stained coat, torn scarf, hair awry under that moth-eaten hat—he's near unrecognizable. Dangerous, that sickly glitter in his eyes. Not a man to be trifled with.

Well, screw that. Captain Consumptive trifled with me first. Same old tale: Eliza gets the charm, I get the temper. No one sticks a knife in Lizzie's face and ends the day smiling.

I retrieve my hissing dragon from the mud. An inch of exposed steel glitters, tempting me to go a-slicing. Damn, I ought to kill 'em both for thwarting me. If Remy twigs I've rid meself of Eliza . . . but I grit my teeth, and sheathe the blade. I know these men. Remy were once my lover. That counts for sommat. Don't it?

"Why'd you do that for?" I hiss. "I nearly had him."

"What are you doing here, Lizzie?" Remy keeps his voice low.

"Doing a job, that's what. And you just screwed it. You and god-rotted Eliza . . ."

He gives a tiny headshake, and flicks a meaningful glance towards François that warms my vengeful heart.

Remy hasn't revealed our secret. Tonight, I see him through *my* eyes, with none of Eliza's cringing excuses, and he's so bleedin' magnificent my head hurts. Hell, we're practically married now. God rot it, can't we just . . .

François the Glass Prince ignores me. "Remy, we haven't time. Get rid of her."

I saunter up, hand on hip. "And who in hell d'you think—"

"Lizzie, peace." Remy's impatience slices. "Which was your target? The tall fellow, or the glass-eyed?"

"Red Cape," grumbles I. "Murdered a friend of mine. Tried to have *me* offed, and all. I'm protecting myself. What's your excuse?"

Silently, they exchange glances and thoughts, as brothers do . . . and my sluggardly wits click into motion.

This is what Remy's lying about.

All that "for your protection" bollocks? Not the wolf, or the Royal, nor another woman, as if his blasted honor would ever countenance *that*. He and Foreign Office Frankie is up to sommat, involving murderous bastards like Red Cape. A secret sommat what could get 'em killed.

It could get *me* killed.

My fists clench. "Tell me what's afoot, or I'll scream blue murder and every lousebrain from here to Seven Dials will hear."

"Be my guest." François advances, fist tightening around that knife.

Remy holds his brother back. "I suppose there's no chance you'll go home and forget you ever saw us?"

I just gives him a greasy eyeball.

Remy sighs. "The man you call Red Cape is Nemo."

"The one in the papers? What blew up that power plant? Well, shuck my arse and call me an oyster."

"Christ," mutters François, "are you always this talkative to a pretty face, brother?" He makes the knife disappear. "Madam, tell me you're what you seem, and not an enemy agent who's screwed my brother's wits away."

I wink. "Depends what I seem, sir."

All I get is a contemptuous flicker of that Lafayette family eyebrow.

I flips him the finger. "You wish." *You can't afford me,* I nearly say, before I recall that he can. "You ain't my type."

"My loss, I'm sure."

I cast an appreciative glance. Bitter bastard, ain't you? I suppose that's what comes of dying before your time. Ain't leaning on no cane tonight, but your breath still wheezes. You're fragile, but ain't letting it stop you. *I don't want it,* Remy told Eliza, about his family's hoard of blood money. Maybe François, too, believes he's got something to prove. Ready to kill me, that's for sure, on the merest whisper of threat to his precious mission.

A driven man. I like that.

François coughs, lips pressed tight, as sick people do. "Do you trust her?"

"With my life," says Remy, without a flicker. Bless his foolish heart. "Lizzie can help us. She's close to the King of Rats."

And here I were thinkin' he wanted me for my fancy-lady airs. "What's that to do with the price of eels?"

Remy explains, swift and low. "The Incorruptibles are meeting tonight, in that house around the corner. You've heard of them?"

I nod. The maniacs what blew up Horse Guards, set fire to Apsley House, shot at them Tories in the House of Commons. A folk hero, is Nemo, down where the *weird* lurks.

Temptation licks my flesh. Someone's gotta rise up against the power-mad pricks at the Royal, or we'll all go down. Let the gutters run with their piss-stinking blood, says I. And I happen to know Eddie Hyde is Nemo's biggest fan.

On the other hand, 'twere Eddie what ratted on Red Cape when I asked him about Becky's killer. Put me onto Mrs. Fletcher's and Rose.

Were Eddie using me? Does he secretly want Nemo dead? Or was I the one supposed to come off second best? Why would this Nemo character kill a small-time thief like Becky anyhow? What in hell's going on?

Then again, if it gets me Red Cape's head on a stick, do I give a moldy fuck?

"What's it to you?" I whispers.

"We suspect Nemo to be a French agent. A sorcerer. *Un agent provocateur.*"

Now I care. I've heard them Parisian horror stories. Rampaging demons in the streets, sorcerers on the hunt, folk turning into monsters and eating human flesh. "Bloody hell."

"Just so, if whatever he's plotting proceeds. That's what we're tasked to uncover. And why we didn't want you killing him." Remy hesitates. "We think Nemo is Harlequin. Using the Incorruptibles for his own ends."

I gape. Not just a French spy. *The* French spy. Only thing them Incorruptibles hate more than the Royal, it's the French. These are criminals, thugs, angry young men. They've no love for sorcery. If they find out he's playing them for fools? This Harlequin cove won't last the night.

But I don't care if Red Cape is Robespierre himself, the original incorruptible, back from the dead with his head under his arm and his gunshot face in a jar. He killed Becky. I want my vengeance. And no piss-ant radical bookworms will take it from me.

Captain Consumptive must've caught some restive look in my eye, because he sidles up, conspiratorial. "See, *chérie,* we can't just kill him. We must let his plans ripen. Expose him red-handed, at the last second, so we can drag his entire foul crew down with him." He grins, utterly merciless. "And *then* we can kill him. Is that agreeable?"

I smile back, sultry. Mayhap he's my type after all. "Why didn't you say so before?"

A few mud-choked alleys away, there's a back entry to that house, down some steps and beneath a crumbling stone lintel, and we use it, first François, then Remy, with me in between.

A single taper burns, jammed on a peg between floorboards overhead. The moldy basement walls crawl with that old-socks stink. Whispers drift from a broken wooden door at the end. François opens it a crack, exchanges brief words, and

I catch the rough lilt of Bow Bells. I gotta admit, François is good. Sounds like a native, talks like a mad fanatic. Which, I suppose, he is. Just not the sort they think.

Inside, candles burn on a low table. Men and women, murmuring in small groups. Some with veiled faces, hats pulled low. Others don't care who sees 'em. At my ankles, a dog snarls. I stretch on tiptoes, searching noses and brows for Red Cape, alias Nemo.

Remy touches my arm. I follow his nod, to a group in the corner. It's Glass Eye, only now he's arguing with . . . Oh.

Glossy black hair, sharp young face. It's Sheridan "paint-you-till-you-scream" Lightwood. Out of twig, in unkempt dusty duds instead of his usual fancy bohemian gent's rig. Huh. Is *that* why he snuck in here t'other night, all secret-like? Artist boy is a radical . . . or a spy.

François is already across the room, in palaver with folk I don't recognize. Without need for words, Remy and I edge closer to Lightwood.

Glass Eye makes a slashing motion, and Sheridan's whisper carries, a mite too loud. "What do you want from me? I did my part. I can't help it if the blackmailing little scum-feeder got himself killed."

"They tore his fucking heart out!"

"Carmine got what he deserved," hisses Sherry. "I don't want to end up like him." He eyes Nemo. "It's too risky. Leave me out of it."

I glance at Remy, breathless. He glances back. We're thinking the same thing.

What if we had it all wrong?

He is a Traitor and Wicked beyond sense. Carmine's letter swims in my mind, fuzzy through Eliza's spectacles. *If we do not unmask Him everything is lost.*

Seems old Dalziel kept strange friends. What if he and Carmine were part of this gang too? What if, instead of some mythical coven master, they meant Nemo?

"You knew," I hiss in Remy's face. It must have blistered, because he recoils. "Nemo killed them two because they found out he's Harlequin! And you just let her make her mistakes. Why, for God's sake?"

A determined headshake. "I only suspected. It's all just conjecture."

Conjecture, hell. Harlequin, French spy and sorcerer, manipulating the Incorruptibles for his own ends . . . and the keeper of that bloodsoaked pentacle ritual. What did Remy call it: a summoning?

My bones shudder in fury, and I grab my blade. "I'll carve the fucker's throat out."

Remy's holding me back, warm and close. "No, wait—"

"But he's the Pentacle Killer! He killed my friend Becky! What d'you want to do, arrest him?" I struggle free, and forge into the crowd.

But a fresh group of men pushes in, jostling me left and right. I can't see past shoulders, hats, shocks of greasy hair. I've lost Remy, I scrabble for his hand but he's swept away.

Nemo jumps up on a table, cape swirling. "Citizens," he calls. "Friends of freedom. You all know why we're assembled tonight. The time for talking is done. We must rally the city."

An angry murmur rises, drowning him. "But the Dials is burning," someone yells. "They're scared. They'll never help us."

Nemo motions for silence. "I told you we had allies. The Rats' Castle . . ."

"God-rotted sorcerers," the same bloke bellows. Seems the majority agrees, because they start yelling, too. "Fairy-arsed bastards!" "Burn all the mutants!" "Won't stand with no fucking freaks."

Picky, ain't they? You'd think anything with a weapon and a heartbeat would do.

Another man leaps up beside Nemo . . . and my heart drops into my guts like a rock. I halt in my tracks. Crooked hat, hunched shoulder, lopsided grin what must once have been handsome—and that deranged storm-gray stare.

Eddie Hyde. Lurking like poisoned eggs laid in the mud, hatching his bloody rebellion. Not much chance he don't know who exactly he's dealing with.

Whatever Harlequin's planning? Eddie's in on it.

Burnings, inquisitions, slave markets and cannibalistic rites. Armies of demon-possessed soldiers, laying waste to the streets. Rebels and Protestants, skinned alive in the public squares to placate some chaos-loving deity.

This is what we're told is happening. What Harlequin and his pack of spell-addled fanatics want to bring to London. A sorcerers' revolution, in all its bloodstained glory.

I remember Eddie's madness, that night the Cockatrice burned. Death-hungry, cackling like a monster. How far would Eddie go, to stick it up the Royal? Just how badly does he want to burn the world?

"Call us freaks, will you?" Eddie roars into the din. "This is our city, too, and we've ripped apart more Enforcers than you've had buttfucks, you glocky sons of dogs. Without us, you're fish food by week's end, every last one o' you. Bloody schoolboys, you've no idea how to fight a war."

A few people shout insults. Hyde howls laughter. "Here's a hard truth, ladies. Run with us, and we'll tear this place apart around the god-rotted Royal's ears. Want to run against us? Be my frigging guests. When the Thames flows red with stinking Royal blood and my crooked arse farts on that throne at St. James's Palace? I'll remember who called me *freak*."

Some people cheer. Then more. Nemo—Harlequin?— yells for silence. "Now's no time for infighting. Let's make peace with our enemy's enemy. One more dawn, that's all. Now go home. Rally your friends. Start the whispers. When the barricades go up, we'll need our allies at the Rats'. One simple question, friends. Die on your feet, or live on your knees?"

They all look at each other. Mutter, nod, fidget.

Oh, for fuck's sake. I suck in a bitter-stained lungful, and scream, "Incorruptible!"

A voice joins me, takes up the catch-cry. More, until the boards shake with it. "Incorruptible! Incorruptible!"

Eddie laughs, uproarious, that demented fire in his eyes. He pounds Nemo on the back. Nemo grins, satisfied, chilly as death. The same black grin he gave when he'd just gutted Becky in the mud.

I shiver, unmade by the same queer sense of *wrong* I got from Moriarty Quick. Nemo's up to something evil.

The crowd mills, congratulating each other, vowing liberty or death. A woman claps me on the shoulder. I smile and nod. A sooty-faced bloke in a greasy tailcoat flings his arm about my neck. "Tomorrow we could be dead," he lisps. "Let's you and I make the most of tonight, eh?"

"In your dreams, granddad." I shove him away. Eddie's dancing on the table, kicking up his heels and waving his hat like a wasp-stung leprechaun. I've lost sight of Nemo. He's gone. Shit.

There. His head, bobbing above the crowd. I grip my cane, fight towards him.

"Lizzie!" Remy's yelling after me. "Wait!"

But I'm already slipping out into foggy night. Moonlight tumbles like falling stars through the mist. Ahead, Nemo vanishes into the glittering dark like a ghost. I sprint down a side lane, around a corner where a starving dog whimpers, too weak to get up. I vault over a broken wall, skid around a barrel on my heels, and back out into the street. Now I'm ahead of him.

I hunker in shadow, easing my muttering dragon free. Here Becky's killer comes, *plop, plop* in the mud like marching death. His face looms from the fog, that hooked nose, the flat empty eyes of a beast.

I step into his path, moonlight dripping from my blade. "Stand and deliver, fucknuts. Or the devil take you."

————◦◦◦————

Recognition alights in Nemo's blackshine gaze. He grins, and goes for his knife.

"Uh-uh." I stand off, arm outstretched. My point slices his windpipe, a crimson splotch.

He freezes, hand hovering over his hip, where that red-lined cape drifts, concealing what's underneath. He's quick, but I'd a head start. "What do you want?" Deep, powerful voice. *Wish you hadn't seen that,* he'd said. Now you're wishing doubly, shitweed. Ha ha!

I advance, backing him to the wall. "Stabbed my friend, you did. Becky Pearce. For her I'll make you bleed."

His cocky laughter just stokes my rage.

Schwick! I stab him through the shoulder, a bright crimson rosette. "But for me, I'll make you *hurt.*"

He gasps a curse. Scrabbles for his knife, but I kick it away. *Plop!* Out of reach.

"Not so bloody cocksure now." I twist my blade deeper, searching for bone. He grabs me, drags me to my knees in the muck. I can smell his sweat, his bitter breath. He's strong, heavier by half than I.

But I've got a blade stuck in him. He don't have one stuck in me.

I cackle like a weed-happy witch. I've still got a goodly hour before midnight, and now that he's at my mercy, I'm itching to know if he really *is* a traitor. "Dirty Froggie *spy,* are you, *Harlequin?*"

He chokes blood. "You've got it all wrong—"

"Shut up." I shove the dragon blade deeper, so the point scrapes the bricks. His sour fear-scent, his panicked heartbeat . . . My breath quickens. I like his pain, the coppery smell of his blood. "Wrong, am I? They discovered you, Carmine, and what's-'is-name. So you killed 'em. Eddie Hyde's my *father,* you smarmy dog-screwer. Rat him out, will you?"

He wheezes wet pink laughter. "You stupid whore. I'm only an underling. It's only just begun. L'Arlequin . . . you'll never catch him—"

Thwock! Blood splurts onto my dress.

Nemo's breath rattles. A curved steel throwing knife is buried to the hilt in his neck.

Only an underling. My eyes boggle. No time to wonder what in hell he were on about. I try to turn, see who threw that, but Nemo slumps onto me, crushing me into the mud.

Fuck, he's heavy. I can't wriggle free. His blood drips onto my face, into my eyes. I'm trapped.

Boots splash in the mud, advancing. *Squick, squock, squick, squock.*

Oi. Where's my dragon? Can't find him. I squirm from beneath all that dead meat at last—Christ, this cove must weigh three hundred pounds—but too late.

Harlequin—for it's gotta be he, the *real* he—Harlequin looms, a moonlit silhouette. Black cloak with a hood. I can't make out his face.

In his gloved fist glints his second knife.

My pulse sparkles wild. I scramble backwards, hands and heels, but terror stabs my spine cold, spikes me numb while my instincts howl for flight. My belly cramps, hell, did I just piss myself?

Harlequin leans over, blocking out the light. Aether drifts, that stormy electric scent . . . and the tingling sherbet sweetness of sorcery.

Oof! A cold punch hits my guts. A tearing sound, *schllp!*, like ripping orange peel.

"I'm sorry." Honest regret, a shake of his hooded head. "You should have left it alone."

And he rips his knife from my belly, and strides away, leaving me to die.

—◦•◦—

I grab my guts. Burning blood gushes. Suddenly it hurts like a bastard.

I shout for help, but only a bloody choke comes out. I fight to crawl, get up, run. Anything but lie here and bleed.

But he's cut the muscles. Nothing happens. I can't move.

Nemo's dead face stares, inches from mine. Already, a fly buzzes around his slack mouth. My courage gasps and drowns. Just a lump of meat in the mud. I can't end like that. Fuck it, I won't die here.

A man's voice shouts a name. Lizzie. That's me. I try to shout back, but all I do is flop like a grounded fish.

Eliza, help me. How I yearn for that bittersweet shudder in my blood. Nothing like a *change* for healing our wounds. Desperately, I search. *Come on, girl, out you pop . . .*

Only blackness, and the retching aftertaste of silvery snail dribble.

Silently, I scream, and curse Moriarty Quick's lies. Temporary, my arse. *Eliza, for God's sake. I didn't mean what I said! I'm sorry! Come back . . .*

But I can't hear her voice. I can't feel her featherlight touch.

She's gone. I've killed her.

I've killed us both.

I clutch the gushing mess that's my belly. It's warm in there, slick snakes of flesh. Those shouts edge closer, footsteps pound. The brothers Lafayette. Remy skids to my side, bunching my skirts to soak up the blood. "Lizzie, stay with me. *François, aide-moi* . . . You have to change, Lizzie. You're bleeding."

Bleeding, bleeding . . . It bounces away, a lost echo. Separated from me, as if I'm trapped in a jar, pawing the glass with bloodied fingers, a fruitless effort to touch him.

God, it hurts now he's here. Eliza's my strength. Always has been. It's more than I can bear alone.

He smooths my sweat-soaked hair. His tears fall like ice crystals on my fevered face. "Eliza, you have to change. You have to save yourself."

The agony munches me like a monster, gobbling up my legs, gnawing into my chest. What's that, getting in my eyes? It's all dim out there. I bat 'em, try to wipe it away. No dice. Christ, a person can live for days gut-stabbed. Can't I hold on just a few minutes more?

Remy gives her a fumbling kiss, desperate with pleading. I want more. Fuck, I want to be *alive* to taste it. But it'd be no use, Lizzie. That kiss weren't for you. Did you truly believe you could steal him from her?

"Change, Eliza. You have to . . ." Over and again, a magic spell that won't work. She don't answer. Too far away. Lost.

"Let me help her." A second man, a lean shadow in the dark. My sluggish blood stirs. Diamond cuff link, red necktie. Sparkling, maniacal green eyes.

Hiss-flick! Remy's pistol, electric purple fire. "Get away from her."

"Do we have time for petty envy? I think not." Steel sings on ivory, a silver-bright flash. "I'd rather enjoy killing you, lapdog. Step aside, or I'll leave you in the mud where you fall."

In hell, Eliza heaves a shuddering breath.

Remy drops his pistol. Half-choke, half-sob. "For God's sake. Do what you must."

Todd's on his knees. He gathers me up, feverish. "Eliza, wake up. Forgive me. Come back."

I don't want him to touch me. Leave me be, Todd. Better for everyone if I die.

But his blackdusted hair falls softly on my face, that uncanny rosy sweetness she adores. His kiss, shy and gentle on my cheek. My lips tingle, and something *awakens* . . .

My heart beats faster, *our* heart, our blood shudders and sighs. Skin rippling, stretching, shedding like a snake, she's struggling against a roiling undertow, yearning for the light.

"Eliza, come back . . ."

ME AND SHADES OF CRIMSON

•●•

WITH A SEPULCHRAL GROAN, ELIZA SHUDDERED awake.

Blinking, she sat up on a verdigris chaise amidst the scents of oil paints and roses. A fire crackled, golden warmth suffusing her aching limbs. Her dark red skirts rustled, echoes of a fading nightmare. Suffocating in a cramped cell, limbs contorted, beating blindly against glassy walls. No room. No air. No light . . .

But in this magical place, light flourished. An old-fashioned candlelit chandelier glittered, and the first blush of dawn shimmered between long magenta drapes. Firelight danced across aubergine carpets and forest-green upholstery, gloated over polished furnishings, glistened on a collection of miniature ivory carvings in a cabinet.

His easel sat by the window, canvas half-hidden, drenched in golden light. A shelf held paint pots, brushes and knives, pencils and charcoal, bottles of linseed oil, a tub of varnish. Beside them, a fresh painting lay drying. *Lot's Wife,* in her moment of decision, storm-gray eyes drawn inexorably to the truth, while behind her, the world burned.

Deep in a sweep-backed armchair, fingers steepled before that scarlet smile, reclined Mr. Todd. The light sought him out, a laughing fire-kiss in his hair, twinkling in his eyes.

"There you are," he said. And that was all he said.

Where was his weapon? What did he want with her? An ugly black splash of alien memory swamped her. Nemo's knife, sinking into her guts—no, *Lizzie's* guts—ripping flesh, agonies unspeakable. Remy's lips on hers, death creeping unstoppably into her bones. Terror, desolation, despair . . . but she, Eliza, had watched it all from the far distance. Helpless. Coiled in cramped darkness, unable to break free.

Her blood slithered with worms. Lizzie had tried to kill her. But where was Lizzie now? To thrash, protest, scream *what are you doing, dimwit, run before he slices you up*?

Nothing. Just crackling flames, and her own perfidious heartbeat.

"I apologize for the state of your attire," offered Todd at last. "I'd have attended to it, but I've nothing else for you to wear."

Carefully, she rose. No sudden movements. "You saved my life. I shan't forget it. Now I really must—"

"I found your message, in my studio. Shadow and I went looking for you, and I confess my intentions weren't friendly. I'd vowed I'd never forgive you. But then I saw what she'd done, and I . . ." His cheeks brightened, a faint flush. "Eliza, the world without you . . . *fades*. I couldn't bear it."

She edged towards the door. "Mr. Todd, I'm forever in your debt, but you must understand. I can't be your friend, or . . . whatever it is you want."

"Mmm. And yet, in that alley outside the theater, you didn't scream. Why?"

A loaded beat of stillness.

Her breath hovered on a dangerous edge. *You terrify me,* she wanted to say. The truth at last. But only half of it. And the other half she'd carry to her grave.

"I'm leaving now." Her voice cracked, and hastily she turned away lest her courage fail. "I'll tell them where you live. I advise you to be gone before they arrive."

He jumped up, a lean shadow flickering on the wall. "Wait. One moment more."

Paper crunched beneath her foot, and she tugged her torn skirts aside. A dozen charcoal sketches littered the floor . . . and before her, the half-finished painting on the easel glistened.

He'd painted her while she slept. Captured the light as it slanted over her form. Hand laid softly beneath her chin, lashes curling on her cheek. Lips gleaming, a loose blond curl kissing her cheekbone. Her scarlet skirts flowed over the chaise and faded to empty canvas, unfinished. An exquisite, luminous princess, just a breath from awakening—or death.

If he'd wanted to kill her—if he'd wanted her blood, flowing fresh and crimson over his hands—he'd had his chance.

Her heart contracted, guilty. And like Lot's wife, she glanced back.

"I met your Lizzie, did you know?" A strange green stare. No deception. Just dazzling clarity. "She behaved rather unpleasantly, and I confess my disgust made me dismissive. But I see now she was correct. This can't continue."

Incredulous warmth flooded her, the sweet seduction of hope. "I'm so pleased. I've developed a treatment regime, and we can begin immediately." She edged forwards, her mind racing. Somehow she'd hide him. Maybe he could stay here. Locked in, of course, until she was certain he'd be safe . . .

"Oh. Not that. Heavens, no." A narrow smile. "Miss Hyde opened my eyes, Eliza. Far too many people know our secrets. It can't be suffered any longer."

She faltered, hollow, her grip on reality slipping. "But—"

"We can't ever be real, Eliza, not while they're hunting us." The room telescoped, shimmering. Suddenly the distance separating them seemed so very small. "I'm afraid they'll have to go. Reeve. Griffin. Finch. Your housekeeper. That lapdog Lafayette, of course." A faint grimace of disgust. "We must kill them all. Soon. Tonight."

Her guts knotted. "No, that isn't what I meant! We can't—"

"We *must*. Or we'll never be free, don't you see?" Todd gripped her hands. His fingers dug painfully into her cold knuckles, his fragrant warmth an assault. "We're special, you and I. We can't allow their idiotic rules to interfere. Half a life is no life at all."

Her flesh crawled. His grip was horrid—compelling, tantalizing. "No. Mr. Todd, please—"

"Don't be afraid. I'll teach you. It's easy, once you know how. All you need to do is . . . act." Fervently, he lifted her fingers to his lips. A single, scorching kiss. "You said the game was growing tiresome. So it does, my love. Time to cease your lies." His eyes glittered, and his mouth curled into an utterly lucid smile. "Either you dance with my shadow, Eliza, or as much as it would grieve me, I'm afraid I must add your name to that list. And we'll see what color you really bleed."

Bitter defeat choked her, the taste of finality. And she tore her hands free and fled from the room.

She stumbled into walls, collided with furniture. Todd's opulent house distorted into a dark labyrinth, stifling her senses, traps and dead ends echoing with cruel laughter. Perfumed drapes swiped her face. A door loomed, and at last she stumbled into glaring sun.

Leafy trees rustled in a cobbled square, fresh in early morning half-light. Not many people were about. One passing lady shot her a disapproving scowl. Unchaperoned in a gentleman's house. How scandalous. Laughter choked Eliza, an ugly cramp . . . and she halted, breath crushed to dust.

Across the street in dawn-lit shadow stood Remy Lafayette. Beside him, the squat bristling shape of Chief Inspector Reeve. She stumbled back . . . and collided with Mr. Todd.

His steely grip closed on her arms, immovable. "I say," he murmured behind her, "what a clever trap. Sweet lady, how you savage my heart."

The idea of Reeve arresting him—breaking those talented fingers, blacking his exquisite eyes—made her want to claw the skin from Reeve's face. Her moment of truth, snatched away. Would she truly have turned Todd in? Now she'd never know.

But Todd's dangerous calm made her shudder. Would he kill her, if he had to? To think she'd pretended she didn't know the answer. "You presume, sir," she ordered shakily. "Let me go."

A little laugh, triumphant. "Shall I? What will you do, Eliza? Run?"

Remy's gaze held hers from across the street. Not upset. Just resigned. Tired.

Her bones stung cold. This wasn't what he thought. It was exactly what he thought. She'd done no wrong. She'd committed the most evil sin in the world. She licked parched lips. "Gentlemen. I—"

"See, Chief Inspector," interrupted Remy coolly, "told you she'd be up to the task."

Reeve rubbed eager hands. "Malachi Todd. Never thought you'd fall for a honey trap. You ought to be more careful whom you associate with."

"So it appears," called Todd over her shoulder. Using her as a shield. "What a foolish fellow I am. Next time, lapdog, remind me to look the other way when I see a friend in need."

From nowhere, constables swarmed, the silver buttons on their uniforms flashing like ice in the dawn. "Don't even think about running, Todd," Reeve warned. "You're surrounded. Pity if we were forced to shoot you on the spot."

Unaccountably, her heart clenched. "Don't. There's no need for—"

"Oh, enough." Peevishly, Todd pushed her aside. "Betrayal is so undignified, don't you agree? Most unworthy of you, my love. I shan't lower myself to make a fuss. Just get on with it, the wretched lot of you."

Her insides curdled. Was he merely keeping up Remy's pretense for Reeve's sake? Or did Todd truly believe she'd tricked him?

She shouldn't care. It was unconscionable to care. But the

idea that Todd might go to his fate thinking less of her—that he might die disappointed in her—carved an aching hole in her chest.

The policemen—four of them, just to be sure, armed with truncheons and electric whips—cuffed Todd's wrists behind his back. One hit him. He gritted his teeth, spat blood. Didn't fight.

Efficiently, a constable patted him down for weapons. Todd frowned. "I say, idiot, have a care what you're poking at down there. Never know what might slice your clumsy paws to ribbons."

The constable turned to Reeve, showing empty hands. "Nothing, sir."

Reeve shook his head in disbelief. "You nutty bastard. Evidence or no, you're still a dead man."

Todd wriggled his clothes into place, and cracked his neck bones, *pop!* "Capital job, men. Most excellent. Shall we be off? I don't have all day, you know, and we've still business to address. Slamming my face into the mud, beating me until I vomit, conscripting some coarse and hairy buffoon to sodomize me for a few shillings. You know the drill. Or have standards slipped at Newgate since last I paid a visit?"

"Shut it, convict." Reeve elbowed Todd in the guts.

Todd doubled over, coughing, and gave a bloody grin. "No?" he wheezed. "I'm so glad. Come, let's get this over with, you beastly little man. That moldy-walnut miscreation you call your suit is making my head ache."

Her eyes stung. Lord, she'd howl like a baby. Just the kind of hysterical fool Reeve thought her to be. And in front of Remy. *Please, not that.*

With relish, Reeve lit a fresh cigar. "That's the Pentacle case closed. It pains me, Doctor, but I'm in your debt. Couldn't have done it without you. Come work for me anytime."

"Don't mention it." She gritted her teeth, kept up the charade Remy had started, probably to preserve her professional reputation, though heaven knew why he cared now.

She'd wanted her job back. Well, now she had it.

Gleefully, Reeve clapped Remy on the shoulder. Probably already imagining the plaudits he'd get from the Commissioner. "Job done, Royal Society. Not just a mouthy arsehole after all."

"Pleased to be of service." Cold, almost inaudible.

The constables marched Mr. Todd away. As he passed Eliza, he leaned close, a whiff of guilty memory. *"Check your pocket,"* he whispered.

And in a few swift seconds, he was gone.

Had the sun winked out? She could barely see, all the world's colors drained dim. In her pocket, paper crackled, wrapped around a small solid object. She longed to examine it. But she wiped her eyes, forced her breath to behave. Turned.

Remy waited, a stormy shadow.

"He saved my life." Small, apologetic. Damn it. She didn't want to apologize . . . but she did. Desperately. As if it would make a difference, remorse without hope of healing. What a cruel barb *sorry* could be.

"As I could not." A small, aching smile. "I'll owe him forever for that. Isn't irony a killer?"

"Remy, we didn't . . . I don't want you to think . . ." But her words stung, toxic in her mouth. All lies. From the very be-

ginning, she'd lied to him about Todd, and this was her re-
ward.

"It wouldn't matter to me if you had." Remy tugged his
hair, weary. "This isn't about you and me. I just can't let that
man walk free."

"I failed." The admission stabbed her heart, a jagged shard
of mirror. Ruthlessly, she forced it deeper. Let her poisoned
vanity bleed out to stain her forever. "I wanted to *cure* him.
Even though I knew what he was, I kept falling for his tricks."

"No. Some sicknesses have no cure. That doesn't mean
you're beyond saving."

How well he knew her. Better than she did herself.

"I said I'd do anything to protect you," he added. "I meant
it. Even if it means you won't ever . . . Oh, Eliza, I am so
sorry."

God, the world was upended. Her shallow, craven soul lay
bared, and Remy was begging *her* forgiveness? "Don't. None
of this is your fault."

"It is." His eyes shimmered. "I should have *helped* you."

Damn it. She wiped her own eyes angrily. Oh, to claw out
her own treacherous heart. He wasn't blind. He knew this
wasn't innocent. She'd betrayed her precious justice. Perverted the principles of medicine. Put lives at risk. Spared
Todd for the sake of a vain, selfish obsession that she'd pretended made her special.

Yet Remy forgave her everything. Even betraying herself.

Why couldn't he be furious with her? Tell her she'd deceived him, corrupted everything she'd claimed to believe.
For the rest of her life, she'd be scrambling to make up for
this. And suddenly the prospect was too awful to bear.

Somewhere inside, a tiny child wept and banged fat fists on the wall. *It isn't fair! Don't make me be the one.*

But this, at least, she'd get right.

She tugged the chain around her neck free. Turned the ring in her fingers, a rainbow flash. "I meant everything I said, Remy Lafayette, and I still do. You're an extraordinary man and I'll be forever humbled beyond belief that you'd ask me—"

"Eliza, please don't."

"No. Listen. You're deceived in me. The principles you admire are illusions. I'm not the woman you think I am."

"Eliza. Stop it. With every breath, you prove yourself ever more that woman."

"I don't deserve your esteem," she insisted desperately. "I have not honored it. I'm weak and vain and foolish. I let pride eclipse my reason. And I lied, Remy. I told you I cared nothing for him, but if that's so, then why did I keep this from you?"

"Don't." His gaze was raw. "For God's sake. I won't judge you. How can I?"

Unnerving, how he bared himself before her. A man who was half-beast, who'd killed his first wife in an animal fit of fury. Who'd lain with Lizzie, loved her, a deeper and more personal betrayal than anything else he could have done.

Still the finest man she'd ever known.

Her throat swelled, choking her. What fatal hubris, to imagine she could live in two worlds. Lord, this was the worst mistake she'd ever made.

"I don't deserve you." Trembling, she held the ring out to him. The stone shone, flawless, blue as summer sky. Uncomplicated, like his heart. "Forgive me, Remy. Because I never will."

Remy tried another smile. "Keep it."

"I couldn't—"

"Please. Do me the honor. It's yours."

Tears half blinded her. She clutched his ring, helpless.

"Oh," he added, "one more thing. I'll probably lose my commission for this, but . . ." A shrug, heedless. "Lady Lovelace is onto Marcellus Finch. I don't know what evidence she has, but he ought to clear out."

"Thank you," she whispered. She couldn't bear *good-bye*. She just turned, and stumbled away.

Somehow, she found her way home, along glaring sunlit streets that blurred and tangled like a maze. Her dim hall was chilly, lifeless. Only Hippocrates greeted her, snuffling dolefully at her skirts. She fumbled to pick him up. His brass body was cold. Blindly, she forced her wooden limbs to climb the stairs. Her study door slammed, a prison echo. The curtains were drawn. No fire, no lights, no warmth. She didn't want warmth. She didn't deserve it.

In the dark, she sank into her chair, and let the tears flow.

FLASCHENGEIST

...

HAD SHE SLEPT? HOW MUCH TIME HAD PASSED? HER eyes stung, her throat hurt from weeping. Exhausted, she teetered back in her chair and poked the study drapes apart. Afternoon sun, red and raw like tortured flesh.

Dully, she set Hipp on the floor. He snuffled in sleepy protest. He'd been slumbering in her lap, cogs clicking as he dreamed.

She leapt up, stumbling in haste. She'd forgotten. How could she be so *selfish*? "Hipp, wake up! Run and telegraph Mr. Finch immediately, in cipher. Tell him to leave town. It's over."

"Finch," croaked Hipp woefully, "leave town." He scuttled out, a flash of brass.

Over. Done. Finished. What a coldly scientific concept. Sick laughter bubbled. She'd imagined herself so logical. Such ugly vanity.

The mantel clock ticked, pressing. She ignored it. What was the hurry? The case was *over*, too, one way or another.

Had Nemo lied? Was he the Pentacle Killer after all? She'd never know, not until another corpse turned up. She'd no further clues to unravel.

Not one.

On her desk, Remy's ring glittered, splashed scarlet by the sun. She wandered over, listless. A flat pasteboard box sat on her blotter, tied with string. Had Mrs. Poole put it there? Where was Mrs. Poole, anyway?

A letter poked from the knot. Wanly, she pulled it out.

Dear Doctor Perfect

Her heart lurched, tipping her from her stupor. Unevenly spaced words, jerky underswirls . . .

I watched you last night, at that imbecilic gathering. What a farce! Saw you run, too. What a sticky end for that fool Nemo! I'm glad that hooded fellow stuck a knife in him. The lying runt deserved it!

Ha ha! Did you think he was me? Wrong AGAIN!

Here's a thing I harvested, just for you. A flash cove this time, just for a change. Take a good look. If you don't want this to happen to you—STOP LOOKING FOR ME.

See you in Hell
The Pentacle Killer
(nice nickname! I'll carve one in YOU)

Her gaze swiveled to the box. Dry-mouthed, she folded
back the lid.

Arranged neatly on a paper lining sat a golden ring, soaked
in gore. A man's finger, severed at the big knuckle, greenish
with corruption. And a pale, soft blob of . . .

She recoiled, sick.

A face. Peeled from its skull like rind from ripe fruit.

Part of one, anyway. One eyelid hung crooked, dark-lashed.
The flesh looked oddly misshapen. As if the pitiable fellow
had a spongy growth around his eye socket.

That headless corpse in Soho had been missing two fingers. Rings stolen, reddish coat torn. *Concealing the victim's
identity . . . or something else about him.*

Images of Seven Dials, gin and guilt. Men playing cards, a
weird-looking fellow in a russet coat, his arm around a lady.
*His face is bulbous, malformed, and he blows me a kiss over
gold-ringed fingers. Willy, you handsome devil.*

The headless corpse was Strangeface Willy. The man who
filed off the manufacturer's marks, reset the jewels, melted
the silver to ingots. Made your stolen loot untraceable.

But why would the Pentacle Killer—who was demonstra-
bly not Nemo—slaughter a petty fence?

New possibilities flowered, the petals of a dark rose. Sir
Dalziel Fleet's closet, ransacked, that yawning safe emptied.
Evidence clearly faked. A burglary gone wrong, Reeve had
insisted, and she'd laughed at him.

Searching for something, I'll warrant, and not only revenge . . .
What if it really was a burglary?

What if the murderer stole something from that secret

cabinet, and killed Dalziel in the process? Something from the safe? Or . . .

Eve and the Serpent flashed through her mind. Taken from a police vault by Carmine Zanotti and his gang of thieves. That frame-maker's shop, the Mad Queen's missing portrait.

Stolen artwork.

The box hit the desk, fallen from her numb fingers.

What if Carmine killed Dalziel, and stole an artwork from Dalziel's fabled collection? Something Strangeface Willy could christen . . . and then *someone else* killed them both to retrieve it?

But who? And what could be worth murdering so gruesomely for?

Fresh determination steeled her nerves, and she headed for the study door. She'd return to Dalziel's, search it top to bottom. Break in, if she must. Find Mr. Brigham and demand to know what was missing from that cabinet . . .

The door blew open, knocking her onto her backside.

"At last!" cried Marcellus Finch. "I've been looking for you all day. I say, what are you doing on the floor?" He hauled her to her feet.

She shook her dizzy head to clear it. "Did you get my telegram already?"

"Eh?" Finch goggled, wild white hair bobbing.

"The Royal are onto you. It's serious. You must leave town right away—"

"Oh, never mind that." He slapped a pocketful of clutter onto the table. "Please explain. Chop chop, don't have all day!"

Her mind boggled. "Marcellus, there's a *face in a box* on my desk. Forgive me if I'm a little distracted."

"So there is. Spectacular one, too, my goodness." He sniffed, dismissive. "Well, forget it, dear girl! Concentrate!" He tapped a forefinger on her forehead. "You really should eat more turnips. Why, you're positively puffy-eyed—"

She warded him off. "Will you kindly tell me what's going on?"

"*That.*" He jabbed an indignant finger at the clutter. Scrunched papers, a ball of string, a wrapped sweet, her collection of sample phials. And a white-wrapped packet labeled LADY GRAY'S FAMOUS PARISIAN ENAMEL. "That *substance* is evil. He's killing them. He must be stopped!"

"Who? Don't bounce, Marcellus. Slow down."

"Moriarty Quick, of course." Finch scrabbled at his hair, raising a white bird's nest. "It's the stuff that killed Sibby! I told you not to trust him, but did you listen to wise Marcellus? Of course not! He's a maniac, I tell you. Souls in jars, heads boiling on the stove . . . Oh, those empty eyes!"

She guided him to the sofa. "Take a breath. Shall I fetch tea?"

She poured a cup, and Finch gulped, not noticing it was long cold. "Haven't anything stronger, perchance?"

I could murder a whiskey . . . "I'm afraid not." Her wine carafe was missing. She sat, but her gaze kept flicking impatiently to Willy's disembodied face. "From the beginning. Who's Sibby?"

"We were to be married. Sibyl Finch, eh? Never cared for marriage, me. Always seemed irrational and pointless. But she was something special."

Vague, Lizzie-flavored memory stirred. "Quick told me she fell ill?"

"I tried everything. Alchemy, of course. Homeopathy, hypnosis, even a witch doctor or two, and you know what I think of that, eh? But nothing helped. Moriarty . . . he wasn't calling himself that then . . . he said he'd distilled a new elemental essence that could restore her."

"Don't tell me: he lied?"

"It *altered* her. She became cold and jealous and cruel. She'd bait people, steal, trick them just to laugh at their pain. I thought her illness had warped her temper, but the more of Quick's essence she took, the worse it got."

"Quick insinuated that he and Sibby . . ."

"Oh, yes," said Finch darkly. "Quite shamelessly. I couldn't understand it. She'd always loathed him. Called him a sly fellow, which for a lady with Sibby's sweet tongue was a veritable rain of curses, eh? But now it was as if they were made for each other. A pair of sniggering devils. And that's when I knew the vile little stoat had tricked us." He sniffed, teary. "Tricked *me,* I should say. Didn't care for her in the slightest."

"So what did you do?"

"I had to look, didn't I? Stay away, Marcellus, Henry told me, there are things we're not meant to meddle with. But I *needed to know.*"

Eliza nodded grimly. She understood that compulsion all too well.

"So one night, I sneaked into Quick's secret laboratory." Finch's face greened. "I'd known he was dabbling with the occult, but I'd never seen anything like it. A shelf of jars, with *things* trapped inside. *Creatures* with pale flesh and staring eyes. Coiled up tightly, straining against the glass, writhing to get out . . . and screaming. Over and over. Not words. Just . . . despair." His voice cracked. "One was Sibby. It didn't look like her. Just a lump of flesh. But I knew."

Icy wire threaded her veins. Those oily silver snail-squeezings, sliding down Lizzie's throat. Eliza's own horrid nightmare of beating against cold walls, trapped . . . Was that what Quick's potion did?

"Moriarty was studying the consciousness, you see. Life force, eh? With every dose of his treatment, the *thing* in the bottle grew, and the rest of her . . . rinsed thin." At last, Finch met Eliza's eye. "And once he'd finished with her—ruined her utterly, of course, to spite me for turning Henry against him— Sibby died. The thing in the bottle withered away, and took her with it."

She swallowed, sick. "I'm so sorry."

"For the best in the end, eh?" Finch's eyes shimmered. "Better die than live in thrall to that maniac."

"So you had him arrested?"

"Not for the bottled souls, who'd have believed that? Human eyeballs in his icebox, kidneys roasting on the spit. No proof of murder, sadly, but enough to get him transported."

"And now Quick's doing it again? That sample I gave you is the same substance?" She blanched. That coveted porcelain-white skin. BEAUTIFUL FOR EVER. Quick was poisoning ladies with that twenty-guinea enamel. They were paying for the privilege of being murdered. "But why? Is he extorting money, or favors?"

Finch leapt up, re-energized. "Who knows? Put a stop to it, say what? You must tell me where you got this right away."

"But I already told you. I found it at Quick's beauty parlor."

He swiped the enamel aside. "No, you nitwit! That's just lead steeped in a barbiturate. Ladies spend their husbands' money, develop cravings, come back for more. A money trap, eh? Not that. This!" He shook the sample phials before her eyes.

Shreds of dark flesh. A ball of bloodied canvas. Coagulated plasma. "From Sir Dalziel's cadaver? It's only Quick's alchemical hallucinogen. From the cigar. Remember?"

"Have your wits shriveled? That scintillating stuff isn't the hallucinogen. It's dark alchemy, imbued in the linseed oil and mineral traces. The same essence that stole Sibby's soul!"

"Linseed oil? But—"

"Only now he's added a retrograde tincture of *aqua vitae*. Made the whole process more aesthetic and profitable." Finch waved his arms. "Don't you see? No one would *pay* to have their soul sicken in a jar while they waste away. No, they want to watch their souls rot with sin, while *they* stay young and beautiful. Never heard anything so repellent in my life. We must stop him!"

Eliza blinked. "But . . ."

Finch wiggled the bottles, frantic. "It's on the canvas the killer stuffed down his throat. It's the paint, dear girl. Paint!"

Her thoughts ricocheted, all the evidence she'd collected zinging with fresh meaning. Arterial spray on Dalziel's carpet, unobstructed by the killer. A crucifix, dangling inexplicably from the dead man's neck. Not the murder weapon. Twin slices under the chin, a neat "X." Left to right, right to left.

Just like the cuts in that scrap of portrait shoved down the corpse's throat. Dalziel's painted face, healthy, years younger than his sallow cadaver.

Paint. Stealing the soul. Murder.

BEAUTIFUL FOR EVER.

"That's why the blood spatter didn't make sense," she whispered. "The killer didn't stab the man. He stabbed the painting! Shoved in the crucifix to hide the fact. And then cut his face off. Not to obscure his identity. So no one would see Dalziel had *aged*."

Finch bounced. "This is what I'm trying to tell you!"

She gripped his arm. "How's it done?"

"Well, you'd have to attune the essence somehow, to the subject's vital force."

Old Dalziel were nutty as a fruitcake. Bargaining for eternal life with the "gray man." LADY GRAY'S FAMOUS PARISIAN ENAMEL. Moriarty Quick. Very funny. "Might an occult blood ritual do the trick? The kind Dalziel attempted at his parties?"

"Bunkum," muttered Finch. "But it's easy enough to make alchemy look like a ritual. Moriarty loves an audience."

"And then your soul"—*your shadow,* she almost said—"your soul would be trapped in the picture, and you'd be immortal? Indestructible?"

"Forever young." Finch shuddered. That's what the retrograde *aqua vitae* is for. "Until you die, that is. Then the link's broken, and everything goes back where it should be. But while you're alive, your painted soul still decays. I'd imagine the portrait would be quite frightful, after a while."

"So frightful, one might kill to keep it hidden?"

"The kind of person who'd pay to have this done? Shouldn't think they'd hesitate, old girl."

"Or had it done against their will," she mused. "An artist's model. Someone in the black-magic coven, who knew Quick's secret. Someone like . . . Oh, my."

Shaking, she unfolded the killer's letter onto the desk. Unevenly spaced hand, jerky underswirls, hooked letters below the line.

Dear Doctor Perfect. Here's a thing I harvested, just for you.

Next, she pulled the sheaf of Dalziel's papers from her bag, and smoothed out the secret milk message.

He is a Traitor and Wicked beyond sense.

Carmine's, they'd assumed. But Carmine was no bleeding-heart republican to be writing letters about traitorous French spies.

In her mind flashed a grim scene of naval warfare, foreshadowing the doom of a revolution. *Nelson at Trafalgar,* the artist's signature in the same jerky letters with that sharp-hooked "G." The laboriously written English, not of a foreigner, but of an apprentice who wanted to be an artist. An intelligent but poorly educated boy, aiming above his station.

She scattered the papers, spilling Dalziel's sketches over the blotter. Fine-lined faces, large liquid eyes, flowing hair and gowns. Beautiful models, all. But particularly one, with perfect cheekbones and striking, sorrowful dark eyes . . .

"I say," remarked Finch, "he looks better in a dress than you do. Handsome lad, say what?"

The prettiest girl in Dalziel's sketches wasn't a girl.

Eliza's throat squeezed tight. She'd thought at the Exhibition that Sheridan looked familiar. She'd thought herself so clever, finding a secret political motive for the Pentacle Killer. But the motive wasn't elevated. It was banal. Hatred. Jealousy. Fear.

Sheridan had done frightful things to win Dalziel's patronage. *The students get it worse,* Brigham had said. What was worse than a beating? Cruelty, humiliation, degradation. Surely these sketches were only the beginning. The kind of sins a penniless watch-maker's apprentice who wanted to be a painter could go to prison for, while a baronet escaped scot-free.

She shuddered to imagine what Sheridan had endured. What he might have done to others, too, covering his anguish with a fake smile . . . and Carmine had just laughed at him. Threatened blackmail, stole Penny Watt's affection, tried to purloin Dalziel's favor with art that wasn't even his.

"Sheridan," she burst out. "Carmine stole a magic painting of Sheridan . . . and Sheridan killed him trying to get it back . . . but Carmine had already sold it to Willy, so Sheridan killed Willy because he was the only one left alive who knew Sheridan's secret . . ."

But one other person knew. The one who'd pointed Eliza towards Moriarty Quick with a cleverly plausible misdirection. Who'd lied all along to keep Sheridan safe.

"Oh, my." Eliza all but tripped again in her haste. "Marcellus, you have to go."

Bewildered, Finch blinked. "But I've only just arrived. Who's this Sheridan?"

"The Royal are onto you. Go! But don't go home, it's no safer than here." She scribbled an address and pressed it along with the sapphire ring into his hands. "The man who lives here is Remy Lafayette's brother. Show him this ring, tell him I sent you. He'll help."

Finch examined the gemstone through his pince-nez. "Egad! Quite flawless. Indian, you know, the only place they find precisely that color. Deep in the Kashmiri jungle, say what? I'm so pleased! Are congratulations in order?"

"Um . . . no. Not really."

His face fell. "You really ought to marry that poor fellow. Put him out of his misery, eh? Foolishness, of course. Highly irrational. But if you insist on falling in love, you could do a lot worse."

"Please, Marcellus, not now. This is important."

"Very well," he muttered. "Not very dignified, all this scuttling about like a rodent. And where are *you* going?"

She slung her bag, already halfway out the door—and tripped over Hippocrates, who'd bounded back from the telegraph with an excited *whir!* "To find Sheridan, before he goes hunting for a friend."

A FACE WITHOUT A HEART

...

A GLIMMERING, REDDISH DARKNESS SWAMPED TRA-falgar Square like a mockery of hellfire. Smoky wind whistled over the pebbled roads, *ooh! ahh!* Arc-lights glittered over the main gallery entrance. Nelson's Column loomed, the admiral casting an evil red-rimmed shadow. A pair of Enforcers strutted before the statue of dead King Charles, red eyes glinting in the dark. Their brassy feet kept perfect rhythm, *clunk! clunk!*

Unholy giggles bubbled in Eliza's throat as she crept along, keeping to the shadows. Fooling the metal monsters was fun. Apart from the threat of sudden death.

Lizzie? Are you there?

Bleak silence.

Eliza stifled another disembodied laugh, and slipped down alongside the gallery. Hippocrates quivered inside her bag, muttering to himself. An owl hooted above, making her hair prickle on end. Somewhere, a rat whickered, claws skittering.

Ahead, a side door led away from the exhibition rooms, the workers' entrance. She stole up the steps, and slipped inside. The Academy's classrooms lay on the first floor. The corridor was silent, gaslights unlit.

Her heart thudded, echoes of another occasion when she'd crept into a killer's lair alone. This was stupid. Would she never learn? She should call the police.

But it would be fruitless. Reeve would never believe her, his smug "apology" notwithstanding. *What's that you say? A magic painting was the murder weapon? Shut up, you foolish chit, and leave police work to the professionals.* And she refused to get Harley Griffin in trouble for helping her. His career had suffered enough. Besides, after her frustrating lack of weapons at Moriarty Quick's sinister theater, she'd brought a small electric pistol as well as her stinger. She could defend herself.

The students' rooms lay at the end. She strained her ears. Voices, from the door at the end, faint light leaking underneath.

She crept closer, tugging the pistol from her bag. Sobbing, a woman's voice. Then a man's, more forceful. "No, Penny, I can't let you . . ." *Smack!* Flesh on flesh, a shriek of rage.

Eliza flung open the door and burst in, weapon ready.

A narrow artist's studio, bright with flickering oil lamps. Not opulent like Mr. Todd's house. This was sparse, with whitewashed walls and bare floorboards. Books, papers, sketches, rolls of linen, ingredients for mixing paint, the familiar scent of linseed oil. Muslin cloth draped the tall windows, translucent for altering the quality of light. On the easel was pegged a large square canvas, shrouded in paint-stained linen.

Sheridan Lightwood and Penny Watt stared at her, interrupted mid-fight. Sheridan's shirt was loose, his dark hair tumbling. He gripped Penny's wrists, as if they'd been struggling. Penny's auburn curls were mussed, her black satin dress in disarray.

Who'd been crying? Eliza couldn't tell. Both breathing hard, their faces reddened, as if they'd been shouting . . . and Penny's lip oozed blood.

"Danger!" yelled Hipp inside the bag. "Murder! Imminent peril!"

Eliza ignited the pistol's charge, *flick-snap!* "Police. Let her go."

Sheridan laughed. "Oh, for heaven's sake."

Penny yanked free and stumbled away, panting. "Thank God. I only came to apologize and he turned on me."

"Christ, Pen, give it a rest." Sheridan dragged back damp hair. "Doctor, get out of here. This is a private matter."

Eliza edged further in and gestured with her pistol. "Step away from that painting."

Sheridan smiled. Like Mr. Hyde, handsome and utterly corrupt. How had she not noticed before? "How about *you* step away? You've no idea who you're dealing with."

"Don't I? That's a portrait of you, isn't it? Painted by Sir Dalziel Fleet, with help from the gray man. Your soul's trapped in it. Shall I go on?"

A smirk. "I feel you're about to."

"Carmine killed Sir Dalziel and stole the painting," she continued. "Probably because he planned to ruin you with the secret of how you truly won that patronage. Oh, I hardly blame you. You just did what was necessary, playing the old man's evil games. But when you tracked Carmine down, he'd already sold it out of greed. So you tortured him until he told you where, and then you killed him."

Penny's mouth trembled. "Oh, God. Sherry, what does she mean?"

"You killed Strangeface Willy, too," accused Eliza, ignoring Hipp's bouncing and yelling, "and took the portrait back. And now here it is. Am I getting warm?"

A strange laugh from Sheridan. "Pen, don't do this to me. Tell her."

Penny just sobbed. "How could you? Dalziel was just a harmless old man. It wasn't his fault he adored you."

"You *bitch*." Sheridan bolted for Eliza.

She squeezed the trigger. *Crrack!* Lightning struck Sheridan's shoulder, flinging him backwards. He hit the floor, blue current forking over his twitching limbs.

Eliza pounced. Recharged her pistol, *hiss-flick!*, and aimed straight down into his face. Static crackled up her arms. "Move another inch, and I won't aim for something harmless."

Sheridan just choked for breath, smoke drifting from his hair. A raw burn snaked on his shoulder, inside his charred shirt . . . and it sizzled, and *healed*. His singed hair *grew back*.

Immortal. Beautiful. Soulless.

"I did it all for her," he rasped. "I only wanted her to love me."

"Sherry, don't," Penny sobbed . . . but then her sobs hiccuped into laughter.

Off-balance, Eliza whirled. The stained sheet lay at Penny's feet, the painting unveiled at last.

An unframed forest portrait, almost life-sized, the canvas pegged out flat. Sheridan, painted in romantic style as a poet, flowing shirt and floating hair . . . but the figure's skin was blotched with decay, the shirt stained with ichor from countless wounds. His spine hunched, twisted forever in pain, his belly misshapen from over-indulgence. That same snake-shaped burn showed raw on his shoulder. His half-smile twisted into a knowing leer, and his teeth bled in rotting gums. His perverted gaze glittered, amused by his own cruelty. Satisfied.

And he wasn't alone.

A second figure completed the painting. Laughing like a maniac, her glossy eyes rolling. Her pretty face was rotted with sin, a dark hole where her nose used to be. Her body sagged, dissolute. Blood coated her arms to the elbows, and began to drip from her lip.

Two figures. Two souls. Two killers.

The real Penny grinned, blacker than midnight. The split on her perfect lip had healed perfectly. Such a beautiful girl.

"An entertaining tale, Doctor. Unfortunately, you made one false assumption." Triumphantly, she aimed her own pistol into Eliza's face. "Carmine didn't kill that filthy old man. I did."

CAIN'S HERESY

· • ·

WHAT?" ELIZA'S MIND RATTLED. SHE'D BELIEVED what she'd wanted to, that Penny was innocent and all the others corrupt. All those lies, insinuations, alibis, designed to frame first Carmine, then Moriarty Quick, then Mr. Todd. Sheridan and Penny, pretending they hated each other, when all along . . .

Penny brandished her pistol. "Drop that gun. One step towards that picture, and I'll burn your face off. What will you do, shoot me? You must know I won't die."

Eliza took a cautious step. "It's not too late. You can still—"

Penny shifted her aim an inch and fired. Eliza yelped, hair springing tight in the stink of burned aether. "I've already killed three people this week," Penny warned. "Tortured one to death, too. Ha! Think I won't do the same to you?"

Still on the floor, Sheridan laughed. "Do as she says, Doctor. You don't know her the way I do."

Stiffly, Eliza powered down her pistol and tossed it away. Her mind scrambled for a new plan. Maybe Hipp . . .

"And the bag."

She dropped that, too, cursing inwardly. Hipp wriggled like a spider, one brass leg poking out.

Penny kicked Eliza's things aside. "Sheridan, stop whining and get up."

Sheridan obeyed. Not a scrap of blood or burn, his sneering good looks unblemished. "Penny, we have to stop this."

"You covered it up," Eliza burst out. "I saw your footprints in the blood. She killed Dalziel, but you returned later. Made it look like a ritual, to fool the authorities."

"Very good." Penny sneered. "The old monster deserved it. Do you think I *liked* being in his thrall? A slave to his every foul whim?"

"Abuse doesn't excuse murder," snapped Eliza. "Why didn't you report him to the police?"

Rage twisted Penny's face. "A baronet? Are you serious? Curse you, and your middle-class ignorance. You've never been penniless. I was destitute. I'd have starved!"

"Plenty of people are starving, They're not all killers—"

"Dalziel flattered us into sitting for him." Oblivious, Penny ranted on, waving her pistol wildly. "He was talented, and handsome, oh yes, with his vile self-portrait keeping him pure. All those pretty lies, about how only *I* could be his muse. What a foolish *ingénue* I was. Once it was done, he had us over a barrel. Literally, sometimes. He didn't care that we'd live forever. All he wanted was a model who'd always be pretty and a slave he couldn't beat to death."

"Pen," whispered Sheridan, "enough. It's over."

"Shut up!" Penny howled. "Think *you* suffered for your art? At least he rewarded you. I had to hide behind a stupid male name. Those cringing fools see my work every day, but I'll never be famous. You got everything and I got nothing and *still* all you do is *whine*."

A look of abject disgust. "You know how I suffered. He cut me. He *hurt* me. Made me do evil things for his diabolical rituals—"

"You *liked* it, you vain little whore. All that play-acting, all the other victims he made you brutalize. It *pleased* you to watch him drool, didn't it? And those men you hurt in Soho, Sherry, after I gave them what I wouldn't give you. Don't pretend you didn't enjoy *that*."

Eliza gaped. That dead yellow-feathered parrot. Pirate Ship Gino.

Sheridan's chin trembled. "You know I did that for you. They *besmirched* you, Pen. How could I let them live—"

"I got on my *knees*!" Penny's face purpled. "I *begged* Dalziel to give me our painting, to set us free. He just laughed at me. Said it was gone, he was going to exhibit it, show everyone what we really were. So I stabbed his precious self-portrait and got my revenge. It was your idea to go back and tear his rotted heart out, Sherry. And that nonsense with the pentacles. What, didn't Professor Quick adore you enough either?"

"We needed to pin it on someone." Sheridan's cheeks flooded with tears. "That Royal agent was already asking questions. I couldn't bear it if they caught you!"

Keep them talking. Eliza's gaze darted, searching for another weapon. "And Carmine?"

"Carmine was as bad as the rest," Penny snapped. "He and his cracksmen cronies didn't even know what they had. Once he found out, he thought he could use it against us." A predatory smile. "I've never heard a man try so hard to scream. Did his heart taste good, Sherry, you devil?"

Sheridan flushed. "Shut up," he muttered. "As if you never *tried* things."

Eliza felt ill. That missing eyeball, the chewed heart . . . "What about Strangeface Willy?"

"The ugly fellow in Seven Dials? He'd seen the painting. He had to die." Penny cackled, empty of emotion. "His face peeled off like apple skin. Did you like it? Good, because it's your turn. Sherry, tie her up. She's wriggling too much for my liking."

Eliza tried to run, but Sheridan shoved her to her knees, binding her wrists tightly behind her back. He was sweating, pale. "Pen, be reasonable. How much vengeance is enough? We'll never be free. What's the point in going on?"

"He's right." Eliza struggled, but his knots were cruelly tight. "You can't just keep killing people."

"But I can." Penny danced up to the painting, blowing herself a kiss. "This ugly crone grows old and rots. *I* can do whatever I want, and get off scot-free . . . Oh, spare me your moralizing!" she yelled at Eliza, a squall of fury. "I saw you at the Exhibition, swigging your hellbrew so *she* wouldn't burst out and embarrass you. She wallows in filth while *you* swan around without a care. Who's got a disposable conscience now?"

Eliza trembled. Was that all Lizzie was? A way for Eliza to sin without consequence? By night, Lizzie raged, indulging every whim fair or foul. And in the morning, Eliza awakened, pristine. Her conscience clear. Remade.

But her stomach curdled. Her conscience was far from clear. She'd been cruel and selfish enough today without Lizzie's help.

"You're mistaken." Still she fought her bonds. Across the floor, Hipp peeked from the bag, flashing his indignant red light, and frantically she tried to warn him off before he was seen. "Trust me. It'll come back to haunt you."

"Ha! I beg to differ." Penny pointed to her own eternally perfect face. "Don't you recognize me? I'm immortal. The angel of vengeance! That's my purpose. I know that now."

Sheridan tugged Penny's arm. "Let's run away together," he urged. "Take the painting with us. Abroad, where no one will recognize us. Spain, or even Egypt. Wouldn't you like to see Egypt?"

"Not with you."

His eyes drained. "But I love you, Penny. Since the beginning."

"Love is a *ghost,* Sherry," spat Penny. "A limb that hurts after it's amputated. There *is* no love, not for people like us."

"No." Sheridan's perfect cheekbones glittered with jeweled tears. "He didn't take that away. I can still feel!"

"Do you think *saying* that makes it true?" Penny grabbed his hair and twisted, forcing him to look at the picture. "Your soul's rotten. Look at it! There's no love left in you, Sherry. You're going nowhere but *hell.*"

"Let him go," Eliza urged. Still the knots wouldn't loosen. "You need medical care. You're not yourself . . ."

"They won't let me be myself!" Penny hurled Sheridan away. She tore her hair, raked sharp nails down her face. Blood

oozed . . . and then the crimson streaks bubbled and healed, and picture-Penny's face began to bleed. The real Penny laughed. "But now, I can be. See? It's all just a game."

Terrible sympathy burned in Eliza's heart. *I don't want to be half of me,* Todd had said. So wrong . . . but right, too. "No. You can't be half a person, Penny. Believe me, I've tried."

Penny waved her pistol. *Boom!* Blue lightning stabbed the tall window, and it shattered, a rush of warm breeze. She recharged, *hiss-flick!,* and jabbed the red-hot barrel into Eliza's temple. "I know: I'll kill you, and Sheridan can eat your body. All of it, not just the heart. No one will ever find you. Brilliant! What d'you think, Sherry, you little monster?"

Eliza's guts heated, a wash of dumb incoherence. She struggled impotently. In a few seconds, the gun would recharge, and she'd be dead.

Sheridan's eyes rolled, abruptly pearly white, as if his mind had snapped. "Don't be cruel, my darling. We can work this out. I just want us to be the way we were."

"I've always hated you, Sherry. Even when we were lovers, touching you made me sick. I'd rather *die.*" *Zzap!* Penny's pistol charge re-ignited. Eliza's guts clenched, and she braced herself . . .

"If you say so, Penn." Suddenly Sheridan brandished a short, sharp knife. The kind that had carved those horrid pentacles.

Penny just laughed. "You can't kill me. I'm immortal!"

Sheridan grinned, ghastly. "So am I." *Snap!* He threw the knife.

It struck Penny in the chest, sinking to the hilt. Penny just laughed harder, and reached up to pull it out. For a moment, her pistol's aim faltered . . . and Sheridan dived for an oil lamp, and hurled it.

Not at Penny. At the painting.

Fire streaked, a bright red arc. The lamp hit the easel and shattered, splashing hot oil across the canvas. *Woof!* Flame exploded, licking up the grisly portrait.

Penny shrieked, clawing her eyes. On the canvas, painted flesh crackled and melted. Faces dripped, eyes slid, hair and skin charred in seething, evil-smelling black smoke.

The real Sheridan and Penny burned, too. They collided, fighting, twin twisting pillars of flame. Skin bubbled, clothing erupted in fire. They rolled together in a boiling red inferno, and at last fell still.

Blackened, smoking husks, clutched in a hateful embrace. Transformed forever into the *things* they'd caused so much suffering to hide.

------◆------

Eliza retched on the stink of burning flesh. Fire ate across the wooden floor towards the broken window, unstoppable. Like red-eyed imps, the flames gasped for air and swelled triumphantly, their low roar rising. Hipp bounded from her bag, and yelped as his feet heated up. "Fire! Exit!"

"Yes, thank you, Hipp." Her hands were still tied behind her. Squatting, she scrabbled up the bag with difficulty, and tried for the pistol, but heat and smoke drove her back. She'd no way to extinguish this. Everything would burn.

Ancient wooden beams cracked as the ceiling caught alight. Flames dripped and cackled, victorious. Already, in the corridor, footsteps banged. Shouts rang. "Fire! Fire!"

Hipp squealed and sprinted for the door, disappearing into thick smoke. She sucked in one last clean breath, and ran.

Crash! A beam tumbled, dragging a curtain of flame. She staggered, coughing. Her spectacles were smeared with dirt. The smoke made her dizzy. The door seemed so terribly far. *Lizzie, wake up. Help me! Give me strength.*

Fruitlessly she kicked debris from her path. Hipp was gone. Her lungs spasmed, aching. No hands. Couldn't see. Couldn't find the exit. Couldn't breathe. What a stupid way to die.

So die, muttered Lizzie. *Best for both of us. Better off without me . . .*

"Eliza!" A scuffle, the bang of timber tossed aside. "Sound off, for God's sake. If you burn to death, I'll kill you."

"Here!" She staggered towards Remy's voice. Vicious heat lashed her face. Surely she was on fire, her skin melting like Penny's. "Over here!"

"I see you . . ." More wood crashed, a rich British army curse. "I'll meet you halfway. To your left. Keep coming . . ."

Awkwardly, she ran, flames grabbing greedily at her skirts. Collided, and strong arms swept her up, carried her into the corridor, down the stairs, into blessedly cool night air.

She choked, gratefully gasping clean lungfuls. Alive. Hipp galloped up, a flurry of soot. "Fire! Seek medical attention! Make greater speed! Fire!"

Around them, in smoke and ash, men ran and yelled, unrolling hoses and pumping handles. Clockwork fire engines cranked. People rushed up and down the front steps, carrying out paintings and etchings to pile them in the square. Gentlemen, scruffy folk, police, children—everyone was pitching in. Except a line of Enforcers, marching by towards Whitehall. Weapons glinting, flesh-grafted brass parts gleaming. Studiously ignoring the blaze, though the firefighters could clearly have used any help they could get.

She nudged at Remy's chest. "I'm all right," she spluttered. "Put me down, sir. I'm not a sack of wool."

He set her down, and untied her hands. Her knees buckled. She steadied herself against his shoulder, slapping embers from her skirts and wiping smarting eyes.

Remy's face was charmingly smudged, his scarlet coat dusted with soot. He was breathing hard, coughing, but still managed a smile and a jaunty tilt of saber. "Don't look so alarmed, Doctor. All free of charge. You needn't faint, or fling yourself into my arms or anything."

But she did. Pressed her cheek against his coat and held him close. His startled embrace felt so warm, so safe. His heartbeat so strong. *Just hold me, and don't look down.*

Her breath raked her throat. Her lungs stung. Smoke inhalation. She'd prescribe a tonic. But it didn't matter. Everything was perfect . . . yet so perfectly wrong.

"I say," she managed, muffled, "rescued again. It's an unfortunate habit."

"No trouble, I assure you." His voice was strangely soft and deep.

"Happened to be passing, did you? Or do you schedule random heroics into your day in a bizarre effort to impress me?"

"Mr. Finch turned up at François's telling a most peculiar tale about Sheridan Lightwood. I figured you'd be here."

She craned her neck to glare. "That's it? You decided to dash into a burning building on the off chance I was inside? Honestly. Haven't we had this conversation?"

He shrugged, sheepish. "Seemed a compelling idea at the time."

"I rest my case. I'm glad we're agreed you're a romantic fool, Remy Lafayette."

"I'm all kinds of fool where you're concerned, Eliza Jekyll." He hadn't let go. Hadn't relinquished his embrace. Why would he, with her body flush against his?

Her fingers curled in his coat. Other ideas seemed quite compelling right now, too. Things she didn't deserve. Let him hold her. Give in and kiss him. Weep.

At her feet, Hipp chortled and danced, teasing. "Eh-eh-eh!"

Flushing, she stepped back and smoothed her claret skirts, which were now charred as well as torn. How she must look. Lizzie would have been proud, once. Lizzie, who'd wanted to die in that burning building.

"Well, I'm glad you're safe." Remy jammed his hat on over tousled hair and glanced at the marching line of Enforcers. "I don't like the look of that. The streets won't be safe tonight."

Eliza wiped her spectacles on her skirt and replaced them. "Well, I don't think we can do anything to help here. Might I walk you home? I know you fear for your life, alone in the dark."

"Would you? I'd feel so much safer." His eyes twinkled—haunted, not so bright, but merry just the same—and he offered her his arm.

Eliza tucked her hand into his elbow, and they headed down the steps towards the fountain. Men ran and dragged hoses, their faces blackened.

The awful *thwock-schllp!* of Harlequin's knife in her guts still echoed, unforgettable. "Last night, the man who stabbed me . . . Lizzie, I mean. He killed Nemo to stop him talking. That was the real Harlequin?"

"We believe he must be." He handed her over a gutter, where the Enforcers marched.

"Nemo claimed to be only an underling. That the war had only just begun. What did he mean?"

"Who knows? The Incorruptibles have gone to ground, so we won't hear anything about it until it happens. Nemo had the ill manners to die, so we can't question him. The Foreign Secretary is furious. François is beside himself. Months of work lost. A mess, in fact." Remy glanced down at her. "So how was your evening?"

She explained about Sheridan and Penny, their horrid portrait. "A mess, as you say," she concluded.

"And to think I got you into this because some sneaking fey thief stole some pictures."

Eliza halted, stunned. "What did you say?"

"The frame-maker's shop. Remember? Harry the Hooligan, or whatever his name was."

"Haunter," corrected Hipp importantly. "Invisible. Does not compute."

She barely heard. Her thoughts buzzed, a swarm of bees. Magic paint. Stolen art. A sneaking fey thief.

Lizzie's memories stirred with her own, green and gold like absinthe and cognac. Wild Johnny's new girl, drifting in the shadows, trailing a glitter-green wake. Even sharp-eyed Lizzie had trouble following her. *Now you see her, now you don't* . . .

Images wobbled, a speeding cinematograph. That night at the Cockatrice, a purse of gold pressed into Johnny's hand.

Lizzie in the matchlight, the bloodied knife in Nemo's fist. *I really wish you hadn't seen that.*

Harry the Haunter was Becky Pearce. She'd had business with Nemo that night, and anticipated a big payday. But instead, he'd stabbed her and left her to die.

Not over nothing. Over a theft Nemo wanted kept secret. An item from the frame-maker's shop, worth killing for.

And Nemo was merely an underling. The servant to a dark master.

"Oh, my," she said faintly.

Remy winced. "Don't say that. It's never good when you say that."

"Nemo killed Harry the Haunter," she burst out. "Lizzie's friend from Seven Dials. To silence her about stealing the Mad Queen's portrait. Don't you see? Penny said Dalziel wanted to exhibit their picture. He sent it to the frame-maker's shop! Where Becky Pearce stole it. By accident. Along with the one she was being paid for."

"So Harlequin has the Queen's portrait? Irritating, but hardly calamitous."

"Didn't you say the Empire's fate rested on solving that case?" She sucked in a breath. "What if it's imbued with dark alchemy? Destroy the painting, and you kill the subject. Not simply a portrait . . ."

"But a weapon." Remy halted, gripping her arm. "Good God. But how?"

"Penny had access to the magic paint. And she adopted a man's name for her commissions. People looked at her work every day, she said, but she'd never be famous. Wyn Patten, the court painter! A pseudonym. An anagram! Rearrange those letters, and you get—"

In the dark, an arc-pistol charged, an ugly purple flash.

Eliza gasped. Behind Remy loomed the white face of an Enforcer. "Look out!"

Ever alert, Remy dodged the Enforcer's swinging brass fist. *Zzap!* Electricity exploded.

But not from the Enforcer's pistol. Current stabbed Remy in the back, knocking him flat. Eliza yelled, and dived for him . . . only to be shoved aside by a slender gray-booted foot.

Lady Lovelace hobbled from the shadows, a pistol smoking in her iron-jointed hand. Firelight glistened on her metal cheekbone, and she stretched cold lips in a creaking smile. "Take Captain Lafayette to the Tower," she ordered, that single red eye glittering. "He has questions to answer. About a certain unorthodox condition he seems to have been hiding from me."

Horror squeezed Eliza's lungs. She struggled to get up, to fight, but something hard and cold thumped the back of her head, an evil echo. Her muscles watered, and as light slipped away, the last thing she saw in the shadows was the gloating, vengeful smile of Moriarty Quick.

———◈———

Minutes later—or was it hours?—Eliza groaned, and tried to rise. Trafalgar Square was a blur, the gallery still aflame in the night, firefighters running madly like ants. Fumbling, she retrieved her fallen spectacles, straightening their bent frames. Hippocrates poked her ribs with a frantic brass leg. "Awake! Emergency! Make greater speed!"

"Enough, Hipp. Stop it." She stumbled to her feet. Quick had betrayed them to the Royal. Remy was taken. Her bag was gone. And Harlequin was planning to assassinate the Queen with a stolen magic painting.

Just perfect.

What now?

Her heart bled at the thought of Remy at Lady Lovelace's mercy. Those electrified cells, bristling with torture implements and truth drugs. He'd feared this more than anything. Not for his own sake. For hers, Eliza's.

Lady Lovelace hadn't arrested Eliza. Hadn't known of her "crimes." Remy had never told. This proved it once and for all. And she couldn't just abandon him.

But the Royal were all-powerful. The police couldn't help her. No one could. She was on her own.

She grabbed Hipp and hurried for home. "Lizzie, wake up," she snapped. "I need you. We must get him out of there!"

Silence. Just an empty, windswept hollow in her heart.

But as she ran through smoky streets, the ghost of Lizzie's imagined laughter mocked her, echoing from the dark. *You and whose army?* Lizzie would say. *What will you do, knock on the door and ask nicely?*

An audacious plan, certainly. Break a man out of the most secure fortress in England. Alone. While inhuman Lady Lovelace and her half-flesh Enforcers had their evil way with him.

Not a moment to lose, then.

I MET MURDER ON THE WAY

• • •

AN HOUR LATER, ELIZA RAPPED ON THE STUDDED door of the Royal's precinct. "Open up!"

A single purple arc-light crackled and buzzed, showering her in the thundery scent of aether. Above, the Tower's vast walls climbed inexorably into the night, and behind her, moonlight streaked the rushing river with silver.

Wild giggles threatened to betray her—Lizzie's delight in danger? or just Eliza's own recklessness?—and she throttled them. Knocking on the door, indeed. As good a plan as any.

The heavy door creaked open, and a seven-foot-tall Enforcer leaned out. It stared down at her, impassive, one brass hand twitching over its pistol holster.

Eliza brandished an iron Royal Society badge. "Miss Burton, to see Lady Lovelace."

Luckily for her, Miss Burton hadn't yet found other lodgings. Eliza had shaken her awake, demanded she hand the badge over. Those blue skirts had proved an impossible fit, so she'd thrown the girl's long black coat on over Lizzie's dress, the hood pulled up. She was betting an Enforcer wouldn't notice the difference. To a clockwork, all humans looked alike.

Miss Burton had offered to accompany her, but Eliza refused. She trusted no one with this task but herself.

The Enforcer peered at the badge. Cocked its head. Pulled the door open.

She strode in, a show of confidence. A chilly low-ceilinged room, poorly lit. Machines needed no heat, no comforts. It smelled of mildew and musty stone. Like a dungeon.

Imperiously, she turned. "Where's the countess? It's rather urgent."

Solemnly, the Enforcer pointed to a down-spiraling metal stair.

She descended, shivering in icy damp. The rust-stained iron walls seemed splashed with blood. *Plink! Plonk!* Water dripped, indefatigable. A queue of rats skittered past her boots into the dark. Somewhere below, voltage sizzled, and a woman screamed.

Eliza's courage scuttled into a corner. This was foolhardy. Irrational. She'd never make it out alive.

At the bottom, a rusted corridor stretched into the dark, lit by flickering arc-lights. A harsh coppery scent assaulted her, some vile disinfectant. Cell doors with tiny observation portals punctuated one wall. At the end, a barred hatch covered a drain or oubliette. She imagined what might languish down there, and shuddered.

She passed one empty cell. In the second, a wailing creature banged its head against the wall. The next held a figure slumped on the corroded floor, alive by its tortured breathing . . . but not Remy. Sympathy stung her, but grimly, she walked on.

From the next cell came the sound of pacing footfalls. *Click-scrape! Click-scrape!* The hitching step of an imperfect machine. She couldn't hear Remy's voice. Nothing, bar the *buzz* and *pop!* of electrics and that sinister, uneven step.

Eliza pulled her hood lower and tapped on the door. "My lady. Miss Burton, with a message from Sir Isaac."

Click-scrape . . . At the portal, eyes glinted. One red, one black. Eliza held her breath . . .

Zzap! An electric switch crackled, and the door clunked open.

Cold light shimmered, a single arc-light trapped in a rusted cage on the ceiling. Eliza edged inside, pulse skipping. Chemical testing equipment waited on a trestle table, a brass calculating machine with columns of cogs, a gleaming microscope and its pile of slides. Test tubes in a rack held bright blood. On the wall, a bank of evil-looking instruments sat ready. Knives, pincers, electric probes.

Lady Lovelace paced, her crooked hip twitching. And strapped to a bench lay Remy Lafayette.

Sweating, pale, his shirt stripped off. Bruised and bloodied, half conscious, his breath shallow . . . but alive. From a tall steel array hung a bottle of white fluid that dripped down a tube, to where a steel needle was jabbed into his forearm.

"Fascinating!" crowed Lady Lovelace. Empty of emotion. A woman with no heart. "Such powerful metamorphosis. I must assess the potential for weaponization. How is the change effected?"

Remy muttered something incoherent, ending with a muddled giggle.

Whatever that drug, it wasn't friendly. Eliza hadn't much time. She sidled closer, clutching a tiny metal object behind her back.

Lady Lovelace turned, *click-snap!* Her steel cheekbone glistened, riveted skin damp with fanatical sweat. "What? Out with it. I'm ready to begin."

Eliza charged.

The half-metal woman screeched, hand flashing for her pistol. But too late. They collided, and Eliza slammed the squirming metal surveillance node into Lady Lovelace's dead black eye.

The node had been thwarted. It was hungry. And *snap!* It reared like a striking spider, and stabbed a dozen wicked wire filaments eagerly into Lady Lovelace's brain.

She screamed, clawing for her eyes. Desperately, Eliza scrabbled for the fallen pistol and aimed it two-handed at that cruel face. *Hiss-flick!* The pistol charged.

But her hands shook, and her trigger finger cramped, just a twitch from murder.

Never mind that this woman tortured and burned innocent people. She, Eliza, wasn't an executioner. This wasn't justice. She couldn't just *shoot.*

But Lady Lovelace knew about Remy's curse. He'd never be free of her. Never be safe . . .

Crrack! Blue lightning erupted, blinding. And it was done.

Lady Lovelace's body hit the floor, metal parts clanging. Stray current crackled over her metal cheekbone, her staring eye just a black hollow.

"That's for Mr. Faraday, too," whispered Eliza. Then she dropped the pistol and ran to Remy.

Conscious, just barely. His skin felt cold and clammy on her palms. Pupils dilated, just a narrow rim of blue. Probably in chemical shock. "Remy, wake up."

"'Liza Jekyll. Just th'lady I wanted to see." He coughed, slurring his words. "Don't feel so well."

She fumbled the leather buckles open. Pulled that horrid needle from his arm, with a bubble of white slime. Soon some Enforcer would compute that gunshot as unauthorized. "We need to go. Now." She struggled to help him stand.

"Right. Cert'nly. I can do that." His legs buckled, and he stumbled against her shoulder. Damp, fevered, fragrant. "Good God, you're beautiful."

"This is no time for foolish flirtations." She steadied him, wiping blood and dirt from his eyes. Bruises swelled his cheek, ringing one eye. He'd fought hard.

"Innit? Seems perfect t' me." He grinned at her, dopey but lucid. "You're 'mazing, 'Liza. Y'don't think enough of y'self. You're so much the woman I love that my bloody eyes hurt."

Her heart sank. But it smiled, too. "Oh, lord. Is that a truth drug?"

He nodded solemnly. "Want some? 'Cause this conversation's 'bout to get *really* int'resting."

"No, thank you." She thrust his shirt and coat at him and grabbed his sword from where it lay in the corner. "Now get dressed, before I drag you up the stairs half naked and get you shot, just to shut you up."

———◈———

A few hours later, Eliza paced in the window of Remy's Waterloo Bridge house, invisible ants of impatience nipping her skin. Outside, morning threatened, eerily calm and silent. No gunfire crackled, no thunder of electric cannon, no screams or smell of exploding aether. Nemo's uprising, running battle in the streets . . . none of it had happened. Not yet. But the bright air thrummed with tension, ready to explode.

She'd managed to get Remy upstairs and almost out of the Tower before the Enforcers raised the alarm. Her singed hair still stank, a shot having missed her by inches. But they'd soon lost the clumsy machines in the festering warren of dockside lanes, and what Remy had lacked in strength, he'd made up for with a bloody-minded determination to escape.

On the way home, they'd seen barricades, erected with furniture, splintered doors, beams, slabs of broken brickwork. Anything the Incorruptibles could find. The stage was set. Either the city would rise, and the rebels would triumph, or the rebels would face the dawn alone . . . and the Enforcers would march on the barricades and slaughter them all.

For the umpteenth time, she peered out between the drapes. Unscrupulous fellows were cashing in on the anticipated chaos. Smashing windows, looting, amidst the clatter of galloping hooves and shouts of "Incorruptible!" and "God save the Queen!"

A pair of dirty hooligans hurtled by on a tandem velocipede, hooting and pedaling like madmen. A trio of brass-and-flesh Enforcers sprinted in pursuit, their heavy footsteps shaking the ground. *Thud! Thud!* Pistols cracked, lightning sizzled, a scene from the electric Wild West. The rear-facing hooligan braced an enormous elephant gun on his shoulder. *Booom!* The velocipede swerved, nearly flinging both riders into the road, and an Enforcer exploded, flesh and jagged brass raining.

Remy shot her a fondly exasperated glance as he buckled on his weapons. She'd cleaned him up, washed the blood from his bruises. Dosed him with a nerve stimulant, too, and the effect of Lady Lovelace's horrid drug had started to ebb. He was still subdued, but strong and almost steady. "Will you sit down a second? You're exhausting me."

Her ragged dress still stank of charcoal and smoke. Her blood scrambled, frustrated, rummaging for something that wasn't there. She needed Lizzie. But Lizzie wasn't talking. "Are you finished primping? Perhaps it's escaped your memory, but Harlequin's about to assassinate the Mad Queen and start a war. We can't just sit here! We must go!"

"But to where? And when? Half the country thinks the Queen's already dead," said Remy reasonably.

"I don't know." She rubbed her eyes, bewildered. "Let me think. There must be some clue."

"Well, if I were a French agent striking Her Majesty down with sorcery, I'd want to do it somewhere conspicuous . . ."

"In full public view," she whispered. *For maximum effect.* "Oh, my. The skyship launch. This very morning!"

"Genius," proclaimed Remy. "Well, you did say you wanted to see that skyship fly."

"Not precisely what I had in mind."

Swiftly, he checked the charge on his pistol, fumbling only a little. Sweating and pale, but collected. Never at a loss. "One's almost forced to admire Harlequin. She dies, a victim of sorcery; the Royal are shown to be powerless to protect her; and it's the perfect occasion for a riot."

She stuffed her stinger into her bag. "He'll get the bloodbath he wanted. And the Philosopher won't be able to stop him . . ."

It'll be quite something, whispered sly Sir Isaac in her ear. *London's never seen the like.*

". . . even if he wanted to," she finished, thinking of that addle-brained Prince of Wales, locked away out of sight in electric-fenced Buckingham Palace. "If the Queen dies, who becomes Regent?"

"You're not serious."

"With the Queen defying the Philosopher to pursue her own diplomacy? I'm deadly serious. It's the perfect opportunity for him to secure his power. We *really* have to go." She fumbled for her cape.

Remy helped her arrange it. "One could do worse."

"You don't mean that."

He grabbed his hat. "He is the cleverest man in England, my love, and a hereditary ruler makes about as much sense as a hereditary doctor. Ought we to have a simpleton in charge, just because his mother was Queen? Who died and put these so-called royals in power, anyway? Five hundred thousand Englishmen in the civil war? Oh, wait. I see a problem."

She flashed a smile. "Careful, Captain. Your radical side is showing."

"Is it? Damn. And here I thought the badge was covering it up."

Hippocrates clattered after them to the front door. "Destination," he trumpeted. "Information please."

"Moriarty Quick's shop, of course," she said. "He's up to his neck in it. The magic paint's his invention, and his upstairs windows have a perfect view of the skyship. Timing will be critical. Harlequin must strike at precisely the right moment." She shared a warm glance with Remy. "Do you think Quick could *be* Harlequin?"

"Perhaps there *is* no Harlequin. Just a mythical name they use to spread fear. Shall we ask him?"

"Let's do that." She was already halfway out. "Hipp, stay behind."

A disconsolate whine, and a rattle of brassy feet.

"Don't whine." Firmly, she pushed him back inside. "Telegraph Captain Lafayette—the other one—and ask him to meet us at Quick's. And tell him to make Marcellus stay put. I don't want him punching Quick's lights out before we can question him."

LET OUR NAME BE VENGEANCE

...

A T TEN MINUTES TO TEN, SPECTATORS CRUSHED into Piccadilly, a throng of black hats and parasols. People thronged the street, hung from casements, clambered on rooftops to secure a better view. Soldiers and Enforcers lurked, weapons bristling. Food-sellers cried their wares, children tumbled hoops, jugglers juggled and sword-swallowers swallowed.

"Like an execution party," she muttered. Then she thought of Mr. Todd in Newgate, and wished she hadn't.

Across the street, the silvery skyship bobbed and strained against its ropes. Heat haze shimmered above the twin engine exhausts. Metallic sails glinted in the smell of aether and hot metal, and engineers and crew scrambled like insects in the rigging. Scaffolding had been erected in the park to hold the royal party, and a frilled sunshade protected the dais where Her Majesty would sit. Ribbons and rosettes fluttered, blue and red, a change from the usual mourning black of state occasions.

Would the Queen really appear? After five years in seclusion, a virtual prisoner? Eliza found herself doubting it. Perhaps it was all a hoax.

She checked her watch. Nine minutes to go. Everything was in place. The perfect killing jar.

Remy waved above the crowd. *"François, ici!"*

The elder Lafayette pushed through. In dress uniform, long blue coat with a captain's golden brocade, white breeches, tricorne hat. "I hope you realize I'm giving up a perfectly good invitation to the Lord High Admiral's breakfast. 'Frankie, you old seadog,' said he, 'you simply *must* come for the launch of my new flagship. We'll have a blast! Flog a few seamen, recite the Articles of War, choke down some gin and sauerkraut. It'll be just like old times . . .' Good God, Remy, what happened to your face? You're a living bruise."

Remy shoved him. "So sorry. Did we interrupt your social schedule to stop a royal assassination?"

"All most inconvenient, my lad." François tilted blue-tinted glasses. He wore an old-fashioned powder pistol at one hip, black cane in his hand. "Still, I'd expect nothing less from you cavalry poseurs. Good morning, Doctor. Still haven't kicked him to the gutter?"

"No accounting for taste."

Another figure wormed through the crush, beaming. "Let's get on, say what? Time's wasting, eh?"

Eliza's heart sank. "Marcellus, what are you doing here?"

Finch tipped his top hat. She'd rarely seen him properly dressed, instead of wearing an apron and dirty shirtsleeves. His dapper black coat reminded her of Henry Jekyll's funeral. "Assassination, dark alchemy, gratuitous gore! Wouldn't miss it for the world. I say, sir," he added, narrowing vague eyes at Remy, "not planning to arrest me, are you? Those chemicals in my shop aren't mine. Never seen 'em before in my life. Planted, eh? Blasted spies—"

"Relax, Marcellus," murmured Remy. "Shan't persecute you today."

"Glad to hear it. Not that you'd have anything on me. God-rotted Royal investigators, you're all dimwits. Idiots, I say!"

François covered a cough. "Doctor, tell me my brother isn't inventing this nonsense about magic paint just to impress you."

"I'm afraid not."

"I told you," said Finch crossly, "it's all perfectly possible. You morose military chaps. Lost your sense of wonder, eh?"

Eliza pointed to Quick's shop. Parliament had declared the day a holiday, in honor of the Queen's appearance, and the place was closed, drapes drawn. "This is it."

François peered into the bay window. "'Beautiful for Ever,'" he read. "For twenty guineas, no less. How droll."

"Most of the shops are renting out their top floors for the view," observed Eliza. "Perhaps Quick hasn't yet arrived."

"Or he's skulking in the dark," muttered Finch, a vengeful glint in his eyes. "We'll winkle the stinky weasel from his burrow and strangle him with tooth floss. After we've arrested him, of course. Justice, all that."

"I agree with Finch." Remy glanced left and right, hand on sword. "Police everywhere, Enforcers bookending the street. Guarding the skyship against long-range gunfire, not searching for assassins, but he wouldn't risk being stopped. If Harlequin's coming, he's already here."

"You've a lot of faith in him," remarked François.

"He's played us for fools so far."

"I daresay." François lapsed into coughing again.

A glow of blue concern. "Brother, are you sure . . . ?"

François cocked his pistol. "Belay your mothering, lad," he ordered hoarsely. "We've hunted L'Arlequin for months. Think I'll miss having the fellow at our mercy?" He gestured grandly to the door. "Stand aside, *monsieur le capitaine.*"

"After all these years you're pulling rank?"

"With Her Majesty in grave peril, and the chief French spy in England within our grasp? Absolutely."

Remy flipped an ironic salute and drew both weapons, *swish-click!* "Aye, sir."

Crash! François kicked the door in. Wood splintered, the lock cracking open. Eliza followed François inside. Then Marcellus, with Remy last of all.

Four minutes to go.

Dim, cool, the polished counter gleaming softly. Eliza ignited her electric light, *bzzt!* Shadows leapt. Somewhere, water gurgled. Drapes whispered. The flowery perfume of soap and bath salt drifted on an undertone of sour corruption.

"Pagh," muttered Finch, holding his nose. "Charlatan. I've always said so. Aconite, lead, tincture of mercury salts. Paste *that* brew on your skin and you'll be sorry."

Efficiently, Remy and François searched the room, leading with weapons and tugging curtains aside. "Clear," whispered Remy. "Shall we get on?"

The stairs lay in back, beyond a bathtub of cold chalky water. Enamel paste and white putty filled a row of jars, beside a tray of sponges and needles. Enameling your skin like a porcelain shell, no doubt engendering all sorts of boils and pimples underneath. Eliza wrinkled her nose. The things women did to stay "beautiful."

Crick! Crack! Up the stairs, the air growing mustier. It smelled dead, empty, inhabited by dusty ghosts. Wind whistled in distant roof tiles, *whoo! whoo!*

On the landing, a door hung ajar. Remy's pistol glimmered purple in the gloom. Eliza gripped her stinger. François sidled up to the door, and they burst in.

A study-cum-laboratory, with wooden benches holding steel surgical instruments, gas burners, flasks of powders and solutions in rainbow colors. Three windows yawned open, drapes fluttering in warm breeze. Below, the crowd ebbed and swayed, awaiting the Queen, and the skyship glittered in dazzling sun. A perfect view.

Two minutes.

Shelves lined the walls, books and stacks of paper and . . .

Eliza's stomach crawled. Jars of preserving fluid. *Specimens*. But what abnormal creatures were these? Misshapen, abortive limbs, limpid skin, horns and hooves and mangled faces . . . and they were *alive*. Fleshy coils tightened, bloodshot eyes blinked . . . and they made *noises*. Plaintive cries, agonized groans, yelps of wretched terror.

Quick's souls. Which jar had she been trapped in, when Lizzie drank that potion?

Sick, she tore her gaze away. The Mad Queen's stolen portrait was pegged to a wooden easel. Freshly painted, new varnish gleaming. The figure wore a fine black gown and diamonds, her expression startled. Just a solitary woman, gaunt and approaching middle age, graying hair pulled back.

Over the far casement leaned Moriarty Quick. Breeze danced in his boyish blond curls. In one hand, a pocket watch. In the other, a long steel dagger. Perfect for slashing canvas.

"Grand," he exclaimed, "you're here. Just in time!"

Somewhere, a clock chimed the hour.

Eliza rushed to the closest window. Below, the crowd flung their hats high, erupting into cheers . . . and a figure in white edged onto the dais. She leaned weakly on the Philosopher's arm, her veil fluttering. His ageless face was twisted into a smile.

The Queen was alive.

Flanking her, like silent sentinels, four hulking Enforcers. Impassive fleshy faces, brass joints, staring red eyes. For her protection, or her imprisonment?

The hurrahs fell to a murmur. The Queen's tremulous voice rang out, but her speech was snatched away on giddy breeze.

Remy and François advanced, two pistols and a sword leveled at Quick. "Step away from the artwork," ordered Remy, "or get what's coming."

Quick laughed, pocketing his watch. "Marcellus Finch, as I live and breathe. Come to see if your hellbrew really works?"

Finch spluttered. "Mine? Curse your oily hide."

François gestured with his pistol. "You heard him. Away."

Quick just raised his hands, standing firmly between the brothers Lafayette and the painting. No one could get a clean shot at him. Bullet or electric bolt, the Queen would be just as dead.

Outside, the skyship's engines whirred, and superheated aether ignited. *Crack-boom!* The crowd gasped as the skyship juddered and groaned, straining at its ropes for freedom.

But Eliza licked dry lips. "Marcellus, what does he mean?"

Finch advanced, gripping a glittering shiv. "How dare you call that abortion *mine?*" he snarled. "You poisoned my formula, Dorry. It was supposed to *recombine* transcendental identities, not sever them completely!"

"You haven't changed, Marcellus," Quick sneered, and in that one sentence, his Dubliner's lilt was gone. Upper-class London tones, slick and mocking. "Still a sniveling coward. Call yourself a scientist? You're a disgrace."

"That awful business twenty years ago with that fellow who painted you was all your fault. I warned you."

"Nonsense," retorted Quick. "I told the lovesick idiot what would happen, but he couldn't *bear* for me, his beautiful boy, to grow old and grotesque. He got what he asked for. It's hardly my fault it ended in tears. And you did *such* a sterling job disposing of his body, old thing. Not a hair left behind."

Remy circled, eagle-eyed. "Finch, back off. Resolve your feud later. We need him alive."

But Finch ignored him and closed in. "You were meant to *fix* the new formula, not try it on Sibby. I hadn't *finished* it. How could you?"

A grin split Quick's face. Not the pleasant smile from her consulting room. A vile, ruthless leer. Eliza shuddered, recalling Lizzie's premonition of *wrongness*. Not a circus act. Soulless. Evil.

Quick threatened with his dagger at the Queen's portrait.

"Sibby was nineteen. Her whole life ahead of her. Die pretty, or live as a monster? She *begged* me." He mocked a girl's high-pitched voice. "'Don't let me die, sir, I'll do anything.' And you know what? *She did.*"

With a mindless yell, Finch shoved François aside and launched at Quick.

They grappled. Quick slashed at Finch's throat with his dagger. Finch stabbed his shiv at Quick's face. They tumbled backwards towards the painting, blades flashing . . .

Eliza ran forwards. The easel teetered. "Marcellus, stop it!"

Outside, the crowd's cheers erupted as the sailors cast off the ropes, and on a shimmer of boiling gas, the skyship groaned upwards.

The picture toppled, exposing the painted Queen. Finch and Quick stumbled against it, fighting furiously as they fell. At last, Quick yanked one arm free, and the gleaming dagger knifed down . . .

Thwock! François's cane cracked into Quick's ribs, arresting his fall. The dagger glanced harmlessly from the easel's wood, missing both Finch and the painting. Remy slammed his boot down on Quick's wrist. *Crunch!* Quick screeched like a mad monkey, and let the dagger go.

In a blur, François dropped his cane, yanked Quick up by the shirtfront, and jammed that pistol into his jugular. "Enough out of you."

"Good job, old man." Remy dragged struggling Finch away in an armlock.

Finch's face purpled. "Let me at him! Tear his nose off, say what?"

Quick chuckled, best he could with a gun shoved under his chin. "Piss on you, Marcellus," he said, dropping back into his false Irish lilt. "Never could take a joke."

François's glasses had fallen in the scuffle, and his eyes blazed. "'Beautiful for Ever,' is it?" he hissed at Quick. "Is that your secret? A portrait squirreled away, keeping you young?"

"Not anymore. You've seen how it works. It makes you too vulnerable. I've other methods now—"

"Good," said François coolly, and fired. *Boom!* Blood and bone splattered his gold-trimmed coat. And high on the bookshelf, at the very top, a writhing white creature in a jar screeched in mindless agony.

Remy didn't hesitate. *Crrack!* Blue lightning stabbed, and the jar exploded in a hail of fluid and pale flesh.

Eliza's stomach rebelled, but it was too late to look away. Half of Quick's face was obliterated, a mess of meat and splintered bone. François made a moue of distaste, and dropped him, tossing his empty pistol aside.

Quick slumped. Dead.

Grudgingly, Finch subsided. "I say," he muttered, "you could have let me."

Remy powered down his pistol, swiping back damp hair with his forearm. "Not ideal, François. We could've questioned him."

"I suppose it doesn't matter now." Eliza reached for the portrait, to roll it for safekeeping . . . but a bright sting under her chin halted her in her tracks.

François leveled his sword unwaveringly at Eliza's throat. His eyes glittered, consumptive fever taken hold. "I can't let you do that."

At his side, his left wrist twitched. A miniature lady's pistol clicked from his sleeve, and in a blue-coated blur, he fired.

The bullet drilled a tiny hole. Right between Her Majesty's painted eyes.

Eliza yelled. Remy made a strangled gulp, and his pistol dropped from nerveless fingers, clattering to the floor.

Outside, in a *wumph!* of exploding aether, the skyship burst into flame.

THE KING OF TERRORS

· • •

BOOM! RADIANT HEAT BLEW ELIZA'S HAIR BACK. Burning aether stung, the rich, stormy scent of thunder. The skyship was burning, and the Empire's new model navy along with it. And on the royal dais, blood trickling from a hole in her forehead, the Queen lay dead.

Along his shining blade, François shot her a crooked smile. A sword stick, like Lizzie's. She should have recognized it. His aim was unwavering, fanatical.

Warily, she raised her hands. With a flick of wrist, he edged her backwards, towards the window. Her ringing ears subsided, and in filtered the chaos of a riot. Yells, commotion, *crack!* and *zzaapp!*, as Enforcers and soldiers fired their guns, hoarse shouts of "Incorruptible!" Dignitaries scrambled on the dais, ladies shrieked, and in the common crowd, people trampled each other in their haste to escape.

"You sabotaged the skyship," whispered Eliza. "Right under our noses. While we *watched*."

François winked. "Knew you were too clever for my baby brother. Back against the sill, that's it. No, Remy, stay back. I should hate to have to kill you. Drop the saber, too," he added.

"Don't try anything. You either, Mr. Finch. Not if you'd rather keep your witty doctor's blood in her body."

Speechless, Remy let his blade fall, and François kicked it and the pistol away.

Remy's face had drained, a sick green. His voice, too, because barely a sound emerged. "Why, François? Why would you . . . ?"

"Because we can't fight sorcery," snapped François. "I met some people in Paris, soon saw the error of my ways. Besides"— he twitched his blade under Eliza's chin and watched her flinch—"what's *science* done for me lately? I'm done playing the hero. Best to join the winning side."

"But . . ." Remy was stunned. Lost for words. Gutted.

"I'm dying, baby brother. Stop pretending I'm not. Do you think I've stayed alive this long from bed rest and brandy?" That vintage Lafayette smile, stained strawberry red. "Don't you remember the war? To hell with surrender, eh? I'm merely adjusting my strategy."

Eliza darted her gaze, seeking options. No weapons within reach. Nothing. "But . . ."

"Come, you're an articulate woman. Say it after me: *the Queen is dead.* The flagship's history, and so is the war effort. The Skyborne Corps was our last hope, and now no one will have faith in it. When the new regime comes, I'll be part of it." François laughed, and spat at the upturned painting, landing a crimson blob on the Queen's face. "Why should *that* be immortal, while I rot? Die pretty, or live as a monster? I'll take the monster any day."

His eyes glittered, maniacal, the last throes of his sickness. She'd seen it before. Not a peaceful death. She had to talk him down, or they'd all perish. "So you used Quick's paints? A portrait . . ."

Another bloodstained laugh. "Foolishness doesn't suit you, Doctor. The paint only freezes the subject in time. What good's that, for a dying man? Immortalized with my lungs rotting? No. I want *life*. And that's where you come in! The day Remy told me you existed, I recognized your name from your father's infamous experiments. Think I'd let that opportunity slip?"

"My elixir," she breathed. "You want . . . No, it won't work. All it does is drive you mad."

"I'm aware." A satisfied smile. "Why do you think I've had Quick experimenting on you?"

Her jaw dropped.

"Come, did you imagine it a coincidence he should appear now? You've been a most obliging subject. Your little brass pet, too. Did he survive my infiltrator? Tell him it was nothing personal. I only wanted to monitor your responses to Quick's potion."

Her blood boiled. She'd nearly *died*. Claw his mad eyes out, pin his fragile body to the floor, yell *I'm not some weak female, hear me? I was engaged to a wolf-man and courted by a razor murderer. Think you scare me?*

But he *did* scare her. She didn't want to die pointlessly, unmourned. And her fear only stoked her anger higher.

"You horrid man," she snarled. "You can't experiment on people without their consent. It's unethical!"

He jabbed his sword point harder, bending her awkwardly so the window sash dug into her spine. "Easy to moralize when you're young and healthy. Show me your principles when you're dying by inches."

"But we're all dying by inches, François." If she'd learned one thing—from the Chopper case, Edward Hyde's madness, Sheridan and Penny and their rotted souls—it was that you couldn't cheat death . . . or hell.

"Only because we've no option." He licked bloodied lips. "Down to business. Mr. Finch, my compliments. On the bench you'll find a bottle of Professor Quick's silver-colored potion. Be so good as to fetch it."

Eliza's mind stumbled. *Lizzie's* potion? What good would that do?

Finch cleared his throat. "My dear fellow, I must warn you. Unless you've already undergone the transcendental process, the effects could be fatal."

François coughed, spattering bloody flesh, and his sword hand quivered. "On the double, Mr. Finch, if you please. A pity if this blade should slip and kill her. I do get so very weary."

"Steady on, eh? No need for violence." Grumbling, Finch retrieved the bottle. The silvery liquid writhed, possessed. "Welcome to it, you foolish boy."

But François just grinned. "Oh, it's not for me. Mr. Finch, you're accustomed to administering medication. Do the honors, if you please."

Eliza's knees shook. She'd be gone. Eaten away by greedy Lizzie, just an unwanted memory. Trapped forever in that glassy nightmare of hell. "No. I can't go back there." Her pleading tone—a child begging not to be punished—sickened her. But she couldn't help it. "Can't we come to an arrangement?"

"Not you." François jerked his chin towards Remy. "Him."

Remy blinked, shocked from speechlessness. "What?"

"The wolf," said François, and laughed at Remy's reaction. "You never could lie to me, brother. I've known since you returned from Calcutta with that preposterous fiction about your wife. Jungle brigands didn't kill her. *You* did. And who knows how many others?"

All Remy's color had drained, his eyes just gray ghosts. "You've no idea what you're asking."

"Oh, I do. You know, I watched what you did the other night, in the moonlight. All that blood, Remy. But it's a risk I'm willing to take. And you're always so sickeningly well. Can you even recall when last you were ill? That creature makes you strong, and I want it." He smiled in half-remembered affection. "You never could deny me, brother."

"Listen." Desperation, born of grief. "The curse is a crippling disease. Contracting it nearly killed me."

A familiar arch of eyebrow. "Hardly seems a worry."

Remy stuttered. "But . . . I can't change here. I'll kill you all—"

"I've no time to argue." François's ruined voice trembled. "Understand? *I've no time.* Anything's better than a useless death."

"Is it? How about living every day in terror that you'll hurt the ones you love?"

"Good God, you're insufferable. I'd *kill* to have your perfect life. For years I've longed to swap places. Well, now I can." François coughed, his eyes unpleasantly red-rimmed. "Drink it," he whispered hoarsely, "or I cut your lady's throat."

Eliza's heart broke. Not Remy, trapped in that hateful, screaming emptiness. She'd die first. "Remy, you don't know what it's like there. You can't."

Remy just smiled, strangely gleeful, and grabbed the bottle from Finch's hand. "Don't waste your concern on me, Eliza. Forgive me."

He thumbed off the cork, and drank.

Eliza yelled in anguish. Finch gaped. François grinned.

Remy shuddered, muscles twitching. His fist spasmed, crushing the bottle to bloody shards. And he *changed*.

He screamed in ragged agony, and it deepened to a growl. His limbs contorted, clothes stretching and tearing over swelling muscles. Fibers snapping, sinews quivering impossibly tight. His knee joints broke and popped backwards. Golden fur sprouted, rippling down his lean frame and bristling at his hackles. Claws erupted from his bleeding fingertips. His jaws stretched and elongated, and wicked saber teeth knifed from his gums, soaking his wolfen chin scarlet.

"Marvelous," breathed François, transfixed.

The wolf snarled on all fours, claws raking ruts in the floorboards, a quivering bundle of rage. His fur sparked with static. His bristling tail twitched. But still his eyes drilled into François's. Chilling, famished, yet bright with sorrow. Not flat and golden like a beast's, but uncanny sky-blue.

Eliza froze, not daring to glance away. She'd no expectation that he'd recognize her. "Marcellus, run."

Finch jigged, fisting his hair. "But—"

"Now. You don't want to see him lose his temper."

Shamefaced, Finch scuttled out. Now they were only three.

Remy arched his furred spine, sparks crackling. François lowered his sword and beckoned with a triumphant smile. "Here, boy."

Eliza didn't dare move. She'd never felt so helpless.

Remy crouched to spring . . . But he didn't attack. He curled his neck and howled, raw and anguished, and the floorboards shook with his torment. The beast had already eaten its fill under the full moon. Now it was bewildered, out of kilter, its instincts befuddled.

He didn't *want* to kill his brother, any more than he wanted to kill *her*. But the hunger was mighty.

François sighed. "Very well. Let's do it the hard way." Swift as a serpent, he grabbed Eliza and hurled her out the window.

Eliza screamed, lurching into empty space. Wolf-Remy roared, and leapt.

But François's fingers clamped on her bodice, arresting her fall . . . and Remy skidded to a halt, claws digging up splinters. "Not so fast," warned François coolly. "Kill me, and she'll fall. Even if she survives, that bloodthirsty mob will tear her apart."

Furious, Eliza flailed for a grip, missing the sill by a whisker. Suspended, inches from death in the quivering grip of a madman.

Pop! Stitches in her bodice began to break. Blood lurched in her skull, pounding. Below swam the rioting crowd, bristling with rage and brandishing weapons. François had it right. The fall mightn't kill her . . .

"Remy, don't." She scrabbled for her stinger, but it was lost. *Lizzie, help me!*

"Gently, baby brother. A simple wound is all I require." François's voice was hypnotic, soothing, as if he calmed a frightened horse. "You're the expert on inflicting pain. You know how much a human body can hurt. Must I torture her to make you obey me?"

Her flailing wrist banged a hard lump in her skirts. Something in her pocket . . . Her groping fingers closed on ivory.

In the madness, she'd forgotten Mr. Todd's gift.

She unfolded it, *ping!* Such a sweet melody. Steel flashed, a beacon in the sun.

Her courage quailed. She'd shot Lady Lovelace. But this was François. Could she, even for Remy's sake? Slaughter his brother without due process, bathe in warm living blood? And then fall to her own grisly death?

Remy would give his life for her. Almost had, in that rusted dungeon. *I've already failed to save one woman I cared for,* he'd said. *Just hold me, and don't look down.*

He'd never agree to this. Never acknowledge her debt to him. For keeping her secret. For Todd. For everything.

Forgive me, Remy, she whispered silently. *But I need to make this right.*

Her fingers tightened on the razor. She inhaled one last breath . . . and Lizzie howled, and exploded into life.

The change takes us fast. A breathless scream, aching flesh stretching, eyes boggling fit to burst. My hair springs wild, my chest inflates, invigorated with the lightning scent of that exploded skyship. Alive. As if I'd never gone away.

I struggle, hanging in mid-air by a fistful of corset above this rampaging mob, and I realize I'm seeing through *her* eyes. The world's livelier, somehow, bathed in different shades. Wondrous, more beautiful . . . but also more frightening.

I can't let her do this alone.

I ain't just the unwanted stepchild. She needs me, to do the things she can't—and to swallow the guilt, too, like sweet fairy absinthe. Because without me, it'd kill her.

But I need her, too. To keep me from sliding into endless darkness.

I'm the shadow in her heart, the rotting portrait of her soul. But I'm more than that. I ain't just half a person. We're two people knotted into one. And for good or ill, we can't be undone.

This is what I'm for.

"Let me up," I growl, "or I'll open your throat."

François shows bloodied teeth. Mad, star-glitter eyes. As utterly off his rocker as Mr. Shadow. "Why, hello, Miss Hyde. Would you really slaughter a sick man? You and I aren't so different. I just want to live. Is that so wrong?"

"You bet it is," I snarl, and slash. Right to left, a glittering razor arc.

With a curse, François springs away. But I clamp my fist on his coat, and like it or not he drags me with him, and I thump to the dusty floor, out of danger.

He staggers. A thin crimson thread paints his throat. It brightens. Widens. Gushes bright blood.

He chokes, incredulous. Blood runs faster, soaking his shirt. The coppery stink of it—fresh, arterial, Mr. Todd's precious crimson—is flowers on the air, delicious predator's perfume.

And Remy's control shatters. He roars, muscles coiling, and leaps.

He collides with François. Growling, slavering, fangs tearing flesh.

I don't look. I just run. Lurch out onto the landing, slam the door. Fall into Marcellus Finch's arms, and listen through my weeping to the snarling, choking, rending sounds of death.

A DEEPER SHADE OF NIGHT

•••

IN THE SUMPTUOUS UPSTAIRS DRAWING ROOM, ELIZA sighed and put her book aside. *Treatise on Dissociative States and Disorders of the Nervous Mind*. She'd recovered the torn pages, pieced it back together. But her concentration danced, fickle like windswept leaves. Her mind kept stumbling over burning skyships and dead queens, finding its way to squalid Newgate where a man had waited to die.

Sun poured over the richly dyed Bombay carpet, shining on the rosewood tea table. Her cup was long cold. Hippocrates jumped onto the chaise, nosing at her skirts, and she petted him absently.

Lizzie peered out the window, impatiently twitching the velvet drapes. "Dullest book ever," she grumbled. "Jesus in a jam jar, I'm snoring over here."

"Get your own book, then, if you're so clever."

Lizzie tossed her hair, jaunty top hat teetering. "From your library? Never a rum tale among 'em. All medicine and science and dead old Greek bastards. Nothing happens."

"Historians," protested Eliza. "Really, Lizzie, not everything needs to be a penny gaff melodrama."

"Don't it? Where are the good books? That *Varney the Vampyre*, for one. A rollicking good yarn. Always waking up in graveyards and bumping off ripe maidens and woe is me. Proper tragic hero, he is."

"I'm sure." Eliza eyed Hipp dubiously. "Perhaps we could both use a walk."

"Walk!" squawked Hipp, bouncing. "Motion! Make greater speed!"

Lizzie flounced her scarlet skirts. "'Bout bloody time—"

"Can I come?" From the doorway, Remy flashed a smile. Weary, but still dazzling. Half dressed, scarlet coat slung over his arm. His bruises had faded, just a shadow under one eye.

By the window, Lizzie smirked. Transparent again, just a light-speckled shimmer. Eliza flushed. She knew Lizzie wasn't real, of course. Sometimes, she just . . . forgot. And always, when she remembered, she was gripped with sadness. As if her best friend had departed on a long and perilous journey.

Eliza cleared her throat. "What are you doing here?"

"This is my house. Attendance is customary." Remy hovered in the doorway. Waiting for permission?

She still thought of it as François's house. But François was dead. And nearly a week later, Remy still muttered and cried out in his sleep. "I mean, what are you doing up? I recall prescribing strict bed rest."

"You did. But I can't stand it anymore." Remy bent to pet Hipp, still moving gingerly, as if he ached all over. "And laying eyes on your fresh and lovely face has already improved my condition no end."

She eyed him sternly. "Is this how we're to proceed? You

thwart my every command, then charm me into forgiving you with clownish flirtations?"

"Precisely my plan. Is it working?"

"It could be worse." She hesitated. "How are you feeling?"

"Sore," he admitted. "I can still taste those vile concoctions Finch forces down my throat. If I didn't know better, I'd think he was trying to poison me." Mr. Finch had restored Remy, with the help of that icy pink remedy and a lot of luck. Not an easy transition. The wolf had resisted, digging in its claws and howling to be free. It wanted life.

"Remy . . . I haven't had the chance . . . I'm so sorry about François. I don't know what to say."

A shadow darkened his face. "I'd rather not speak of it, if you don't mind."

Eliza swallowed. Crimson rivers, ragged flesh, that awful rending sound . . .

"But on that subject," added Remy softly, "I owe you an apology. I told you I couldn't let a killer go free. I meant it. And that includes me."

Her heart whispered, uneasy. Newgate Prison had burned in the riots, and in any case, the chaos meant the authorities—whoever those were, with the Mad Queen dead and the Philosopher the new Regent for a half-witted, underage King who slobbered and gaped—whoever was in charge, they had more urgent things on their minds than arranging a hanging.

And in her pocket lurked a letter from a certain froggy-fingered bailiff, detailing where she might—if she chose—pick up a certain collection of sketches and an unfinished oil painting. The bailiff had commandeered them, a favor in return for Quick's vexatious lawsuit. She hadn't yet retrieved the collection. Maybe, she never would.

But Mr. Todd was lost. A ghost. Denying your dark side couldn't absolve you . . . but Remy was different. Wasn't he? "I'm not listening. It was self-defense and that's that."

"But—"

"François wasn't himself, Remy. He attacked you. He attacked all of us."

A pause. "But—"

"There you are, then. And stop saying 'but.' I'm not a goat."

He bit his tender lip. "I once promised I'd never hurt you, do you remember?"

His ring hummed in her pocket, accusing. She hadn't put it back on. Hadn't insisted he take it back either. "Please, don't say it—"

"I must." Gentle, earnest. "I can't keep that promise. You saw what happened. The moon isn't the only thing that awakens this creature. What if it happens when I'm not expecting it? I can't trust it. Not now. Not ever."

All that blood, François had said. It made her shiver. But whatever Remy had done was as much her fault as his. She couldn't just walk away. "I know you're trying," she insisted. "Those candles, that incantation, or whatever it was? Don't lose heart, Remy. Mr. Finch is optimistic for a cure. When the next full moon comes . . ."

He didn't need to speak. He'd already tried spells, amulets, medicines. *When the next full moon comes . . . what?*

She cocked hands on hips, a defiant Lizzie-like gesture. "I won't hear of it. We have the cage. We'll triple the locks if necessary. And we'll keep trying until the thing is done."

"But—"

"Ah." She cut him off with an upraised finger. "Doctor's orders. Think you'll be rid of me so easily? And don't even think about turning yourself in," she added, "or other such gallant foolishness. No matter that your secret died with Lady Lovelace. You're still under enough suspicion at the Royal as it is."

"I can't promise I won't do that."

"Fine. Then this conversation isn't ended. And it won't be until you forgive yourself, Remy Lafayette."

Remy's eyes shimmered. "I really am the luckiest man alive. Aren't you even the tiniest bit afraid of me?"

Behind him, Lizzie snorted. "After what we've been through? Not a chance. Now bloody well kiss him until my eyes boggle, or I'll throttle you."

Laughing, Eliza reached up to brush her thumb across his lashes. "Lizzie says I ought to kiss you now."

"Oh." His smile flashed, glorious. "Well, forgive me, madam, but that's impossible. We're not engaged."

She slipped the ring from her pocket. The stone sparkled in the sun. Ridiculously blue, like his eyes. "Yes," she whispered, "we are."

He took the ring, and slipped it onto her finger. And she kissed him until she couldn't breathe.

• ACKNOWLEDGMENTS •

Like every author, I couldn't be one without my fabulous team of enablers: Kelly, Caroline, and the gang at Harper Voyager; Marlene, agent extraordinaire; and Sean, bringer of chocolate and kisses. Oh, and cheers to the staff at the Alnwick coffee shop where I spent many hours writing this book, who called me "Sheila" and wondered if they were in it.

· ABOUT THE AUTHOR ·

Viola Carr was born in a strange and distant land, but wandered into darkest London one foggy October evening and never found her way out. She now devours countless history books and dictates fantastical novels by gaslight, accompanied by classical music and the snores of her slumbering cat. She is the author of *The Diabolical Miss Hyde*.